What are they saying a

This is a "page turner." The author shows a great deal of understanding of human nature without having people lose character. They all behave well. This book deserves a large audience.

—Charlotte Ryan

The narration made me feel as if I were reading Our Town.

—Betty Aidicon

I knew before I had finished the first three pages, I was in for a pleasurable "read."

Rose-Marie Provencher Burns

We all like the book and enjoyed spending time with the characters. It held everyone's interest.

A positive story. Writing is exceptional, especially perceptive regarding women and children.

The country fair is excellently portrayed. We were all there with them. Thanks for the memories.

Delightful and sensitive without being sappy.

—The Great Books Club of Orange, Massachusetts

With a story-telling style akin to poetry, Jay Kendall paints a recognizable landscape. His people make mistakes, fall down hard, break dishes and each other. They live and die rising whole and forgiven – what we'd wish for ourselves. I didn't expect to cry, certainly not more than once. I didn't expect to be unable to put this book down. Jay Kendall seems to know equally and intimately a child's way of thinking, a woman's heart, a man's soul. It's a surprise reunion. It's a keeper.

– Candace R. Curran

At the back of the room she saw Clay stacking boxes in a pool of light that came from a naked overhead bulb. As she approached him, she watched the graceful movements of his body, the firmness of his muscles. . . She wanted to reach her hand out and touch the sweat stain on his shirt at the small of his back, but instead she began speaking just as she had planned, "Clay Holden?"

"Yes," he turned, saw her, and smiled. Arlette bathed for a couple of seconds in his smile. It didn't matter to her that everybody got the same good-natured smile; she decided to receive it as a gift. And she favored him with the gift of her own smile,
which not everybody received. . . .

"Please, don't stop working. I promised Mrs. Pearson that I wouldn't interrupt your work." . . .

"Oh, no problem," he chuckled. "Forget it."

"But I can't forget it. When I saw you yesterday, . . . standing there with your box of groceries, . . . you just took my breath away!"

"Really? . . . Uh . . . "

"Really! And I was thinking, . . . maybe next Thursday when you come by, perhaps we could talk about . . . a time when we could get together."

"Uh, I don't know, I . . . " He was dazed; he wasn't sure he understood. She moved in closer and pressed on.

Jay Kendall
(623) 214-7645
12927 West
Jadestone Drive
Sun City West
AZ 85375

THE SECRET KEEPERS

Jay Kendall

Haley's
Athol, Massachusetts

Haley's
Post Office Box 248
Athol, Massachusetts 01331
1.800.215.8805

Cover quilt by Carole Paye.
Cover photography by Robert Mayer.
Printed by the Highland Press.

Library of Congress cataloging-in-publication data:
Kendall, Jay, 1940-
The secret keepers / by Jay Kendall.
p. cm.
ISBN 1-884540-39-2 (pbk.)
I. Title.
PS3561.E4229S43 1998
813' .54--dc21 98-38947
CIP

For my sons Matthew and Aaron

Contents

Acknowledgments

Much encouragement and assistance in the writing of this novel has come from family, friends, colleagues, the Western Massachusetts Writing Project, and especially my students.

For their significant contributions I wish to thank Ellen Arrison, Beulah Ball, Kaye Bedard, Richard Belsky, Judith Curley, Douglas Dawson, Marcia Gagliardi, Carolyn Jenks, Anna Karola, Aaron Kendall, Matthew Kendall, Ray Kendall, Solange Kendall, Marcia Larocque, Faye Morin, Betsy Pelz, Ineabelle Perez, Medora Reed, Raymond K. Sauls, M.D., and Lorraine Seymour.

Prologue

Just as fabrics, patterns, and colors combine to create a patchwork quilt, different points of view, memories, and commentaries were stitched together to make up this story. The voices of my grandmother, my mother, and a woman whom the whole town called Aunt Mabel tell much of the story. My own memories and perceptions I relate from the perspective of an adult recalling the world of my childhood.

For me and for others who were also children at the same time, the story was like a jigsaw puzzle that we put together over a period of years. We received different pieces at different times and rarely in the right order. We gathered and stored away bits of information that grownups passed around among themselves in our presence.

And for all of us children the story began on June 2 , 1943, the day the twins were born. It was a morning in the middle of a much larger story of which we were a part. The country was engaged in a war that touched and changed the lives of every American, even those of us who lived in a northern New England border town. Though the adults tried to maintain a sense of normalcy and to shield us from the wars raging around the world, they were themselves engaged in secret, private conflicts that we couldn't escape.

Chapter One

Breakfast with Grandfather

• *Michael Holden* •

I don't know when my grandfather began speaking to himself and referring to himself in the third person. Maybe he did it all of his life. But I do remember the first time that I became aware of that unusual habit of my father's father. He was standing in his kitchen doing his morning stretching and deep-breathing exercises. The early breeze that blew through the open window carried the clear, fluty melody of a wood thrush's song. I didn't know then what sort of bird was singing; I was five years old.

As if in answer to the bird call, grandfather announced, "He thinks he's hungry; he thinks he needs something to eat." I wondered if he was talking about the bird, about himself, or about me. And then to add to the confusion, grandfather turned to me and asked, "And what about him? Is he hungry as well?"

"What?" I said. I knew that I didn't understand, but I wasn't sure why. I thought the puzzle just needed more time.

"That boy, is he hungry too?" My grandfather almost never called me Michael. He seldom referred to any members of our family by their names. He called my father "his son" and my mother "his son's wife." My grandmother he called "that old woman" or "his good woman," and he referred to himself as "this old man." So what he was saying was not a surprise to me, just a puzzle. "Does that boy need breakfast as much as this old man?"

"Maybe," I managed weakly. Now I understood who was who, but breakfast with my grandfather was dangerous territory, and I knew it. Breakfast to him might be cold, sliced mutton and pears. The pears would be green and hard as rocks, "a challenge to the teeth," he would maintain. Mutton was a chore for me at suppertime when it was hot; cold at breakfast, it was a penance.

Or my grandfather might decide to cook. He rarely cooked except when my grandmother wasn't home, and this morning she wasn't home. She had gone with my mother to "help bring Arlette Handy's third baby into the world." For this reason I was brought in the dark of morning half asleep to my grandparents' sofa, where I woke later feeling newly born and wondering where I was and if I were still the same person.

Perhaps if I thought I were somebody else, I might speak to *myself* in the third person as grandfather Holden did. I wouldn't be Michael; I'd be "that boy" who was worried that "that old man" might decide to cook. My grandfather was accounted a good camp cook, but he wouldn't be cooking bacon and eggs for breakfast, or pancakes and sausage. His idea of a good breakfast might be boiled potatoes and liver, pig's liver.

But just as I was worrying about what I would do with pig's liver, my grandfather said something as wonderful as the bright music of the wood thrush's call.

"He thinks his good woman said there was an apple pie in the pantry." Now, there was my idea of breakfast! Not my mother's, who thought that "those people" did not know how to eat, and "whoever heard of pie at breakfast?" Mutton and liver she was right about. Pie was different. But my grandfather thought that apple pie should be accompanied by a wedge of cheese. He believed that "a ripe, sharp cheddar complements a slice of apple pie," but in my opinion what the cheese offered to the pie was not a "compliment," but an insult—a sour, bitter, pungent sensation that obliterated every memory of cinnamon, sugar, or apples.

"Does he want to join him in a piece of pie?" My grandfather had achieved such economy in his life that one good set of pronouns was as serviceable to him as a Swiss Army knife. I needed to be cautious and attentive to understand the context of his words. He taught me the value of listening carefully to understand the meanings of words and the thoughts of other human beings.

By the time grandmother returned home, the apple pie had all but disappeared. After grandfather and I finished the first piece, he asked me how the pie had tasted. From the way he asked the question, I believed that I needed to consider it seriously and answer thoughtfully. The pie had tasted the way grandmother's apple pies always did—delicious. It wasn't too sweet or too tart. She always used both nutmeg and cinnamon, and I liked that. The apples were just right; the crust was flaky. The bottom crust had soaked in some of the juice; I liked that. Grandfather's questions always made me think. I finally responded that it had tasted "very good." I offered this cautious response because grandfather's face seemed to suggest that there was definitely a problem. Grandfather ruminated about my answer.

"Very good? Hm-m-m. Good. No, he can't say that 'good' is the word he would have used to describe the taste of that apple pie." His face became a study in mystery. He said, "No. He thinks that the word is 'more.' He thinks that it tasted like 'more.' Now, what does that boy have to say to that? What does he think about that word to describe his grandmother's pie?"

There was an obvious challenge in his voice, and my duty to assist my grandfather in his line of inquiry was clear. My response was just as clear, "Yes, Grandfather, you're exactly right; it did taste like more."

"Just as he thought!" my grandfather thundered. So we each set to on another piece, and as we ate, I thought of how clever my grandfather's reasoning had been.

After the pie there were several games of cards. We played a few games of "war," which my grandfather called "everlasting." Then my grandfather began to teach me how to play double solitaire, a game that called for a good deal of vigilance in order to avoid a penalty. Grandfather seemed to enjoy tossing the penalty card in my direction, when I failed to see a play or made a mistake.

Unlike every other adult I knew, grandfather never let me win just because I was a little kid. Grandfather always played to win, and he "gave no quarter." If I won a game with him, I knew that I had won fair and square on my own merit. When I did win, grandfather congratulated me on a game well played, but he never made a big deal of it. I always felt as though it should be treated as a big deal, but grandfather helped me temper my understanding of victory. He never made a big deal of his winning either. He would just say, "Well, he seems to have played that one right."

When he tired of cards, my grandfather decided that he needed to take a short snooze. He suggested that, if I were not like-minded, I could look through the little drawers in the shed at his collection of nails, screws, bolts, nuts, wingnuts, washers, hinges, hooks, latches, locks, and keys. Grandfather had more rings of keys than I had ever seen. I loved looking at his "collection," and grandfather knew what would keep me amused, whenever he needed a little private time.

Grandfather sat in his rocking chair, tipped his head back, closed his eyes, and "breathed heavily." He didn't snore! He had been careful to point that out to me a number of times. He didn't snore; *grandmother* snored. I sorted through his hardware while grandfather breathed heavily for a while. When he finished his nap, grandfather decided that we needed a little "something" to tide us over until lunch. We saved grandmother a sliver of her pie.

Just as we finished our final mouthful, she and mother swept in looking tired, but satisfied. Grandmother ruffled my hair. "What have you two been up to, Michael?"

"We've been eating pie," I answered.

"I'll bet you have. That sounds like a good idea, though. How about a piece of apple pie, Angela?" grandmother asked mother. My mother agreed, and I thought it was interesting that my mother didn't say what she always used to say to my father about his mother's apple pie—that it had too much nutmeg and would probably be better without nutmeg altogether. But right on the heels of that thought, I remembered that there was practically no apple pie left. I was wondering what would happen then, but my grandfather brought this fact to light first.

"Well, good woman, it's probably going to be a fairly small piece. That boy's a growing boy, and this old man has had a powerful hunger today."

My grandmother frowned at grandfather, and then she sighed a great sigh which said that she was not at all surprised to learn the pie was gone, and that living with this man had accustomed her to such trying eventualities. Her face was serious, and her disappointment was obvious. She put both of her hands on the table, as though she were dizzy and thought she ought to sit down. Her left hand crept feebly to her brow. Then she straightened up as though it were painful for her to do. She sighed again, shook her head, and began walking slowly toward the pantry.

I thought that grandfather looked a little sad or guilty. The kitchen was deadly quiet. Then grandmother returned from the pantry. She was carrying the plate with the small sliver of pie in her left hand, but in her right hand she was bearing a brand new apple pie. "It's a good thing that I know the two of you; I had an idea that I had best make a spare, if I wanted any left over."

Grandfather looked at me, and his face was filled with wonder, "Now where in the world could that have been?"

"You don't know all my hiding places yet, old man, and I'm not about to give you any idea where they are. You might as well face the fact that I'm usually about two steps ahead of you." Grandmother turned her attention to my mother. "See what you think about this pie, Angela. I used some of those Northern Spies I dried last fall. Of course in this house you have to think like a spy in order to salvage a piece."

Grandmother was enjoying herself. She liked drama. She relished the little play of disappointment before she brought out the pie, and she enjoyed the triumph of producing a second pie and watching grandfather's face. She cut a slice of the pie for mother and one for herself, and then she turned to grandfather. "Would you care for another piece, Ward?" She said it as though she were talking to her favorite person in the world.

"Another piece? She just wants to see him bust wide open! That's what she wants," grandfather countered.

"You bust? The idea!" grandmother snorted. "Idea" was grandmother's favorite word: "The idea! What an idea! I've no idea. Have you any idea? I've got an idea. Now there's an idea!" She said the word with an "r" on the end of it, "idear." She poured some coffee for mother and herself, then sat down and took a bite of pie. "Whoo, what a night!" She began eating her pie and gave it her complete attention.

I knew she was waiting; I don't know how I knew, but I knew. I also knew that grandfather knew the same thing, but he wanted the moment to be special for grandmother. So he was waiting too. It was always interesting to be present when my grandparents talked, like watching a dance. Sometimes the moves were predictable; sometimes they were startling and new. Grandmother chewed slowly and sipped thoughtfully. The pie and coffee provided her with something to do while we all waited.

Finally grandfather broke the silence, "How did that woman leave Arlette Handy?"

"Why, through the front door. How would you suppose?" my grandmother answered innocently.

My grandfather followed up without missing a beat, "And how is Arlette?"

"She's doing fine."

"How is the baby?"

"Arlette didn't have a baby," grandmother said flatly.

"Didn't she and daughter-in-law go to help Arlette Handy bring her third baby into the world?"

"That was the idea."

"Did Arlette lose her baby?" grandfather asked doubtfully, because grandmother's mood did not seem to suggest this as an appropriate avenue of conjecture.

"No, I wouldn't say that. Would you say that, Angela?"

My mother managed a weary smile. "No, I don't think I would say that, Mother Holden."

"But that old woman said that Arlette didn't have a baby," grandfather persisted in his attempt to solve the mystery.

"You're in the right church, but the wrong pew, Ward." Grandmother was getting ready for the revelation. "I said that Arlette didn't have 'a' baby."

"Ah!" said grandfather. He clearly relished riddle games. "If she didn't have 'a' baby, then did she have more than one baby?"

"Now you're getting the idea!"

"Did she have two babies?" grandfather asked with confidence.

"That's about the size of it!" Grandmother gave him the victory.

"Boys or girls?" grandfather continued.

"No, you have to guess!" Grandmother spoke as though grandfather had tried to cheat in the next phase of the game.

"All right, one of each. That's my guess."

"Bingo! On the first try! Very good, Ward!" Now she would be ready from this point to tell the rest of the story herself. My grandparents never tired of these sorts of games; I didn't either.

After my mother finished her pie, she took me home, and then my grandmother told my grandfather about her night at Arlette Handy's. I had already heard as much as I was going to hear that morning. As far as my mother and grandmother were concerned, their little Michael was "way too young" to witness such a recounting at that point in my life.

Whenever grownups became aware that I was listening and not absorbed in my coloring book, my drawings, or my trucks, my grandmother would say in a knowing way to my mother, "Little pitchers have big ears." She did not differentiate in the pronunciation of "pitcher" and "picture," and both words were pronounced the same way my grandfather said baseball "pitcher." It was years before I understood what my grandmother meant by that saying, which was always clearly pitched in my direction. In any event the little pitcher was not present to hear recounted the events of my grandmother's night.

"Where do babies come from, Mom?" Michael had a sense of this question's delicate nature, and he asked it into his coloring book, hoping an off-hand approach would secure the answer he sought. Carefully he colored the outline of a watering can's long blue spout, while he waited for his mother to formulate her response. His tongue protruded slightly from the left side of his mouth as his crayon bore down skillfully.

It was a question he had asked her on other occasions, and he had never yet been satisfied with her reply. But now with the birth of the twins, the question seemed a timely one, and he was more hopeful that her answer would help him connect the bits of information he had, just as she had helped him connect the dots to reveal the image he was now coloring.

He looked up at Angela and realized that she had not heard him. Her eyes were unfocused, and he for a moment watched her hands moving her coffee cup around in its saucer in small, clockwise turns, as though her fingers were the mechanism controlling an escape wheel. Those gestures indicating his mother's preoccupation were not unfamiliar to Michael. He knew she was thinking of the man she loved, his father who was on the other side of the world fighting in a war. At such times he thought her beautiful, distant, and sad—sometimes angry and sad. Lately she was often angry with Michael, and he didn't know why. He dared her anger because the question was important to him; he repeated it louder and again quickly returned his attention to the watering can.

"What?" The word sounded worn and tired, as though it had traveled a great distance to arrive at the kitchen table, where they were sitting.

"I said, where do babies come from?" Michael looked at her; perhaps the direct approach was better after all.

Angela turned her head in Michael's direction and blinked her eyes. "Where do babies come from." She repeated the question as a statement. Parts of her seemed to be slowly reassembling themselves. She tipped her head back, and her neck cracked. She sighed. "Oh, Michael, we've been through all this before." There was a weary reluctance to repeat a familiar process.

"But I want to know!"

"I know you want to know. And I've told you that you will know. When you're old enough, you'll know."

"But how will I know, if nobody'll tell me?" He was exasperated. This was the very response he had dreaded.

"Michael, I don't want to deal with this right now. Trust me; you'll know. That's it."

"Grandma says, Arlette swallowed too many watermelon seeds." He spoke the words slowly, carefully, trying to gauge precisely an innocent quality in his voice.

Angela took a quick, sharp breath. Her gray eyes became sudden points of steel. "Honest to God, one of these days that woman is going to drive me right up a wall! That is right up there with her babies-come-in-the-doctor's-little-black-bag story!"

"But did she?"

"Did she what?"

"Did she swallow too many watermelon seeds?" Michael's innocent confusion was masterfully controlled.

"Of course she didn't swallow too many watermelon seeds! That's just foolish talk to keep you from asking questions."

"At least it's an answer," he said quietly. This statement was a key element in Michael's strategy.

His mother's voice rose a decibel, "But it's not the right answer, and there's no point in giving an answer if you can't give the right answer. Honestly, Michael, if I thought that the time was right for you to hear the answer, I'd give it to you. But *I* don't think it is! And *I'm* your mother, and *I* make that decision. Is that *clear*?"

"I guess so." He noted to himself, not for the first time, how she always won with volume.

"Besides, your grandparents have plenty of animals. I know you've seen kittens being born in the barn, and God knows what else you've seen over there. You just want me to put it into words. And I'm not ready to do that! If you want an answer, go ask your grandmother. She's probably got a couple other old wives' tales tucked up her sleeve." She knew that this was a safe thing to say. She knew that Michael knew better than to repeat any part of this conversation to his grandmother.

Chapter Two
Grandmother's Night

• *Grandmother Holden* •

Ward always says that I snore, but he was dead to the world and making all kinds of racket when I sat bolt upright in bed from a thudding noise on the kitchen's outside door. It must have been just after three o'clock in the morning when Alder came to wake us up. I couldn't imagine what that pounding on the back door was. He'd come across the field because it's quicker than using the road, and the back door is closer than the front door to the field.

I thought that that trek was brave for a boy who wasn't quite ten years old. Not that the field's not usually safe enough. During the day it seems a friendly place, but after dark it's a little queer and spooky in the mist. You could break your leg in a woodchuck hole if you're not careful. But I think that the only idea that was in little Alder's head was that he needed to hurry.

He'd certainly had to grow up in a hurry in these last few months since the accident. He'd had to take on more than a boy his age should have to, but he seemed to take it in stride. He was bigger than a ten-year-old, and everyone had the idea that he should be more responsible than a ten-year-old—even himself.

When I opened the door, he almost fell into the kitchen. Since all of his energy had been bent on going forward, it was as though he couldn't stop himself. He plunged into the room as though he were under water. His hair was plastered to his forehead from running in the night damp. The words burst from his lungs as though he'd been holding them in all the way across the field. "It's Ma!" he blurted.

Well, I had an idea right away what the matter was, and I caught him by the shoulders before he could collapse onto the floor. "It's all right, Alder. Catch your breath and get steady," I said. I kept hold of his shoulders with my hands. It struck me how skinny they were, and how much they needed a firm hand. His shirt was damp, and I was afraid he'd catch a chill.

Holding onto his shoulders like that, it was almost as though I could see in my mind's eye how that boy had run at full tilt across that dark field, without any idea of himself—just his Ma, his message, and his need for speed. It's funny the ideas you get and how much can go through your mind in an instant like that, as though the clock has slowed down and you have all the time in the world.

It was just a few seconds that I held him that way, but I felt a change come into his little body. He calmed down right away, and his breathing became more regular. I've seen horses at the county fair do that, when the driver's hands on their necks and shoulders seem to communicate to them that the race is over. When he spoke again, Alder was in control of his voice, "Ma sent me, Mrs. Holden. She said her labor's started. She asked if you will call the doctor and if you will come yourself. Ma said, 'Ask Ida if she please will come.'"

I don't know just why I felt so emotional. Maybe it's because I think of a birth as such an important time, or maybe it was because Alder was such a grown up little man all of a sudden. Anyway I felt my heart tighten, and I had a hard time controlling my own voice. I felt a connection with this boy, and for just an instant there, he reminded me of our Clay when he was that age.

I put my arm around his shoulders and pulled him into the sitting room. "Everything will be all right now; you'll see," I said. "We'll take care of everything. Now you sit here in this rocking chair with this blanket around you, so you don't catch your death of cold. I'm going to put on some milk to warm for you. Then I'll call the doctor. While I'm getting dressed, Ward will go across the way and fetch Angela to help. I'm sure that we'll be in time. I can certainly see that you haven't lost any time in getting here, and that's good. Your mother's got a lot to be proud of in you, Alder." He smiled, and his face began to lose its rosy flush from the race he'd just finished.

I wanted to leave him here while Angela and I went to help bring Arlette's baby into the world. It's hard enough on grownups to be present or in the house when a birth is in progress; it's something a child shouldn't have to witness. I had an idea that Alder was already growing up too fast. I wanted to spare him this experience, but he wouldn't hear of it.

"I need to be there," he said. He seemed to take my thought from the look on my face, because he added right away, "I don't need to be in the room, Mrs. Holden, but I need to be in the house. Maybe you'll need me to run an errand; you never know. I can run fast. Maybe you'll need me to do things."

I had an idea right then that it was no good saying no to him. If we left him here, he'd just wait until we went down the road, and then he'd cut back across the field. I couldn't bear thinking about that boy going across that field again in the dark. If he fell and hurt himself or, God forbid, broke his leg, I'd never forgive myself. I'd feel so responsible. So I decided it would be better if we took him with us.

He was a help, too. He got wood and made a fire in the kitchen stove. He pumped water and put it on to heat. He found the newspapers that Arlette had collected and saved for this day. Maybe he shouldn't have been there, but maybe it wasn't a bad idea that he was. On the way over to his mother's house, he carried the extra kerosene lamp that Angela brought over, and he set a pretty fast pace, as we went around by the road. It was chilly for June. Of course you expect that in northern New England, but Alder kept us moving right along, so we didn't feel the cold. He didn't say much as I tried to reassure him that babies take time to be born; I could tell how anxious he was.

I was glad that both Angela and I brought flashlights. They were a comfort on the part of the street with street lights and houses fairly close together, but they were a necessity further on. Arlette's road was dark as a pocket, because theirs was the only house and there were no street lights.

I was glad, too, that Angela had thought to bring a kerosene lamp. She said that without electricity we might need the extra light for the birthing. It was a shame they didn't have electricity over there yet, but Arlette said that she and Mark couldn't afford what the electric company wanted in order to run wires past their house. So I guess that's just the way it had to be, until somebody else built on that street and helped come up with the money.

When I was a girl, we didn't have electricity either. There were only four farms on our road then. And those were far apart and surrounded by land like Arlette's. But over the years the acreage was chopped up to make homes for farmers' children. Or the land was just sold off. Now there were eighteen houses on our street. A few like ours had barns, and most of them owned a good bit of land out back. But there was only one real farm left, and that one wasn't as big as it used to be. I never thought things could change so much.

The only thing that had stayed the same was the river. I didn't know that years later they would even change the course of the river when they built the access road to the super highway. They took some of the steepness out of the roads down either side of the hill and took out one of the bridges as well. But that night on the way over to Arlette's as we walked the river road and crossed three bridges, I thought about how the river seemed to flow all around us and through our lives. Its sounds, its smells were the background of our daily thoughts. In early spring it overflowed into the meadows and looked like a lake. In the late spring and summer, people fished along its banks or went into the water up to their hips in their waders to fish.

In the fall we watched brightly colored leaves float down the current, and we thought about another summer gone and winter coming on. In winter the water near the river's banks froze, and the river seemed to shrink to the size of a small brook, and in the depths of winter the river might disappear altogether under ice and snow. People skated on the oxbows and tobogganed down the hills that led to the river.

On summer days mallards floated on the water and clamored at passersby for food. Sunrises and sunsets turned the river's waters rose and gold. It was a beautiful, peaceful place to live. But when mothers couldn't immediately locate their children, for some, their first thoughts were of the potentially dangerous river, which might have drawn their innocent, unresisting children into its swift waters. But it seemed to me that the river was less interested in robbing us of our physical lives and more interested in affecting our souls.

When the three of us got to the house, we didn't knock or anything. Because little Alder was with us, we just walked right in. Arlette was sitting in that big, easy chair in her front room. She was in her nightgown, and she had a sweater on. Her head snapped up, and she looked for just an instant like a wild creature at bay, but when she realized who we were, she heaved a sigh. Her smile and the pain in her eyes drew us into the room. She held up the crocheting which had lain in her lap. I could see that she'd been trying to keep herself busy while she was waiting for us; now she felt relieved.

"Oh, Lord, I'm so glad you're here! You have no idea! Come in; come in. Oh, I'm glad you brought another lamp; I thought of that after Alder had left, but then there was nothing I could do about it. Thank you for thinking about that." She set the crocheting aside, and supporting her great belly with her left hand, she pushed herself out of the chair with her right hand. She struggled partly upright and reached out for her son. "Alder, would you go set it on the chiffonier in my bedroom. Thank you, you are such a help to me, my sweet boy. I just don't know what I'd do without you."

She paused a minute to breathe, and she indicated the other chairs in the room with a weak wave of her hand. "You two, Ida, Angela, sit down. Thank you . . . both for coming. I'm so blessed . . . to have such good neighbors. Sit down on the sofa there, or anywhere you find a place. You might as well . . . make yourselves comfortable. It's not just yet; it's going to be a while. I've been keeping myself occupied, you see, crocheting a little on this christening dress. It's almost done now."

She lifted the snow-white dress to show us, and just as she did, she straightened up. Her eyes went wide, and her left hand shifted around to her back. I looked at my watch. Her face went slack, and she got that look of concentration, as though she were looking inside herself at the pain and beyond the pain to the child on the other side of it.

I knew she had been worried, and the words that had come pouring out of her just now were like a relief to her. I could see that she needed to talk, but she kept pausing in the middle of sentences to sort of collect herself, so she could go on. She seemed to have difficulty breathing, even when she wasn't in the midst of a pain. When you get those pains, it's as though you're in a completely different place, where you're all alone with just you and the pain. Sometimes it seems as though only the pain is there. When it passed, she blew her breath out and breathed and seemed to come back into the room. I pulled the rocker nearer to her chair, and I sat down in it and took her hand.

"How far apart are they now? Have you got a good idea?" I asked her. She looked at the clock on the mantel and thought, still coming back to herself.

"It was nine minutes between the last two."

I patted her hand. "Good. We've got a little time then." Just then Alder came back into the room. I got the idea that he had been in the doorway the whole time his mother was having her pains, and he just stayed there and waited as though he knew without having to ask that she was beyond the reach of his concern. And now he came up to her and asked the question he'd been swallowing like a lump in his throat, "Are you okay, Ma?"

Arlette reached for him and pulled him to her. "I'm fine, sweet boy. Everything's going to be all right, but these things take a while. And it's not easy—for anybody." She looked at us. Her right hand seemed to wander from her belly up to her breastbone, and her face was worried by a new thought. "Maybe I should send Alder over to Aunt Mabel's."

I had a good idea just how far that was going to go, even before Alder spoke, "Ma, I'm not leaving; you can't make me go." I understood somehow what he was going through. He'd been through too much, too many losses in the last little while, to leave his mother's side while she was like this—in danger as he saw it and, I guess, as I saw it too. So I told Arlette that we could really use Alder's help. I said there were quite a few things that he could do to help us out.

"Alder, I want you to write down the time I tell you, every time your Ma gets a pain. You get a pencil and paper and write it down. That way we'll be accurate, and nobody'll forget. And there are other things for you to do, too." It's hard to be somewhere where you've just got to be, especially if you've got nothing to do and you feel useless. "Arlette, I'm going to get Alder to make a fire and get some water heating, and he could make us all a cup of tea. I'm going to let you and Angela talk, but you let us know when you get a pain, so Alder can write it down."

They both caught the drift of what I was trying to do. I went into the kitchen and got Alder going on his tasks and got some cool compresses ready to put on Arlette's brow while Angela timed the pains and let us know when each one started. I knew that Arlette had been scared before we got there. Now that we were there, she got her nerves under control. She didn't have to work so hard in her mind to keep the baby from being born before we got there. Not that she could really have done anything about it, but in your mind you feel as though you can. The pains themselves are bad enough, but being alone at such a time can be terrifying.

She'd been through it twice before, so she knew more or less what she was up against, although I've known mothers to say that each birth was a little different: one birth was easier or harder than another, with one birth the pains were in the back, with another the pains were in the front, for some births the labor was longer than for others. I've always thought that it's too bad men can't experience it, because really they've no idea. No birth is easy. Oh, I've heard of women who supposedly drop their babies like kittens, but I've never met one, and I've been present at a lot of births.

Doctor Bonsecours hadn't arrived yet, and I wondered if he would get there in time. When I talked to his wife, I apologized for calling in the middle of the night. But she said not to give it a second thought; after all these years, she said she was used to it. She said the doctor wasn't home, that he'd gone over to the part of town we called Stovepipe City to be with a woman who was dying. She'd try to get a message to him, and she knew that he'd come as soon as he could. Then she said, "I know that you know just what to do, Ida; Arlette couldn't be in better hands if the doctor should be late." I thanked her, because I knew that she meant what she said, but she had no idea how nervous I always felt in these situations, having some notion of all the things that could go wrong.

Arlette was walking now, pacing back and forth in the room. She was having a tough time, breathing hard, holding onto her stomach. Beads of perspiration dotted her forehead, and little moans and grunts escaped her lips. I watched her walking. I understood her need to walk, but it looked as though that act itself was painful for her. I thought her legs were probably sore; I couldn't get over how big she'd gotten. Arlette had always carried a little extra flesh, but that's not what I was thinking about. Her belly was just "big"! It was my idea that this was going to be a really large baby and that we were all in for a rough time of it.

Between pains, she crocheted a little on the christening dress and talked with Angela while I kept Alder busy. We drank our tea, and when Angela told him, Alder wrote down the starting times of the pains. As they got closer and closer together, I decided that we needed to move into the bedroom. Alder and I had lighted all the kerosene lamps we could find and set them around in the bedroom. Arlette had gotten them all out beforehand, and she and Alder had filled them and cleaned the chimneys. Everything was ready now, and there wasn't much to do but wait. While Angela talked with Arlette, I thought I'd look around for some other little thing to do around the house just to keep busy. But that little house was immaculate. Alder said that just the day before, his mother had cleaned the whole place from top to bottom. It's funny how it is with us women just before we give birth. We get this burst of energy enough to clean three houses. I went back into Arlette's room and waited. She was twisting her body in the pain, and it struck me to wonder if we really are God's favorite creatures; frogs and fishes seem to have it so much easier. Between the pains Arlette kept saying that all along she'd had a feeling that she would lose this baby; she didn't know why, but she'd just had that feeling. Even now that it was about to be born, she wasn't sure it would live.

"I've made twelve christening outfits already since I've been in the family way," she said, "but, every time I got one done, someone would see it and say they wanted to buy it. Of course, with the way things were, I could use the money, so I sold it. But it really wasn't because of the money. I just kept feeling that I shouldn't get my hopes up. My mother always said that bad things come in threes, and I thought: first Janine, then Mark, and now I'm going to lose the baby. That's what I kept saying to myself. Then last night I decided that maybe I was going to have this baby after all, and I'd better get to work and finish this dress. But somehow I'm still not really hopeful. I've just got this feeling." She gasped and another pain took her.

Arlette was lying in the bed, and she was holding Angela's hands when the pains came. I thought that she would turn Angela's hands black and blue from squeezing them. It's amazing what strength we have when those pains take us. I tied some sheets to the sideboards of the bed for Arlette to pull on when she felt the need. That would save Angela's hands, I thought, and also it would free Angela to help when the baby came.

Meanwhile I was thinking about what Arlette had said about her losses, about the loss of her husband Mark and especially about her loss of little Janine. I think that it's especially hard, when a woman has lost one child, for her not to think that she will lose another. But Janine died of spinal meningitis when she was four and a half years old; it's not the same thing as a death in childbirth. They're both hard. I don't know which is harder.

I thought about Janine and her golden hair and about being there when she was born. She was a strong, healthy child then. I thought about saying something about that, about Janine's death being something that happened later, not in childbirth. But I decided that it was not a good idea. Arlette needed to have her thoughts on life right now.

So I told her how proud she should be of Alder, what a responsible young man he was, how he had grown, what a handsome boy, what a good job she had done with him. She seemed to take some comfort from my words. I knew, when the pains came, that she was trying not to make a lot of noise out of consideration for Alder (who I knew was fretting in the kitchen), but she was having an awful struggle. She was working very hard. Her body was awash with sweat, and the pains were coming closer and closer together.

She couldn't talk anymore between pains; she slept or was unconscious, and then her body was wracked again. It went on and on, until it was just one pain right after another. She couldn't control the noises coming out of her mouth. She arched her back and screamed, "I can't take it anymore! I can't take it!" She pulled on the sheets as though she'd rip the sideboards off the bed. She was breathing hard and fast; each breath had a moan on the end of it. "Oh, Lord! Oh-h-h! G-o-d!"

Arlette's quick shout brought me back to myself. "Ida!" she gasped, "It's coming." She was feeling the need to push, and the baby was on its way. Right then I thought a sharp thought to myself, "Where is that blessed doctor?" Everything was ready, and for a while all of our attention was on the birth. Even though the doctor wasn't there, we couldn't do anything about that. Babies have their own time, and they don't ask anyone if it's convenient right now for them to be born.

When the head started to come, I had the strangest feeling. You know how sometimes you get a feeling that you've seen something before or done something before? Well, it was like that, but still it wasn't like that at the same time. When I saw all that golden blond hair, it was eerie because I'd just been thinking of little Janine, and this was just like seeing the birth of Janine all over again. When the hair is wet like that, it doesn't look blond, but when you've seen as many births as I have, you know what that really golden-blond hair looks like on a baby being born. I just knew it was a little girl, and my idea was right. She was all red and wrinkled, just like Janine. Arlette had drifted into that peaceful moment without pain. At that point the door opened, and the doctor came in.

"How are we doing in here?" he asked.

"Well, how like you, doctor! You've arrived just in time to do your part in the ribbon cutting ceremony," I said. I always like to give him a smart remark, just so he knows I'm not overawed by him. I had just used the twine to tie off the cord, when he came in. I tied it in two places, so all he had to do was to cut in between. I was glad it was almost over, because Arlette was exhausted.

The doctor checked the baby, and while he examined the afterbirth, Angela took charge of bathing the little girl. Oh, she was a healthy baby all right; she had a set of lungs on her that could shatter a window pane. A beautiful baby girl—five and a half, six pounds—the picture of Janine. But still, I was surprised; I had thought from the size of Arlette that this would be a much bigger baby.

Just when I thought it was about over and we could all get some rest, Arlette had another "contraction." The doctor didn't call them pains; he called them "contractions." But he was a man; a lot he knew about pain! Anyway, right at that point, I looked at the doctor. I looked at his face, and he looked surprised. It was an expression that stayed on his face for just an instant, and then it was replaced by that confident "everything's under control" look.

He felt her belly with his hands; he listened with his stethoscope, and then he passed an examination on her with his fingers. He looked at Arlette, and he said quietly that there was another baby on the way. I was helping to clean up Arlette, while Angela was taking care of the baby girl.

Then Dr. Bonsecours asked me if I would go out to his car with him to get some medicines. He said that he needed someone to hold a flashlight for him. I thought there was something a little fishy about this because it was light out now, but I went with him without saying a word. I had an idea that he wanted to talk to me. Alder was in the kitchen; he'd fallen asleep in spite of himself. The doctor went straight through the kitchen and outside to his car. He stopped by his Hudson, but he didn't open the car door.

"Ida," he said, "This second baby's coming back end first. It's struggling, and its heartbeat is irregular. Arlette has been through so much in this past year, I wasn't sure if she would carry this pregnancy to term. I didn't think that she needed to worry that she was carrying a baby she might lose, not after Janine, not after the accident. She's not strong. I don't know if that second baby is going to make it. For that matter, I don't know if Arlette is going to make it. She's exhausted right now."

"Is there any way to turn that baby around, Doctor?" I asked. It seemed to me I'd heard about that somewhere, turning a baby around while it was still in its mother's belly.

"No, Ida, it's too late to do that now. The baby is already engaged. It's ready to be born, and it's going to be born back end first. A breech birth is never an easy delivery."

Now, I was really glad he was there. He'd studied this; he knew what to do to help Arlette better than I could, but I couldn't stop my mind from having its own ideas. Did he think the first birth was easy? Did he think any birth was easy? They don't call it labor for nothing. It's work! It would be the hardest work he would ever do! I'd like to see him have just one. All these thoughts went through my head in a flash, but I kept my lips shut tight to keep any one of them from jumping out at him like a great toad.

"Now, Ida, we're going to go back in there and put the best face on this we can. I'm going to drop some chloroform on a handkerchief, and you're going to hold it to Arlette's nose and pull it away, the way we did for Helen Rickert, you remember? And I'm going to try to help her deliver that baby. That's all we can do. After that it's not in our hands anymore."

I had an idea that the doctor had taken more into his hands than he should have, not telling Arlette that she was going to have twins, but just then I remembered the look of surprise on his face, and I wondered if he even knew. He didn't say one way or the other, but I got the idea that he wanted me to think he knew all along. I'm not a doctor; I don't know. Maybe he knew best. I nodded; I didn't say anything. He got something, some medicines, out of his car so that he wouldn't look like a liar. Then we went back inside to tend to Arlette. We'd only been away a couple of minutes.

When we went back into the kitchen, Alder jumped up awake, "Is something wrong? Is my Ma going to be all right?"

The doctor told Alder that he had a little sister and that there was another baby on the way. He said, "Your mother is very tired, Alder. She's having a difficult time right now; she's experiencing quite a bit of discomfort. But we're going to do our best. Maybe you could ask the Good Lord to give us a little help."

"Discomfort?" I thought. "Discomfort, my foot!" What a word! I wanted to spit. We went back into the room. Arlette was moaning, clutching at the blankets, turning her head from side to side. She was sweating like a butcher. My mother used to say, "Horses sweat, men perspire, women glow." Well, Arlette was glowing all right, but she was also sweating, a lot. Angela was trying to keep a cool compress on her head, trying to talk to her, trying to soothe her. But Arlette was delirious with the pain. Discomfort! The doctor gave me the chloroformed handkerchief, and I used it on Arlette. He was right about one thing. Arlette needed to be out of this, out of this pain. It was too hard! I wondered if births were getting harder, or if I was just getting less able to bear them.

It was not an easy time, I can tell you, but anyway, that baby was born. The cord was wrapped around its neck three times. It was white as a sheet. The only idea that came to my mind was, "Oh my God, it's dead!" I didn't even know that I had said it out loud, but I had. "Oh my God, it's dead!" The words hopped out of my mouth right into that room. I must not have been paying much attention to what I was supposed to be doing with the chloroformed handkerchief, because Arlette heard me say those words. She brought her hand up to her mouth and uttered a little cry of grief. I came to myself right away, and put the handkerchief back to her nose.

The doctor carefully unwrapped the cord from around the baby's neck, and he laid the baby down on its back. He didn't cut the cord; he just left it attached to the baby. There was no sign of life or movement in that little body whatsoever. That baby was so white, it was almost blue, if that makes any sense.

As that baby lay there, the most amazing thing happened. The color started to come into its little body. It started right at the cord—where the cord attaches to the baby, and it sort of worked outward like a ripple. His little body started to pink up, and he had like a little spasm. Doctor Bonsecours picked him up and gave him a gentle pat on the back. Then the baby let out a weak, little cry like the mew of a kitten. Honestly, he made me think of a kitten. He was so small, scrawny, dark haired. He was delicate: three and a half, four pounds, no more. He didn't look anything like the little girl. I told Ward, "When they grow up, nobody will even be able to tell that they're sister and brother."

I had to hand it to the doctor, though—much as it griped me; he knew what he was doing. He saved that baby and Arlette, too. Sometimes he just got under my skin, but he did a good job that day. Arlette was coming to herself, and the doctor told her she had twins, a little girl and a little boy. "But the third one died," she said. "What was the third one?"

The doctor looked puzzled. "There was no third one, Arlette. You have twins. They're both living."

"But I heard Ida say, 'Oh my God, it's dead!'" Arlette said. That's when I knew what opening my mouth had done. It took us a deal of explaining to convince her of what had happened. And I'm not sure she ever really was convinced.

Arlette got to hold both her babies. She said she needed to think about names for them. She didn't think that a baby should be named until it was looked at and held for a while. She said that she had some ideas, but she just wanted to think them over.

We put the little girl in the crib that Arlette had ready. The little boy we wrapped in cloths and put him in a box in the warming oven, because Dr. Bonsecours said that he was too little to make enough of his own heat. The doctor told Alder that his prayers had helped, and Alder just beamed. He hadn't had much sleep, but we sent him to get Aunt Mabel to come and stay with Arlette and the babies.

Aunt Mabel is wonderful with babies and taking care of sick people. She's no help at all at a birthing, but once the babies have arrived, you couldn't ask for them to be in more capable hands. After Aunt Mabel came, we talked for a while, and then Angela and I decided to head for home. We would take turns with Mabel and spell her for a while, but right then we both needed some sleep.

On the way home Angela and I talked about how much the little girl looked like Janine, but that the little boy didn't favor Alder or Janine. He was the spitting image of Mark. Arlette must have thought so too. When she looked at him, all she could say was, "Oh, Mark! Oh, Mark!" as though she wanted to cry. Angela said that Arlette had talked a lot about her husband Mark while she was in labor. She missed him terribly. Angela said, too, that thoughts of Mark came into her mind as soon as she saw Arlette sitting in Mark's special chair.

"There. Right there. Just like that. Oh, God, that feels so good!" Ida sat on the edge of the bed while Ward, kneeling behind her, massaged the muscles of her neck and shoulders. "Oh, God!" she sighed. "I think I'm getting too old for this baby business. I'm so tired! It'll be so nice to take a nap before we eat."

"It was a long night," Ward said soothingly.

"Yes, it was; it certainly was."

"But everybody lived through it. And everybody did a good job. Even the doctor?" Ward's question was spiced with mischief.

"That bastard!"

Ward heard energy surge back into Ida's voice, and he felt tension cramp her neck muscles again. He moved his fingers expertly over the muscles, untying the knots of a memory. For a moment he thought she might not talk about it this time. But then she began to speak; her words were level, practiced, predictable. She still needed to get it out.

"I never deliver a baby with him but what I remember that time with Adela Burns. That was a night pretty much like last night. He didn't come, and he didn't come. And the baby was born. And I did everything I knew to do. And I was just about to cut the cord when he shows up. 'So, what are you doing here, Ida?' he says to me. 'Delivering babies without a license again? You know, I could have you arrested for that. But I suppose it's all right, so long as you haven't cut the cord.' And he cuts the cord. And he gets paid for that, cutting the cord. That's all the work he did!"

"He was probably just kidding."

"Well, if he was kidding, he doesn't do it well, I'll tell you that. He got my dander up in good shape! The idea! Telling me he could have me arrested! I said to him, I said, 'Well, maybe you know, and maybe you don't, but babies have their own schedule. They can't wait around for you, when you're ready to show up.' And he was probably off with some woman. That's no secret! How his wife puts up with him, I'll never know. And the whole town knows what he does in his office, when women don't want their babies. And he's going to have me arrested?"

"Hearsay is one thing; proof is another." Ward worked his hands down her back and then returned to her neck.

"I know; I know. Never believe anything you hear and only half of what you see, but I can't abide that smug attitude of his." She relaxed again into Ward's hands. "Oh, my, that feels so nice. Don't stop."

Ward began taking the pins out of her hair. As his hands went about their business, his face seemed to be working on its own thoughts: how to ask a question without leaving another question behind. "And Angela did all right?" His voice was bland, conversational; his fingers slowly massaged Ida's temples.

"Yeah, she did all right, I guess. She's not a great help, but I think she tries. She's an odd duck; I never know quite how to take her. She seemed okay while she was talking to Arlette. Actually Arlette did most of the talking. All Angela had to do was to ask her enough questions to keep her going. And that was all right. But after the baby was born, she acted odd. I don't know another way to put it, just odd. Maybe it was the sight of all that blood. She's not like Mabel; she doesn't pass out at the sight of blood. But she doesn't like it either. And babies are born covered with blood and Dutch cheese.

"When I handed the little girl to her, you would have thought I was handing her a grenade that might go off any minute. She looked at that baby as though she didn't know quite what to do. I said, 'If you'll take charge of cleaning up the baby, I'll see to Arlette.' After I said that, she seemed to be okay again. While she was bathing the baby, I could hear her talking to it, 'It's not your fault, is it? Let's get you all cleaned up now. No, that's right; it's not your fault. You're a nice, little girl. No, don't take it away yet; I need to wash that hand. I know; I know. It's not easy, is it? But it's not your fault.' Of course, we all do that, crooning at babies while we wash them. But she was crying through it all; it just seemed so odd. She can be so cold and so emotional at the same time. I can't figure her out."

Ward was combing one hand through Ida's long hair, his other hand explored her back, her sternum, the curves of her breasts. "This old man can think of something that might be very relaxing for his good woman before she takes a nap."

Ida captured one of his hands and brought it up to her lips. "Oh, I'll just bet you can!" She smiled and pressed the hand to her cheek. "You're the king of relaxing."

Chapter Three
Angela's Thoughts

• *Angela Holden* •

I was watching Alder walk ahead of us with the lamp and one of the flashlights. He was stepping right off. Mother Holden was too busy breathing to talk much, so I had my thoughts to myself. I guess that really I started thinking about Mark even before Ida and I walked into that house, because I was thinking about how he'd built that house with his own hands.

He built it in the same style as the neighboring farmhouses, but it's not a big house. But he said that he'd built it so that he could add on to it, as he needed to and had the money to. He worked really hard on that house, and he was very proud of it. It was a dream come true for him. His uncle had left him this piece of land, left to the last of the Handy line. He said if you went back a way up the family tree and came down a different branch, there might be some other Handys somewhere. But of the Handy family around here, he was really the last.

I guess that was why he was so pleased when Janine was born, because now there was a Handy to carry on. I remember that I reminded him that Janine's children wouldn't carry the Handy name. But he said that that didn't matter. What mattered was that she was a Handy, and now there was hope for the future. And, who knew, with a bit of luck there soon might be a whole houseful of Handys, and maybe there'd be boys as well. But boys or girls made no difference; the Handy family tree was in flower again, and that was cause for celebration. I guess everybody knew he liked to celebrate; sometimes he celebrated a little too much.

But, you know, I always liked Mark for that. Not for the celebrating part, but for the way he felt that girls were just as good as boys for carrying on a family line. I respected him for that. Most men make you feel that the only reason for a woman to exist is to take care of them and give birth to boys to carry on their precious names. But Mark was genuinely pleased when Janine was born. There was no disappointment in him at all, and Arlette didn't have to say that maybe next time they'd be lucky and have a boy. He didn't need any apology. Not that it's any woman's fault, but some men need that.

Mark was a different kind of man. Maybe he did drink a little too much, I don't know; but it was always comfortable to be around him. He made women feel that they were as smart as he was, that they were as good as he was. Most men don't do that. He was a different kind of man. He would have had to be. He treated Alder as though Alder were his own son. It didn't seem to bother him that Arlette had had a child out of wedlock. I think that it honestly didn't matter to him. He loved her, he wanted her to be his wife, and that's what was important. In fact, when he found out that she was pregnant with his child, he leaped at the chance to marry her. Some men would've made a big thing out of that. He didn't. Anyway, I'm getting ahead of myself.

When Mother Holden and Alder and I walked into that house and I saw Arlette sitting in Mark's chair, I couldn't help thinking about Mark and the day that I sold that sitting room set to him and Arlette. I was working for Chamberlain and Drew's Furniture at the time, and they came into the store. It was only a few weeks before Janine was born, and they were still living in one of Aunt Mabel's apartments until their house was finished. They didn't really have any money; they'd put everything they had into that house. But they said that they were looking for something new, something nice for the sitting room, something special for their new home.

I began showing them the sets that we had, but Mark's eyes went immediately to that chair. Arlette's a shopper, and even though she was very pregnant, she wanted to look around at all of the different choices. But every time I looked at Mark, his eyes were on that one chair, and I knew that he was just waiting until we got around to that set. I don't know if Arlette noticed it or not; she was just very interested in looking at different sets and comparing prices and thinking about how they would look in her front room.

Anyway, I wasn't in sales for nothing. I could see where my sale was going to be, so I decided that I'd show them every other set first. And Mark didn't rush me. He didn't say, "I like that chair. Let's go look at that set, Arlette." I could see that he wanted her to be able to do her shopping, but his heart was set on that chair, and his mind was already made up. So we went through every other set, and I'd tell them the advantages and special features of each piece of furniture.

All the time, I was watching Mark steal looks at that chair. He was trying to look interested in what I was saying, trying to pay attention to Arlette's questions. He even asked a few questions himself about buying on time, how much money they would have to put down on the set, and how soon a set could be delivered once we reached an agreement.

As a new bride myself, I understood Arlette's need to consider all the choices; she was looking for the set that would be exactly right for them. I felt the same way; Clay and I were so perfect for each other that I wanted the furniture in our house to be as perfect as our love. My mother wanted to give us her old living room set to start out with, and I knew that in terms of our finances it made sense. But like Arlette, I wanted something that was uniquely "us," a kind of celebration of our union.

I always liked Mark and Arlette, and I knew that I'd be able to get Mr. Drew to give them a good deal. But I also loved selling. I thought probably that Arlette would go along with whatever Mark wanted, if it really mattered to him; so it was just a matter of setting up the sale. And what makes it nice is when you're pretty sure you have a sale, when you know that people are really there to buy.

It's not like waiting on somebody who's just stopped in to look around and pass the time of day. Although that can be fun too, when you succeed in selling somebody something they didn't even know they wanted, needed, or were going to buy. That can be an interesting challenge. It's a matter of observing your customers and listening to what they say and don't say with their mouths, and understanding what they're saying and not saying with their bodies and their faces.

Anyway, Mark's face was an open book to me. Arlette was a much harder nut to crack. I always knew that there were a lot of thoughts going on behind her face that she didn't let me see. At the time I didn't know and couldn't have guessed how many. Arlette was the kind of person who didn't let her defenses down very often; she showed you only what she wanted you to know. She'd had a life that had trained her in just how to keep her thoughts to herself.

So my selling job here was to appear to be selling furniture to Arlette, but underneath it all, I was really selling to Mark. And finally I brought them over to the set Mark was interested in, and he was having a tough time trying to look as though it didn't matter to him whatever Arlette decided. In something for the house, it's usually the woman's decision that prevails.

Lots of times the men don't even bother to come with their wives to pick out furniture, since the wives will wind up getting what they want anyway. Often the wife brings her husband in to look at something only after she's already made up her mind. And then she convinces him that this is the best piece of furniture in the store and the best buy, and then he pays for it, and they leave. Most men just aren't that interested, but with Mark it was different.

Mark sat in the chair, and if he'd been interested before, now he was in love. It fit him to a "t." It was one of those wing chairs with a high back that made it look big, but its seat was actually set fairly low to the ground. Mark was strong and wiry, but he wasn't a tall man, and a lot of couches and chairs felt too high for him and cut him wrong in the legs. But this set was "just right." It was like watching Goldilocks sit in the little bear's chair. It wasn't too big, it wasn't too small, it was just right. It was only a two-piece set. Mark liked the chair, and Arlette liked the couch; so that settled it, and they bought it. And that was always "Mark's chair."

While Mark was alive, nobody ever sat in that chair when Mark was at home. And not very many people ever sat in it when Mark was not at home. I always had the notion that it was more Arlette's rule than Mark's, but Mark went along with it. He liked having a particular spot in the house that was all his own. And he used to sit there in the evenings and read the paper or listen to the gramophone, which sat on top of the radio beside his chair. The gramophone was a wind-up machine, but the radio didn't work, because they had no electricity in their house.

The night that Janine was born, however, he was listening to the radio, because they didn't move out of their apartment until a couple of weeks after Janine arrived. That night he was listening to the boxing match between somebody and Joe Louis. He'd bet his whole week's wages on Joe Louis, and Arlette was upset about that, and she was in labor.

I guess he'd had a few too many to drink when he made the bet, but around here when you make a bet like that, it's serious business. If you lose, you pay up. And they didn't have much money, any more than most people around here have. If he'd been my husband, I'd have wanted to kill him. Anyway, he sat in that chair glued to that radio while Arlette was having Janine. And after Janine was born and Joe Louis had won, it was hard to tell which Mark was happier about. He had a baby girl and an extra week's wages, and it seemed like everything in the world was going just right for them. Arlette was almost as relieved about Mark's winning the bet as she was about having a healthy baby. In a way I didn't blame her; it was a lot of money.

When we entered their house to help with the birth of another baby, I saw Arlette sitting in Mark's chair, and that other night came back to me so clearly of Mark's sitting in that chair, frowning at the radio, with his dark chin resting in his hand, and of Arlette's pacing up and down the room holding onto her belly. "Oh, good Lord! A week's wages! Oh, good Lord!" she kept saying. She didn't seem to be angry with Mark; it was more like a prayer. And now seeing her sitting in that chair, I wondered if she was thinking of that same night. Arlette would never have sat in that chair while Mark was alive, but now I wondered if she was sitting in it to somehow be closer to him.

I didn't plan to say any of this to Arlette. I figured that this was not the right time to be talking about Mark and reminding her of the accident or reminding her about little Janine's death either. (Besides, I wasn't sure that I really wanted to talk about Janine.) But Arlette was the one who brought up both Mark and Janine. Somehow she seemed to need to talk about them.

"I'm sitting in Mark's chair tonight," she said. "Actually I sit in it a lot nowadays. In some way it comforts me to sit in his favorite chair. You were the one who sold us this set. Remember that, Angela? Lord, how he loved this chair! Tonight I was sitting here remembering the night Janine was born and that damned Joe Louis fight. Remember? Oh, Lord, I was so discouraged thinking we might lose all that money. Somehow the money doesn't seem so important anymore. There are a lot more important things that you can lose." Her thoughts returned to the crocheting which lay in her lap, and her fingers moved like lightning, while she added another row onto the bottom of the christening dress she was making.

"My, that's beautiful!" I said, changing the subject. "You do such wonderful work, and you're so fast at it."

"Crocheting is one of the few things my mother left me," Arlette said. "She could crochet like an angel. You put a crochet hook in her hand, and she could make almost anything, gorgeous things. And if you think I'm fast, Lord, I couldn't hold a candle to her. You couldn't even see her fingers move. And now she's gone. I don't even know where she is, or even if she's dead or alive. Can you believe that? Can you believe that a mother could just disappear like that? She took off with a traveling salesman and never came back.

"She never wrote to me, not even one line. She sent Aunt Mabel a couple of letters, but she never wrote to me. And you know, I can't remember that we ever had a cross word between us, my mother and me. We always got along. I was all she had in the world; she was all I had. I was sixteen when she left, and she never looked back, at least not at me so far as I can tell. I can't imagine walking out on a child of mine that way. But she did; somehow she was able to do that, and I've lost her too."

Mother Holden was looking in from time to time and keeping an eye on Alder and Arlette at the same time. Arlette and I were visiting, but actually I didn't have to say very much to keep her distracted. She seemed all wound up and needing to talk. Her talk wasn't all connected and smooth the way I'm going to tell it, and I'm not sure now which pieces of the conversation came first and where the pains interrupted. So what I'm remembering here is the gist of the things that she said over the course of the time she was in labor. I do remember asking her where her father was and then wishing that I could have taken the question back.

"My father?" Arlette repeated my question. "I guess that you could say that that's another loss, except that I never knew him. My mother never talked about him; I'm not even sure that she knew who he was. Maybe that sounds awful, but I think it's the truth. When I say that she didn't talk about him, I mean that she didn't talk about a *real* him. Every time I asked about my father, which was often when I was little, she would tell me a different story.

"Once he was a down-on-his-luck gold miner, who was looking for a lost mine in Texas, and when he managed to find his gold mine, he would send for us. Once he was an important businessman, whose business took him all over the world. They'd always kept in touch, but she'd misplaced his letters at the last hotel she worked in. He was away on a long trip right now, but when he returned from India or Afghanistan, he would look us up. It was always somebody far away, who had some good reason for staying gone. Once he was a handsome carnival barker, who was too much in love with Ferris wheel lights and the marvels of the midway to ever leave them and settle down. I suspect that that was closer to the truth."

"Well, it was lucky for you that you had Aunt Mabel," I said.

Arlette's eyes went soft. "Aunt Mabel has always been wonderful to me. If it hadn't been for her, I don't know where I would have turned when my mother left. But she was always there. She'd hold me while I cried, and she'd hug me when I laughed. She's been like a mother to me and more. She taught me how to cook. She gave me some of her recipes that she never shared with anyone else in the world. She showed me how to make a bed. She taught me how to clean, how to wash, how to take different kinds of stains out of different sorts of cloth. If I can make my own clothes today, it's because of Aunt Mabel. She's such a special lady. She's always good humored; I've never heard an angry word fall from that woman's lips. No matter what, she's always been there for me. And you know what? She always smells nice. Isn't that a funny thing to think about? But it's true; she always smells nice."

When we moved into the bedroom, it was lighter than day with all the kerosene lamps Alder and Mother Holden had placed around the room. The bedroom set was a beautiful old set, dark oak with marble tops on the dresser, the chiffonier, and the commode. I had never seen a set like it at Chamberlain and Drew's. It was much too old for that. "This is a beautiful set. Where did this come from?" I asked.

"Isn't it beautiful?" Arlette agreed. "This came from Mark's uncle's place. I think that it was the only really beautiful thing he owned, and it was always special to him. He left Mark everything, including this piece of property that we built the house on. But except for this bedroom set and the land, nothing else was worth very much. He was very good to Mark; Mark always spoke very highly of him."

"How did Mark happen to be raised by his uncle?" I asked.

"Good Lord, I thought everybody was familiar with that story!" Arlette said.

"Well, my family hasn't always lived in Duncansboro. There are quite a few stories that I don't know, that everyone else in town seems to know by heart."

"Mark's mother died when he was born," Arlette began, "and after that, his father was never quite right in his head. From what Mark told me, his father blamed Mark, and he also blamed himself for his wife's death. Mark didn't have a lot of clear memories of his father; much of what he knew, he learned from his Uncle John. Anyway, Mark's father just got stranger and stranger. He'd go through long periods of being depressed and silent, and then sometimes he'd yell and holler and break up the furniture and punch holes in the walls. He tried to commit suicide and almost succeeded. Finally, he had to be committed to the state asylum, where he passed away when Mark was still a boy.

"The state took Mark's parents' property to pay for the care of Mark's father, and if it hadn't been for his Uncle John, Mark would have become a ward of the state and gone to a foster home. His Uncle John was his only family, and he wouldn't hear of Mark's being placed in a foster home. So Mark went to live with him in the tenement he rented in the old Charlan Block. His Uncle John was really good to Mark; he taught Mark how to be a good father."

This was pretty much all of the conversation we had before the babies were born, except for the talk about losing the baby. When Mother Holden came into the room just before Arlette went into hard labor, Arlette talked about the superstition of how bad things always happen in "threes" and for that reason she was going to lose the baby. At the time nobody (including the doctor) knew that it was going to be "babies." In fact the talk about losing the baby nearly turned out to be right when the little boy was born. That was a close call.

After the babies were born, Arlette just kept looking at them both, but mostly she looked at the little boy and kept saying, "Oh, Mark! Oh, Mark!" When we were alone, Arlette said to me, "That night that Janine was born seems like just yesterday, and now they're both gone, both Janine and Mark. I don't think that I ever appreciated Mark enough, that I ever loved him enough when he was alive. Sometimes his drinking would get in my way, not that he was ever really mean or cruel, and he always provided well for both Alder and me. He loved us both, and he was just crazy about Janine. He was a wonderful father; Alder's been just lost without him these last few months. I wish that I had loved him more and had thought about myself less. I just wish I had it all to do over again." She began to cry, "I'm going to have to do my best to make it up to these little ones. I just don't know if I have the strength."

During that morning I saw into Arlette more than I ever had. Arlette had a way of being friendly but of keeping to herself at the same time. For one thing I had never seen her so willing to talk. She started talking a blue streak from the time we came in, and she just kept going. Being about to bring new life into the world, I guess, had put her in mind of those who were gone; and her sorrow, her pain, and her joy seemed to open her up.

When I mentioned that to Mother Holden on the way home, she agreed. She said, "When the pain takes you, you're completely surrounded by it, but when it leaves, sometimes you get the idea that you want to hold on to the people around you. That's probably why she talked so much and let her hair down to you."

Frankly, though, in later years I often wondered why she talked so much about herself to me that night, how she could have felt comfortable doing that. Maybe she just needed to talk, and I was the one who was there. I don't know. Of course, I was dealing with my own pain, which I didn't mention to anyone. It's strange the things we keep to ourselves and the ones we choose to reveal.

We left a little while after Aunt Mabel arrived, but not before we'd had a cup of tea with her and told her everything that had happened. We were tired, and all for leaving, but she wouldn't hear of it: "I know; I know. I'm imposing on you, after all you've been through, but don't you know, I've got to hear it all first hand from you. I'll have the tea ready in a twinkling, and while we're waiting, you can go over with me everything I need to do, especially for that cunning little darling in the warming oven there." We talked and told Aunt Mabel about our night.

She just had to hold "both those little darlings" and kiss Arlette and tell her how proud she was of her. "Isn't this wonderful! I've just written it down, so I'll remember to put it in my date book—a new birthday, June 2, 1943. They've been born during a war, but that's a blessing—a double blessing! That's what it is. And after all you've been through, my precious love, you deserve it. It's time to put the past behind you, Arlette, and celebrate your blessings. It's time to look ahead, don't you know. But after a cup of tea, I want you to get some sleep, young lady. You need your beauty sleep. That's what's most important right this minute. And I've got to send these two good women home to get some rest as well. I'll get Alder packed off to bed, too. School will keep until tomorrow. He's had about enough excitement for one night. And don't you worry about the little darlings; I'll take good care of them. I've got nothing else to do today but look after things here, and unlike all of you I've had a good night's rest. I know your house is spic and span as usual, but I'll find something to keep me occupied. Don't you think you're going to stay awake and entertain me. If I run out of things to do, I've got my memories to keep me company."

"Why don't you have a baby, Mom?" Michael looked up at Angela as she bent over and tucked in his blankets. She sat down on the bed and kissed his forehead.

"I already have a baby. I have you."

"I know, but I'm not a baby anymore. Why don't you have a *baby* baby?"

"Hm-m, that's probably not such a good idea while your father is away." She smoothed her dress over her knees and smiled to herself at Michael's sweet innocence. A part of her wished he didn't have to grow up.

"But Arlette had two babies, and Mark is away. Grandma said he's in heaven."

"Yes, that's true enough." She swallowed to ease a sudden pain and to keep her voice even. "But that's just the way things turned out." She paused, searching for a way to forestall further questions. "And . . . speaking of turning out, I'm going to turn out this light and let you get some sleep. Good night, my big boy. I'm sorry that I was cross with you earlier. It's been a long, tiring day for me." She gave him an apologetic smile, hugged him, and pressed her cheek to his. Sometimes when the pain was so sharp, it helped her to hold her son close. He was so seldom willing to be hugged.

"Good night, Mom." Michael watched his mother switch off the light, and the click of the switch seemed to touch off another idea in his mind. "I know what you could do! You could have a baby and surprise Dad when he comes home from the war."

"That would be a surprise all right." She was already retreating from the bedroom.

Michael hugged himself. "That would be great! You could have a baby and surprise Dad."

At the threshold, Angela closed the door part way. As she turned, she addressed herself quietly to the newel post at the top of the staircase, "It would serve 'em all right if I did!"

"What, Mom?"

She was descending the stairs, clutching at the banister for some sort of support. "Nothing, Michael, I was just talking to myself."

"You do that a lot."

"I know; it's a bad habit. Good night, dear." At the bottom of the stairs, she moved her hand thoughtfully from the banister to the newel post. Then she turned down the hall to the kitchen. She walked through the kitchen and circled through the dining room and living room, until she encountered again the newel post at the bottom of the stairway in the hall. She had made a complete circuit of the house.

She told herself it was exercise, and she started on a second round. This walking was a ritual—almost every night. Sometimes she took a dust cloth with her on her rounds, sometimes the carpet sweeper, sometimes the broom. And sometimes like tonight she just walked, but she was always going around in the same direction. She was like a soldier on angry patrol near the crest of a cold escarpment. On her tenth circuit tonight she began muttering to herself.

"Yes, I do talk to myself a lot. I certainly do. But who else can I talk to? Who else would listen? I tried talking to my mother. That was great advice she gave me, wasn't it? My own mother! Damn it! And, I can't talk to you, can I? Oh, God, I wish you were here right now, you son of a bitch! I'd like to rap you a good one.

"No, it's only me. I'm the only one I can talk to. There's nobody else. That's just the point—nobody else I know. Some wouldn't even believe it. 'Oh, no, I can't believe that!' Some wouldn't care. 'Too bad for you,' they'd say. And what about them? What do they know, huh? What are they keeping to themselves? It would be like talking to the wall. What do they care anyway? They're condoning it. That's it! That's exactly it. They're condoning it.

"And I can't talk to you. You're not here. But you could be here. Couldn't you? You could be here, you no good, rotten . . . " She took a swipe at the newel post. "You didn't have to go. They told you, you didn't have to go. But you did. You went anyway. You left me. You left us. You wanted to go. That's it, isn't it? You wanted to go! And maybe this is exactly why you wanted to go.

"And where does that leave me, huh? Where? You want to know where? You want to know the answer to that one, pal? Well, I'll tell you the answer. It leaves me walking around this house at night, talking to myself—Angela Holden, crazy woman.

"I shouldn't take it out on him. He's just a baby. I know that. And I find myself saying things I shouldn't say. I should know better. But what do you want me to say? What do you want me to do? You just want me to take it, and take it, and take it? Of course, that's what you want. You're not here. What do you care?

"So what do you expect of me? What? Of course I talk to myself. Why shouldn't I? Who wouldn't? If I had you here, I'd cut your slimy heart out and open it up just to see what makes it tick. God, I hate you! Do you hear me? I hate your guts!" She took another swipe at the newel post. "You . . . *jerk*!"

"It's not their fault either. But I don't understand how that happened. That was strange. Really strange! But I saw it with my own eyes. Didn't I? I did. I'm going to have to find out about that. But there it was. The proof! The proof of what a stupid, blind idiot I am.

"And what about her? All this time! What's that all about, huh? You want me to talk to her? What should I say to her? Talk about the things we have in common? Huh? You want to know the one I blame for this? That's it. You got that right, buster—*you*. You're the one I blame. Honest to God, I can't believe you did this to me! I can't believe you're putting me through this.

"And you're not here. And I can't talk to you. And I can't write it in a letter. My letters to you are supposed to be morale boosters. I'm not supposed to write about problems at home. I'm supposed to make you feel good, make you feel loved, support you, support the war effort. And I'm so dumb, that's what I do! Angela Holden—Citizen of the Year. And who makes me feel loved? Who supports me? Who supports me, when you knock the pins out from under me?

"What would I say in a letter anyway? How can I write about this? I can't even talk about it with anybody. How am I going to write about it? No. It's not the sort of thing you write in a letter. Not if you want answers. Truthful answers. I didn't even talk about it when you were here. I'm so stupid, I didn't even see it." Her fist came down hard on the top of the newel post.

"Oh, I knew about that! That was obvious, once I had a clue. I knew about that, and I just tried to forget it. Forgive and forget. Things were different now. Let it go. Just lock it away somewhere. Lock it away and forget it. Put it in a little room and close the door. But I never did forget it. And it was bad enough already. Now it's worse!

"This is the worst! Do you hear me? Now I know—all this time, all this time. And I believed you. I believed in you. Is that what you wanted to do—make me believe in you so you could make me crazy? Well, you've done it. Now you've got your wish. You've succeeded! Do you hear me? You've gone and done it. Here I am. Walking around this house talking to myself. I've gone right off the deep end. I'm nuts!

"Crazy as a bedbug, walking from room to room. Room! Hunh! I saw that room. Oh, yes. Oh yes, I did. I looked at everything in that room. It's in my mind now. It's burned into my mind. I memorized it. I'll never forget it as long as I live! That's the room, isn't it? That's the room. God, I hate you!" Angela struck out at the newel post, which tonight she had taken a habit of whipping every time she walked by it.

"But I don't know why you did this to me. I really don't. I tried so hard! Tell me why. How could you do this to me? I just can't believe it! How could I believe it? How could anybody believe it? It's too much to be believed!

"And I loved you so much! I thought it was so good, so perfect. Wasn't any of it good for you?" She stifled a sob. "Didn't I do anything right? I tried. God knows, I tried! And I loved you." The tears that had gathered unbidden in her eyes interfered with her vision and slowed her pace. "I did. I loved you so much. I really did. I would have crawled through a knothole for you." She stopped at the bottom of the stairs and wiped her eyes. "I thought we were the best! And I'm so stupid, I thought you felt the same way about me." Slowly she sat herself down on the bottom step and wrapped her arms around the newel post.

"Oh, God! It hurts so much!" She put her cheek on the post and rocked her body to keep herself from crying.

"I must be crazy. God help me, I still love you." Hugging the newel post, she surrendered herself to her tears. Words erupted intermittently, more and more slowly between sobs.

"Where are you, tonight? I miss you. I need you.

"Wherever you are, I hope you're safe, you snake.

"What am I going to do? Just take it?

"Jesus, I hate myself so much!"

Such a release of tears was an unusual occurrence in her nightly vigils. It was like watching the promontory of a glacier suddenly break away and melt in a moment. But the next day, a silent pool of ice shone in a winter sun. Somehow it gave her little comfort to remember that it hadn't always been that way. A single word had opened her eyes and changed her life. Now she felt cold, and she didn't know if she'd ever be truly warm again.

Chapter Four
Aunt Mabel's Memories

• *Aunt Mabel* •

Do you know what a paradox is? Well, you probably do, but bless your heart, I'm going to tell you anyway. It's something that doesn't seem to be true, but when you really think about it, it turns out to be true. I like that word because it fits me. I probably learned it in school, but it didn't really strike roots in my mind, don't you know, until I saw the local schools do a production of Gilbert and Sullivan's *The Pirates of Penzance*.

All the schools in the whole town get together and do a musical production every year—all the grade schools and the high school put together. They're wonderful shows; I wouldn't miss them for the world. They put so much work into them. The mothers sew for hours on the costumes. Townspeople work for days building sets and painting scenery. And the children learn these songs and dances, and they always look so happy and full of life. It's got to be a job-and-a-half to pull something like that all together; that music teacher must have the patience of Job. He puts on a show every year that I'm sure even Gilbert and Sullivan would be proud of.

Anyhow, in *The Pirates of Penzance* there's this boy who has been apprenticed to a band of pirates until his twenty-first birthday. Then on his twenty-first birthday, he learns that his period of apprenticeship is not over. It seems that he was born on February 29, so he's really only five years old. And the woman who raised him sings, "A paradox, a paradox, a most ingenious paradox . . . ." I think what made my ears prick up was the fact that he was born on the twenty-ninth of February, because that's my birthday, too. Then I got to thinking about it, and I said to myself, "My life is a paradox!" I'm really nobody's Aunt Mabel, and yet I'm Aunt Mabel to anybody in the town who knows me. Now, wouldn't you call that a paradox?

I've been Aunt Mabel so long, I almost can't remember when I wasn't Aunt Mabel. Well, of course I can, if I put my mind to it, but you know what I mean. For one thing my hair went white when I was just in my early twenties. I never colored it like some folks would, going white so early like that, don't you know. And that was the reason that they started calling me Aunt Mabel.

At that time I was working in the Lakeview Hotel in the part of the hotel that's mostly under the street, which was called then the Lakeview Grill. After prohibition was over, it was called the Lakeview Bar and Grill, but nowadays most people just call it "the Pit." Anyhow, people would come in there for lunch, and I'd be working at the grill. And because I looked so much older than I was, they commenced to calling me Aunt Mabel.

My mother said to me, "Why do you let them call you that, Mabel?" But, you know, I never minded it, even though in the beginning they started it to get my goat. But they never did get my goat with that name; I liked it. It seemed to fit me, and the name stuck. My mother said it made her feel old, hearing me be called Aunt Mabel. I remember thinking to myself that she *was old*. She was forty when I was born, and my father was forty-four.

They had never had children, and they had sort of come to terms with the fact that they weren't going to have children. And then I came along. I was a real surprise, I can tell you. When my mother went to the doctor and he told her that she was going to have a child, she told him to his face that he was crazy as a loon. She was too old to have a child! I guess he kept his composure, and he told her that apparently she wasn't too old, and that it sometimes happens as a woman approaches the change of life. And there I was. They called me the gift of their old age.

And, when my hair went white, my mother was in her early sixties, and I thought she was old. Of course, I look back on it now and think that really she wasn't that old. I don't feel old, but I'm not about to tell you just how old I am. Actually, if you go strictly by the number of birthdays I've had, I'm just a slip of a girl.

When I was a girl, most of my time was spent in the Lakeview Hotel. My mother was the cook there before me. My father was a railroad man. Those were the two big things in Duncansboro: the railroad and the hotel. Actually there were three hotels, but the Lakeview was the grandest. In my parents' day it was a big tourist town. The Lakeview was always full from the first of May to the end of October. Boats went back and forth to Quebec on the lake. The train station was always bustling. It's not like it was then. Time passes; things change.

By the time I was twenty-five, I'd lost both my mother and my father. My father died first, and then, just a few months later my mother followed him. She used to wait on him hand and foot, but once he was gone, she never recovered. She just dwindled away.

I'd been living at the hotel for a few years then. I could have lived at home with my mother and father, but I guess that I felt the need to be independent. There are quarters in the hotel where the help live. To tell the truth (and I haven't told a soul this for years), I was setting my cap for a young man who also worked at the hotel; that was part of the reason I moved there. But nothing ever came of that, and I was never sure why. He never married; I didn't either, but we were good friends for a long time. I used to hear from him even after he moved away—often at first, and then only a letter at Christmas time, and then it stopped altogether. Oh, I had other chances, but somehow it was never the same for me.

Well anyhow, after my folks died, I stayed on living at the hotel. My folks had owned a tenement house, and I probably could have moved into their part of the house and made out just fine, but that just wasn't my way. I enjoyed my work. So I rented out their part of the house, and I decided to stay on at the hotel and put some money by for my old age. I always worked, and I never really wanted for anything.

I was never rich, but I was always comfortable. And sometimes I had the means to do a bit of good with the little extra I had, to make life a little better for someone else. It seems to me that that's what life is all about, helping others. That's what the Good Book says, and I believe it's true.

I was able to help Arlette and her family, and I was glad to do it. I remember when Arlette and her mother first moved into the hotel; Arlette couldn't have been more than eleven or twelve years old. That was right after Mr. Champion bought the hotel. I think his name used to be Champignon, and he changed it to Champion. That happens a lot near the border here: Boisvert becomes Greenwood, l'Esperance becomes Hope, Desruisseau becomes Rivers or Brooks. They translate the name or they just change it like Chabot to Cabot or Champignon to Champion. Anyhow, Mr. Champion bought the hotel.

Arlette's mother had worked for him in another one of his hotels, and she and some of the other staff from that hotel moved here. Arlette came with her. Some of the staff from this hotel were transferred to the other one. They do that when they buy a hotel so that they have their own staff who know the way they want things done. I stayed right where I was. I was the head cook, and Mr. Champion always said that one of the reasons he bought the hotel was because of my cooking. He used to say that I was the best cook in three counties. He was probably just saying that to hear himself talk, but I liked hearing it anyway, don't you know.

Arlette's mother Mrs. Luce was the head housekeeper. She never let anyone call her by her first name; she was always Mrs. Luce. I happen to know that her name was Sadie, but I never in my life called her anything but Mrs. Luce. She called me Aunt Mabel. When Mrs. Luce was busy, someone else would have the care of Arlette. Like most children who grow up in the servants' quarters of a hotel, she was sort of passed from hand to hand, bless her heart. Anyhow, she took to staying around the kitchen. She never bothered me; I liked her. We got along just fine. When she wasn't in school or with her mother, she would most likely be found in the kitchen with me. And she began to learn how to cook; she picked things up very fast. She seemed to be interested in everything, and as time went on, she was a big help to me.

Sometimes, after my shift was done, she'd come up to my room and just sit and talk. I'd ask her what she was learning in school, and she'd ask me to tell her about things I remembered, stories from when I was a girl, the "olden days" she used to call them. I remember once she came into my room, and I was reading a book. That seemed to strike her as an unusual thing to do. She'd seen people reading newspapers in the hotel lobby, don't you know, or looking at magazines or railroad timetables. But I don't believe that she'd ever seen anyone reading a book just for pleasure. She thought about reading as something a body only does in school, bless her heart. She never remembered having seen her mother read a book, she said. Well, I said that her mother must have read to her when she was younger, and she allowed as how that had never happened. So I began reading to her in the evenings.

Oh, we read lots of books. She absolutely loved Dickens; she seemed to feel some kinship with his sad children. It got so after a while she would read on her own, but she still wanted me to read to her. She was getting to be a big girl. In some ways she was very grown up and too serious; she was brought up mostly around older folk with no children her own age to associate with very much, except in school. But in some ways, it seemed to me that she hadn't ever been a child, and she needed to be. She missed that somewhere along the way, don't you know. She felt it, and I understood it. So, even by the time she was fifteen or sixteen, I was still reading to her. We'd sit on the bed wrapped in blankets, and she'd curl up beside me like a girl half her age and listen to me read.

As time went on, though, I did notice a change in her. She commenced to become interested in the romance part of the story. Big as she was, she still loved fairy tales, and especially ones where the handsome prince won the hand of the beautiful princess and carried her off to his castle to live happily ever after.

And then her mother left. And I mean, she left. She'd been seeing this gentleman who sold supplies to the hotel. This had been going on for, oh, a couple of years off and on. Arlette wasn't very struck on him, and he didn't seem to like her too much either. Well, this one day, I was in my room resting between the lunch and dinner rush, and Mrs. Luce just walked into my room without so much as a knock or a by your leave.

"Aunt Mabel, I'm leaving," she says. I had been dozing, and it took me a minute or two to get my bearings. She just stood there in that kind of grand way she had. I thought she meant that she was going out shopping, but that seemed strange, because she'd never explained her comings and goings to me before. She seemed to be waiting for some sort of response from me, and I felt I just wasn't catching her meaning.

"You're leaving, Mrs. Luce?" I said. I didn't know what else to say to her.

"Yes, I'm leaving," she repeated. "Would you look after Arlette for me?" Now, that seemed to me a very strange request. Arlette was sixteen; she pretty much looked after herself at that point. I must've looked as perplexed as I felt, because after a pause she added, "I'm going away with Mr. Warner. He's asked me to marry him. We've put together a little money, and he wants to go to California and try his hand at the hardware business. I'll let you know where we are, and when I can, I'll send for Arlette. I can't take her now; I've got some things to work out with Mr. Warner first. I've talked with Arlette; she understands."

"Why, well, of course, I'd be happy to look after Arlette," I said.

"Thank you very much. I appreciate that," she said. And with that she turned on her heel, and away she went. I got a letter from her from Kansas. She said how flat the land was and how poor the people were. There was another shorter letter from Colorado saying they liked the mountains and the trees, and she wasn't sure if they were going to California after all. She never asked about Arlette, and I never heard from her again. I knew it hurt Arlette, but she always tried hard not to show it. I'm not going to say that Mrs. Luce was a bad mother, because she really wasn't. She had always seen to Arlette, but I suppose she came to a place in her life where she just had to make a choice, don't you know. I can't judge her, I didn't live her life, I don't know.

So Arlette and I went on, and I was her Aunt Mabel. We were closer than ever. She told me all of her girlhood secrets—the teacher she had a girl's crush on, the cute boy who had come to work for the hotel. By this time Arlette had been working in the hotel for some time herself.

Even before her mother left, she'd worked as a chambermaid and as a kitchen helper, wherever she was needed. Now, with her mother gone, she needed to work for her keep, you see. Mr. Champion could be generous to a point, but like most hotel owners he was not in business to have charity cases living in his establishment. But Arlette was a good worker; he knew that already. It seems that Mrs. Luce had settled with Mr. Champion that Arlette would be able to stay on and work for her room, board, and laundry, as well as a small allowance.

When Arlette graduated from high school, I was there in the place of her mother to see her accept her diploma. She was just radiant that day. I was so proud of her! A lot of young ladies didn't make it that far. When her mother left, she talked about quitting and going to work full time, but I wanted her to stay and get her diploma. So she did it for me.

School was only compulsory until a body finished the eighth grade or was sixteen years old, don't you know. So the fact that she stayed and completed all of her courses was quite an accomplishment. I think that it's important to finish the things that you start. One of the big lessons you need to learn in life is how to stick to a task until it's complete. And she did it, and I think it made a difference in how she looked at herself. She had some confidence that she could see a thing through.

Arlette had talked about being interested in boys from time to time. There were periods when it seemed as though that was all she talked about, but it was all just talk. She had gone to her senior dance with a young man who had no one special to go with, and because Arlette had no one either, it was a good match. But it wasn't a date or anything; it was just a dance and a convenience for both of them.

Now, I always loved to dance, and I went to functions at the Grange or other dances in the town, and sometimes I would take Arlette along with me. And she would dance. In fact she got to be quite a good little dancer. Sometimes old men would ask her to dance, and she never said no. She would dance with them, and of course she danced with young men as well. But it was always just a dance, and nothing ever came of it. She was a pretty girl; she wasn't what you'd call beautiful. But she was pretty enough; she wasn't plain. She was never slender, but I wouldn't say that anyone could have called her fat. But in the town, Arlette was an outsider, you see. She and her mother weren't from the town, and they had worked and lived in the hotel, and that kept them on the outside.

Arlette had gone to the high school in the town, but that wasn't enough to make most people feel that she was really a part of the town. Nobody knew her father; her mother had gone off and left her. People in the town who knew the story and knew that I'd taken her under my wing may have felt sorry for her, but that didn't mean that they would have felt encouraged if their sons had taken a second look at Arlette. Now and then, she would tell me about young men who showed some interest in her, but for some reason she never seemed to be very interested in them.

I thought about it some, but it never seemed to bother her. She had her work, and she kept busy. And no young man seemed to turn her head until young Clay Holden came into the picture. It's funny how there are some things you don't remember at all, and then there are some things you remember so clearly. I remember that day as though it were yesterday; it was a Thursday in mid-July, 1932. Arlette was up to her elbows in the big sink scrubbing out pots and pans; her hair was hanging in her face, and her face was flushed from her work.

Women always think they look a mess at such times, but I honestly think those are the moments when men find women most appealing. At any rate, there was Arlette in her soiled apron busy scrubbing pots and pans when young Clay Holden came in with a big box of groceries he was delivering for Pearson's Market. He'd been delivering groceries on Thursdays for a little while; Arlette just hadn't ever been there before when he'd made a delivery.

He came through the side door and spoke to her. He said, "Where would you like me to set these?" The counter where he usually set the groceries was full of the pots and pans which Arlette had just cleaned.

She said, "Oh, I'm sorry. Let me clear a place for you." And she cleared away some pots and pans, while he stood there holding onto his box of groceries and looked at her. It took her a few minutes.

When she had finished, he set the box down and said, "Thanks."

"It was no problem; I'm sorry things were in the way and you had to stand there and hold that heavy box," she said.

"I'm used to it; it happens all the time," he said. He smiled; she smiled. She blushed, and he cocked his head to one side.

That was almost all of it. He brought in the rest of the order from Pearson's Market. Arlette returned to her pots and pans.

When he had finished, he stopped at Arlette's sink and said, "You take care of yourself, now."

And she answered, "Oh, I will. You take care of yourself, too." He smiled; she smiled. She blushed, and he cocked his head to one side.

"Thanks, I always do," he said, and he was gone.

It doesn't seem like such a remarkable conversation that I should remember it so clearly. I was working at the steam table, where I could see the whole event. And I probably would have dismissed it from my mind and not remembered it at all, if it hadn't been for the next thing that Arlette said. The door had no sooner closed on that young man's back when Arlette turned around and looked at me. Her eyes were shining; her face was all lit up like a Christmas tree.

"Oh, Aunt Mabel, isn't he just the most beautiful boy you ever saw?" she asked. She'd already made up her mind to what she was saying. It wasn't really a question, don't you know. I knew that she expected me to say something, and I wasn't sure just what to say.

"Usually when we're talking about a young man, we say that he's 'handsome,' not 'beautiful.'" That's what I said.

"Oh, no! He's way beyond handsome. He's beautiful! He's the most beautiful thing on two legs!" she said. She put her hands together as though she were saying a prayer, and she twirled once around and went back to her pots and pans.

Well, there was no question about it; she was smitten by that young man. He was a nice boy. And there was no question about his being handsome, or beautiful, as Arlette put it. He could have been a movie star. I guess he could've given Clark Gable a run for his money.

Clay was tall, blond, blue-eyed. He had a warm smile and a confident air about him. I couldn't help thinking that he was the type of boy that was just born to break women's hearts, whether he meant to or not. He was a couple of years younger than Arlette. I knew that; I knew him, for that matter. I remembered when Clay Holden was born; I knew his father Ward and his mother Ida. Unlike Arlette, I was born and raised in this town, and I knew most of the people in it. I thought that that young man would never be a match for Arlette, but I didn't say what I thought.

If I'd known then what I know now, I might have said something. I might have said a lot of things and done a lot of things that I didn't do. Of course, that's easy to say, looking back; but I don't know. It always seems easier when we look back, don't you know. It's not so easy when we try to look ahead. I might have said something or done something that would only have made it worse than it was.

My mother used to say, "Don't stick your nose in where it doesn't belong, Mabel." Sometimes it's hard to know where your nose belongs and where it doesn't belong. So as a general rule, I've tried to keep to myself and not to interfere with other people's business. I haven't always been successful in doing that, but I try. My mother also used to say, "You can catch more flies with honey than you can with vinegar."

I remember one time when she said that to me, I said that I wasn't interested in catching flies. Who wants to catch flies, anyway? I just want them to keep out of my kitchen. But I knew what she meant, and I've tried to live by those words. They're not high and mighty phrases, you might say, but they seem to work for me. They "speak to my condition"; I think that's what the Quakers say. They speak to my condition. Those two rules and the Golden Rule all seem to go together, and I've tried to stick by them. So usually I keep my thoughts to myself, and more often than not I'm just as glad that I did. Maybe I did wrong where Arlette was concerned, but then again maybe things happened the way they were supposed to.

At that point, of course, there wasn't really anything I needed to do or say. Arlette just seemed to be struck on this boy, but she'd had crushes before, and they had passed. I certainly didn't think that I should tell her that I thought nothing would ever come of her interest in Clay Holden. I didn't think that he was the type of boy to be interested in her.

As she had said, he was very handsome. He was a star athlete at the high school, a football player, and a popular beau with the young ladies. And he was a couple of years younger than Arlette. I didn't think that Arlette would stand a chance with him. But there was no way in the world that I would ever say such a thing to Arlette. She had a right to her dreams just like everyone else. If she liked the boy and took pleasure from his smiling at her, then there was no harm in that.

Well, time passes; things change. Now Arlette had her hands full with a ten-year-old boy and two babies. Clay Holden had married Angela Surprenant, and they had a child of their own, little Michael.

As she opened the door to Pearson's Market, Arlette's cool, gray eyes made a quick inventory of the store. At one time it had been a good-sized general store, but now it had almost completed its transformation into a food market. It still retained a notions counter near the front on one side and a small hardware section toward the back of the other; these were vestigial women's and men's sections from a time when the establishment had served more of a social function than it did today. Arlette had not been focusing on the shelves of canned goods or the small, attractive displays; she was interested primarily in the store's population. There were five people present, none of whom was Clay Holden.

Arlette's disappointment didn't show on her face, and she busied herself with "looking around," while she thought of adjustments to her plan. It hadn't been a real plan anyway. It was only an idea, a wish, a hope. "Not much hope," she thought, but then she straightened her back and reproved herself, "'Nothing ventured, nothing gained' or as Aunt Mabel always says, 'The answer's always no, until you ask.'" At least she could get information; she could find out when he worked. She was turning a card of rickrack over in her hands, and she started when a voice interrupted her thoughts.

"Can I help you?"

Arlette replaced the rickrack in a basket and looked up at an expanse of white apron, which she was sure had taken a whole bedsheet to make. Mrs. Pearson stood beside the counter. She was a large woman in her late fifties, and her pasty face maintained a pleasant but no-nonsense business look. There was a pencil over her glasses in her henna-dyed hair.

"Oh, yes." Arlette's voice was an apology. "Could you tell me please if Mr. Clay Holden is working here?"

"Friday's freight day; he's in the back rotating stock." Mrs. Pearson dispensed the answer almost automatically, but her eyebrows moved closer together, and the look on her wide face narrowed a little.

Arlette's heart leapt, but her countenance maintained a look of apology. "Oh, thank you. I was wondering if it would be at all possible for me to speak with him for a moment. I'm afraid that I rather inconvenienced him yesterday when he delivered groceries to us at the Lakeview, and I just wanted to apologize."

"Oh, think nothing of it," Mrs. Pearson dismissed the apology. "He's paid to be inconvenienced a little. It's just part of the job."

"I'd feel much better, though, if I could just say that I'm sorry in person." Sensing a small cloud of objection gathering between them, Arlette tried to minimize it with sincerity. "I wouldn't need to interfere with his work; I could just say my piece and leave."

"Well, suit yourself then. The door to the stockroom is through the back there." She waved her hand in the general direction, but she rode over Arlette's "thank you" with a warning, "But don't forget, he's paid to work, not to flirt."

"I just want to say I'm sorry." Arlette hoped she looked appropriately dismayed at such an implication, but she realized that this round woman was sharper than she looked.

Fortunately, Mrs. Pearson was too busy at the moment to follow her, as Arlette walked toward the back of the store. She passed Mr. Pearson at his butcher's bench lopping chops off a pork loin. A tall stick of a man, he wielded his cleaver with deadly accuracy. The Pearsons reminded Arlette of Jack Sprat and his wife. Mr. Pearson pronounced a pleasant "good afternoon" without breaking his rhythm or attempting to impede her progress towards the stockroom.

The stockroom was somewhat darker than the store itself, and Arlette took a moment to get her bearings. At the back of the room she saw Clay stacking boxes in a pool of light that came from a naked overhead bulb. As she approached him, she watched the graceful movements of his body, the firmness of his muscles, and she worked to hold onto the speech she'd prepared for this moment. She felt lucky beyond belief. She wanted to reach her hand out and touch the sweat stain on his shirt at the small of his back, but instead she began speaking just as she had planned, "Clay Holden?"

"Yes," he turned, saw her, and smiled. Arlette bathed for a couple of seconds in his smile. It didn't matter to her that everybody got the same good-natured smile; she decided to receive it as a gift. And she favored him with the gift of her own smile, which not everybody received.

"Please, don't stop working. I promised Mrs. Pearson that I wouldn't interrupt your work." But he *had* stopped, and that encouraged her to go on. She was also encouraged by the calm control she heard in her own voice. "I came by to apologize for inconveniencing you with all my pots and pans at the Lakeview yesterday."

"Oh, no problem," he chuckled. "Forget it."

"But I can't forget it. When I saw you yesterday, . . . standing there with your box of groceries, . . . you just took my breath away!"

"Really? . . . Uh . . . "

"Really! And I was thinking, . . . maybe next Thursday when you come by, perhaps we could talk about . . . a time when we could get together."

"Uh, I don't know, I . . . " He was dazed; he wasn't sure he understood. She moved in closer and pressed on.

"I've never been with anybody else, Clay. You would be the first. No strings attached. Well, . . . except for one condition."

"What's that?" he managed. Nothing like this had ever happened to him before in his life. This was like a dream. He was fascinated, but a little leery; he wondered what the condition was.

She smiled conspiratorially and spoke in a low voice. "This would have to be very private, just between us. You'd need to agree to that. Will you please think about it and let me know next Thursday?"

"All right. I guess. Sure." Private was good! No strings attached was good! He'd have time to think it over. She said he'd be the first! Wow! His mind was shooting in too many directions to be articulate.

Arlette had kept one eye on the door to the store, and in that instant she saw Mrs. Pearson's bulk fill the entrance, like a quizzical snowman in a rusty wig. Arlette's posture changed abruptly, and her voice was all business in an instant, "Well, thank you, Mr. Holden, for being so understanding. I don't want to take any more of your time, but it did bother me, and I wanted to apologize to you in person."

Immediately Clay had grasped the cue and bent over to pick up a box. He was straightening up as she finished speaking. His voice was flustered, "No problem. Don't give it a second thought, Miss . . . Miss . . ."

"Luce. Arlette Luce."

"Luce." He set the box on top of his stack. Arlette had turned and started back to the store. "Oh, Miss Luce?" Clay called to her back. She turned. "I would appreciate it, though, if you could make sure that everything is all clear for next Thursday. That would be a big help." He was in complete control of his voice now, and his smile was genuine.

"I'll make sure that it is, Mr. Holden." To Mrs. Pearson, who had backed out of the doorway to let her pass, Arlette's demeanor spoke of relief and gratitude even before her charming voice said pleasantly, "Thank you very much, Mrs. Pearson; I appreciate your letting me apologize in person. Now I feel so much better!"

"That's perfectly all right, dear. You're very welcome, I'm sure." Mrs. Pearson realized that Clay hadn't even known Arlette's name, and now she was puzzled with herself for having harbored any sort of suspicion against the tender conscience of this polite young lady.

Chapter Five

Opening Doors

• *Michael Holden* •

My mother wrote to my father every single day. On some days she wrote him two letters. My father was a seaman first class in the Pacific theater. He could read her letters, but I couldn't. I didn't know how to read, but I could sign my name—in cursive. I didn't know yet how to print. Except for my name, I didn't know how to write yet either. When my father first enlisted, I used to write to him, too. I'd fill up a sheet of thin stationery with lines of continuous m's and u's. My mother would ask me what I had written, and I would tell her. At first it surprised me that she could read my father's letters, but not mine. She tried without much success, so because I didn't want to hurt her feelings, I would read her my letter.

Dear Dad,

How are you? I am fine. I hope you are fine, too. I miss you. Pepper misses you, too. I can't throw a stick or a ball as far as you can. Pepper says to say, "Hello." I hope the war is over soon so you can come home.

Love,
Michael

Later, my mother would read me her letter. It didn't seem strange to me that she could read her own letter. I could read my own letter. But I couldn't read hers, and she couldn't read mine. That made sense to me, and it satisfied my idea of fairness. In her letter my mother always told my father what my letter said. That did not make a lot of sense to me.

It seemed to me that if my father were smart enough to read her letters, then he should be smart enough to read mine as well. My mother had told me that she needed to say as much as she could on one sheet of paper, because the letter was going by airplane. I thought it was a waste of space for her to tell my father what my letter said. I didn't know the word redundant then.

Then as my father's letters came, it began slowly to dawn on me that my mother could read his letters, but I couldn't. My grandparents could read his letters, but I couldn't. My grandparents could read my mother's letters, but they couldn't read mine. I read my letters to them, or my mother told them what my letter said. Grandmother Holden always smiled and said what a nice letter it was; grandfather always just said, "Hm." "Hm" was one of my grandfather's noncommittal words that made me think, and I began to put two and two together.

I realized that I was a fraud, and that my mother and my grandmother were indulging me. It was the same kind of thing as adults' *letting* children win at games. It was fun in the beginning, but it stopped being fun after a while. It stopped having any meaning. So I stopped writing letters to my father. I would just sign my name, because everyone could read that. I don't remember when I learned to sign my name. It seemed to me that I had always known. I didn't tell my mother or my grandmother why I stopped writing letters. Somehow I felt that they didn't deserve to know.

I told my grandfather, "I've stopped writing letters to Dad, you know." He didn't ask me why.

What he said was, "Would he like to learn the letters of the alphabet?"

"Yes, I would, Grandfather," I answered.

Grandfather began to teach me letters, but I soon could see that it would take forever before I could really read and write. I had not yet learned to cultivate the virtue of patience. That's when I discovered that I could draw and use crayons. And I didn't have to explain to anyone what the pictures were.

Everybody understood my pictures; this was real and very satisfying. So after that I would draw a picture on the airmail stationery and sign my name to it. Sometimes with grandfather's help, I would put a title on my picture. I remember sending my father a picture of Pepper with d-o-g printed on the top and my signature written on the bottom.

A few days after Arlette Handy's twins were born, my mother was having a two-letter day. I had drawn a picture of an Eskimo outside his igloo looking at the northern lights. This was for the first letter. My artistic creativity was sufficiently drained so that I did not feel compelled to produce anything for the second letter. To avoid listening to my refrain that I was "bored, bored, bored," my mother assigned me the task of dusting the living room while she wrote.

This was her standard gambit: give Michael something to do, which will keep him out of my hair and make him think twice about bothering me. Nevertheless, I made short work of the dusting, and soon I was at my mother's elbow requesting her attention again. She was too preoccupied to check over my dusting or to direct me to another chore. Instead she simply suggested that I go play with Pepper.

I had written to my father that Pepper wanted him to throw a long ball to him, but that was really what I wanted. I wanted my father to be there to throw a long ball, and I wanted Pepper to be interested in going after it. In reality Pepper didn't like to be outside very much anymore, unless he could be right beside me or my mother. Mom said that he couldn't see very far. But Pepper and I still played an indoor game of fetch which consisted of my rolling a ball across the living room floor and his retrieving it, often from under the couch. So we played fetch until Pepper needed a nap.

Pepper was older than I was; he was twelve. Mother said that Pepper was old for a dog. He was my father's dog before he was my dog. But when I was born, Pepper decided that he was my dog, or that I was his boy. It was hard to tell who was in charge with Pepper. He used to sit by my crib and growl at anyone who approached to look at me, until either mother or father told him that it was all right.

As I grew up, Pepper took all kinds of abuse from me with incredible good nature. Insensitive to his pain, I sat on him, rode him, pulled his hair, bit his ears. But Pepper never nipped me or tried to retaliate for what I put him through. He would simply walk away if I became too much for him.

Pepper was my best friend. He wasn't called Pepper because he was black or gray. He was a multicolored dog: black, white, brown, gray. Mother called him a crossbreed; grandfather called him a mutt. But grandfather said that mutts made the best pets, because they had better dispositions and were healthier than purebred dogs. But neither Pepper's breed nor his looks had anything to do with his name.

Pepper had gotten his name from his habit of bowing and sneezing whenever he greeted my father. My father thought that he sneezed as though he had just sniffed some pepper. When I was little, Pepper started to do the same thing with me. Every morning when I got up, he would stretch his front paws out in front of him and sneeze. I always did the same thing as a greeting to him.

But this afternoon Pepper was tired, mother was busy writing a letter, and I was bored. So I asked my mother if I could go over to grandfather's. My mother was deep into her letter.

"M-m-m, that's fine; I think that he's home this afternoon," she said. As I started to leave, she added her final suggestions, "Don't make a pest of yourself. And be a good boy, Michael."

I don't think that I ever left the house in my life without that parting imperative from my mother, "Be a good boy." Although these words did not guarantee that I behaved, they always hung over me like a banner, whatever I did.

When I got to grandfather's, he and his "sidekick" Ira had several locks spread out on the kitchen table. Grandfather was a locksmith, and he was teaching Ira to be a locksmith as well. From his childhood grandfather had been fascinated with locks, and over the years he had gradually taught himself to be a locksmith. He knew everything about locks, but in a small town such as ours it was not a skill that was in demand sufficiently to provide one with a living.

In those days many townspeople didn't even have locks on their front doors. So grandfather had a cleaning business as his primary occupation, and locksmithing was more of an avocation, although he predicted that the day would come when people would feel the need to lock their doors. Grandfather had locks on every door in his house, not because he was paranoid about the quality of the neighborhood, but simply because he loved locks.

Ira was a good person to be grandfather's sidekick, because he enjoyed studying locks almost as much as grandfather did. Grandfather was the one who called Ira his sidekick. Actually Ira had become a partner in the cleaning business that grandfather had started. Grandfather and Ira had several contracts to clean stores and banks, as well as the post office, the courthouse, and the armory in town.

They worked mostly after business hours, and that often gave them some time during the day to work with locks. Fortunately, it also often gave grandfather time during the day to talk with me. I had some difficulty thinking about grandfather and Ira washing floors, polishing furniture, and cleaning windows, because grandfather never did any of those chores in his own home.

Grandmother said that she didn't need any of his interference in her work and that, if he felt a compelling urge to clean something, there were several other places in the town that certainly needed cleaning more than her house. Grandfather was always very considerate of grandmother's feelings, and he refrained from demonstrating his cleaning talents in her house. To the best of my recollection, I do not believe that grandfather ever felt possessed to lift so much as a dustcloth against my grandmother's furniture.

When I walked into grandfather's house, grandfather and Ira looked up from the locks on the kitchen table. From the hallway to the kitchen I could see that there were several locks on the table, but none of them were taken apart the way they usually were when grandfather and Ira were studying together. They had been looking at the locks, but somehow I had the feeling that their attention hadn't been on the locks. They looked surprised to see me.

"Well, Michael, Michael, Michael!" Ira was the first one to speak. "So, how is my favorite little artist today?"

"Fine," I said. I put my hands into my pockets and walked up to the table.

"Fine. That's great! Fine's a good way to be. Wouldn't you say so, Ward?" Ira continued. "What're you up to today?"

"Mom is writing a letter, and I'm bored," I said.

"Boy, I wish I had the time to be bored like you, Mikey boy. Maybe, someday you'll be like your grandfather and me—too busy to know the meaning of the word bored," Ira chuckled.

"This old man remembers being bored, but it was a long time ago," grandfather said finally. "Sometimes, he wishes he were back in those days." Grandfather sighed. "But it's no good wishing for what can't be."

I pulled out the chair facing grandfather and sat down. "What're you doing?" I asked.

"Oh, we were just studying some old locks, Mike, my lad," said Ira. "With locks you're never done; there's always something new to learn, wouldn't you say, Ward?"

"Always something new," grandfather repeated reflectively. "Something old, something new."

"Something old, something new, something borrowed, something blue, eh? Ha, ha, ha!" Ira joked.

"Hm," said grandfather. Grandfather picked up a lock and turned it over in his hand. He set it back down and looked at Ira. He looked back at the surface of the table, and he picked up a key. "Does that boy know what this is?"

"It's a key," I answered.

"This is a skeleton key," grandfather said. "A skeleton key opens many locks. This key will lock and unlock every door in this house, except for the outside doors. Why doesn't that boy see what he can do with this key?"

"Can I lock and unlock any door I want?" I asked.

"That's the ticket, Mikey boy. That's just the ticket. There's lots of doors to lock and unlock in this old house. I'll bet you that would be loads of fun! What do you say you start with the ones upstairs?" Ira encouraged.

I took the key from grandfather's hand. His hand was trembling a little, but I didn't think much about it at the time. I went upstairs and began exploring the locks in the house. I wondered if this was how grandfather had gotten started on his interest in locks. I discovered that I had to be careful just how far I inserted the key into the lock. A key inserted too far didn't work; a key not inserted far enough didn't work either. It took practice to insert the key just the right distance into the lock to lock the door.

I locked and unlocked every door several times. After I locked them, I tried them, and sure enough, they were locked. Then I would unlock them and try them again, and they would be unlocked. I wasn't bored anymore; I was enjoying myself. I locked and unlocked each door when it wasn't closed to watch the bolt slide out and retract. Having the skeleton key was like having a magic wand in my hand. It was a powerful feeling. After I had experimented with every lock in every door on the second floor, I decided to try the locks downstairs. When I got to the bottom of the stairs, I could see that the door between the hallway and the kitchen had been closed behind me, when I went upstairs.

That closed door at the end of the hallway gave me an idea. All of a sudden the kitchen had become the jail. I was the sheriff. I crept through the living room as quiet as a mouse. It was really two rooms joined together, but at the end of that space was another door to the kitchen. I would close that door and lock it and return to the hall door and lock that too. My prisoners would be safely locked in. I got to the door between the living room and the kitchen, and very slowly and quietly I began to swing it shut.

I heard my grandfather say, " . . . hard to see just how it will all sugar off. Well, they've got their own lives, but they've made a mess of them, seemingly. This old man feels sorry for them."

I stopped and listened.

Ira said, "I think that I feel more sorry for everybody else, especially the children."

I continued closing the door slowly. The door creaked.

Ira spoke out, "Hey, hey! Mike, my lad, how did that key work?"

"You're the prisoners," I said. "This is the jail, and I'm going to lock you in."

"It's the jail all right," said grandfather.

"Ho, Mikey boy! Lock us in. That's a good one, lad. Don't forget, your granddad here is a locksmith. He could probably get out of any jail, wouldn't you say, Ward?" Ira gloated.

"Sometimes he thinks, and then again, he's not so sure," grandfather sighed. "There are all kinds of jails."

Just then grandmother opened the door to the hall. "What are you men doing all shut up in the kitchen?" she asked.

"This is the jail," I said.

"Well, I guess I've had that idea a time or two myself," grandmother said, "especially when I'm surrounded by laundry, the washing machine, and set tubs."

"How is Arlette?" grandfather asked.

"Well, she's still got six days in bed to do. She's weak; it took a tuck out of her, I can tell you. But she's finally come up with names for those babies," grandmother announced. "It's taken her four blessed days to settle on an idea, but it's finally done. Arlette said that she had thought about Janet for the little girl, because she looks so much like Janine."

Here Ira gave my grandfather a meaningful look, but my grandmother continued without noticing. "And she thought about Marcus for the little boy, because he's the spitting image of Mark. The more she thought about those names, the more unhappy she was though. She felt that if she named them Janet and Marcus, she'd always be reminded of Janine and Mark, and so would everybody else. Then she thought of Sadie for her mom, and John for Mark's uncle. But she didn't like that either. What she decided was that those babies needed a fresh start, names all their own that didn't remind anybody of anybody else. She named the girl Nadine and the boy Nathaniel. Now I like those names, especially because of the idea of their being twins and all."

"Is Mabel with her now?" grandfather asked.

"Yes, she is," grandmother answered. "Actually, Aunt Mabel brought her suitcase with her when she came today. She said that she's decided she had better move in for a while until Arlette is back on her feet and able to look after the babies and her own affairs. Aunt Mabel doesn't think that Arlette is doing as well as she might. She's got milk leg bad. But we just got to hope for the best. Mabel asked if Angela and I would keep coming by. She's got an idea that Arlette could use the company."

"What's milk leg?" I asked. I knew that mothers nurse their babies. I had seen kittens nursing from mother cats in the barn. Grandfather had explained that kittens were too little to eat on their own and were getting nourishment in the form of milk from their mother's nipples. We got our milk from my grandfather's cow Buttercup; I had often watched grandfather milk Buttercup. Grandfather pointed out that cow's udders are like cat's nipples and that, of course, human beings have nipples too. So I knew that different animals have nipples in different places, but my knowledge of these things was not very sophisticated. The term "milk leg" suggested to me that Arlette had nipples on her legs. It was years before I untangled this mystery. The ailment was thrombophlebitis, but everyone I knew called it "milk leg." No one, including my grandmother, seemed to know exactly what was physically wrong with Arlette's legs.

"Milk leg is what some women get when they have babies," grandmother said. "Their legs get sore and give them a lot of pain. It happens when women are nursing or when the milk for the babies begins to come in, so I guess that's why they call it milk leg. All I know is that it's very painful for poor Arlette."

Ira was sensitive to most of Ward's moods, and he could tell just from the way that his best friend pushed his wide floor-cleaning mop that Ward was deep in thought, concerned. Ira had no doubt that Ward was disturbed about the information that Ira had shared with him earlier that afternoon. Under the circumstances, though, Ira had felt that he could no longer keep what he knew to himself. In the beginning he had thought that he would take his secret with him to his grave, because Ward was his best friend. And now, ironically enough, for the very reason that Ward was his friend, Ira had felt compelled to share this intelligence with him.

He knew that he had upset Ward, and the moment had been made more awkward by the interruption of little Michael, but still Ira felt relieved and cleansed to have finally confessed to keeping this knowledge from this man, whom he respected as he had no other in his life. He had tried to explain his reticence by saying that everything before was old news, but that the birth of the twins changed the way everybody had to look at things. Actually, Ward hadn't blamed him at all for not being open before. Ward even said that he saw Ira's point in not speaking out earlier. But that was like Ward, Ira thought; he was a man who listened with his heart and not just with his ears. Ward had thanked the messenger, even though the message was a bitter one for him to hear.

Ira polished furniture in Ward's direction, until he was near enough to Ward to speak, "I'm sorry, Ward. I know you're upset. I-I just wish there was something I could do."

"If wishes were horses . . . " Ward sighed. "Well, it's hard for anybody to know what to do."

"Did you tell Ida?"

"No, not yet."

"Are you going to tell her after work tonight?"

"This is a puzzle that needs some careful thought. Now is maybe not the best time to tell her."

"But won't she be mad if you keep it from her?"

"Yes, she will, but she'll be mad no matter when she hears it."

"What'll she do, do you think?"

"Oh, she'll fly around the house a few times, no doubt. And, while she's doing that, she'll come up with a few new ways to string cuss words together. Eventually, she'll come back to earth, though, and talk about it."

"And you don't think that it might be better to get it out in the open and get it over with?"

"It's hard to tell what's better. Just wait and see might be the best course right now. Truth can be a gift or it can be a curse. There's truth, and then there's truth. And whatever the truth, the one who receives it has to be ready for it. Otherwise it has no value, or it has the wrong value. The question is, 'Does she even need to know?'" Ward sighed and thought about a secret he'd known about their son and kept from Ida for more than ten years.

There was no one in the hotel's great kitchen downstairs. The help's dining room was empty. Upstairs, people were sleeping, taking naps in the middle of the afternoon. Everything was as quiet as a church. Then there was a scuffling noise and whispering voices in the narrow enclosed stairway.

First a woman's voice.

"Sh-h-h! Quit that! We've got to be quiet!"

"I haven't said a word. Have I said a word?"

"It's not what you're saying!"

"Then, what's your problem?"

"It's what you're doing."

"And, what am I doing?"

"C'mon, cut it out! Sh-h-h!"

"You're the one who's talking, not me."

"Yeah, but you're the one who's pinching me."

"Me?"

"All the way up the stairs."

"Just now?"

"You always do."

"And you love it, don't you?"

There was a quick squeal and a giggle.

The stairs creaked.

It was quiet; then the man's voice—husky.

"Tell me that you love it."

There was a long pause.

"Unh-h, I love it."

The register of her voice was lower than before.

"Oh, God!" she said. "I love everything you do."

There was a longer pause.

No noise.

The stairs creaked.

Silence.

The woman's whisper, this time sharp.

"Not here, Clay! C'mon, not on the stairs."

A protest? Or an invitation?

"It's okay. Just relax."

"What if somebody comes?"

"Everybody's asleep. Here, give me your hand."

"Oh, my God!"

Whispers.

Scuffling on the stairs.

Whispers.

Inaudible.

Quiet.

Creaking sounds.

Muffled sounds.

Whispers.

Footsteps descending the stairs—two sets.

Quiet.

Footsteps ascending the stairs—one set.

A pause.

Arlette opened the door from the stairway to the second floor. She looked down the hall and then around the door, up the hall. The hallway was empty and silent. She breathed a sigh of relief and stepped quietly into the hall and closed the door behind her. Her hair was disheveled. Her clothes were in disarray. She was alone, but she didn't look lonely. She was radiant; she had never looked lovelier.

Just as she passed the common bathroom, Aunt Mabel stepped into the hall. Aunt Mabel's eyes were wide open. She had not been napping. She looked at Arlette; she didn't speak. Arlette didn't speak either; she just continued on her way down the hall to her room.

Chapter Six
Aunt Mabel's Children

• *Aunt Mabel* •

I figured that I might as well move in with Arlette's little family until she got on her feet. As it was, I was there more than I was home anyway, don't you know. There was nothing really that tied me down at home, and Arlette needed someone there full time. Ida and Angela were wonderful about helping out with Arlette and spelling me, but I was sleeping there every night. So after a few days of coming and going, I decided that it just made a lot more sense for me to stay put at Arlette's, until she could take things in hand for herself.

The doctor's orders were that she had to stay in bed for ten days. And after that she would be weak and unable to do for herself for another little while. Especially with twins, I knew that she was going to have her hands full. The babies were doing just fine, both contented and happy little creatures, just as cunning as they could be. And eat! Why, I tell you, those little darlings could eat like two little pigs. Arlette wasn't nursing them, so she didn't have that to contend with. We took turns bottle-feeding them.

I was worried at first that little Nathaniel would have a difficult time. He'd given everybody such a scare when he was born, don't you know, and he was so little that he slept in the warming oven for two weeks. But that baby never gave a minute's trouble. He wasn't colicky or fussy or sickly at all— just a quiet, contented baby. Of course, he would fuss a little when he was hungry or needed changing, but that's normal. I don't consider that fussy; it's just part of being a baby.

As you know, I never had any babies of my own, but I have taken care of quite a few little ones in my time. (I wasn't called Aunt Mabel for nothing, you know.) And from my experience I can tell you that that little Nathaniel was a positively serene baby. When he did cry, which wasn't often, he made just this little noise, as though he didn't want to bother anyone very much. Ida said he sounded like a cat, and

I guess that was a pretty accurate description of Nathaniel's way of crying. He was always a quiet baby.

Nadine, on the other hand, was another story altogether. I don't mean to say that she was any real trouble at all, but she wasn't quiet like Nathaniel either. She was a talker, you might say—a talker and a smiler. Some people will tell you that babies don't notice things or smile or talk until they're a few weeks old, but I swear to you that that little girl was born "curious."

Right from the start she was looking around noticing things, commenting on everything, just curious. And, whenever she needed to eat, she wanted to eat right now, and she'd begin scolding at me, if I wasn't moving fast enough for her. She didn't really cry, don't you know; but she certainly knew how to scold a body when she needed attention. Now, nobody can tell me that that little girl didn't know what she was doing! She most certainly did! And then, when she got the attention she wanted, she'd smile from ear to ear and kick her feet and wave her little hands. And I mean from day one! People say, "Oh, babies only smile because they have gas on their stomachs." Well, I say maybe that's *their* babies. This baby smiled; she smiled because she was happy, right from the beginning.

Oh, but you know, babies really are a lot of work. They're a joy, but they're still a lot of work, too. It's not all just rocking and playing and having tea parties. The washings alone can keep a body busy. And Arlette had no electricity, you know; so that made it more work. And with two of them it's twice as much work.

Now, I have to say that Alder was a big help when he was there, but he had just a few weeks left in order to complete his fourth grade in school. Arlette wouldn't hear of his staying home and not going to school, and of course, neither would I. He'd stayed home the day the babies were born because he'd been up most of the night, don't you know. That's the way it had to be, and that was understandable to everyone, but that was the only day of school that he missed. In fact, except for that day, I'm pretty sure he had perfect attendance for the school year.

I was thinking though, that by the time Alder was finished school for the summer, it would be about time for Arlette to begin taking hold, and then Alder could be a big help to his mother with the babies, because he'd be home every day. I could move back home and just stop over to help out and give them a breather, don't you know. Then, by the time Alder was back in school and the summer was over, Arlette would be pretty much back to herself. That's the way I expected it to work out.

It was really too early yet to say anything or to get too worked up, but Arlette didn't seem to be doing so well as I hoped she would. She had that milk leg, you see. The doctor said ten days in bed. Of course, that was the way they did things in those days—ten days in bed. Well, I got to thinking about that milk leg, and I asked the doctor if it wouldn't do Arlette some good to exercise it; by that I meant walk on it a bit.

What was behind my thoughts was my lumbago, you see. Sometimes I get the lumbago something fierce, and when it acts up, if I just baby myself and take to my bed, it doesn't get any better. In fact, I think it gets a good deal worse. But, if I can keep myself going, walk around and do for myself and all, it seems to help me, don't you know.

Well, I thought that it was an interesting thing. So I decided to take it upon myself to talk to the doctor about what I had experienced. Well now, let me tell you, he let me know in no uncertain terms that *that* was absolutely the worse thing in the world we could ever do for Arlette.

He said he wanted her in that bed for ten days, and he meant ten days! And on the tenth day he just wanted her to dangle her feet some and maybe sit in a chair for a spell. He told me to keep her leg wrapped up, and that would be the best thing we could do for it. If exercise helped my lumbago, he said, that was just fine for me, but having a baby wasn't quite the same thing as having the lumbago.

Well, I probably should have kept my thoughts to myself, but I went ahead and told Ida what I said to the doctor and what he said to me, and she said she was inclined to agree with me. She said that just because he was the doctor never stopped her from having her own ideas. She said she didn't always agree with him, and sometimes she even told him to his face. Nevertheless, she allowed as how she thought we had still better do what the doctor ordered. "Aunt Mabel," she said, "I honestly don't disagree with a thing you're saying. In fact I agree with you one hundred percent. I've got an idea that you're on the right track, but he's the doctor. That's what he went to school for. If we followed our own thoughts and something went wrong, how would we feel? So I guess we'd better do it his way. He may be right. I'll tell you, I certainly thought that little Nathaniel there was a goner, but the doctor pulled him through. He knew what to do, and he saved that baby. After that he went up a couple notches in my estimation. So I guess maybe we should follow his advice. That's what he's paid for."

Well, I had to agree with her, don't you know. She was right; I wouldn't know what to do with myself if I convinced Arlette to go against the doctor's orders and she had a setback or something terrible happened. So I left it alone, but you know, I began thinking about a story my mother told me about my Aunt Sarah, when she had my cousin Louise. That was an interesting story, and I thought of telling Dr. Bonsecours about it, but I thought he'd probably pin my ears back good and proper, so I didn't tell him.

Anyway, my Aunt Sarah and her husband Emile had a farm just west of here. And my Aunt Sarah was going to have a baby, and it was haying season. Maybe you know, when you're haying on a farm, you need about all the hands you can get. Well anyway, after she made breakfast for the whole crew, she packed a lunch for everybody, and off she went to help with the haying with her husband, her sons, and their hired hand. On a farm they start work early, and she worked in that hayfield the whole morning, and she didn't stop. She didn't say anything to my Uncle Emile, but she was in labor the whole time. And it turned out to be one of those really hot, hot summer days, and the sun was just beating down.

At noon she stopped working in the field, and she went back to the house. She had her baby by herself, and she had supper on the table when the men came in that night. There was no ten days in bed for her. Now, I'll have to admit that Aunt Sarah was a tough old bird; she never stopped going in her whole life. She felt that it was their living, don't you know, and she had to keep going. She lived to be eighty years old, so I guess it may be true when they say that hard work doesn't kill you. She worked hard. Of course, I never had a baby, so I can't speak from personal experience. And I'm not trying to say I thought Arlette should go out in the hayfields or anything like that, but looking back on it, I don't think that it would have hurt her to have moved around a little. I'm not sure that lying in that bed all that time was good for her body, and I'm more than positive that it wasn't good for her mind. But that's water under the bridge, as they say. So that was why I decided to move in to be there to help out and to make sure that she was able to stay in that bed the way the doctor wanted her to. As I said, there was no reason that I really needed to go home. There was someone there, but he looked after himself. He didn't need me to be there.

By the time the twins were born, you see, I'd been living back in my parents' old home for three years. It was funny how that came about, and it was quite a scandal in Duncansboro. A small town doesn't have too much to talk about, as a rule, so sometimes they have to make more out of a story than there really is, just to give their mouths something to do and, as we say, to keep the hair on their tongues worn down.

As you know, I had been renting out the bottom floor, which had been my parents' part of the house. I rented it out to a Mr. Noah Ames and his family. Actually, his wife Mary was all of his real family that lived with him, but that house was always just full of children. They were children that were "on the town" or "on the state," as we used to say. The town or the state paid the Ameses something, not a lot, to take care of children. You didn't get rich doing this; it was more a labor of love. I guess the Ameses couldn't have children of their own, and they felt they couldn't afford to adopt. Mr. Ames said that there had been some "financial reverses" in Mary's family that were very expensive for them. But they both loved children, so they took them in. And, the way things were, the children were always changing, some going, some coming, but while they lived with the Ameses, those children had a good home, one of the best. The Ameses were both just nice people.

Mr. Ames, like me, worked in the same place all his life; for him that would be the Cote Drug Store just up on the hill. From the time he wasn't more than a child, he was stocking shelves there, sweeping the floors, and cleaning up around the place, then later on working at the soda fountain. Later, as the druggist, he still did all those things. Everybody in town knew him. Then when he and Mary got married, and they took in all those children, people took to calling him "Dad." Even though he and Mary didn't have any children of their own, they certainly did have a lot of children anyway, so people called him Dad, Dad Ames.

Well, about the time Arlette's Janine was born, Mary Ames died. She'd been sick for a while. She and Dad hadn't been taking in children for almost a year, because Mary was feeling poorly and needed to give it up, you see. And, when Mary died, that left Dad living alone in that big tenement. He had eight rooms to himself, but still he didn't really want to move; he was at home there, don't you know. He'd been there twenty-six years, and there were a lot of memories there for him.

After a little while, though, he commenced to talking to me about giving up the tenement and maybe taking the little upstairs back tenement that Mark and Arlette had lived in until their house was finished. He said that it pained him to be thinking that way, but the place was a lot more room than he really needed. It had been worth the rent when Mary was alive, but now he could do with a smaller space, and he could always use the extra money.

I got to thinking about it, and Dad Ames and I got to talking things over, and what we finally came up with was moving in together. Now, it wasn't what everybody was saying it was. I was getting ready to retire from the hotel. I still loved the work, and I was still able to keep up fairly well. But I think that you just come to the end of a thing, and you need to recognize that it is the end and then move on, before it gets to be a burden or before *you* get to be a burden, don't you know. So it worked out well for me. I was needing a place to live; I was used to living in the hotel with people around me.

I owned the house, after all; but still my parents' old apartment was too big for Dad, and it was too big for me all alone. Living together seemed like the perfect solution for us both. Dad wouldn't have to move; there'd be enough space for both of us, and yet there'd be company for both of us, if we wanted it. And it would be cheaper for Dad because he'd be sharing the place with me, you see. I knew that Dad was the sort of man that I could live with, and I guess that he felt the same about me. We became friends. That's what there was to it, and that's about all there was to it. But, if you think about it, that's really a lot.

So here we were, Aunt Mabel and Dad Ames moving in together. Why we were the talk of the town! We weren't getting married. No, sir, we were just going to live together. Well, I'm telling you, the gossip just flew around the lake and up the river, as they say around here! All of a sudden, after all these years, Aunt Mabel had decided to become a scarlet woman. They were saying things like, "Maybe we didn't know Aunt Mabel as well as we thought we did," "Maybe, she's just finally showing her true colors," and, of course, "There's no fool like an old fool."

Dad was bothered by the talk. I think that he was more bothered for me than he was for himself. It seems to be a feather in a man's cap if he has a woman, but the woman's the one who generally has to bear the blame and the shame, don't you know. So he asked me how I felt about it and what we should do about all the talk that was going around town. Well, I told him that if he didn't mind, I thought all the talk was just wonderful, a compliment almost. I guess that I have a strange sense of humor, and I've got a hide as thick as a rhinoceros, don't you know. What did I care what they thought! "Dad, let them talk," I said. "While they're talking about us, they're giving somebody else a rest. You and I know what the truth is. And what business is it of theirs what we do? We're old enough to do as we like."

And people did talk about us and speculate about what they thought we were up to. It's a funny thing about small towns; folks are much more interested in the doings of the people in the town, the people they know, than they are about anybody outside the town. It's almost as though they feel that they've got not only a right, but a duty to discuss what's going on in the lives of the ones they consider their own.

Someone outside the town doesn't seem to touch their lives in the same way at all, don't you know. And I think that's the reason that there was hardly a peep in the town when Arlette had little Alder. People didn't even speculate about who the father might be. And the reason for that was that Arlette wasn't part of the town. Because she worked in the hotel and she lived in the hotel, she might as well have been a gypsy passing through, for all the attention they paid to her. It was almost expected that one of those hotel hands would have a baby, and no one would know or care who the father was. Their thoughts were that it was probably someone who'd stayed overnight at the hotel, left his calling card, and moved on.

Out-of-towners who lived and worked in the hotel were outside of the moral considerations of the townsfolk. They just shrugged it off, because it was what they expected, don't you know. Now, almost everybody in town knew that I had looked after Arlette, but do you know, not one of them, not one ever asked me who I thought Alder's father might be.

The wonderful thing is that it's as plain as the nose on my face that Alder is Clay Holden's son. You don't have to be any kind of a genius to see it; he's got Clay Holden's signature written all over him. And it was amazing; nobody could see it! I am convinced, as sure as I'm sitting here, that Ida and Angela had no idea, absolutely no idea that Alder was Clay's son.

They were good to Arlette because they knew Mark, and when Mark and Arlette built their home on Mark's uncle's land, the Holdens were their nearest neighbors. That means a lot in this town; we help our neighbors. We take care of each other; it's just a fact of life. The fact that Ida and Angela Holden were so good to Arlette, I saw as one of life's little ironies. I used to think that if Ida knew, it would be a difficult choice for her whether to go through the roof or to go through the floor. I didn't know then which it would be.

Alder is Clay's child for anyone who has eyes to see, but who could see? His identity was completely hidden, except from Arlette, from me, and from Clay. And Ward Holden also knew, or at least he had reason to know, but he chose to keep it hidden as well.

It was as though Alder was hidden right out in the open, don't you know. That's one of the best places to hide anything. That was the point of Mr. Poe's short story "The Purloined Letter," which I once read to Arlette. The letter in that story was hidden right out in the open where everyone could see it, but where they wouldn't think to look. And of course, little Alder didn't know who his father was. You see, after that day when Clay delivered the groceries to the hotel, Arlette didn't talk about him anymore. She had always talked to me about the young men in whom she was interested, but now she closed up tighter than a clam. She talked to me about other things, but not about what was becoming most important in her life. After that day she always made sure that she was present when Clay came to deliver groceries.

In front of me their talk was always pretty much the same as it had been on that first day, but when he left, she would follow him outside and talk. They didn't talk long, and she didn't say what they talked about, and I didn't pry. She had known Clay from school, of course, but he was younger, and they weren't close then. Now, however, I suspected that they were beginning to become close.

And, after a time, I knew that Clay was visiting Arlette's room. He never took her out anywhere, but he did sneak up to her room. Now, that's not so difficult to manage as you might think. In the hotel the help's dining room adjoins the kitchen. A door from the dining room leads up the enclosed stairs to the servants' quarters, where Arlette's room and my room were located. Between the noontime rush and the preparation for the evening meal, the help all go for a walk or take a rest, and there is usually no one around the kitchen. That was the time when Arlette would let Clay into the kitchen, and they would go up to her room.

Arlette pulled the sheet up over them and let out a long whistling sigh, "Wow!" Clay took a long drag from his cigarette, exhaled contentedly, and looked down at her covered breasts.

"Don't cover them up; I like to look at them."

She pulled the sheet down so that he could look. "It's hard to believe, isn't it? But every time it just gets better, Clay!"

"And it's so-o good already!"

"Do you feel that way, too?"

"Yes, ma'am. I do, *too*." He laughed. "And *two* is just the right number." He leaned over and kissed each of her breasts.

She dug him in the ribs. "C'mon; be serious. Will you? I'm trying to be serious here."

"Oo, I can be serious; I can be very serious." He kissed her ear and ran a hand over her body.

"But Clay, we just finished! How can you be . . . " She saw the look in his eyes and followed it down the sheet. "Oh, my God! You don't stop, do you?"

He nuzzled her neck. "Baby, I pray to God I never stop."

"But your cigarette, you just lit it."

"So, I've got more."

"No, c'mon; finish your cigarette. I want to talk. Really."

"You want to let this go to waste?" He indicated the rise in the sheet.

"It won't go to waste; I promise. Neither one of us would let that happen." He was nibbling at her ear again. "C'mon, Clay, sit up straight for a minute and talk to me."

He sat up and took another drag from his cigarette. "All right, I'm all ears."

"No, you're not all ears; you're all . . . No! I'm not going to say it; I'll just get you started up again. No!" She took his hands from her breasts and put them on his lap. "I wanted to talk about sex."

"Oo, so do I. It's my favorite topic."

She laughed, "Don't I know it! No, I mean . . . I wanted to ask you . . . Hm-m-m." Now that she had his attention, she felt self-conscious about her question. "I wanted to ask you . . . am I really good . . . in bed?"

He rolled his eyes and blew out a long, thin stream of smoke. "Oh, baby, you're good!" The groan of his voice echoed hours of pleasure.

"Have you been with lots of other women?"

"Not lots. A few."

"Am . . . am I as good as they were?"

"Honey, you're the best!"

She smiled and let his words sink in. "Am I really?"

"Really! No-o contest!"

"What . . . what makes me the best? What do I do that's different?" Her voice was earnest. She wasn't fishing for a compliment. It seemed to her that she made love from instinct, from need. But she thought other women knew something that she didn't. Because of her limited experience she had no way to gauge the quality of her performance. Clay suddenly understood all of this, and he had the good sense and the good manners to respond seriously to her questions.

He butted his cigarette in the ashtray. "You know what makes you different, Arlette? You really enjoy yourself. I mean, you want it as much as I do. You're a . . . you're a natural. Other women, other women I've been with, aren't like you. It's like they don't want it, or they have to pretend they don't want it. I don't know which. And a guy has to talk them into it, and beg, and then he winds up apologizing for it afterwards. With you it's different. Sometimes it's so soft and gentle, and other times it's like a wrestling match. And whichever way it is, it's just right. It's so great! There's nothing I want to do with you that you don't want to do with me. Sometimes I think you've got a better imagination than I have!"

"That just goes to show what a good teacher you are."

"Sometimes I don't know who's the teacher, Arlette. I'll never forget the day you came into Pearson's. You really knocked me for a loop that day. I didn't know what the hell was going on. But, man, I'm sure glad I didn't let that opportunity pass me by! I would have missed the best time of my life."

"Are other men like you?"

"In what way?"

"Do they enjoy sex as much as you do?"

He smiled mischievously at her. "I can't be sure. You see, the truth is, Arlette, I haven't been with that many other men."

She gave him an elbow in the side. "Be serious!"

The glint hadn't left his eyes. "Well, to hear them talk, they enjoy it a lot. But, I'll tell you what I could do for you. Maybe I can find out. I could take a survey. It'll probably take me a couple of weeks, but . . . "

She pounced on him. "Shut up! Will you just shut up!" Arlette was pounding on him, and Clay was laughing as they rolled around on the bed.

"You're an Amazon! I'm being attacked by an Amazon!" He managed to get hold of her wrists, turn her over onto her back, and straddle her. "All right! Now that I have the upper hand, you Amazon, I'm going to have to take you down a peg!"

She laughed, relaxed, and moved under him. "Oo, what peg are we talking about, hm-m-m?"

• *Aunt Mabel* •

I guess that Clay Holden wasn't the only one sneaking around, you might say; it was a two way street. Now, I wasn't spying on Arlette, but I'm also not stupid, don't you know. I'd known Arlette for a number of years. She was twenty years old; I'd known her since she was a child. And now she was different, you see. She would stop before a mirror and look at her reflection as though she were seeing herself and appreciating herself for the first time.

That young man made her feel special. He made her feel like a woman. I didn't know if she was in love with him or not, but she had that young man under her skin, as they say. What could I do? She was a woman grown. I wanted to warn her; I tried to warn her, but at the same time I felt that she had a right to her own life, to her own dreams, to her privacy. Lord knows, my own life had not gone the way I'd wanted it to go when I was her age. I didn't know what I should do, and of course, I had a concern that whatever I did might not be the right thing to do. Whatever I did, I might just make it worse.

So what I eventually decided to do was to go to Clay's father Ward Holden and to tell him about my concerns and about my uncertainty regarding what I should do. He said that he would talk to Clay. He didn't seem angry or upset. He didn't say that he objected to Arlette, but just that he would talk to Clay. I didn't know what else to do. And I believe that Ward did talk to Clay, but I think that both Arlette and Clay were beyond hearing anymore. And about a year after that first day when Clay delivered the groceries, little Alder was born. And he was such a delightful child that certainly nobody could ever wish that he had not been born.

Arlette watched Clay getting dressed, and for a minute she thought that she was going to let him walk out the door without saying what was on her mind. How to say it? There was no easy way. Maybe she should wait until next week. By then maybe she could think of the right words. No. *Just say it!* she told herself. *Just say it, and get it over with.*

"Clay, I've got something I need to tell you." There, now she was started.

"Hm-m-m?" He was adjusting his tie in the mirror.

"Clay, I'm pregnant." There, now she had said it.

"What?" The words hit him like a blow in the solar plexus. His head swam; his face went slack. He spun round and looked at her. She wasn't joking. *That isn't a joke!* his mind warned.

"I'm pregnant."

He had no words. He felt like a trapped animal clawing at his cage, looking for a means of escape. Maybe . . . maybe there was some mistake. A mistake. Yes! Now the words tumbled out of him, tripping over themselves racing for a way to freedom. "Are you sure? I mean, are you sure it isn't a false alarm? I mean, that happens sometimes, doesn't it? False alarms . . . women think they're pregnant because they're late with their periods . . . or even miss a period and . . . "

"I've missed two periods, Clay. I'm pregnant." She pronounced the words distinctly, deliberately, and to Clay they sounded like the slow tolling of a bell.

But wait! There had to be a way. He was eighteen years old; this couldn't be happening to him. "But have you gone to a doctor?"

"I don't need to go to a doctor to have him tell me I'm going to have a baby. Sometimes a woman knows these things without seeing a doctor. And it's more than the periods. I know I'm pregnant."

"But don't you think you should go to a doctor?"

"Yes, I suppose I'll have to go."

"You should. You should! Maybe there's some other problem. Maybe it's a mistake." There was still hope.

"It's not a mistake!"

He knew in his heart there was no hope. "Am . . . am I the father?" His mind shouted, *Stupid question!* Or was it? Maybe it wasn't.

Arlette took a long breath. She turned away from him and looked out the window. "No, Clay, you're not the father." There was a long pause. He breathed a sigh of relief.

Arlette began speaking again very softly. "You're not the father, Clay. One morning just as the sun was rising, an angel from heaven appeared to me in a golden cloud, and he said, 'Arlette, you're going to have a baby.'" She spun on him; her face was fierce. "Of course, you're the father! Who else could be the father?" Her fist shot out and punched him in the chest. "I've never been with another man! Don't you know that? Maybe you don't believe it, but it's the truth!" She turned back to the window.

At that moment something woke in Clay. He had no name for it, but it was something beyond the boundaries of self. Clay always thought of himself as a basically good person. He had been raised to demonstrate and even in some measure to feel the attributes of kindness, generosity, courtesy. But the very gifts of personal attractiveness and charm that had always opened doors for him and strewn flowers in his path had in some way hampered his inner growth. Now he looked beyond himself and saw Arlette with her face in her hands, and he felt a tenderness. It wasn't love, but it was an understanding. Not pity— something like grief perhaps, but not for himself—a feeling for her, a longing to comfort her, to encompass her feelings—her pain. It was an awareness of her plight, of their plight. She had done him no wrong; they had done this together. What "this" was he still couldn't bring his heart to say, but he felt responsible. Still though, something in him warred against this realization, the intruding strangeness of these new sensations, but they held him for a time.

Clay put his hands slowly on her shoulders, feeling her flinch at first and then relax. "I do believe that, Arlette. I know it's the truth. I-I deserved that—that punch; it was . . . a really stupid thing to say."

She took a deep, shuddering breath. "Well, I'm glad that you realize it, at least."

"I do. I'm sorry!" He turned her around and held her. "What are we going to do?" *Oh, God, what a mess this is!* he thought.

"I honestly don't know. I'd only gotten as far as telling you. I decided that was about as much as I could handle for today."

Jesus, what will my mother say? What will everybody think? Clay thought. *This isn't going to be easy.* Whenever he heard of others in this predicament, he faulted them for a lack of common sense. Now others would think of him in the same way. But he could brave it out. He could marry Arlette. Arlette was a good person. They were good together. What did it matter what other people thought? It wasn't the life he would have chosen for himself, and he didn't feel at all ready for it. But he had brought it upon himself, so he pushed the words out into the room . . . a question, "Do you . . . do you want to get married?"

"Now, that would be stupid!"

"What do you mean?" He felt as though he'd said the right thing.

"Clay, you don't love me."

"But I . . . "

"No, don't say anything! But you know what, Clay? I don't love you either. I've thought about this a lot. We don't love each other. We make love. No, let's call it by its right name. We have sex. It's great! It's wonderful! I don't want it to stop. But we're not in love."

"But, if we've got great sex, we could learn . . . "

"We haven't learned! And we've been having great sex for five months now. We can't make it happen, Clay. I don't think it works like that. I think it's either there or it's not there. I don't know. I care about you, I don't want to see anything bad happen to you, sex with you is great, but I don't love you. Now, can you honestly say that you feel different about me?"

"Arlette, I . . . " How could he answer this question?

"Honestly! Please."

"No." Clay looked at his shoes.

She lifted his face with her hands. "All right. Thank you. So there you are."

"But I'll marry you, Arlette. Really, I will." He was looking for ways to make this acceptable to himself. "I mean, we've got great sex. How many marriages don't even have that?"

"And it's the decent thing to do." She hugged him. "Clay, thank you for trying to be decent; I think I needed that." She pulled away and held him at arms' length. "No! Actually I was sort of hoping you'd be a complete bastard, so I could tell you to get the hell out of my life. And I'd feel justified." She turned away from him and looked at herself in the mirror. "Proud and disdainful. I was telling myself some such stupid story in my head. I don't know." Turning back to him she added, "But what I do know, what I'm very clear about here is that we shouldn't get married."

"Why not?" He looked concerned, but she could feel that he was relieved.

"Because I don't want us to look at each other in ten years and wonder why we hate each other so much. Because it doesn't feel right."

"So what are we going to do?"

"I don't know." There was a long silence. "But we might as well keep on having sex. I'm already pregnant." She laughed; Clay didn't. "All right, I'm sorry! I was just trying to lighten the mood here." She sat down on the bed; Clay sat down beside her.

A thought came to him. It was like the hopeless wish of a drowning man, a wish that he could turn back time to the moment when he still felt firm land under his feet, before that last desperate struggle as dark water closes over him. "Maybe if you went and talked to Dr. Bonsecours, Arlette. People say that sometimes he helps women that . . ."

She put her hand on his lips to stop him from completing the sentence. "No! No, Clay." She saw him remove the hand and hold it in his own. She looked into his eyes whose deep, radiant blueness so often left her breathless, and she saw a frightened boy. She found herself feeling sorry for him. "I thought about it, you know . . . about seeing Dr. Bonsecours. That would *solve* your problem, but then I don't know if I could live with myself afterwards. I'm not going to do that. I'm going to have this baby, Clay."

Everything had gone wrong, terribly wrong. But he didn't want her to suffer, and he felt the need to satisfy his sense of honor. "But if you don't want to get married, how are you going to manage? What do you want me to do?"

She finally knew what she wanted. "I don't want you to do anything. When I started this, I told you 'no strings attached,' and I meant it, Clay. This is my baby. So it's not your problem."

"But I'm the father, Arlette."

"Yes, and I wanted you to know, but that's the end of it, as far as I'm concerned. No, Clay, I have to do this my own way. Will you let me do that? Will you let me do this my own way? I don't want you to do anything. No strings attached, remember?"

"Are-are you sure it's really what you want?"

"I'm sure. Really." She looked at her watch and gasped. "Oh, my God, look at the time! You've got to get out of here!"

"We should talk about this again, Arlette."

"No. Let's not, and say we did. Okay? Now you've got to go." He turned to leave; her voice stopped him, "Clay?"

"What?"

"Will I see you next week?"

"Do you still want to?"

"Absolutely."

• *Aunt Mabel* •

When I first realized that Arlette was in the family way, I asked her what her plans were, if Clay was going to marry her. She said that she'd decided that she didn't want to marry Clay, that she didn't love him, and that she didn't want to tie him down. She said that she was all right and that she planned to raise her child in the hotel the way she was raised. After all, it hadn't been such a bad life for her, she said. And so, that was that, don't you know. And that's what she did, you see, until she married Mark.

It's funny sometimes how things turn out. Time passes; things change. Now here was Arlette living near the Holdens, but Clay was gone to the war. And Clay's mother and wife were visiting Arlette almost every day without any knowledge of her connection with Clay and without knowing whose son little Alder was.

Chapter Seven
Visiting Arlette

• *Michael Holden* •

My mother had a whole list of daily duties which I had to accomplish before I sat down to breakfast. Most of them had to do with personal hygiene, and she had a litany of questions which she recited to determine that these tasks had been done:

Did you brush your teeth?
Did you wash your hands and face?
Did you wash your neck?
Did you wash behind your ears?
Did you clean your fingernails?
Did you put on clean underwear?
Did you put your dirty clothes in the hamper?

Sometimes there were more questions, and she didn't ask them always in the same order, but she did ask most of these questions every single morning. A couple of times I tried affirming that I had completed a neglected task, but I soon learned that words alone were unacceptable to my mother.

It was less complicated simply to perform the duties than to look for ways around them. I believed that my mother must keep somewhere a great, black, leather-bound ledger like grandfather's where she recorded all of my responses and the accomplishment of my daily requirements. In my mind that made her part of a triumvirate with Santa Claus and God, whom I also saw as glorified accountants keeping track of my life in their enormous ledgers. They were spiritual beings who had a more direct line of communication than my mother, who needed to resort to these regular quizzes in order to acquire her information.

An additional question that my mother always asked in the final position was one that seemed to me of a very different sort. For one thing all the other questions had to do with tasks which were supposed to be performed that morning. Her last question had to do with a "function" which should have occurred on the previous day. The question was, "Did you move your bowels yesterday?" I always answered the question for the benefit of my mother's black ledger, and I reasoned that being a mother permitted her to ask very personal questions.

Interestingly enough, there was no punishment for answering this question in the negative, but that answer always elicited a couple of responses. My mother would feel my forehead and ask me to stick out my tongue. What further information she derived from doing these things, she didn't say, although eventually I gathered that she was concerned about my health. Sometimes she would follow these actions with an additional question, "Are you feeling all right?"

My mother was always wanting to see my tongue to know if I was all right. Once I witnessed another kid who stuck his tongue out at his mother when her back was turned. I thought that his mother must be very clever to be able to ascertain the state of his health without even actually looking at his tongue.

It occurred to me that my mother might want additional assurance of my health, and that perhaps from time to time I should just show her my tongue without her having to ask me. That way she would know if I were becoming ill or if I were maintaining my good health. I have a very clear memory of the single spontaneous exposure of my tongue to my mother; I learned about the taste of soap.

I remember one morning when my mother had already asked her bowel question. Breakfast was over, and my mother asked me to put Pepper's leash on and take him outside so he could perform his daily duties. Pepper's only duties were to make sure that he didn't have accidents in the house. My mother could be severe when he forgot, although sometimes she wondered if his age contributed to this growing problem. I put on Pepper's leash and took him outside where I soon met my grandmother.

"Are you taking Pepper out for his morning constitutional?" my grandmother asked.

"Yes, Grandma," I answered. "Mom doesn't want him to have an accident in the house again."

"Well, that's a good idea! I can't say as I blame her," grandmother said. "I just hate having to clean up after an animal." I thought about grandmother's chickens, her rabbits, her pigs, and her cow Buttercup. She and grandfather both cleaned up after them.

"What about Buttercup?" I asked.

"Oh, well, that's a different idea altogether," grandmother retorted. "I was talking about in the house."

"Oh," I responded.

"Say, Michael, you want to walk with me? Maybe you'd like to go over to Arlette's to see the twins," grandmother wondered.

"I'd like that very much, Grandma."

"All right, why don't you let me hold Pepper, while you go ask your mother if it's all right with her," grandmother said while reaching for Pepper's leash.

"Oh, it's okay," I assured her.

"Well, maybe it is, but your mom needs to be the one to say so," grandmother rejoined. "Go ask her."

I went quickly back to the house. I had forgotten that mother would probably need to record this sort of information in her black ledger. Grandmother's words reminded me, and I skipped off to get mother's permission. I was right; it was okay.

I said to my mother, "I told grandma it would be okay, but she said I had to ask you."

"She's right; I need to know where you are," my mother said. I wondered where she kept that black ledger. "You be a good boy," she called at my back.

On the way over to Arlette's, Pepper managed to accomplish the performance of his daily duties. In fact he sniffed at bushes and lifted his leg so many times that grandmother began to become impatient with him. Pepper wasn't moving very fast today anyway.

"At this rate, it'll be suppertime before we get there," grandmother said. "I marvel that he's got any liquid left in him at all."

But he did. I tugged him along to try to keep grandmother from getting annoyed with him. At one point Pepper became fascinated by a dead and decaying bird on the side of the road. He walked around it and smelled at it and bent his front legs to try to touch it with his neck.

"Don't let that dog roll in that dead bird, or your mother will have a conniption fit! And I can't say that I'd blame her. I can't think of anything right now that smells worse than a dog that's rolled in some dead or rotten thing. You'd think it was perfume to them or something." Grandmother helped pull Pepper away from the bird carcass. Pepper grumbled and looked back longingly, but he followed us nevertheless. I couldn't help thinking again of my grandparents' chickens, rabbits, pigs, and Buttercup. I wasn't sure that their smell was much of an improvement over the dead bird.

When we got to Arlette Handy's, Arlette was just sitting up for the first time since the babies were born. She was feeding Nadine. Aunt Mabel had just finished changing Nathaniel and was rocking him. She stopped so that I could take a good look at him. I had never seen a tiny human being close up before.

Nathaniel was a cute little guy with lots of fuzzy, black hair. I became fascinated by his delicate ears and his long miniature fingers, which he wrapped around my thumb. Aunt Mabel said it was his way of shaking hands and making friends. His fingernails were so tiny and perfect, and it looked as though he'd just cleaned them that morning. As far as his "daily duties" were concerned, they were all accomplished. He had just been freshly bathed; he had on clean underwear, and he didn't need to brush his teeth, because he didn't have any. Nathaniel looked at me and stuck out his tongue between his toothless gums. I wasn't sure how my mother would have reacted to that tongue, but I decided that he was just letting me know that he was spontaneous and enjoying good health. I liked him.

When Arlette finished giving Nadine her bottle and burped her, I got to take a good look at her, too. She didn't look like Nathaniel at all. I had a concept of twins, and I thought that they were supposed to look alike. Nadine's hair was white gold, and she was fat, smiling, and wiggly. She was cute, and she seemed to like looking at me, but she kept her fists closed and didn't shake hands. She bounced her arms up and down and made squeaky noises. I liked her, too.

While I was looking at Nadine and talking with Arlette, Alder came into the bedroom to tell his mother that he was going to go fishing. It was Saturday, and Alder was home from school. Arlette hugged Alder and said, "Oh, wouldn't it be nice to have some perch for supper." She said it as though she wanted to sound happy and excited, but I thought she sounded tired and sad at the same time. "Alder, maybe Michael would like to go with you?" Arlette added. This was a neat thought, but it was a little scary for me at the same time.

"Would you?" Alder turned to me. "Would you like to come fishing with me?" Alder was a big kid. He was almost grown up from my point of view. I couldn't imagine that he really wanted me tagging along behind him, but his voice seemed to be genuinely inviting.

"I-I don't have a fishing pole," I said. I was embarrassed. I didn't know how to fish; I'd be sure to do something dumb.

"Oh, that's no problem. You can use mine. I'll use my dad's," he smiled. He had a way of making problems, embarrassment, and fear disappear almost as if they had never been.

"I'll need to ask my grandmother," I said.

"Sure. Okay, let's go ask." He put his hand on my shoulder and pulled me into the kitchen where grandmother was holding Nathaniel.

We asked grandmother, and I was afraid that she would say that we would have to go ask my mother. I wasn't sure if Alder would be willing to wait for me or to go to my house with me to get permission. And I also wasn't sure that my mother would give her permission for me to go. I quietly blessed my grandmother when she said, "I guess that it will be all right. But you two be careful around that river, now. Alder, I know that you can swim, but that current can be really swift. I'm concerned about that river." Grandmother had given her permission, but now it seemed that she was beginning to worry and have second thoughts. I was about to raise my voice in protest, but Alder handled it with self-assured ease.

"Oh, we'll be fine, Mrs. Holden. I know a place where the river is slow and shallow, and there's a nice fishing hole right near there. It's always full of perch, and it was one of dad's favorite places. We won't go in the water." Alder was twice as old as I was, but he really wanted to take me with him. It was the best day of my life.

Just then I thought about Pepper, who was sitting on my foot. Pepper wouldn't be comfortable staying at Arlette's house. He wasn't happy in unfamiliar surroundings without me, but I was afraid that Alder might not want to take him with us. He might think Pepper would get in the way or would scare away the fish or something. Alder saw me looking at Pepper, and he bent down and ruffled the hair on Pepper's head.

"Hey, Pepper boy, I guess you'd better come with us. You can keep an eye on us and maybe help save us, if it looks like we're going to drown." Alder laughed and swept a look at grandmother and winked. Pepper sneezed; I'd never seen him sneeze at anyone except my father and me.

At Alder's words, though, I felt a stab of fear that grandmother might change her mind on the spot, but she laughed. Alder seemed to have a way of putting her at ease, and grandmother took the gibe with a smile.

"Get along with you, you two scalawags!" grandmother chuckled. Alder went to the shed to get the fishing poles. I stopped by the door to attach Pepper's leash to his collar, and I overheard grandmother tell Aunt Mabel that "somebody" was a charmer. I closed the door behind me, and Alder and I walked together down to the river.

Our section of Duncansboro was called "Skunk Hollow" by people who didn't live there. And also by those who did live there, although some preferred the name "Pleasant Valley" or simply "the Hollow." Sculpted by glacier and river, the hollow was fertile bottom land nearly surrounded by hills and bluffs that separated it from the rest of the town.

For those who lived in the hollow, the river was a focal point and a fact of life. Grandmother and I had crossed the river three times to get to Arlette's house. We could have taken the road up the hill and then back down the other face of the hill and have avoided the river altogether. But the hill was steep and daunting to grandmother, and we both enjoyed the walk along the river.

The river was a short walk from Arlette's house, but it took us a while to get to Alder's fishing spot because Pepper was going so slowly today. We were on the second twin bridge before I mustered up the courage to tell Alder that I had never fished before. He said, "I'd never fished before either, until my dad took me. My dad used to say that fishing isn't just for catching food, but it's for thinking about things. You put the worm on the hook, and it makes like a question mark, and while you're waiting for a fish to answer, you ask yourself about what's important to you."

We sat on the banks of the river and fished and thought about what was important to us. Alder talked about his dad, who had taught him how to build things and how to listen to himself. Alder asked me what I remembered about my dad. It was strange to think that both our dads were gone away, but Alder's dad would never come back. And even though my father was gone away on the other side of the world, I still heard news from him almost every week. Alder wanted to know what I remembered about my father.

What came immediately to mind was a badge on father's left breast pocket and a long nightstick which he held in his right hand as he kissed my mother. Then he would shut off the lights, open the front door, and leave us in the dark. My father was an air raid warden. He walked all around our section of town making sure that all the lights were out in all the houses. If he could see light, he would knock on the door of that home with his nightstick and remind the inhabitants of the air raid.

During the day father still wore a badge and carried a nightstick; he was a policeman. One afternoon, a few days after Alder's dad died, my father came home with pictures of soldiers in uniforms, different uniforms for the different branches of the armed services. And he asked my mother which one appealed to her most of all these uniforms. My mother said that she preferred the sailor uniform and asked why he was interested in her opinion on this subject. He said that he was just curious about her taste in uniforms. The next day he came home and said that he had enlisted in the armed services and would be leaving on the day after Thanksgiving. He had enlisted in the navy, because my mother had chosen that uniform.

Alder and I caught five fish, five perch. He caught three, and I caught two. I was so happy and excited when my line first went taut. "What do I do now? What do I do, Alder?" I yelled.

"Just hold on. Give the fish time to get good and hooked, and then reel it in real steady." Alder watched me reel in the fish. "It's a beauty! It's a big beauty! It's your first fish, and it's a big, fat beauty. Just look at it." Alder was just as excited as I was.

I baited my hook the second time myself the way Alder had shown me. I swung my pole and released my line the way Alder had shown me, and the bait swung right into the center of the fishing hole.

"Wow, Michael, you're a natural at this. Are you sure that this is your first time?" Alder thumped me on the back.

I smiled, and it felt like the biggest smile I had ever smiled in my life. Alder caught three fish before I caught another one. It was an exciting time, and they were all beauties. We would have stayed longer and caught more, except for what happened then.

While we fished, Pepper had been sleeping between us on the bank at the edge of the water. He stood up and coughed. It wasn't a sneeze; it was a cough. He wobbled back and forth as he stood there. He coughed again and vomited up his breakfast, or whatever was in his stomach.

I said, "Pepper, what's the matter with you?"

"He's sick!" Alder said.

Pepper staggered as he walked the few steps between him and the river. He walked through his vomit. He didn't seem to know where he was going. He didn't seem to see that he was about to walk off the bank into the river. It all happened very fast. Somewhere I heard Alder saying, "He's going to fall into the river!" We both dropped our poles and lunged for Pepper. I caught him around the neck, and he twisted in my grip and bit me on the hand and on the cheek. But I didn't let go.

His body was shaking all over, but he didn't try to bite me again. I was holding him and crying; he was making moaning sorts of sounds. We half carried, half dragged Pepper to Arlette's house. Alder had had the presence of mind to gather the fishing poles and the willow branch with our string of fish. I'd forgotten about the fishing poles, the fish, and fishing altogether. It was the worst day of my life.

Chapter Eight
Pepper's Passing

• *Michael Holden* •

It's funny how it is with sleep. At first when you wake up, you think that everything is all right, that everything will be healed and all the bad things will be gone away. You have the sense that everything will be whole and fresh and clean again. That's the way I felt on the day after I had gone to visit Arlette and Alder and the twins with grandmother and Pepper. But when I was fully awake, I remembered the events of the day before, after Pepper became sick.

After we got Pepper to Arlette's, I wouldn't leave him to go home with grandmother. Alder and I stayed with Pepper in the shed; Pepper couldn't be in the house because he kept having convulsions, and he had no control over his bladder or his bowels. Grandmother went home and let mother know what had happened, and she sent grandfather and Ira back with the Model T to get Pepper and me. Grandfather had put a canvas on the back seat, and he and Ira lifted Pepper gently and put him on the seat. As I was getting into the car, Alder put his arm around my shoulders.

"I'm really sorry about Pepper, Michael; but I just want you to know, I enjoyed going fishing with you today." Alder was trying to bring a kind of balance to things. Some part of me must have heard him, but most of me was unable to attend or understand. I didn't say anything. My throat was scratchy and hurting, and I didn't feel good. I didn't know if it was from crying or from trying not to cry.

"Looks like old Pepper's got the collywobbles, eh?" Ira said.

When we got home, my mother was very upset about the bites on my cheek and hand, but I didn't care about the bites. Those were superficial things. I was worried about Pepper, because I'd never seen him sick like this before. I sat numbly while my mother bathed the bites with hydrogen peroxide and painted them with tincture of iodine and bandaged them. The iodine stung, but I didn't let my mother see me wince, because she would blame Pepper, not the iodine.

"Now, let's just hope those bites don't get infected," my mother said.

"What about Pepper?" I asked when she finished with me. I wanted her to cure Pepper, not waste any more time worrying about me. "Have you got some medicine for him, too?"

"Your grandfather is going to have Dr. Mills stop by later, Michael. He's an animal doctor, so he'll know better what medicines to give Pepper."

"What's the matter with Pepper? What has he got?" I thought my mother had the answers to these questions.

"I don't know. Maybe he just needs to rest his tummy a bit. But I want you to know, Michael, that I'm very upset with Pepper for what he's done to you." Sometimes my mother had no sense of what was important.

I went up to my room, but Pepper wasn't there. He wasn't on my bed or in his bed on the floor. I looked in all of Pepper's favorite places, but I couldn't find him. "Where is he?" I asked my mother. "Why isn't he here?"

"I told you, Dr. Mills will stop by later."

"I don't mean him; I mean Pepper! What did you do with him?"

"He's tied up out in the back yard."

"He should be in his bed! If I was sick, would you tie me up in the back yard?" Sometimes she didn't have any sense at all. I started for the back door. "Pepper is a dog, Michael. And I won't have him making messes in the house, no matter how sick he is! Let him be; just don't go too near him."

I let the screen door bang behind me on her voice. I didn't want to hear what she had to say. I wasn't feeling good; my throat hurt. I figured if I told her about it, she'd probably get another chain and tie me up beside Pepper. When I saw what Pepper was doing, I was even more upset with her. I watched him for a few minutes. Then I scooped him up and brought him inside; he was heavy, but I managed it. My mother was upstairs, so I yelled up the stairs to let her know how negligent she was.

"Mom, do you know what he was doing? He's so hungry, he was eating grass and throwing up! He threw up his breakfast before. You should have given him something to eat."

"If he's eating grass, that's probably a good thing. Sometimes animals know, better than we do, what they need to make them well. Just leave him outside for a while; he'll probably be all right," she called from her room.

"I'm going to put him in his bed." I was half-way up the stairs. I was struggling to keep from losing my grip on Pepper.

"No, just leave him outside, Michael. I told you, I won't have him making messes in the house." She didn't know that I had Pepper with me.

"I'm putting him in his bed," I grunted. It was all I could do to manage the words and Pepper and the stairs. Just as I reached the top step, my mother issued from her bedroom.

"Michael! I told you not to go near that dog! What are you thinking of? He's already bitten you! I expect you to listen to me when I talk to you! That dog is going back outside *now*!"

I put Pepper down and sat down beside him exhausted. Pepper made a little moaning sound; he was asleep. "He's sick; he shouldn't be outside."

"Then he'll have to go in the shed."

"I'll stay in the shed too, then," I said.

"I don't want you near Pepper in case he should decide to bite you again."

"He's sick!" I cried. "He didn't bite me on purpose! And, anyway, I don't care if he bites me! He can bite me all he wants to!" I wasn't in a reasonable frame of mind. I almost never gave my mother any backtalk, but I was very clear about not leaving Pepper, and that was that. My mother would have to tie me up and lock me in my room. I was not going to leave Pepper's side.

Finally, it was settled that Pepper would be put in my room on grandfather's canvas *in his bed* and that he could sleep there that night, so that I could sleep *in my bed*. My mother said that she understood how concerned I was about Pepper and that she was willing to try to work something out with me. But under no circumstances was Pepper to be in my bed, nor was I to sleep on the floor next to him. Now, was that perfectly clear? Mother had a way of making things perfectly clear.

That afternoon old Dr. Mills, the veterinarian, stopped by and spent a few minutes examining Pepper as he lay on the floor of my bedroom. The doctor looked serious and said, "Hm!" a lot. He asked me questions about how Pepper had been acting lately and what had happened, and I told him the answers. He looked more serious and said, "Hm!" some more. When the doctor finished, he turned to leave.

At first I wasn't going to ask him how Pepper was; I wasn't sure I wanted to hear the answer. I didn't feel good, and I didn't feel like talking any more anyway. But when the doctor had almost reached the top of the stairs, I realized that I couldn't let him go without asking.

"What's the matter with Pepper?" I didn't look at him. I just sat on my bed and looked at Pepper. The doctor stood for a moment as though he were trying to think of something to say.

"Well, Pepper's a pretty sick dog. Pretty sick. I'm not sure there's a lot we can do for him. He's quite an old dog too, isn't he?"

I didn't respond. My elbows were on my knees, my chin was in my hands, and my eyes were on Pepper. The doctor stood for a minute longer and then turned and went downstairs. I heard him downstairs talking to my mother. He asked her questions, too. Some of the words he said were "not rabies," "too old," "too bad," "could linger for weeks," "your decision."

That night I pulled Pepper close enough to my bed so that I could sleep with my hand touching his shoulder. Somehow I thought that action would help make him well. After I woke up and remembered what had happened, I tried to wake Pepper up too. He moaned, opened his eyes a little, and closed them again. He didn't sneeze the way he usually did, but he did manage to wag his tail a couple of times. I took that as a hopeful sign. I did my daily duties, and I went down to breakfast to tell my mother that I thought that Pepper was getting better.

Mother said, "Michael, we need to talk about Pepper."

I began to speak rapidly, excitedly, trying to avoid listening to her. "He's getting better, Mom; he really is! He wagged his tail—twice; he knew me. Maybe—maybe he just needs some medicine . . . and some rest. Ira said it's just the collywobbles. I can keep him in my room. I can look after him. He's a good dog. He's no trouble. I can take care of him."

My mother spoke again; this time her voice was quieter, "Michael, I know that you love Pepper very, very much." Tears welled up in my eyes. I had tried to stop her from talking, because I was afraid of what she was going to say. "Michael, Pepper isn't going to get better. Pepper is suffering, and the doctor said that he could go on suffering for a long, long time, but that he'll *never* be well again. Sometimes he's not going to know who you are again, and he could bite you again. And you may say that that's all right with you, but it's not all right with me. I have to think about what needs to be done, for you—and for Pepper. I know you don't like this; I don't like it either. I wish I didn't have to be making this decision. I love you, Michael. I love Pepper, too; we all do. But we need to do something about Pepper, and we need to do it soon."

"What are *you* going to do?" I began to cry. I knew that *I* wasn't going to do anything.

"This afternoon, your grandfather and Ira . . . are going to put Pepper away," my mother answered.

She continued to talk at me, but I was thinking about those words, "put Pepper away." They echoed in my mind. Put your clothes away, put your toys away, put Pepper away. It struck me as strange that the same words could mean such different things. I decided that I didn't want to talk to my mother for the rest of the day; just thinking about talking to her made my throat hurt. I went up to my room and lay down beside Pepper and petted him. When my mother called me for lunch, I didn't respond. She came up the stairs, and I just stayed where I was. She stood in the doorway for a few minutes, and then she went away. I must have fallen asleep, because the next thing I knew, Grandfather and Ira were coming up the stairs. Pepper was asleep, too.

Grandfather said, "It's too bad when a boy has to lose his best friend!"

"I'm sure sorry we have to do this, Mikey!" Ira added.

I didn't say anything; it hurt me just to swallow. I kissed Pepper and hugged him, but he didn't wake up. Then they lifted him in the canvas and took him down the stairs. My mother went with them in case Pepper woke up or knew where he was. Pepper always needed my mother or me near him. My mother said that I was to stay in the house, and under no circumstances was I to follow them. She didn't need to worry; I didn't want to follow them.

After they left, I sat in the middle of the stairway. There was a window there that looked out at my grandparents' house. It was a diamond-shaped window halfway up the stairs. The window had squares of different colored glass surrounding a clear central pane, like a pattern in a patchwork quilt. It was too high for me to see out of; I didn't want to see out anyway. Even though I knew that they would probably take Pepper down to the field to "put him away," it just seemed to me that if I were sitting near the window that I would be closer to Pepper.

My throat, my whole body seemed to be in pain. I sat on the stairs, and I waited. It didn't matter where I waited; I thought that I could have been on the other side of the world with my father and I would still know when Pepper was dead. Pepper had been my father's dog, and I wondered if my father would be able to know when Pepper died. My father was in a war where they were shooting guns and killing people, but for me the war was going on right near me in my grandparents' field—inside me.

I knew that grandfather would not be able to shoot Pepper; Ira would have to do it. It seemed as though I waited a long time. I was feeling hot and sick; my throat was really sore. Then I heard the shot, and it seemed to me that I felt it in my heart. I went upstairs to my bedroom and went to bed. When my mother came home, I was asleep. She woke me to try to talk with me. I was sick; I had a fever. She made me sit up in the bed, and I threw up.

The next few weeks were like a dream to me. Time flowed over me and around me like the river, and I was adrift in the middle of the stream. I had a sense of people coming and going in my room, of people trying to feed me, bathe me, talk to me. I remember drinking hot liquid that tasted like peppermint. The doctor came and examined me more than once, but I have no clear memory of those visits.

I had a bad case of strep throat, but drifting out in the middle of the river, I didn't feel it. Where I was, nothing could touch me—no feeling, no pain, no sadness, no joy. The world floated by, and nothing mattered. The colors of the voices and sounds in my room muted and flowed together the way people's talking does when you're falling asleep.

I didn't know that Alder came every day to spend time with me. He sat in my room and talked to me. He sat like a patient fisherman on the banks of my river and talked. It didn't matter that I couldn't hear him and didn't know what he was saying. He talked about what was important to him. He asked questions and wondered about the answers. And while I was dreaming, maybe a part of me was awake and listening to Alder talk. Perhaps I grabbed onto one of his questions as it floated by and let him reel me in, because my first clear memory after the day Pepper died was of Alder sitting in my room talking to me.

" . . . not getting better like you," he said. "She doesn't sleep all the time like you do, but she's always tired, and she stays in bed all the time like you. Aunt Mabel says that my Ma caught the same kind of sore throat you had, strep throat. Aunt Mabel says that you should both be all better by now, but my Ma says that she just doesn't feel good. She hasn't felt good since the twins were born, really. And you, you don't say anything. You just sleep all the time. Nadine and Nathaniel sleep a lot, but they do wake up sometimes and smile and laugh and look around. And they drink their bottles and fill their diapers. But sometimes my Ma is sleeping in her bed, and the babies are sleeping in their cribs, and Aunt Mabel is sleeping in the rocking chair, and I'm the only one awake. Why is everybody always sleeping all the time?"

"I'm awake," I said.

"You're awake?" Alder asked. "Wow! That's a surprise. You've been sleeping for three weeks!"

"Three weeks?" I echoed.

"Yeah, you lazybones. How are you feeling?" Alder asked.

"I don't know," I said. I felt weak; I felt numb. My throat didn't hurt anymore, but I still didn't feel good. I was awake, but I was still sick.

"Do you want to go fishing?" Alder asked.

"I don't think so—not today."

"Well, get better so you can," Alder ordered. "I'll come back tomorrow." Alder got up to leave.

"Alder?" I stopped him.

"What?" Alder turned around.

"I'm glad you came."

"That's okay. I'll see you tomorrow, Mr. Lazybones."

Alder did come back the next day and the next day, but I didn't go fishing with him. I was awake from time to time, but I still slept a lot, and I didn't get up. I used a chamberpot in my room; even the bathroom was too far.

Dr. Bonsecours came and checked me over. He looked in my throat. He listened to my heart and lungs. He touched me and poked me and asked me if I hurt. He left some vitamin pills and told my mother to get a bottle of cod liver oil and to give me a tablespoon every day. He said that I should try to do as much as I could—get up and walk around a little bit. He said that he was stumped, but that maybe the strep throat had just taken a tuck out of me, the way it had Arlette.

My mother made all of my favorite foods to try to entice me to eat more, but she became exasperated when even my favorites, beet greens or custard pie, didn't do the trick. "Michael, you have got to eat; you can't get better if you don't eat." My mother looked worried and old. "I'm not hungry," I answered.

"Oh, honey, everybody's been so concerned about you. I've been worried sick. You were so ill, and you didn't wake up, and you didn't eat, and I didn't know what to do. At least now you're awake, but you're still not eating enough, and I still don't know what to do," she said.

"I'm sorry!"

"Michael, I'm not asking you to be sorry. I just want you to get well!"

After I woke up, it was three more weeks before I really got out of bed. I spent my time with my trucks, pushing them around hills in my blankets, which I made with my knees under the bedclothes. I drew pictures and I colored. But mostly I looked at pictures through my grandparents' stereopticon. They had pictures of New York City, Niagara Falls, the Grand Canyon; I was fascinated by the three dimensional look of the pictures. I took the vitamin pills and the cod liver oil, but I was still listless.

Then one day when I woke up in the morning, there was a pumpkin sitting on the bottom right hand corner of my bed. "A pumpkin?" I wondered. "What's a pumpkin doing on my bed?" I thought maybe I was having a dream. I tried to think if maybe it was Halloween. Maybe it was; I didn't know. I sat up and rubbed my eyes. But the pumpkin was still there. I pushed my blankets off, so I could get a closer look. Then the pumpkin moved!

I shook my head and blinked. The pumpkin uncurled itself and stretched and yawned. It was a puppy, a fluffy ball of fur the exact color of a pumpkin. The puppy walked up my legs and licked my hands and face, and I named her "Punkin" on the spot. Punkin was Dr. Bonsecours' latest prescription, and it worked.

Dr. Bonsecours had talked with my mother about my illness. He said that he had been very concerned for a while, because strep throat could have some nasty complications. He explained that he still had some concerns but that the strep throat was better and that there didn't seem to be any physical reason I should still be in bed after almost six weeks. After six weeks he thought I should definitely be "out of the woods."

"I understand that he's lost a lot of weight and he's weak, but what I don't understand is why he's just not interested in getting better," the doctor said.

"There's got to be something we can do, some medicine, some therapy," my mother prompted.

"This seems to me to be more an emotional thing than a physical thing. It's like a depression. I'm not sure, but I've seen something like this before. It's almost as though he's lost something or he's missing somebody," Dr. Bonsecours ruminated.

"His father is in the Pacific in the navy," mother offered.

"No, I don't think that can be it. Clay's been gone since last Thanksgiving. I'm suspecting that this is something more recent. Has he lost somebody or something recently that was very important to him that he might be grieving over?"

"We had to put his dog Pepper away."

"Well, Angela, then I think you'd better get that boy another dog. And I'm willing to bet that Michael will get better," the doctor explained.

With the advent of Punkin in my life I did begin to get better. At first I felt tall and dizzy and wobbly on my legs, but within a few days I was running around the yard with Punkin at my heels. And Punkin and Alder and I went fishing in the river. When I looked in the mirror, my face looked long and sort of bony around the eyes, but I felt better.

When my mother reported to Dr. Bonsecours concerning the success of his prescription, he said, "Well, I'm really pleased to hear that. That's good to hear! I hope we have the same kind of success with Arlette."

Chapter Nine
Aunt Mabel's Worries

• *Aunt Mabel* •

I never figured come August I would still be living at Arlette's, but the way things were, there was really no way that I could leave. Arlette hadn't been out of bed enough to say so, since the twins were born in early June. There were a few days when she got up and sat in a chair for a while, but then she got sick with that strep throat.

She was sick, and for Arlette she was thin. Now, if she hadn't been carrying the twins, Arlette wasn't really up to her usual dress-size when the twins were born, don't you know. She was big because she was carrying them, but all in all, she had lost some weight. Then after the little ones came, she kept right on losing, because she just wouldn't eat right.

I was taking care of them, so she didn't have them to think about very much, but I almost believe that it would have been better if she'd had to put her mind onto looking after them by herself. Not that I minded taking care of the little darlings; they were just as cunning as they could be. And for twins they weren't so much care as you would expect them to be, but still and all, there was always something to do. And if Arlette had had to do it, she might have gotten her mind off herself and what was eating at her. It was clear to me even before the babies were born that something was wrong.

Of course she had lost her daughter Janine to spinal meningitis in January of '42, and she lost her husband Mark in November of the same year, don't you know. Little Alder had turned nine in July, and here she was in the family way with the twins. All that would be enough to discourage anybody.

As a carpenter Mark had been beginning to make a decent living for them, but when he died, there was nothing coming in. Of course, the land and the house were paid for, because Mark's uncle John had left him the land and Mark had built the house himself. Mark built it with money he had and with money his uncle John had left him.

He started building that house before he and Arlette were married, and he sort of built it on his own between his paying jobs, you might say. He got help here and there when there was something in the construction that he just couldn't handle by himself, but for the most part he put that house together himself. Then Mark and Arlette moved in shortly after Janine was born.

Sometimes, while he was building it, he used to take little Alder with him to work on the house; he used to say that he wanted Alder to feel that he had a part in building their home. And if you asked Alder, he would tell you that he helped to build that house. So Mark did accomplish what he set out to do. Of course, Alder was only four years old when Janine was born, so you can see that he probably wasn't much real help in building that house. But Mark would have him sit on a board while he was sawing it; he would tell Alder that he needed somebody to help keep the board steady. Then he would encourage Alder to pound in nails where it wasn't going to show, don't you know. So that child really got the sense that he worked on their house, and in a manner of speaking he did.

What Alder did learn, though, starting from that time, was an understanding of working with tools and a feeling for building things, just from watching Mark and having Mark explain things to him. Then, between then and the time Mark died, Alder managed to pick up quite a bit of carpentry. Mark was a very patient man with children.

Anyway, after Mark and Arlette moved into the house with Alder and Janine, they were on a week to week basis as far as money was concerned. Mark had pretty much used up all the money he had, you see. And Arlette had never been one for saving a lot of money. Of course, she'd always kept herself and Alder in nice clothes, and what she did have put away, she spent before they moved in—on linen and curtains and draperies and such. Those things may not look like a whole lot, spread out around the house the way they are, but put all together, things like that can cost you a pretty penny. And, to tell the truth, Arlette had tastes that were a little on the expensive side. When she bought, she liked to buy nice things. So, for that reason, she really didn't have any money left either, you might say.

They got by, of course, and they weren't in need really, but there wasn't a lot of money left over for extras, don't you know. They didn't have a lot, but they didn't owe a lot either. One thing Mark didn't like was being in debt; he said that, as far as money was concerned, he liked to walk down the street and feel that he didn't owe anybody a blessed thing.

The fact is, though, that they did owe something. They had bought their living room set on time, and that bothered Mark like a sore tooth. It wasn't a big debt, and it wasn't anything they couldn't handle the payments for, but it was just the idea that he owed somebody money and that he wasn't free and clear, don't you see. He'd carry on to Arlette and say how he hated being beholden. Now, I'm not saying that's a bad way to be. In fact the world could probably use a few more people like Mark, but to my way of thinking he almost went overboard with it.

Well, one morning a couple of months after they'd bought the living room set, he was carrying on about how little headway they were making on this debt and how much it bothered him. Then, I happened by for a visit after he'd gone off to work on that same day, when the whole harangue was still fresh in Arlette's mind, and she told me about it. Well, I got to thinking about that, and I decided to do something that maybe I shouldn't have done, but I did it anyway. I went that day up to Chamberlain and Drew's Furniture, and I paid off the note. And that evening I went by and presented them both with the receipt inside a card that I'd done up with a fancy bow.

I knew that Mark would have some problems with my paying for the living room set, so I tried to fix that up as best I could. I told them that I had never given them a proper wedding present and that I wanted their living room set to come from me. In fact I included in cash the difference of what they had already paid, so that the whole set came from me, you might say.

Of course, Mark started to put up a fuss, saying I'd already done enough by charging them so little rent for my upstairs, back tenement, but I put him in his place by reminding him of all his Uncle John had done for him and how many things he had in that house that came from his Uncle John, and that I wanted something major in that house to have come from Arlette's Aunt Mabel. The fact is that I felt like her aunt, even though I wasn't really her aunt, don't you know. Well, he closed his mouth right then, and that was the end of that. And that chair in Arlette's front room became Mark's very favorite place to sit in that house, so I don't think that he ever held a grudge against me for going behind his back and paying that bill.

Actually, when Mark died, they did have a little bit put away in the bank, mostly because of the way Mark was, but it wasn't much more money than would see you through one, long, hard winter. Mark had had a small insurance that his Uncle started for him and had kept up. It was enough to bury him and a little more, but it wasn't a lot by any stretch of the imagination. So Arlette had a right to worry about how she was going to manage with two babies and a growing boy, now that Mark was not around to provide them with a living.

I would have helped her with money if she had asked me, but I knew Arlette well enough to know that she'd never ask, unless she were in extreme need. She was proud that way, and I don't think that's a bad way to be either. I think it's good for people to stand on their own two feet. And Arlette was a very capable young woman, don't you know. She had talents, and she knew how to work.

She had worked in the hotel, and if she needed to go out to work, a way could have been found to manage that. I'd have looked after the babies and Alder; that wouldn't have been a problem. Arlette could have taken in sewing and washing; she was a marvelous cook, and she could clean a house and make it just shine. There were things that Arlette could do to get by. Even though she might have wondered or worried about what she was going to do now that Mark was gone, it wasn't as though the situation was completely hopeless or that she was helpless either.

So, with that in mind you see, I didn't think money problems could be what was gnawing at Arlette. But something certainly was gnawing at her, and that was pretty clear to me. For one thing, from the time those babies were born, she just didn't seem to have any spunk left in her; it was as though all the sparkle had gone out of her. She just wasn't herself, don't you know.

I realize that sometimes after women give birth they go through a time when they feel sort of down and blue. And she lay in that bed, and she thought. And I'm thinking that the things she thought about made her even more depressed. As I said, she had lost her daughter and her husband in a very short space of time, and those were terrible, terrible things to go through. But these little babies and her growing boy should have been something for her to anchor herself to, something to live for, but she was drifting. From the day those babies were born, I saw her just sort of drifting.

She kept living in the past and talking about Mark. It seemed to me that Mark was more present to her now than he ever was when he was alive. I don't mean that she didn't love him when he was alive, because I know that she did, but she never talked about him so much when he was alive as she did after he was dead. She talked about Janine some, but mostly her thoughts dwelt on Mark, so it didn't take a genius to figure out that it was something about Mark that was bothering her. I had my own thoughts about what it could be, but it was a while yet before I got the whole picture, you might say. I didn't discourage her from talking about Mark, because I thought that just maybe it might help her to talk and get what was bothering her out of her system.

Of course, I always felt kind of responsible for her and Mark's being together, because I was the one who introduced them and encouraged that relationship, you might say. Now, that's kind of an interesting story all by itself. Arlette had already had Alder in July of '33, and she had decided not to marry Clay Holden. Actually, to tell the truth, I'm not sure that he ever asked her to marry him.

Be that as it may, she had decided to raise Alder in the hotel on her own, the way she was raised. Of course, it wasn't really completely on her own, because everybody in the hotel helped out. Little Alder would always stay with me when Clay came to see Arlette. She didn't marry him, but she didn't stop seeing him either. He knew that he was Alder's father, but I'm not sure that he ever laid eyes on his son close up, except maybe as a tiny baby. After that Alder was always packed off to my room before Clay came by.

Arlette wasn't interested in having Alder know who his father was. Right after Alder was born, I'm pretty sure that I said something about Clay's being nineteen and able to help out with the expenses for the baby. I seem to remember there was something for the baby that she wanted and felt she couldn't afford, and I thought maybe Clay should help out. He was working, and after all, it was his child.

Well, let me tell you, I guess I must've said the wrong thing, because I touched a nerve. She told me that Alder was *her* baby, that she didn't consider Clay responsible for *her* baby in any way, that she was not interested in having Clay contribute to the care of *her* baby, and that she didn't see any need for Alder to know that Clay was his father. Whatever her reasons, she had thought about them, and she was very clear about how she felt. So that was that, and Clay still came by about once a week. I took care of the baby and tried to keep my thoughts to myself.

Now, 1933 was the year prohibition officially ended, and in the next year Duncansboro voted to go "wet," although towns all around it remained dry for years afterwards. And, I think I told you, the Lakeview Hotel had this sort of half-cellar arrangement called the Lakeview Grill that sold reasonable lunches to the men and women who worked downtown, or to shoppers. Actually, for a long time it was a fairly popular place to go for lunch.

Well, after the town went wet, the hotel had to get in on the business, don't you know; and the Grill became the Lakeview Bar and Grill. The hours got considerably extended, but of course I never worked in the Bar part, so I didn't ever work very late. Every other week, when it was my turn to be baker, I would help out in the Grill part for the lunch from 11:00 a.m. to 1:00 p.m. and for the evening meal that they had added from 4:30 p.m. to 6:30 p.m. That was one of Mr. Champion's ideas that the head cook and the baker swap jobs every week, so that nobody got rusty and in a pinch a body could work both jobs.

The point that I'm trying to get to here is that it was in the Bar and Grill that I got to know Mark. Of course, I'd known his Uncle John Handy, and I really knew Mark and his whole story, but the fact is that I hadn't seen him for years. And people grow up, and you forget even what they looked like, don't you know.

Well, after Mark's uncle passed away in the spring of '35, Mark took to coming in after work to have supper at the Bar and Grill. Before that he'd always taken supper with his uncle, although if the truth be known, he did used to frequent the bar once in a while later in the evening, pretty much from the time the bar opened. But I didn't know that, because I only worked until 6:30, you see.

Anyway, this young man started coming in for the evening meal, and he always sat at the counter, never in a booth, because he was always alone. Of course, he called me Aunt Mabel right away, and I said to him, "I should probably know who you are, but I can't seem to place you."

He said, "Aunt Mabel, I'm Mark Handy, John Handy's nephew."

"Well, land sakes!" I said, "You're all grown up; I don't think I've set eyes on you since you were still in short britches." And then I remembered and added, "I'm sorry about your Uncle John; I saw in the paper where he passed on."

Well, that was the beginning of his and my relationship, you might say. When he came in, we always exchanged a few words, and if it wasn't too busy, we'd have a chance to visit a little. Whenever I came back on duty after being off for a week, he'd always say, "Aunt Mabel, where were you last week? I missed you! It's just not the same the weeks you're not here." Over the space of a couple of months, I got to know quite a lot about Mark Handy. He was twenty-five now; he was still single. He said that he felt that his uncle had needed him, and besides he hadn't found the right woman. He had worked in the veneer mill from the time he was sixteen until he was twenty. Then he decided that he wanted to be a carpenter, so he went to work as a carpenter's helper. And after five years of learning his trade and working with some of the best craftsmen in the area, he felt ready to be out on his own and working for himself.

Now, I don't know if you've ever noticed this, but over the years I've noticed that people seem to come into my life just when I've really needed them. And that's the way I felt about Mark. He came along just when I needed him. You remember that I told you about my parents' old house, the one I rented out. Well, that house has this porch in the front that wraps around to the side. Now, that porch and the back stoop were just on the verge of giving out completely.

Dad Ames had already replaced a couple of boards on it, but he said the whole porch and stoop needed to be looked at by somebody who really knew what they were doing. I got to thinking that one of the tenants or one of the Ames's children might step on a rotten board and get hurt, don't you see. So I asked Mark if he would take a look at it and make me an estimate of how much it would cost to fix it. And he did, and the price seemed reasonable, and he did just a wonderful job. So, over a period of time, I got to know Mark pretty well, you might say.

One day I happened to talk to Mark a little bit about Arlette, but Mark didn't seem to know Arlette. He was four years older than she was, of course, and in school you really don't tend to know that many people who are younger than you are. But you might recognize several people who are older than you are, don't you know. As it turned out, Arlette remembered who he was, so maybe that proves my point.

Anyway, I talked about Arlette from time to time, and he could see that she was very important to me, so he got so he would ask me how she was doing, just by way of making conversation. And so, I would talk a little more about her. I didn't hide the fact that she had a child, but I didn't go into a lot of details either. So, with time, one thing led to another, and the day came when he said that he'd like to meet her. And so, that's how it happened. Now I don't want you to think that I just grabbed up the first available man to get Arlette married off. I had been talking to Mark for almost a year before I introduced him to Arlette. Arlette used to say that I had really tried to keep him for myself.

What Mark did was, he took Arlette on a date. That may not seem so remarkable, but it really was. It was the spring of '36, Arlette was twenty-three years old, and I can't remember that she'd ever had a real date before that date with Mark. She'd gone to dances, but that's not a date, you might say. Now, Mark was no dancer, so he'd never seen Arlette at a dance.

For their date he took Arlette to the movies, and I don't remember now what the movie was, but I do remember that it was a "talkie." You see, when Arlette came into my room from her date to pick up little Alder, I asked her where she and Mark had gone on their date. When she said that they had gone to a movie, I asked if it was a talkie. Well now, she looked at me as though I were a relic in a museum, don't you know. She said, "Why, Aunt Mabel, what are you thinking of? All they make nowadays are talkies! They don't make silent movies anymore." Time passes, things change. I can't be expected to keep up with everything.

Anyway, after that first date, Arlette and Mark began to go out almost every week, sometimes twice a week. And sometimes, when she could get away from her work and had someone to watch Alder, she would meet him in the Bar and Grill and sit with him while he ate his supper. Like all of us, Arlette took her meals with the help in the help's dining room. Everything seemed to be going fine between Arlette and Mark. Mark had met Alder, and the two of them seemed to take to each other right away.

There was a fly in the ointment, however. Arlette did not stop seeing Clay. I thought she would, once she met Mark and got to know him, but she didn't. There was something about Clay that she just couldn't let go of. I was trying to keep my thoughts to myself, but I was having an awfully hard time of it. It got toward the end of summer, and Mark let me know that he'd started to build a house on his uncle's land for him and Arlette. Well, I thought about Clay, and I wasn't sure just what to say.

I said, "Mark, have you asked Arlette to marry you yet?"

"I don't want to get married until I get the house built," he said.

"But what if she says no?" I asked.

"Well, if she says no, the house will still be mine, and I can live in it or I can sell it. Why? Do you think she'll say no?" he asked.

"I'm sure I don't know," I said. "That's between you and her; I was just wondering if you'd thought about all the possibilities."

In November when Mark told me that he had bought an engagement ring to ask Arlette on Christmas eve for her hand in marriage, I felt that I couldn't stay quiet any longer. I went to Arlette, and I told her that I thought that she needed to make a choice between Mark and Clay, and that she needed to think very carefully about what her choice would mean for her future. Well, as it turned out, she did listen to me. Near the end of November was the last time that she saw Clay in her room as far as I know.

Clay stretched full length on the bed and settled himself with his arms folded around the pillow behind his head. He closed his eyes and took a deep breath, and then he turned to look at Arlette. He could feel the comforting warmth of her body all down his right side. "So this thing with Mark sounds as though it's getting pretty serious."

"Yes." Arlette seemed to be studying the central ceiling fixture of her room. "Yes, it is."

"Do you love him?"

"You know, as strange as this may sound to you, I do; I really believe I do love him."

Over their years of lovemaking, Clay's and Arlette's relationship had deepened. Whereas in the beginning the sexual act was the sole purpose of their meetings, now their focus had shifted, and they saw more of each other's interior lives. Their lovemaking was still rich and intense, but they had come to care about each other as people. They had taken their times together to share pieces of themselves, and they had become friends, although neither of them would have called what they felt "love," the word that had just passed between them concerning Arlette's feelings for Mark.

"How is it different with him from the way it is with me?"

"It's funny you should ask that. I was just wondering the same thing myself, probably because I knew somehow that you'd ask me, and I'd need to put it into words."

He didn't press her; he waited for the words to come. Neither of them felt the need anymore to fill the silent spaces of their time together with touching or talking. Sometimes each knew what the other was thinking and could finish the other's sentences, but this time Clay wanted to hear Arlette's response to a question that he was struggling with himself.

Just as Arlette had told Clay about Mark, Clay had told her about Angela, the woman he had been seeing for two months. He was comfortable now with Arlette, but his feelings for Angela were different, and he wasn't able to articulate even to himself what that difference was. He saw Arlette's face pinched together in thought, and he realized that his was also, as they both worked on the same puzzle. But the question had been asked of her, and it was she who spoke first.

"Okay, don't laugh; I didn't prepare this, so it's probably not going to be all nice and neat and packaged together. What I'm going to do here is sort of think out loud. Now, being with you is easier in a way, because—because we know what we're here for, and that's what we do. We're always together in this room. We make love, and we talk, and then we each go our separate ways. It's nice. It's never the same really, but it's like . . . variations on a theme. Being with Mark is not easy in the same way. I have to think more; in some way I have to be more—more of who I am, . . . more of who the two of us are together. In some way we share more of who we are. We're together in a different way—more ways. And I know that he cares about me in a way that you don't. And I don't mean that as a criticism of you, but it's a difference. And it's a difference . . . that changes the way I feel about him, and about myself. I see him and me together in a way that I don't see us together. I feel you and him in different places in my body. With you it's always been very physical. When I think about you, I feel . . . well, I get wet."

She looked at Clay as though she expected to see him smirking at her, but he wasn't. He was giving her his complete attention. "But when I think about Mark, I feel him . . . " She touched her bosom. " . . . here, in my chest, in my . . . heart. And I can tell that he feels me the same way. And I want to be with him . . . completely, . . . not just in bed, but doing things together. Walking around in the world together." She stopped talking and let her mind review these thoughts she'd just had about another man in her lover's presence.

"You feel that you share more with him than you do with me."

"Yes, I do. Do you understand that? Does that make sense to you?"

"Yes." He was quiet. He seemed to drift out of the room for a moment, and when he came back, he took up where he'd left off as though no time had passed. "Yes. I know exactly what you mean. That's the same way I feel about Angela, but I hadn't put it into words. When I'm with her, I don't want to be anywhere else. I feel really alive for the first time in my life."

He knew that he didn't need to apologize to Arlette for these feelings, because he knew that they were both experiencing the same thing. They lay beside each other in that bed where they had shared so much passion, each absorbed in thoughts about a loved one who wasn't present in the room. Neither could have said how much time passed before Arlette spoke.

"He wants to marry me, you know."

"Has he asked you?"

"No. Not yet. He's sort of talked about it. But he told Aunt Mabel that he wants to marry me. He told her he wants to build us a house first."

"Well, he is building a house . . . on the little road across the field behind my folks' house."

"That's the one."

"So, what're you going to say when he asks you?"

"I'm going to say yes, Clay."

"Have you slept with him yet?"

"No. Isn't that strange? But no, I haven't yet. Somehow it hasn't been what we're about so far."

"Arlette, I know you too well. It's going to have to be about that at some point. That's a pretty important thing. Don't you think before you tie the knot you should know how that is? Would you buy a pair of shoes without trying them on first?"

"Well, I guess I've been feeling that we've got plenty of time, that we're just getting to really know each other, to love each other, and that sex will be part of that in its place. I haven't felt that there's any rush. Have you slept with Angela?"

Clay blushed, "No. Not yet."

Arlette laughed, "So, are *you* going to buy a pair of shoes without trying them on first?"

"Touché!" They both laughed. It was comfortable; they understood each other.

There was one more subject that Arlette felt she needed to bring up before they agreed not to see each other again. It was a subject which they had avoided for almost four years, because of her insistence that she was the sole parent of Alder. Now if she should marry Mark, Mark would become Alder's father. So at this moment of parting with Clay, Alder stood between them as he had never done in all the afternoons and evenings of lovemaking, while the child had been out for a walk or just down the hall in Aunt Mabel's room. Arlette decided just to plunge in.

"Mark is just wonderful with Alder."

"Mark knows about Alder?" Clay hadn't thought about Alder—Alder and Mark.

"Of course, he knows about Alder. He's known about Alder from the beginning. I couldn't hide something like that from him."

"Does he know that I'm Alder's father?"

"He's never asked, and I've never volunteered any information."

"And he's spent time with Alder?" Somehow the thought of another man spending time with his son, being "just wonderful" with his son, sparked a feeling of proprietorship in Clay which he had never before experienced or acknowledged.

"Yes, we do things together."

"What do you do?"

"Oh, I don't know. Nothing special really. We go to the park; we take walks together. Mark takes us out for ice cream cones. Little things. But Mark has a way with children. He's already like a father to Alder."

"But I've never even seen Alder, except when he was a baby. And those times we pass on the street, when we make like we don't even know each other."

"Clay, you know that I didn't want Alder to become confused. I didn't want him thinking that you were his Uncle Clay or some such foolishness. We needed to be discreet. And not just for Alder. For me. And for you as well, so you could go on living in this town as though Alder never existed. Except for Aunt Mabel, nobody knows who Alder's father is."

"Oh, c'mon, Arlette! No matter how careful we've tried to be, people in the workers' quarters here have seen me coming to your room—or leaving. Don't tell me they're so stupid that they couldn't put two and two together."

"People in the hotel quarters are a different breed of cats. Aunt Mabel is the only one here who has any ties to this town. The rest of us just live here, where we're in a little world all of our own. We keep to ourselves, and we keep our secrets to ourselves. No one here would think of telling Alder that you're his father, even if they knew. Alder has no idea who his father is. That's the way I wanted it, and that's the way it's going to stay."

"But I am his father."

"Are you telling me that you're ready to say that to the world, Clay?"

She had him there, and now Clay understood where she was going and why she'd brought up this subject, which they always avoided and pretended did not exist. "So Mark is going to be Alder's father. Is that it?"

"Yes, Clay. When Mark asks me to marry him, I want Mark to be Alder's father. And I want you to promise me to let it be that way. 'No strings attached,' remember?"

With things the way they were, Clay knew that this was really the best decision for himself. Acknowledging that he was Alder's father might be even more awkward for him now than it would have been when Alder was born. Still a part of him thought that it might be good to make a clean breast of it and finally get everything out into the open. He didn't know, however, if his relationship with Angela was strong enough to bear this kind of weight, and he didn't want to risk losing the woman he loved from his life, a life he now saw as meaningless without her.

He didn't even know Alder, and Alder didn't know him. It was better that way. But Alder was his son. What did that mean to him, really? Every time he tried to think about that, he got all muddled up. And to keep himself from dealing with important considerations, his mind veered away from the subject of fatherhood and narrowed upon a small question that had nagged him since Alder's birth. The question was a non sequitur, but he grabbed at it to save himself from ambivalence, as a tired swimmer reaches for a floating spar. "Why did you name him Alder?"

"I like the name; I like the way it sounds."

"But Alder? Alder is the name of a tree, for God's sake!"

"So what? People name girls after flowers: Iris, Violet. What's wrong with naming a boy after a tree?"

"But why Alder? Because Oak and Pine didn't sound good to you?"

"Actually, I thought about that name a lot, Clay. All right, I didn't pick that name just because it sounded good to me. If you really want to know, I chose that name because an alder is a tree that will grow in some pretty poor soil, in soil where most other trees won't grow or can't grow. And there's something about an alder that makes that soil better, just by its growing there. And I didn't consider myself to be very good soil, not good soil at all, but this baby, this beautiful, sweet boy has made me a better person. Every day I feel blessed by him. And he's lived up to his name. I'm much better soil now than I was when you planted him. Maybe people think it's an unusual name, but he's an unusual child, a special child, and he needed a special name. So, now that you know, what do you think?"

"I think it's wonderful!"

"And you promise?"

"I promise."

• *Aunt Mabel* •

Shortly after Clay Holden stopped visiting Arlette's room, Mark Handy started visiting her room. So I was still babysitting Alder, which I never minded, don't you know. That wasn't a problem. I can't really say that I approved of either situation, but Mark really suited my fancy better than Clay. "Well," I said to myself, "the other man never even took her on a date; and this one wants to marry her." And he did marry her.

As a matter of fact, he married her somewhat earlier than he expected to and before his house was completely finished. In February, Arlette told Mark that she was in the family way. Well, he wasn't upset about that; he was excited about it. He had wanted to marry her anyway; now that he was going to be a father as well, he just couldn't wait. They were married on March 6, 1937, and they moved into my little upstairs, back tenement. Janine was born on August 30th, and a couple of weeks later they moved into the home that Mark had built. Arlette said that Janine was born a month earlier than expected. I took one look at Janine, and I took a look at Alder, and I remembered how he looked as a baby. Those two children were like two peas in a pod; they looked so much alike. Well, I shut my mouth and kept my thoughts to myself, and I never ever told Arlette herself what was on my mind.

Mark loved that baby to distraction, and he thought that Janine was his, and I never let on any different to him or anyone else. Now after Janine died, Mark almost went out of his mind, he loved that child so! Then when Mark died, Arlette nearly went out of her mind as well. And with all that, I thought I had a pretty good idea of what was gnawing at Arlette, don't you know. Then I would look at those twins, and then I wasn't sure what to think.

What I knew, though, without any doubt, was that Arlette was truly sick. She was sick in her spirit, but she was also very sick in her body as well. In July she developed a rash over her body, and then she commenced to complain that her joints were sore. It pained her to move, she had no energy, and there was no doubt that she was sick. Doctor Bonsecours had treated her strep throat, and he said that the very thing that he had been so worried would happen with little Michael Holden had happened to Arlette. Her strep throat had turned into rheumatic fever.

Chapter Ten
Bits of August

• *Michael Holden* •

My dog Punkin knew how to be a guard dog from the moment she came to live with us. She would lie at the foot of my bed and listen to the noises in the house. Any unfamiliar noise that no one else could hear would make her grumble. If the noise continued or was louder, she would make a comment which sounded like, "M-m-boof!" Her next level of alarm was, "Woo, woo, woo!"

She was a kind and friendly dog, but every stranger who came to the door was greeted by a grimacing, snarling, barking gatekeeper who had her teeth bared and her hackles raised, until she was released from her duty and restrained by being told by my mother or me that it was okay, that the visitor did not present a threat. Then she immediately became docile and prancing and interested in the newcomer. Mother said that Punkin had a natural instinct for protecting her family.

What Punkin did not have was a natural instinct for climbing stairs. From the very beginning I had to carry her up and down the stairs. I tried leaving her downstairs while I went upstairs, but even though she was eager to accompany me, she wouldn't try the stairs. She would stand at the foot of the stairway and whine. If I left her upstairs and went downstairs, she would stand at the top of the stairway and whine. No amount of coaxing from the other end of the stairway would induce her to attempt to ascend or descend. Since she didn't seem to understand how to do it, I decided that I would need to teach Punkin how to go up and down stairs. I got down on my hands and knees at the bottom of the stairs while Punkin stood beside me with a question on her face, eager to play the game.

"Come on, Punkin, let's go upstairs," I encouraged. I started up the stairs on all fours, "Come on, Punkin. Come on." Punkin bounced in her excitement and seeming willingness to follow, but she did not start climbing. I started over again from the bottom, "Come on, Punkin. Let's go." Punkin put one paw on the first step, and wiggled, but then timidly retracted her paw. "It's not hard; you can do it. Come on." She was enjoying the attention; her eyes sparkled and she smiled.

She was one of those dogs who knew how to smile, but she didn't know how to climb stairs. I put her front feet on the stairs and pushed her and moved her legs in the way I had seen Pepper move to climb stairs. "That's the girl! See, you can do it. First this foot and then this foot." I pushed her from behind, "And then this foot and this foot. And there, you did it! Isn't this fun? You can do it! Let's try it again." She looked happy, but she still didn't try the stairs. "Come on, Punkin. Don't be a scaredy cat or a lazy bones. Just try!"

We worked most of one day, but by the end of the day Punkin could climb the stairs. It wasn't her favorite thing to do, but she could do it. Sometimes she got halfway up, and she would stop and whine for me to come and get her. But I wouldn't pick her up. I would just put her feet on the stairs, and I would help her with a boost. Eventually, she managed to get to the top. I showed mother what Punkin had learned, and mother said that I was a good teacher.

I had taught Punkin to climb the stairs, and after a few days she was able to climb as though she had always known how. But descending the stairs was much more intimidating, both to Punkin and to me. When I got on my hands and knees at the top of the stairs and tried to go down that way, I found that it was much more difficult than going upstairs. My lower legs were in the way, and my head seemed to be at a precarious angle. But I couldn't be a scaredy cat or a lazy bones either, so I had to try to teach Punkin to go downstairs.

At the time when I was trying to teach Punkin to go downstairs, she was a smaller dog than Pepper had been. Pepper had used all four feet, one after another to go downstairs, and I thought that that was the way Punkin needed to do it from the very beginning. I tried teaching her in basically the same way as we had ascended the stairs, one foot after the other and a little push. By now she was confident that I knew what I was doing, but it didn't seem to be working very well. With my positioning Punkin's legs and helping her with each step, we had worked our way down the stairs to within four steps of the bottom. At that point I lost my grip and tumbled down the last four steps.

I landed at the bottom of the stairs with a bruise on my arm and a bump on my head. Trusting and eager to follow, however, Punkin launched herself into the air, tumbled down the steps, and landed on my stomach. My mother came running just in time to find us in a heap at the bottom of the stairs, Punkin sitting on my stomach, laughing and wagging her tail.

Within a few days Punkin did learn to come downstairs, but at first she managed it by putting two feet on the step below her and then moving her back end onto the same step and repeating the process. It took a while, but eventually she got there. And with time she did learn to use all four feet the way Pepper had done. The lesson I had learned was that teaching by example can be hazardous.

When grandfather and Alder came one day to pick me up to go to the county fair, I showed them what Punkin could do. I went up the stairs and Punkin followed; I came back down the stairs and Punkin followed.

"See, she's not scared anymore, and she likes to go up and down now," I said. "I showed her how."

"That boy's done a fine job of teaching his dog how to use the stairs," grandfather encouraged me.

"That's really neat, Michael," Alder said.

"Michael's worked very hard," said mother. "He deserves a day off, so I'm glad you're all going to the fair."

"What they need is a day for disporting themselves!" grandfather proclaimed.

"That's what my Ma said," Alder agreed.

Everybody knew that Alder's Ma had been very sick and that Alder had been worrying a lot about her. He had been staying around home and not doing all the things he used to do. But Alder's Ma and Aunt Mabel were worried about Alder; they said that he was brooding too much. They thought that Alder needed to get out of the house and get a fresh outlook by putting his mind onto other things. They mentioned it to grandmother who told grandfather. Then grandfather suggested the idea of going to the county fair, and everyone thought that that would be just the thing for Alder.

"How is your mother doing today, Alder?" mother asked.

"She seems a little better today," Alder said. "She sat up in bed for a while. She said it still hurts her to move, but she thinks she's on the mend."

"She was in good spirits yesterday, according to his good woman," grandfather added.

"Well, I'm glad to hear that!" mother said. "That's a hopeful sign."

"And now, it's county fair time!" grandfather announced.

"The three of you have a good time now," mother said. "And Michael?"

"Yes?"

"You be a good boy."

So grandfather, Alder, and I were in the Model T on our way to the county fair. Alder and I each had two dollars to spend on rides, food, and amusements. Grandfather said that he would pay our entrance fee and that maybe we would like to leave our money with him for safe-keeping. We could come back to him and get more as we needed it. When we got to the fair, grandfather said we would be on our own after he took us on the grand tour, and then we would only need to check in with him every hour. He gave Alder a pocket watch to keep track of the time.

"Now everybody will know what time it is." grandfather said.

"I'll be sure to take good care of your watch for you," Alder assured him.

"He should take good care of it for himself; it's his own watch now."

"Really? It's mine? To keep?"

"That's what the man said." Grandfather smiled.

"Wow! Thank you, Mr. Holden. That's really great. I will take good care of it."

Alder and I both admired Alder's new watch, and grandfather must have read my mind, because he said, "This old man has one for the young grandson too, when he gets old enough to take care of it."

"You do, grandfather? How old do I have to be?"

"We'll see; that depends. Responsibility always depends. So, what do they like best about a fair?"

"I like the Ferris wheel," Alder said. "I love it when you go up so high and you can see way, way off. It seems as though you're on top of the world."

"I like the cotton candy," I said.

"Just a few more miles to the Ferris wheel and the cotton candy!" grandfather crowed.

"What do you like best, grandfather?" I asked.

"The animals, mostly, but the horses most of all—the pulling contests and the sulky races. This old man grew up on a farm and always loved horses." Grandfather sounded wistful.

"You have other animals. If you like them, how come you don't have horses?" Alder asked.

"One doesn't keep what he doesn't need and can't afford," grandfather said as though it were a key maxim of his life. "On the farm, horses were necessary; on his bit of property they'd just be an expense."

When we got to the fair and grandfather was parking the car, Alder and I were both having difficulty containing our excitment. We just couldn't wait for the fair to assault our senses. There was so much to see, we could hardly take it all in: barnfuls of animals, produce, preserves, crafts; games of chance and skill with banks of colorful prizes; great machines to take us on marvelous rides; people in exotic costumes; canvas paintings of intriguing marvels.

Our ears invited the calls of several carnival barkers at once: "A prize every time!" "Step right up! Step right up!" "Hot dogs! Hot dogs! Get'em while they're hot!" "Hear your past; learn your future!" "Round and round she goes; where she stops, nobody knows!" "Get your tickets! This way—right here!" "Guess your weight; guess your age!" "The eighth wonder of the world!" "Try your luck—a penny a pitch! Hey, mister, you look lucky!" "See it all on the inside!" "These little ladies will make you dream!" The sound of the barkers was superimposed on a backdrop of music from the calliope, the carousel, the country band, and the fiddlers' contest, which were competing with the many noises of farm animals and people. And then there were the smells of animals and straw, frying hot dogs and hamburgers, fried onions and french fries, fried dough, cotton candy, candy apples, perspiration, and manure. It was wonderful.

Grandfather accompanied us on the "Grand Tour" around the entire "Midway" and through all the barns. "Always make sure to see everything first before settling on something to do. That way nothing gets missed and the suspense builds. It makes the whole experience more enjoyable," grandfather explained. One of the sights we did see was a blue ribbon on grandmother's caramel pickles. "Third year she's won the blue ribbon, but nobody should spill the beans to her. Let her see it for herself." Grandfather was pleased with grandmother's blue ribbon, and I wondered if he would be able to keep this a secret from her.

After the grand tour, grandfather gave us each a portion of our money, showed us where he would be in the grandstand, and left us to our own devices. Alder and I each got cotton candy and took it with us on our Ferris wheel ride. As the ride filled up with people, we stopped at places on the way up and ate bunches of cotton candy and looked around. It was exciting to be up so high above the crowd, to be able to see everything from above. There was only a stick holding us in, and it wasn't really holding us in. When gusts of wind made the seat rock at the top of the Ferris wheel, I was holding onto the stick more than it was holding onto me. But Alder was really enjoying himself, and he didn't seem scared at all, so that helped. The ride was a great whirl of music, sights, and sensations. Alder was right; it was wonderful! A little scary, but wonderful.

When our Ferris wheel ride was over, we walked around a bit. Grandfather had told us that if we didn't walk around some, we would spend our money too fast and have nothing else to do but walk around. So it was better if we spread things out. We watched men and women pitching pennies at golden plates that looked as though they had rainbows in them. We didn't participate. Grandfather had said that that was something you did just before you left—pitching pennies and trying games of chance. If you did it earlier and you won something, you had to carry your prize around with you the whole time, and even prizes got tiresome to carry. Grandfather told us that most games of chance were rigged so that you just lost your money on them, but pitching pennies at plates was all right to do, he said.

We stopped in front of a side show where a barker with a small black moustache and a bowler hat was explaining what the townsfolk would see on the inside. Alder and I stood with the crowd gathered around the outside stage and watched a man eat fire as though he liked it as much as cotton candy. After that we watched a woman put a long knife down her throat. I had never thought about eating my mother's silverware. There were many more marvels promised on the inside, including a fantastic four-legged woman, the only one in captivity. Alder said that we might never have a chance to see such wonders again, so we parted with a quarter each to see them.

"It's a lot of money, but it'll probably be worth it!" Alder reasoned.

It was definitely worth it. The people let Alder and me stand in the front row, because we were little kids, so we got to see everything up close. The fire-eating man ate a lot more fire, and the sword-swallowing woman swallowed a lot more swords. A magician made silk handkerchiefs disappear one after another into his fist and then showed us his empty hand. And then he put his hand into his pocket and pulled all the silk handkerchiefs out all tied together in a long line.

Then the magician took three metal rings and asked Alder to examine them to make sure they were solid with no holes in the rings. Alder examined them thoroughly and said that they were solid. The magician asked if Alder was sure there were no holes in the rings, and Alder said that he was sure. Then the magician stuck his hand through the center of one of the rings and said, "Well, here's a hole I think you missed." People laughed; they thought that was funny.

The magician waved his hands over the rings, and then he tapped them together while he said the magic words, "Hocus! Pocus!" And all of a sudden the rings were joined together. This time he asked me to check them over to see if I could discover how they had been joined together. "Can you explain how I joined them together, young man?" he asked, after I'd looked them over carefully. The rings were solid, so I could think of only one explantion.

"By your hocus, pocus!" I said. People thought that was funny, too.

After the magician had finished, the barker announced the advent of the bearded woman. He whipped aside the faded red curtain to reveal her to the crowd, and as it brushed past her face, the curtain swept half her beard to the floor of the stage. A gust of wind blew through the tent and carried it into the crowd. The half-bearded woman stood there holding the naked side of her face while the crowd laughed and jeered good naturedly, as the disgruntled barker hurriedly reclosed the curtain.

Last of the marvels was the four-legged woman. The carnival barker twirled his black moustache and said that she could run twice as fast as a normal woman so that she was twice as hard to catch. "But man, if she wants to catch you, look out! You're in trouble!" he announced. Just to be on the safe side, he said that they had to keep a leg iron on one of her legs to restrain her.

There was movement behind the curtain, and the barker said that some of the four-legged woman's attendants were wrestling with her to get her onto the stage and restrained. Once she was restrained, he explained, she became quite docile. He said that she would even talk to the crowd and answer questions about herself and what it was like to have four legs.

Just before he pulled the curtain to show us the four-legged woman, he said that there was one additional wonder. For one more nickel people could go into an adjoining tent room and get a close-up look at naked Siamese twins joined together at the spine. He said that he would collect the nickels now, and Alder and I each gave him our nickels. We didn't realize that we had a choice. Then a man in the crowd called out, "Let's see your four-legged woman first, before we decide if we want to spend any more money."

Everybody agreed, and then nobody else would give the barker their nickels, so he got angry and drew the curtain aside to reveal the four-legged woman. There sat a wide-shouldered, wide-hipped woman in a tent-like, blue dress, the skirt of which fell to about mid-calf to reveal four legs in cotton stockings, ending in two pairs of sensible shoes like my grandmother's. Her plain face suggested none of the ferocity I expected to see from someone who had had to be wrestled to the stage and restrained by a leg iron on one ankle.

As she talked, I noticed that her head was set off to one side of her shoulders, and her left arm seemed to lack the mobility of her right. She gestured with her right hand and for the most part kept her left hand on her midriff. She moved her feet one after the other to show that they were real, and she told the story of how difficult it was for her, growing up in a society where most people had only two legs. Adults shunned her, she said, and other children were terribly cruel to her. To the request that she walk around a bit, she explained that the narrow stage did not afford her much room and that of course she was restrained. I was disappointed, because I wanted to watch her walk around, and I wanted to observe how she moved her feet to go up and down stairs.

Someone wanted to know if she could at least stand and move her legs a bit. She rose to comply, and something very strange happened; her left side seemed to fall away from her like an avalanche. Her left arm was swallowed into its short sleeve; her left breast fell to her waist; her hips separated, and one set of her legs nearly fell to its knees. The breeze coming into the tent filled and lifted the dress's wide blue skirt to reveal a second woman struggling to right herself under the dress.

People booed and hooted and called out, "Fake! Fake!" and left the tent, while the barker tried to call them back, as he fumbled once again to close the red curtain. Everyone left except for Alder and me.

"We're not leaving," said Alder holding my arm. "We paid our nickels to see the naked Siamese twins."

"What are Siamese twins?" I asked.

"I don't know, but if they're naked, it might be worth a nickel to see them," he reasoned. He raised his voice to the departing barker, "Where are the Siamese twins?" The barker jerked his thumb indicating a tent flap on our right, as he disappeared into the curtain behind which a muffled argument was already in progress.

Alder and I went through the tent flap into another tented space, which held only a stool and a cupboard. We stood for a few moments until a tired-looking woman came in.

"What're you boys doing here?" She looked surprised to see us. She looked older than grandmother. She had small patient eyes, deep lines on either side of her mouth, and salt and pepper hair caught in a pug at the base of her neck.

"We're here to see the naked Siamese twins," Alder said.

"Unless you're accompanied by an adult, you have to be twelve to see the Siamese twins," the woman sighed. "How old are you, anyway?"

"We're twelve," Alder answered quickly.

"Maybe you're twelve, but your little brother here can't be twelve," she responded.

"We're friends," I said.

"That's a good thing for brothers to be," she countered.

Alder smiled at the carnival lady, "We've paid our money, and we're the only ones here." Alder opened and closed his eyes in a way he had that made everyone like him right away.

The lady pursed her lips as though she were about to object again, but right away I said, "Grandfather said that we have to stay together."

"Well, all right, since your grandfather gave his permission. He did give his permission, didn't he?"

"Yes, of course he did," Alder lied.

The lady went slowly to the cupboard. She opened the cupboard doors, pulled the stool closer to the cupboard, and sat down. "These are the Siamese twins," she said. The only thing that the cupboard contained was a great glass jar. Inside the jar like pickles were two naked, little boy babies, who did indeed seem to be joined at the spine. They were back to back, and their hands held out a little before them seemed almost to touch the sides of the jar. They're eyes were closed, and they were all wrinkled and pruney. The woman touched the jar, and the babies bobbed a little and turned in their liquid environment.

"Did they drown?" Alder asked.

"No, they died shortly after they were born, and they were put in this jar in a special fluid to preserve them, so that people could see them," the lady said in a quiet, patient voice.

"What are their names," I asked.

"They died before they were given names," she said flatly. "They're little twin boys who share a part of their spine." She patted the jar.

"Are they real or fake?" Alder asked.

The lady didn't take offense at the question. "They're real enough," she said. "This is something that happens sometimes when twins are forming inside their mother. Sometimes their bodies do not separate completely. When that happens, we call them Siamese twins. It's rare, but it happens."

"How come they died?" Alder asked.

"There must have been something wrong with them," the carnival lady said. "Sometimes babies die if something is wrong with them. Siamese twins don't always die; some live to grow up and lead some kind of satisfactory life even joined together."

"What if they decide to separate later on?" Alder wondered.

"Doctors would have to operate to get them apart, and that's not very often possible to do," the lady responded.

A flash of inspiration occurred to me. "The four-legged lady must have been Siamese twins, and she just separated. Just now! We saw her! Didn't we Alder?" I said.

The carnival lady laughed, and the skin around her little eyes crinkled. "I think that that was something different," she chuckled.

Alder and I left the side show and bought French fries. The man asked if we wanted vinegar on our French fries, but he was already sprinkling it on, so there was really no choice. Alder and I both agreed, however, that they tasted good that way. After a ride on the merry-go-round, we returned to grandfather to check in with him. He was absorbed in a horse race, so he just handed us more money. Then we continued to alternate food, rides, and amusements with walking around. The next time we checked in with grandfather, he was between races, so we told him about the Siamese twin boy babies and the four-legged woman who turned out to be Siamese twins also.

"Well, that sounds like quite an experience!" he said. Then we admitted that our money was almost all gone. Grandfather looked puzzled, "Do they really know how to count? It seems as though there is still some left." He reached into his pocket and pulled out two one-dollar bills. His eyes were sparkling with mischief.

I took the money and handed one of the bills to Alder. "Thank you, Grandfather," I said.

As we were leaving, it was Alder's turn to look puzzled, "Wait a minute; I know we didn't have any more money. How could we have a dollar left?"

"That's just grandfather," I said. "Grandfather gave it to us. That's just his way."

The carnival and the fair were wonderful. When we left, the lights were coming on all over the grounds turning it into a fairyland. Each of us was carrying a golden rainbow dish that we had pitched pennies for. Alder had successfully won his own, but I had not been so successful, and grandfather had helped win one for me. In addition Alder had a small glass piggy bank and a bird whistle. I had a little plaster dog, that looked a little like Pepper, and a woven tube that held onto your index fingers and didn't want to let them go. Alder and I slept on the way home, but when we got home, we woke up and couldn't wait to tell mother and grandmother all about our adventures. Grandfather said that he couldn't remember if grandmother's pickles had won a prize or not.

"Oh, Ward, you're a marvel at keeping secrets," grandmother said.

Before I went to bed, I drew a picture of the Siamese twins joined together in their bottle to send to my father who was separated from us by the whole world. Toward the end of August we got a letter from my father. Mother read it to me; father said that he was glad mother had gotten a new dog for me and that I was feeling better. He said that he had been very worried about me. He said that he missed us all very, very much and would be glad when the war was over and he could take us in his arms again.

Dear Clay,

I've just gotten Michael settled down for the night. It wasn't easy, because he's been fretting all day about you. This afternoon we got your letter saying that you had been wounded when your ship was strafed. I could tell that you were making light of the incident when you said that they dug a few fragments out of your thigh and you were as good as new, but that it did sting for a couple of minutes. I know you know that Michael looks forward to your letters and that I always read them to him, so I had a sense that you were minimizing this for him, maybe also for me. But Michael didn't minimize it.

Ever since Pepper died, he has been haunted by the idea of death – not his own, but everyone else's who's important in his life: What if Ward dies? What if Ida dies? He and Alder went to the County Fair, where they saw dead Siamese twin babies on display in a bottle. He went around for a couple of days worrying that Arlette's twins might die, like the twins in the bottle. It's been rather grim living with him. He drew a picture of me lying in my casket holding a bunch of roses. Behind my head there was an ornate candelabrum casting a rather ghastly glow on my features. We had had a disagreement, and I chalked his drawing up to wishful thinking. And now today he was beside himself with the thought that you might die in the war and he'll never see you again.

Uncertainty is one of the constants in life, and death is ultimate certainty. We never know what's going to happen. It can be dangerous just getting out of bed in the morning. Michael is learning to deal with that, and I know that at some point he'll reach a balance in his thinking. I guess we all do. But it struck me that he is right – that we may not see one another again. It wasn't a new thought, but it struck me with renewed intensity. If you don't come back, Clay, no purple heart or other medal is going to make up to Michael or to me for your absence. I haven't forgiven you yet for going in the first place. I'll hold it against you for as long as I live if you don't come back.

And then I think, what if you do come back and you're not the same person who left? I know that I'm not the person you left behind. You wouldn't believe it from the letters I send you, but I've turned into some kind of weird harpy, circling through the house at night, slapping the newel post with my dust rag, muttering imprecations to myself—cursing you, cursing your parents, cursing my life. I go around feeling sorry for myself because you're not the man I thought you were, and I don't feel as though I know anymore where I stand in your life. Or for that matter where you stand in my life.

Michael's fussing today about your impending death somehow brought me to a real standstill. I started listening to him go on and on, and I suddenly realized, "My God, it's me!" I don't know if he's heard me at night or not, but what he was doing was definitely me. And I started wondering about the effect that negative thinking has, wondering if it generates a negative effect, an opposite positive effect, or no effect at all. I realized that Michael's carrying on definitely affected me in a negative way. At one point I wanted to slam him up against the wall. I tried reasoning with him; I tried distracting him, cajoling him. Finally I just decided to let him go on until he ran down. I did this by pretending that he really belonged to the neighbors and that I was just babysitting him. In that way I could be kind and objective and uninvolved.

Are you surprised to hear me talk that way? Well, let me tell you, sometimes a precocious five year old can be a sore trial to a single parent. Of course, you wouldn't know that, because you're not here to experience it. And if you were here, you wouldn't be alone as I've been, unless I were somewhere else. Don't think that that happy thought hasn't occurred to me once or twice.

But I'm getting off the track here. That's easy for me to do; I feel derailed most of the time, or as if I'm two trains careening down different tracks. And sometimes the two trains collide; the results are never nice. Unfortunately, Michael is the one who probably sees the most of that behavior. He seems to know what buttons to push to send me crashing over the edge. (I've got to be more observant. I've got to find out where those buttons are and what their labels are. And then I've got to hide those buttons from Michael. A five year old shouldn't be in control of my buttons!) But now, I'm off the track again.

All right. Here we are. The track I'm trying to go down here (both trains at once) has to do with this idea of negative thinking, or negative thinking vs. positive thinking. As you know, I've never been terribly religious, and when people say that they're praying for this result or that result, I think, "Well, that's okay! It'll make them feel good about themselves – that they're doing something, and their activity doesn't do anybody any harm." So the net effect of that is positive. The person praying feels positive about her (or his) intervention. Then if the intervention doesn't work, that person can usually let it go by saying that the outcome was God's will. So the effect is still positive because they did their best. I guess I wish I could feel that way, that I could deal with my anger and frustration in a way that has a "positive effect."

Ever since the twins were born, what I've been doing is negative thinking. A lot of negative thinking! I cuss you up in a heap when I'm by myself, and I've been thinking that that's good, because I need to get it out of my system. But I don't seem to be getting it out; I seem to be just grinding it in deeper. On the surface I go around acting as though nothing's wrong and trying to be nice, but I find myself snapping at people. It's as though I'm trying to keep the lid on so tight that every once in a while some steam just has to escape. Yesterday Michael and I were having a row because he wouldn't pick up a mess he'd made, and in the middle of it (like salt on a wound) your mother came over.

She asked if Michael could run an errand for her, and as soon as he was gone, she said, "Angela, what's wrong?"

I wasn't up to telling her what was really wrong, mostly because I think she already knows, which makes her a part of it. So I snapped out, "Nothing!"

"Well, something is certainly wrong. You've lost control of that boy. You just can't let him get the upper hand like that."

"It's too bad we can't all be as perfect as you are!" I snapped again. What I thought was, "Who does she think she is? Grandmother Perfection? I've seen her temper a few times."

"Well, I thought maybe I could help, because his father was a handful too, but if that's the way you're going to be, I'm just going to let you stew in your own juice," she said, and she started to leave.

Right then I realized that, like it or not, I have to live with this woman next door to me, so I apologized for snapping and said that I just felt harried by Michael. Now, believe it or not, she was the one who suggested that I pretend that he's the neighbor's child when he's driving me crazy. It sounds dumb, but I'll tell you what – it works. She said it was Ward's idea on how to deal with you.

"One day I just wanted to kill Clay," she said, "and Ward said to me, 'Killing him will only make it worse. Now if he were the neighbor's boy, what would she do?' And I said, 'I'd scold him good and proper, and then I'd pack him off back home to his mother in a hurry.' Ward said, 'But what if his mother's not home and won't be home for days? And this good woman has the care of him. What should a body do? Older and smarter folk need to be able to outthink a child, especially one that's not their own.' Well, the more I thought about Ward's idea, the more I liked it," she said. "It gave me a different perspective to think that this little brat was not my own. He was just being rotten, and I wasn't to blame for it. Thinking about it that way helped me relax a bit and take a different look at him. It doesn't always work, but in those times that it doesn't, it's still a comfort to remember that this little monster is somebody else's kid. And after a while I came to realize that Clay really wasn't mine. He was God's child; I just had the care of him."

I felt better about her after that, but this morning I snapped at Arlette because I'm so full of these negative feelings. When Mother Holden can't go to help Aunt Mabel, she asks me to go. And I get so angry while I'm there that sometimes I just let it out. I was helping Arlette with her bath, and she was going on about Mark and how she wished he could see how his children have grown. "They're not all his!" I snapped. She didn't answer a word, but the look on her face was indescribably sad. I don't know how I thought she was going to look – smug maybe, because she's borne you more children than I have. But she looked hurt. And a nasty part of me thought, "Good, I'm glad you're hurt; now *I'm not the only one hurting." But that just goes to show you how sick I am.*

All this anger, this negative energy in me isn't making me any happier, and it wounds other people. But it's not only wounding others, it's wounding me. Primarily me. I was happier before I knew any of this. I was happy with you; I was happy with me. And now everything I touch is rotten. You're rotten, and I'm rotten. And I've never been this unhappy in my life. And I can't go on this way. It's not that I've lost control of Michael; it's that I've lost control of myself.

I was thinking about that, only half listening to Arlette go on and on about how she wished Mark were still alive and how you never appreciate happiness until you lose it. I was sort of agreeing with her there, but Aunt Mabel piped up and said, "You can't do anything about what was or already is; you just have to hang onto the now and hope to Glory for what will be." Now, I thought that was a good bit of positive thinking.

Ever since the twins were born, I've had almost nothing but negative thoughts, and all kinds of bad things have been happening in my life and all around me from that day on. I'm acting crazy. I snap; I lose my temper. Pepper died. Michael got sick, and that was really scary for me. Arlette got sick, and I felt as though I wished it on her. Now you've been wounded, and I felt as though I wished that (or worse) on you. Mind you, I'm not taking personal responsibility for all these bad things, but it sort of makes me wonder if our negative thoughts somehow help structure the events around us.

I remember when I was working at Chamberlain and Drew's, there were times when something would be wrong in my personal life, and I'd try to plaster a smile on my face and go out to wait on the customers. Some older woman might come in to look for something – an end table, and I'd try to be pleasant and helpful while she considered and considered and wasted my time. And I'd think, "If you're not going to buy something, why don't you go somewhere else and do your considering." Whenever I couldn't forget about myself and focus on the customer, my frustrations just seemed to leak out around my fake smile, and I usually lost the sale. But I guess what's happening now is that I'm losing the sale with myself. And with Michael. I love Michael too much for that, and I wish I loved myself more.

I know, dear Clay, that this letter is rambling, but I think the point of it is that it doesn't matter that I think you've acted like a dink. What matters is that I'm letting it ruin my life. I've been writing nice, cheerful letters to you, pretending that everything is just fine between us. But I don't even know if there really is an us *anymore. But I do know that there's a* me *and that* me *needs to get healthy. No matter what you've done, I need to be healthy again. For myself, and for Michael. So, I'm going to try to turn over a new leaf: get sane by remembering that Michael is somebody else's kid (God's child), by "hanging onto the* now,*" and by just letting you "stew in your own juice." Maybe I'll even pray. Meanwhile I hope you keep safe and that you are really as good as new. (Please note that positive parting thought. I do still love you, Clay; I don't understand it, but I do.)*

Love,
Angela

P.S. I'm not going to send you this letter. I need to keep it so that I can read it over when I get off the track. I'll write you a different, more positive letter and send it out tomorrow.

Chapter Eleven

Aunt Mabel's Conversations

• *Aunt Mabel* •

By the end of October, Arlette was no better. She had her good days and bad days of course; but on the whole I'd have to say that she'd lost ground. Over the past few months I'd watched her just waste away, don't you know. Before the babies were born, she'd lost some weight, but now she was frail. Anyone could see that it was going to be a long, hard struggle for her before she'd be back on her feet again. She was always tired now, always hurting, unable to do for herself, let alone for her little ones. There was no question of my being anywhere else but where I was—at her side, helping out however I could.

Her little ones needed her, and I encouraged her to put her mind on fighting to get better. I'm a great one for believing that if you really want something with all your might, then you have a better chance of making it happen. Arlette was trying, but a part of her was still brooding on the past, and she hadn't been able to turn the tide yet against the rheumatic fever. Dr. Bonsecours was in and out now almost every other day to check on Arlette. He seemed frustrated by her condition. That last Saturday of the month when he finished his examination, I asked him what he thought. He just shook his head.

"I don't know, Mabel," he admitted. "Nothing I try seems to keep her from slipping away from us."

"Maybe I should keep my thoughts to myself, doctor," I said. "I keep waiting for Arlette to take a turn for the better. Sometimes she's in good spirits, but generally she just doesn't seem to take enough interest anymore. I keep telling her how much the little ones need her. I wish I knew what else to do to reach her, to make her want to take hold."

"What makes you think that she doesn't want to take hold, Mabel?" Dr. Bonsecours asked. "I'm asking because I've thought the same thing myself."

"Well, I'll tell you, doctor; I've known Arlette for a long time," I said. "She and Mark went through an awful time together after Janine died, but then when Mark died only a few months later, that seemed to me to be the last straw for Arlette," I explained. "The whole time she was in the family way, she wasn't herself, don't you see.

"Most women about to have a baby think about the life growing in them, and they commence to make plans and think about the future. But not Arlette, her mind was in a bad place. She got it in her head that the child she was carrying wasn't going to live, you see. Now, after the babies were born and they were healthy, I thought she'd come around.

"Then, of course, she got sick; but even before that, her mind was drifting, pining for Mark and what might have been. She wasn't eating right; she wasn't putting her energy into getting back on her feet. I tried to get her to put the past behind her, but that's just what she can't do. It seems to me she's haunted by the past."

Dr. Bonsecours considered my words carefully, and then he looked at me as though I'd just told him a secret. I realized then that maybe I'd said too much with my talk about the past. He began speaking almost to himself, "Death and loss are always hard to deal with. Experience teaches us that if we put one foot in front of the other, then in time the pain becomes easier to bear. Arlette lost a child to spinal meningitis. It was a terrible thing; there was nothing anyone could do for that beautiful little girl.

"Then her husband fell and hit his head in the Bar and Grill. When they brought Mark into the hospital, he was already dead. There was nothing anyone could do. I can understand how difficult this all was for Arlette, but still I'm stumped here." The doctor looked straight at me, "There's no question that death is very hard, Mabel; but I'm suspecting that something else is at work here.

"Arlette lost her mother when she was younger. Her mother didn't die, but for all intents and purposes, she might as well have. But Arlette dealt with that; as young as she was, she dealt with that. She's not dealing with this, even though she has at least three good reasons to want to live—her children. Is there anything more you can tell me that would shed some light on why, as you say, she doesn't want to 'take hold'?"

It was probably only a moment before I answered him, but it seemed a very long moment for me. I didn't really want to tell him what I knew about Arlette, or what I thought I knew. I was struggling with my own thoughts, don't you know. I'd had some thoughts about what was bothering Arlette, but I'd kept it all kind of locked up inside myself. I had let her talk, but she hadn't said what I believed she needed to say. And now I realized that what Arlette had needed to do to get better was to get that poison out of her system.

Somehow I had known that all along, but I hadn't quite put my finger on it the right way. I wished I'd mentioned it to the doctor before, but then I remembered how he had treated me when I suggested that it might be better for Arlette to get out of bed before her ten days were up. Now, however, the doctor had had this thought himself about Arlette's secrets. This was a positive turn of events, and if Arlette would cooperate, getting those secrets out into the open might be just the ticket to put her on the road to recovery. The doctor was waiting for my answer, and eventually I got around to answering him. "Whatever there is to tell is really hers to tell, I think. Do you believe, doctor, that it would really help her get well if she got what's bothering her out into the open, whatever that is?" My response was cautious, but at last I was feeling truly hopeful again. I felt that we were finally about to turn a corner. I could have kissed Dr. Bonsecours for suggesting a way to reach Arlette and make her better.

Now it was his turn to take a long moment to respond. I couldn't read his expression, but after a bit he looked straight at me again and said, "To be very honest with you, Mabel, I don't think that anything can help her to get well. For Arlette it's really only a matter of time, now. But talking out whatever it is that's bothering her may give her some peace of mind, and I believe she needs that very much at this time."

I looked at him and drew my breath in. It finally dawned on me then that he had been trying to break this to me from the beginning of our conversation, when he said that she was slipping away. And I hadn't understood, maybe because I didn't want to understand. I knew she was frail, but I always thought there was hope.

Up to that point I hadn't really faced the possibility that Arlette would not eventually get better. Maybe there was a part of me that suspected this, that really knew it, but I'd held onto the hope that after a time, after a long struggle, she would come back to herself and be well again. I tried to speak, but my throat closed up on me. I wiped at my eyes and managed to choke a couple of words out, "How long?"

"It's hard to say." Doctor Bonsecours voice was gentle and sympathetic. "Days, weeks, maybe as much as a month. In these cases, so much depends on the patient. I've sensed, though, that she's contending with something that's not the disease, something that's making everything much harder for her. I wish she could be easier in her mind; it might make it easier for her to let go."

"What should I do, doctor?" I asked. The world seemed bleak to me; I had no hope.

"Maybe you can get her to talk about it and to put her affairs in order," he said.

After the doctor left, I went to my room and had myself a good cry, don't you know. Then I thought about what needed to be done, and I dried my eyes and put my face back together. I had to tend to the little ones and make supper, even though Arlette was eating like a bird. I decided to wait until the babies and Alder were in bed. Then Arlette and I would have to have a talk. In the meantime, I tried to think about what I needed to say.

Alder and I did up the supper dishes and then sat down to play a game of dominoes. He got to start first because he had the double sixes, and from the beginning the game was going all his way. I kept having to select pieces from the boneyard; that's the name we give to all of the dominoes that are face down and not in play. Every time I had to pick from the boneyard, I thought about Arlette and how she would soon be in the boneyard. Arlette had been like a daughter to me, don't you know. And now she was dying in her bedroom, and Alder and the twins would be left without a mother.

Somehow I kept myself from breaking down in front of Alder, and I made it through the game. After he won, Alder went into his mother's room and kissed her good night. I said good night to Alder and then got the little ones all set for the night. Nadine went right to sleep; Nathaniel was being fussy, which was unusual for him. I rocked him and got him settled down; then I made tea and took it in to Arlette. She had fallen asleep, and I had to bustle around and make a little noise in the room in order to waken her, bless her heart. "Aunt Mabel, is everything all right?" She knew something was the matter.

"Arlette, I've made us each a cup of tea," I began. "I thought that we ought to have a talk." I had set my face; I was determined that I was not going to cry. Arlette studied me for a moment. Then slowly she sat up in the bed. I helped arrange the pillows behind her and handed her her tea.

"This sounds serious," Arlette began weakly. "Oh, Aunt Mabel, I feel so guilty just lying here, giving you all this work to do. I wish I felt better and could do something to help. I wish . . . "

"If wishes were horses, beggars would ride," I cut her off.

"What's happened? What's gone wrong?"

"Well, Arlette, my precious love, that's just what I was asking myself, 'What's gone wrong?'"

"Are the babies all right? Is something the matter with Alder?" she asked.

"Alder and the precious darlings are fine," I said. "I was talking about you."

"Oh!" She looked puzzled. "Well, the doctor says it's the rheumatic fever, that it's . . . "

"Arlette," I stopped her again. "Arlette, this is not easy for me." I put my hand up to keep her from speaking while I tried to control my voice. "Please hear me out. This is the most difficult thing I've ever had to do in my life. I want you to know that I love you. I couldn't have loved you more if you were my own daughter. The rheumatic fever . . . the rheumatic fever is . . . progressing. It's . . . the doctor says . . . Arlette, the doctor says that you're not going to get well, that you don't have much time left."

I had said it. I held my breath and watched Arlette's gray eyes flicker in her pale face. "I'm sorry, dear; I'm not used to saying these things." After a few moments a little color came back into Arlette's cheeks.

"I know, Aunt Mabel," Arlette said quietly. She put her hand on mine; her hand was thin and cold. I lifted my eyes and looked at her closely. Her face worked a little, as though she were trying to solve a problem. "I know," she repeated. "I guess that really I've known for some time."

"There's more," I said. I had intended to be matter of fact, but this conversation was more difficult than I had expected. I felt as though tears were clogging my throat. "It's not just the sickness, love. There's something bothering you; there's something preying on your mind." She looked up at me and frowned. "Sometimes when you start talking to me, I think you're talking to keep yourself from saying what's really on your mind, what you really need to talk about."

Arlette shook her head slowly, "But, Aunt Mabel, I don't . . . "

I put my hand up again to stop her from speaking. "Arlette, I don't think that you can accuse me of meddling a lot in your life. I've tried to keep my thoughts to myself, to keep my tongue in my pocket and not interfere, you might say. But I do see, Arlette, and I do think. I've watched you for quite a spell. I've watched you struggling, not just with the illness. I've watched you struggling with something else. And I don't know to whom you need to tell this thing. I'm not saying that you have to tell me, but I do believe that you need to get it off your chest and put your mind at peace. The doctor said that you need to think about putting your affairs in order, and he feels that it might help if you get whatever's bothering you off your chest. There, I've said it!" I stopped talking and took a sip of tea to cover my feelings.

"Oh, God, I've made such a mess of things!" Arlette said. "I never intended to harm anybody, but I've made such a mess of it."

"Is there anyone you need to talk to? Is there someone you'd like me to get for you? What would you like me to do? Whom should I send for?" I felt as though I was rattling on, and I stopped myself to let Arlette take the lead.

"If I should talk to anyone about this," Arlette began to speak as though she were thinking it through. "If I should talk to anyone, it should be to you, Aunt Mabel. Maybe there are others I need to tell as well, but certainly I need to talk to you. You've always been there for me; you've been an angel. But I just haven't been able to talk about this. Sometimes I've wanted to talk about it with you, but I just couldn't. I felt guilty; I felt all wrong in my head. I don't know; I guess I thought you'd think less of me. Except somehow I think I knew that anything I told you wouldn't come as a surprise to you."

I took another sip of tea and waited. I didn't feel like an angel.

"Aunt Mabel, Janine was Clay Holden's baby." She said it fast looking at her knees, and then she stopped and looked up to see what my reaction was. But I kept my face set, don't you know, and I just sat there waiting.

"When I was carrying her, I didn't know she was Clay's baby," she said. "Maybe you think that sounds stupid, but I really didn't know. Yes, I was sleeping with Clay. I'm not particularly proud of that, but it's the truth. I was. And you knew that I was, even though I was seeing Mark at the same time. Somehow it was as though they were completely separate things to me. I liked Mark; he was a nice guy. He was the nicest man I'd ever met. He was kind and considerate; he was good to me. He cared about me.

"But I had this incredible thing, this passion for Clay; I don't need to tell you. I knew that Clay was mostly interested in just one thing, but if I'm being honest here, I have to say that I was mostly interested in the same one thing. I didn't really love him. We had an understanding—a kind of friendship and our passion, but I didn't love him. Does that sound terrible? Well, it's true. That's why I didn't want to marry Clay when Alder was born. I don't think he wanted to marry me either. I wanted to have the baby; I have to admit that. I wanted Alder, and I wouldn't trade having him for the world. Alder has been such a blessing." She stopped talking as though she'd lost her train of thought.

"So what happened with Janine?" I prompted.

"When you came that night and told me that I needed to choose between Clay and Mark, I knew you were right," Arlette continued. "I was going out with Mark and sleeping with Clay. I guess I was really messed up in my mind. Anyway, the next time I saw Clay, I told him that we couldn't see each other anymore. He was going out with Angela, you know, and I guess that he was beginning to feel guilty about our relationship, too.

"Instead of being smart and shaking hands and saying good-bye to each other, we made love one last time. That was the way we said good-bye, and that was the beginning of Janine. But I didn't know that then. I hadn't slept with Mark yet, and I didn't sleep with him until after I'd had my next monthly period. I didn't know that you can have a period when you're pregnant, but you can. Did you know that?" she asked.

"No, I don't guess that I did know that," I said. We had never had such a frank discussion in our lives. It's one thing to know about something, but I wasn't accustomed to just saying things out like that, don't you know.

"Well, I didn't know that either," she said. "But I've found out since from other women, that I'm not the only one that's ever happened to. There were quite a few I talked to who had periods while they were pregnant. Anyway, I had a period, and I thought that I was safe. And after that I started having relations with Mark. It was my idea; it wasn't his. He was willing to wait until after we were married, but I just didn't feel as though I could wait. I'm sorry; I'm probably shocking you, Aunt Mabel."

I was working hard to keep my face just right, so that I wouldn't interfere with what she was saying. "It's all right," I said. "You say what's on your mind, love. Don't you worry about me. I'm more broad minded than I look. You just go on ahead and talk." Arlette took a deep breath and a sip of tea and changed her position in the bed. I knew that her hips were hurting her. Her hips and her knees seemed to bother her a lot. Then she began speaking again. "All my life it seems, I've felt different from other women, or at least from what I see of other women. All those fairy tales you used to read me where the handsome prince carries off the beautiful, innocent young maiden—well, I always felt like the handsome prince.

"I don't mean that I felt like a man, but I was always the one doing the carrying off. When Clay and I started seeing each other in my room, it was my idea, Aunt Mabel. I made the advances; I carried him off to my room, and I wanted him to keep coming back. I got the idea that women were supposed to be sweet and innocent and retiring, but I didn't feel like that.

"I felt as though I were made different from other women. Whereas other women permitted it, I was pursuing it. I felt guilty, I felt dirty, but I didn't stop. I felt as though I was doing what I had to do. I've only been with Clay and then with Mark, but in both cases I was the one who started it. Oh, they didn't object, but I started it.

"Then I found out I was pregnant again, and I was sure it was Mark's baby. When I told Mark that I was going to have a baby, he was so excited, he was beside himself. He wanted to get married right then, that day. We figured that Janine had been conceived at Christmas time when he asked me to marry him, and he started calling the baby his Christmas present. He said that a baby was the best Christmas present he could ever wish for. He didn't know it wasn't his. I didn't either, or I never would have let him marry me." Arlette started to weep.

I went to the bed and took her in my arms. "It's all right, love. It's all right," I said.

"When Janine was born at the end of August," Arlette continued, "I thought she had been born a month early. It didn't matter to either of us that people would talk about our only being married since March. I've heard people in town say things like, 'The first baby can come anytime; the second one takes nine months.' I knew I wasn't the first woman to get married in the family way or even to have had a baby before she was married, the way I did. But none of that was a problem for Mark. I used to worry that it might bother him what people said, but that stuff just rolled off his back. He was such a sweet man, Aunt Mabel; he was one of a kind!"

I hugged her. "Yes, he was," I said. "He certainly was."

"Well, I took one look at Janine after she was born, and my stomach twisted," Arlette continued. "She looked just like Alder; she looked just like Clay. No one else seemed to notice it. To Mark all babies looked alike; he didn't see what I saw. I thought that she had been born early, but then I counted back and realized that it was just about nine months before that I was last with Clay. I didn't understand then, but I felt in my heart that this was Clay's baby.

"But Mark was so enchanted by Janine, I didn't know how to tell him, and I didn't really want to tell him. I had fallen in love with him, but I had this awful secret from him. I didn't know how to deal with it. So I just kept my mouth shut and let him think that Janine was his. For Mark the sun rose and set on Janine, and as far as Janine was concerned, her daddy hung the moon.

"I decided that I would take that secret to my grave rather than come between them. Janine was such a beautiful, loving little girl, and Mark was so proud of her. He took pictures and pictures of her 'special occasions': the day she took her first step, the day she said 'da-da,' every birthday and lots of days in between. Then Janine got sick, and in no time she was gone, just like that. Four and a half years old, and on one cold January day she was dead. And Mark just went nuts!

"He was inconsolable; he'd put so much into that little girl—so many dreams, so much love. And she was gone, and he was lost—lost almost as though he were lost in a great forest. It was as though they were lost together in the woods. I used to think of the story of Hansel and Gretel lost in the woods, and I think it was Gretel who said, 'It is dark, and we are lost.' I don't remember much of my high school German, but I do remember that line, *'Es ist dunkel und wir sind verloren.'* I would say that to myself, 'It is dark, and we are lost.'

"Mark wasn't the only one lost; I was just as lost myself. I loved Janine too, and I missed her terribly. But I was even more lost without Mark. Darkness closed around him, and he just brooded and brooded. He worked late every day, and when he came home, he stayed up and drank and slept on the couch. He didn't sleep with me anymore; he stayed away. I needed him; I needed his closeness, his touch.

"I tried to break through to him, but nothing I did seemed to work. Everything seemed to drive him further away from me. I kept myself busy. I looked after Alder. I kept the house so clean, you could have eaten off the floor. I tried to make all of Mark's favorite foods, which often went uneaten, by him anyway. By the end of summer I was at my wits' end. He never said that he loved me anymore; he hardly even spoke to me. I would talk to him, and he would grunt or not reply at all.

"Finally, I had the idea of sending Alder to spend a couple of days with you hoping that, if we had the house to ourselves, Mark might feel freer to talk or make love, but it didn't make any difference. Then, when I got up the next morning and I was making breakfast and waiting on this scowling man that I didn't even know, all of a sudden I just couldn't take it anymore.

"I put his plate down in front of him, and I said, 'Mark, I just can't take it anymore. It's been seven months since Janine died, and in all that time, you've hardly said a civil word to me. I loved her too; I miss her too. But it doesn't matter how much I cry or feel sad, I can't bring her back. And neither can you. Mark, I love you, but I can't live with this perpetual gloom that you seem to be surrounded by. If I were the one dead, I would hate to think that you would have neglected Janine while you mourned everlastingly over me.

"'We're lost, Mark. We're lost in the dark woods, but we've got to find each other soon. I can't stay lost any longer; I want us to find our way out. I want you back—the real you, the you that I married.' Mark didn't say a word—nothing; he ate his breakfast and then got up and went to work. I cried most of the day, and when Clay Holden stopped by with a message for Mark that Clay's father had a couple of jobs lined up for Mark to take a look at, that's how Clay found me—crying and at the end of my wits."

"Did Clay often visit you?" I asked, trying to keep my voice level.

"Clay sometimes stopped by with a message for Mark," Arlette answered. "His father Ward often kept Mark in mind when he or his clients needed some carpentry done. If they didn't know where Mark was working, either Ward or Clay would stop by with a message. And, if you're wondering if Clay and I kept on having sex after Janine was conceived, the answer is no. But we had known each other for ten years, and we had shared a lot over that time, and we were still friends.

"He was Alder's father after all, even though I never wanted him to be involved in Alder's life. I guess I wanted Alder all to myself, but I knew that Clay sort of kept tabs on him from a distance. He knew how I felt and he respected that, even though I think it worked out the way he wanted it, too. For the rest of the town we kept our distance from one another, but with each other we were always honest and never pretended that nothing had happened between us. Even if it wasn't love, over the years it became something more than just passion."

Arlette finished her tea and closed her eyes. I knew she was tired, and I suggested that we continue the next day, but Arlette said that even though she was tired, she felt she needed to finish.

"When Clay found me, I was a mess," Arlette took up her story again. "I had been crying. My eyes were red, my face was puffy, I hadn't even gotten dressed. I was still in my nightgown and housecoat. He asked me what the matter was, and I told him. I told him that Mark had not been able to deal with Janine's death, that he spent his time drinking and brooding, and that ever since the day she died, Mark had not been a husband to me.

"'He loved her so very much,' I said to Clay, 'and the ironic thing is that she wasn't really even Mark's daughter, even though he thought she was. She was your daughter, Clay.' Clay looked stunned; I hadn't meant to tell him that. Clay said that he was sorry; he sat down beside me on the couch and took me in his arms. What followed then, you can probably guess.

"I had felt so alone for so long, and I was hungry for a man's touch. At first Clay was just comforting me, and it just happened. Neither one of us meant for it to happen, and when it was over, we were both confused and unwilling to talk about it. We had each been unfaithful to our marriage vows for the first time. I tried to tell myself that it hadn't happened, but I knew that it had. Neither of us had intended for it to happen. It was . . . I guess it was just the way we'd always communicated with each other."

Arlette looked straight at me. "Do you think I'm terrible, Aunt Mabel?" Her eyes filled with tears.

"Arlette, I don't live in your skin," I said. "I'm not you; I've got no right to judge you. Nobody in this world does." I hugged her and held her until she was able to go on. Then I asked her the question that was on my mind, "Tell me, dear, were you ever able to tell this to Mark?"

"I didn't tell him that day," Arlette answered. "I couldn't. When he came home, he arrived with a bouquet of roses and a box of chocolates. He said I'd given him a lot to think about that morning. He knew he was troubled, but he just hadn't known how to stop, how to get out of the dark place he was in. 'But it's over now,' he said. 'You helped me; you made me see.'

"Oh, Aunt Mabel, he was like his old self again. We had a wonderful evening together; we were closer than we'd been before. It seemed to me that he had been needing me as much as I'd been needing him. After that things were the way they were before. No, that's not true either; actually things were better than they were before.

"And then the following month, I missed a period. I tried not to think about it; but, when I missed my second period, I knew that I was in the family way again. I didn't know what to do. What if it was the day that I'd been with Clay? I'd been with Mark on the same day, though. Of course I'd been with Mark lots of times afterwards. The odds were that it was Mark's baby, but there was a chance that it was Clay's. For one thing, Mark and I had never had a baby, and it wasn't for lack of trying. But I had given birth to two babies that Clay fathered.

"I knew that I had to tell Mark; I didn't want to have any more secrets from him. I was through with secrets between him and me. I had to tell him, whatever the consequences were, even if he decided he didn't want to stay with me anymore.

"It took me a few days to get up my courage. Then I waited until a weekend, when we could have some time together. I'll never forget that day—Saturday, November 7th. Maybe you remember that I sent Alder over to spend the weekend with you again. Well, now you know why; I sent him so that I could tell Mark. Anyway, that day I told Mark everything, everything, Aunt Mabel. I told him about Clay and Alder and Janine and about being with Clay on the day of the roses and the chocolates, everything—just as I've told you.

"We had one awful row; we'd never had a row like that. Never before. He didn't lay a hand on me though. But he yelled, and he smashed the wall and crashed around. I had never seen him in that state before. It was so sad to see him like that; I was so sorry. I told him that I would leave, if he decided that that's what he wanted. 'Mark, I can't believe how much I've hurt you,' I said to him. 'Honest to God, Mark, I never intended to hurt you at all. I never loved any man until I met you. You can believe it or not, just as you like, but I've never been so sorry about anything in my life.'

"Well, you know what? He stopped dead still right in the middle of what he was doing. He'd just knocked over a chair; he bent over and picked the chair back up and set it down on the floor the right way. He said, 'I can't talk about it right now.' And he took his jacket off the hook and went out the door. Well, I was sure he was going to go get drunk. But he didn't; he just went out on the stoop and had a cigarette. He walked around the outside of the house a couple of times, and then he came back in.

"I said his name and started to say something to him, but he said, 'Arlette, I can't talk about it right now.' And he went to bed. It was the middle of the afternoon, but he slept until the next morning. I didn't go to bed with him; I slept on the couch. I didn't know what I should do.

"When he got up, I had breakfast ready, but I really didn't know how things were going to go. I had cried so much that I didn't have a tear left in me. I served his breakfast, and I didn't know whether to leave him alone or to sit down beside him, so I just stood there. He patted the place next to him, so I sat down.

"'You know,' he said, 'I've been thinking a lot about my father lately. And I've been acting just like him. I remember him, brooding for days on end, just the way I was doing after Janine died. He was always sad; he never recovered from my mother's death. I was little when he was doing that, but I remember. But you saw me through that, and you got me out of that brooding. Then yesterday I was yelling and smashing things up, but when you talked to me, it stopped me.

"'Then all of a sudden I remembered it so clearly. It all came back to me in a flash—my father in one of his violent moods: yelling, crashing around, breaking things. And I realized that I was my father. Isn't that strange? I was doing the same things I saw my father do, the same things that I was afraid of as a child and that I hated. I had to think about it. I had to think about a lot of things.' I put my hand in his. He took it, and he took my other hand as well. 'Do you really love me, Arlette?' he asked me.

"'Yes, God help you, I do,' I told him.

"Then he said . . . Aunt Mabel, he said, 'I love you too, and that's what really matters.' I started to cry, and he picked me up and carried me to the bedroom. He was so strong. He could carry me a lot easier now, couldn't he, Aunt Mabel?"

"Yes, I'm sorry to say, he could," I answered her. At first I thought that she was finished with her story, but then she started to talk again.

"Afterwards, when I was making lunch, Mark said to me, 'You know yesterday you said that Clay is Alder's father.' I froze; I didn't know what he was going to say, but he started speaking again right away. 'Well, Arlette, I want to tell you something right now. Clay Holden was never Alder's father, and he wasn't Janine's father either. Anybody can plant a seed, but it takes a real farmer to grow a crop. I am Alder's father, and I was Janine's father, and I'll be the father of this baby.' Oh, Aunt Mabel, I loved him so much right then.

"And the next day, the very next day, he was dead. November 9th. Then when the twins were born, I took one look at them, and I thought, 'Oh my God, one of them is Clay's, and one of them is Mark's, and neither of them will have a father.' I don't know how that happened, and maybe I'm crazy. Do you think that Nadine looks like Clay and Nathaniel looks like Mark, or am I just seeing things, Aunt Mabel?"

"No, I don't think that you're seeing things," I answered. "If you are, then so am I, because I've had the very same thought from the day they were born. It made me think of the story of Helen of Troy, don't you know. Maybe you remember that her mother had four children at the same time. What do you call that? Quadruplets? Actually, what she had was two sets of twins—two boys and two girls. The father of one of the boys and one of the girls was her husband. The father of the other boy and the other girl was Zeus, the king of the gods. Helen of Troy's father was Zeus. I knew that this had happened in a Greek myth, but I didn't know that such a thing could happen in real life."

Chapter Twelve
Learning Secrets

• Grandmother Holden •

There was a knock at the back door, and when I answered it, I found that it was Alder. I was reminded right away of the night he'd run across the field when Arlette was in labor. He had come across the field again today, but this time it was a bright Sunday afternoon, and he hadn't been running. "Why, Alder," I greeted him. "It's too early in the day for 'trick or treat.' Maybe you smelled my Halloween cookies all the way over at your house. Is that it?" I asked laughing.

"I wouldn't want to miss your Halloween cookies, Mrs. Holden," Alder said, "but I really came over on an errand for Aunt Mabel." His shining, mischievous, blue eyes wandered past me to the cookies cooling on the kitchen shelf.

I put my arm around his shoulders, drawing him to me. "I'll tell you what. You come in and have one of these Halloween cookies while I take this last batch out of the oven, and you can tell me about your errand." As I said, he hadn't been running, so I didn't get the idea that his errand was terribly pressing, though with his mother as sick as she was, it wouldn't have surprised me to be asked to come in a hurry. I knew that Aunt Mabel had her hands full over there.

Even if Alder's errand had been pressing though, I would have offered him a cookie, and I wouldn't have let him see me look worried or upset. I think it's important for grownups to keep their composure in front of children, especially in times of crisis. It doesn't do for the people children respect to be falling to pieces in front of them when things go wrong. I glanced at Alder, who was nibbling on his jack o' lantern-faced, raisin-filled cookie to make it last, while I was moving the last of the cookies from the baking sheet to a wire rack to set. "So now, tell me about your errand," I said.

Alder pulled an envelope from his jacket pocket. "Aunt Mabel wrote you a letter," he said.

He held out the letter to me, and as I crossed the three steps to take it from him, several ideas went through my head. A letter? Now that was curious, I thought, that Mabel had written me a letter and sent it by Alder. Alder could certainly be trusted to remember a spoken message and to deliver it accurately, so the fact that the message came in a sealed envelope piqued my interest. "Well, how nice for Aunt Mabel that she's got her own personal mailman! And you even deliver on Sundays; just imagine that!" was what I said. "Here, you take another cookie while I read it." I took the letter and perched on the high stool by the sink while I read it.

Dear Ida,

Arlette has something that she needs to talk over with you, but it is important to her that she speak with you alone. I don't know if you are free to come over now, but if you are, perhaps you could leave Alder with Ward. Or I could send him on a errand to Dad Ames when you get here, if that works out better for you. If you can't get away right now, please let Alder know when you will be able to come over. It is very important that you come soon. Arlette is very sick. She is holding her own right now, but the doctor said yesterday that it is only a matter of time now. I haven't told this to Alder yet.

Sincerely yours,
Mabel

Ward had gone over to Ira's right after dinner, but I had an idea that I could send Alder over to spend some time with Michael. Even though he was older than Michael, those two boys seemed to get along just fine. So I suggested that he might like to stay at Angela's and play with Michael and Punkin for a while. "You know, Alder, Michael's been keeping his Halloween costume a big secret from me, but maybe he'll show you what he's going to wear this evening. Perhaps the two of you would like to make plans to go out trick-or-treating together. What are you planning to be for Halloween?" I asked.

Alder flashed me one of his big grins. "I'm not telling, Mrs. Holden," Alder said. "That'll be a surprise when you see me, and maybe you won't even guess it's me."

I decided to go with Alder over to Angela's to ask if Alder could spend some time with Michael. Before I even got the words out of my mouth, Michael and Alder were off in a corner whispering and giggling together. Angela laughed and said of course Alder could stay. I took Angela aside out of the view and hearing of the boys and showed her Aunt Mabel's note. Angela read it, sighed, and put it back in the envelope.

"I knew that Arlette was very sick, but I really didn't know that it was this serious or so close," Angela breathed in a voice just above a whisper. "Poor Arlette! She hasn't had it easy, has she? It never rains but it pours. Oh, Mother Holden, whatever is going to happen with those children? I don't know if Aunt Mabel is really up to taking on all that responsibility full time."

"Well, I wouldn't count Mabel out just yet; I've got an idea that there are a lot of good years still left in that old bird," I said. "Besides, she has been taking care of things pretty much full time since the babies were born back in June. But I suspect you're right, though; I suppose it is wearing on her."

"Well, if things are wearing on her, I'm sure it's not just taking care of the house and the children. It must have been awfully hard on her these last few months watching Arlette go downhill the way she has; Arlette's been like a daughter to Aunt Mabel," Angela said.

"Yes, I'm sure that it hasn't been easy for her. Sometimes life has a way of dishing up meals that are very hard to digest. It makes you wonder," I said. "Well, if Alder is all right here, Angela, I suppose that I'd better go over to Arlette's to find out what this is all about." I put the letter back in my purse and set out for Arlette's. I had no idea what was waiting there for me on this Sunday afternoon. I don't think that I would have guessed in a month of Sundays.

When I got to Arlette's, Aunt Mabel had just put the babies down for a nap, and Arlette was eating toast and having a cup of tea. Mabel thanked me for coming and made a cup of tea for herself and for me as well, and we sat down by Arlette's bed. I asked Arlette how she was feeling today.

"Oh, well, I guess that I've had worse days," Arlette said. "I know Aunt Mabel wrote you that it's only a matter of time for me." Her words were kind of flat and tired.

"Yes, she did," I said. "I'm so very sorry to hear it, Arlette. Lord knows, you've been through so much." I stopped talking. It was so hard to know what to say. Nobody said anything. It was an awkward moment during which Arlette stared at her tea and stirred it with her spoon. Finally, I decided to just jump in and find out why I was asked to come. "Mabel wrote that you wanted to see me alone, Arlette. I left Alder playing with Michael."

"That's good. He and Michael get along so well." Arlette paused, and her eyes seemed to focus inside herself for a moment. "It's partly about Alder that I wanted to talk with you; the doctor said that I need to put my affairs in order." Then she began to tell me things that she had never told to anyone before, except to Mark and Aunt Mabel.

She told me her whole story. I'm not going to say that I wasn't shocked by the things she told me. They came as a complete surprise to me; you've no idea. I caught myself more than once with my jaw dropped open. I saw Mabel looking at me with my mouth agape as though I were catching flies, and I shut it tight. But still, at the same time I believed every single word Arlette was saying; I knew it was the gospel truth. I've no idea how I knew; I just knew. But even though I believed it, it was not easy for me to listen to. I didn't really know what I was feeling—mostly bewilderment at that point, I guess . . . and sadness: for Arlette, for the children, for Mark, for Clay, for the world. For myself.

One of the more distressing things for me to hear was something that Mabel added—the fact that Ward had known all along that Alder was our grandson. That was a hard notion to swallow, that Ward had kept that information a secret from me, even though I had an idea that he was just trying to protect me. At the same time, I now knew why Ward had thrown every carpentry job he could in Mark Handy's direction. It all made sense to me now. Mark Handy wasn't just a neighbor; he was the stepfather of Ward's grandson.

When Arlette was finished, I thanked her for telling me, and I told her that she had given me a lot to think about. I felt kind of tongue-tied, and that's not a common feeling for me. I said that I needed to go home and talk with Ward but that I'd be back tomorrow. I hugged Arlette and Aunt Mabel, and I left. When I got home, both Ward and Ira were there. Ira might be Ward's partner, and he might know a lot about the family, but I didn't feel right talking about all of this in front of Ira. I was in no mood to sit around and be pleasant and wait until he left. I might have sounded rude, but I told Ira that I needed to talk with Ward, and I asked him if he would leave and give us some time alone together.

"Well, sure thing, Ida. I guess you and Ward need to exchange some thoughts about what you're going to wear out trick or treating tonight, huh?" Ira said in typical Ira fashion.

"Something like that, Ira," I answered.

"No problem. I need to go check on a couple of jobs anyway. Is it okay if I come back in an hour or so to let Ward know where we stand for tomorrow?" Ira asked.

"That would be fine, Ira; thank you," I said. Ira left, and I planted myself beside Ward and thumped my elbows down on the table.

"That good woman seems to have something important on her mind." Ward looked askance at me, furrowed his brow, and pursed his lips.

"Ward Clayton Holden," I began. That made him look around and face me. "Our son Clay is Alder Luce's father!"

"That was an accident," Ward said.

"Ward, why is it that you never told me that Alder is our grandson?"

"Ah, that's what this is all about."

"Yes, that's what this is all about, Ward, or at least a part of what this is about. And did you know that Janine was our grandchild, too?" I asked Ward.

"Yes," was all he answered.

"You did?" I wanted to hit him. A part of me wondered how he could have known that, but I was in the middle of asking questions, and I just couldn't stop now. My questions were like stones rolling down a hill. You can't stop stones in the middle of an avalanche.

"And—and, Ward, I don't pretend to know how this is possible, but it seems as though one of the twins, Nadine, is our granddaughter, too. Did you know that as well?"

"Yes," Ward answered again.

"You knew?" I stood up and glared at him. "How could you have known? How come you never told me any of this, Ward?" I picked a plate up off the table and threw it at the back door. It smashed into bits. "How could you have kept a thing like that to yourself and not told me?" I turned and took a couple steps away from him so that I wouldn't smack him. "Have you any idea what I've been through this afternoon?" I was beside myself; I just couldn't believe my ears. He was sitting there at the table as calm as you please answering yes to having knowledge of information that seemed to have turned my life inside out in an hour's time. "How come you never told me, Ward?" I came at him, and my hand came crashing down on the table. "Answer me that!"

"Would it have made her life better to have known before now? Would her life have been happier or more fulfilled?" Ward asked me.

"Ward, life isn't just about being happy. Everybody can't be happy all the time. Life is about sharing with each other and about the truth. What about the truth, Ward? I want to know why you've kept this from me?"

"Truth has its own time, it seems to this old man," Ward said. "At the right time the truth makes sense to talk about. At the wrong time, it can hurt for no good reason. He wasn't keeping it, so much as he was holding it, carrying it until the right time came."

"How is it that you know about the children? And how long have you known, Ward?" I demanded.

"By putting two and two together. About the lad, since before he was born—from Mabel. About the others, just after the twins were born—from the description that that good woman gave of the twins and from information that Ira told him. His sidekick told him, because he felt that the time was right; with Mark gone Ira felt that maybe Arlette might need help with the children." His voice was steady and reasonable. I was having difficulty just breathing; I felt as though I'd run a race.

"Ira?" I didn't understand what Ira had to do with this. "How does Ira come to know these things? I don't understand, Ward."

"His sidekick heard about the mess they made of their lives. He was present when Mark was talking to son Clay in the Bar and Grill just before Mark fell and hit his head. Ira was in the next booth; he heard everything they said to each other."

"Mark and Clay? But that was a year ago. What did Ira hear? What did he say he heard, Ward?" I was struck by the idea that this whole day had taken on an unreal quality; the room seemed to be swirling with ghosts out of the past. Part of me wanted to hold onto my anger, part of me wanted to cry, and part of me didn't know just which end was up.

"Ira should tell about this himself when he comes back." Ward got up and filled the kettle and put it on the stove. Then he began sweeping up the smashed pieces of the plate by the back door. I watched him, and I didn't say anything until he finished. I just sat there calming down while he made tea.

"Did you know that Arlette is dying, that the doctor says that it's only a matter of time for her now? Did you know that, Ward?" I said to his back.

Ward turned to look at me, and his face was somber. "He did know that she was very sick," Ward said. "That's too bad. Who . . . what arrangements are being made for the children?" He set the tea on the table and sat back down in his chair.

"None yet, so far as I know, but I've been thinking about that on the way home, Ward." I wasn't sure how Ward was going to react to the idea that was in my head. I took Ward's face in my hands. "They're our grandchildren, Ward. Don't you think that we have some responsibility here?"

"They're his son's children, at least two out of three. They're really his son's responsibility," Ward answered.

"Well, yes. Of course they're Clay's responsibility. I know that, but Clay isn't here right now, and right now is when those children need looking after, if and when Arlette dies. And don't you think Arlette needs some peace of mind about what will become of her children, Ward?" I knew that Ward was not refusing to help the children; this was just his way of looking at all the angles of a problem.

"And what do they tell his son's wife about the children?" Ward asked.

"I don't think that it's our place to tell Angela. That's Clay's responsibility, and I mean to see that he faces up to it. After the war is over, he'll have to deal with it, when he comes home," I said.

"Ah! Then truth does have its own time, doesn't it." Ward pointed this out as though he'd won an argument.

"All right, old man, you've made your point," I admitted.

"And what if their son doesn't come home? Their son is in a war," Ward added.

"Oh, Ward, I hate it when you talk like that. We have to believe that Clay will come home; he's got to come home," I said.

"And if he doesn't, what do they tell his son's wife about the children?" Ward persisted.

"Then, as far as I'm concerned, Angela will never know." I was adamant.

"Agreed," Ward said simply.

I got up and kissed Ward on the cheek. Somehow I wasn't angry anymore. I knew why I'd married this special man. I had the idea that now that we'd settled this business, Ward would tell me what Ira had learned, but he insisted that we wait for Ira to come back and tell me himself.

Ira returned promptly when he said he would. "Well, have the two of you got your costumes all figured out for tonight?"

"Yes, Ira, I think we have," I said. "We've decided to go as the grandfather and grandmother of Arlette's children. What do you think of that, Ira?"

"Well, . . . yes, I guess that would work." Ira was trying to cover his discomfort.

"Ira, Ward says you've got a story to tell me about the day Mark died. He said that you'd tell me yourself when you returned. So I'm all ears; what's the story?" Ira shifted his feet and looked even more uncomfortable. He looked over at Ward, and Ward nodded. Ira looked around the room and then at me and cleared his throat. "It's not a pleasant story, Ida."

"I'm not asking you for a pleasant story. What I want to know is the truth." I could see he needed prodding.

"It mostly concerns a conversation I overheard between Mark and Clay," Ira said. "Some parts of it are kind of rough, Ida."

"I appreciate the warning, Ira; but I think that I can take it, whatever it is," I said. "You just go ahead and tell me what happened."

"Well, let me see," Ira began. "It was Monday, November 9th, and somehow it had been a long day for me, and I wasn't feeling very sociable. So after work I went to the Bar and Grill for a bite to eat, and I took the last booth, and I sat facing the wall. I'd just started eating when someone came in and sat in the booth behind me with his back to me. I didn't know then that it was Clay, but I found out later that it was.

"Evidently he'd just gotten off duty; by then it was a little past five. He ordered a coffee and a jelly donut. When I heard his voice, I knew that it was Clay, but as I said, I wasn't feeling particularly sociable, so I just kept on eating. The waitress no sooner brought Clay his order than Mark showed up. I knew it was Mark, because I recognized his voice, too. Mark ordered a beer, and he and Clay spent a couple of minutes exchanging information about how their day had gone.

"Then Clay said, 'So Mark, I got your message that you needed to meet me here to talk as soon as I got off duty. What's on your mind?'

"Mark said, 'Clay, I want you to stay away from my wife!'

"I had been hearing their conversation, not really eavesdropping. But those words got my attention in a hurry, and I pricked up my ears.

"Clay said, 'What are you talking about, Mark?' But he said it in a kind of husky voice, as though he had to work at trying to sound casual.

"Mark said, 'Don't you try to hand me a load of crap, brother. Arlette has told me everything.' I could tell that Mark had already been drinking more than was good for him. There was a kind of slur in the way he was talking.

"Clay said, 'And just what has Arlette told you?' Clay had his voice under control now; he was using his matter-of-fact policeman's voice.

"Mark said, 'Well, for one thing I know that you're Alder's father.'

"By now I'd forgotten about my supper completely. I couldn't chew and listen at the same time to what was going on in the booth behind me. So I just gave up eating altogether and listened with all my ears.

"Clay said, 'If that's true, and I'm not saying it is, it happened before you even met her.'

"Mark said, 'It's true all right, and you know damn well it's true. I don't mean you're a real father, because a real father wouldn't have abandoned his kid. But you know what I mean. And it turns out that you were Janine's father too, but Arlette says that neither of you knew about that at the time Arlette and I got married.'

"Clay said, 'So, where is this all going anyway? Just what is it you want from me, Mark?'

"Mark said, 'I don't want a damn thing from you, except for you to stay away from my wife.'

"Clay said, 'You already said all this happened before you were married, so what's your problem?'

"Mark said, 'My problem, mister man, is that last August 1st did not happen before we were married. And the fact is that Arlette is pregnant again, and she can't be sure if she's carrying your kid or my kid. She said it was all an accident. Now, I love my wife, and I want to believe what she said. But I just want to make damn sure your fly doesn't come unzipped by accident anymore around my wife, so I want you to stay the hell away from her. You think that's clear enough, or do you want me to put it in writing, so you can show it to your wife?'

"Clay laughed and he said, 'Man, you must've had too much to drink today. You're talking like a crazy man! I pity Arlette having to put up with you!'

"Then I heard Mark sort of growl, and he said, 'You miserable son of a bitch!'

"I knew then that he had stood up, because his voice wasn't coming from the same level as before. My curiosity got the best of me, and I looked over the top of the booth. Mark was part way out of the booth, and he had grabbed Clay by the lapels of his uniform. Clay's arms came up quickly from under Mark's hands and pushed them off.

"Clay said quiet-like, 'You get your damn hands off me and keep them to yourself!'

"Right then Mark lost his balance and pitched over backwards, catching his leg on the corner of the booth seat. He reached out to Clay, and Clay tried to grab his hand, but they didn't connect. His eyes had a startled and pleading look. He called Clay's name and started to fall, and he seemed to fall forever. He didn't seem able to catch himself on anything.

"And he hit his head on the floor. There's only a thin layer of tile covering that concrete floor. And his head smashed like the sound of a muskmelon hitting a wall. Clay was already on his feet, and he ran to check Mark out. He yelled to the waitress to call the ambulance. It was amazing how fast people gathered around in just a couple of minutes; I was just one of the crowd then.

"Clay was off duty, but he was a policeman on the scene, and the story was that he and Mark had been talking. He said that Mark had had a lot to drink and that, when he got up to leave, he lost his balance and fell and hit his head on the floor. Actually, as far as it went, the story was the truth. Clay hadn't hit Mark; he just pushed Mark's hands off him with an upward motion of his arms. When Clay said that he couldn't find a pulse, I had a feeling that Mark was already dead. And he was.

"There was no point in my saying what I had witnessed. It would have hurt people, and it wouldn't have helped anybody. It was an accident. That's the way I saw it, and that's the way everybody else saw it too. It was an accident."

Ira's last sentence echoed in my mind. It was an accident. I'd heard that sentence or ones like it several times in the course of the day. It was an accident. Alder was an accident. Janine was an accident. The twins were an accident. Mark's death was an accident. It was an accident that Arlette's strep throat turned into rheumatic fever. It was an accident. Somehow that idea seemed to be the key that had unlocked the door on this day and let all the skeletons come tumbling out of the closet.

As soon as it was dusk, troops of little ghosts and goblins began a parade past our door offering us the familiar option of 'trick or treat.' I told the first group that I'd had my fill of tricks that day, and so I guessed I'd better treat them. I was kept busy for a while doling out cookies to the costumed children of the neighborhood. I'd no sooner sit down than there would be another knock at the door. "Trick or treat! Trick or treat!"

I opened the door after one particularly loud knock, and there stood a very strange, hunchbacked man. He had on buckled, black, rubber overshoes and an oversized gray coat, which I recognized as Clay's. Even pinned up the coat reached below the tops of his boots. The hunchback had a bag in each hand for collecting his booty. The sleeves of the coat were rolled up, and out of a great muffler at the coat's collar sprouted two identical heads, each topped by a battered hat.

"Trick or treat! Trick or treat!" each head sang out. Each face had been reshaped by being stuffed into a ruined, silk stocking."

"Well, land sakes, what have we got here?" I asked, pretending that I had no idea who it was, or rather who they were.

"I'm a two-headed hunchback!" announced the first, *younger* head.

"Well, you certainly are; I can see that," I said. "Ward, you'd better come and have a look at this little man who's at the door. I don't know if we should give him a cookie or just send him packing."

"Two cookies! Two cookies!" the first head cried out.

"I need a cookie for each head," the second head confirmed with a wink and a smile. "Both heads get hungry, you know."

"Well, you'd better come inside then," I said. "I want my husband to meet you, mister two-headed hunchback. Ward, take a look. What do you think?"

"It wins the first prize as the most original costume of the year," Ward announced as though he were on stage performing the duties of a contest judge. Ward made the little hunchback turn around so that he could see him from all angles. "What happens when he gets tired of carrying his hunch?" Ward inquired.

"My hunch isn't heavy," the second head said.

"But if it gets heavy, that's easy to fix!" said the first head, and immediately the first head disappeared down into the muffler, abandoning its hat. It looked as though the head had been swallowed by the great muffler. As the hunchback's hunch and extra head fell away, he adjusted his muffler and added the extra hat to the one on top of his remaining head.

"Now I'm a four-legged man with two hats," the remaining head said and grinned. It was a winning grin even behind the silk stocking. Below the hem of the coat there were four feet in buckled, black, rubber overshoes.

"That's quite a transformation!" said Ward.

"I'll say," I said. "I think it deserves four cookies, two for each bag."

"Thank you," said the four-legged man. Another muffled "thank you" echoed from somewhere inside the oversized coat. "That's just my stomach talking," the four-legged man said with a grin. And with that he wished us a good night and turned and walked away, obviously very practiced at walking on four legs.

Alder and Michael (and Angela also) had kept the secret of this Halloween costume very well. It struck me that the idea had never occurred to me before how much those two little faces looked alike. Even misshapen in silk stockings, it was obvious to me now that they were the faces of two brothers.

Chapter Thirteen
Making Decisions

• *Grandmother Holden* •

The next day I started out for Arlette's to tell her what Ward and I had talked about. It occurred to me on the way over to Arlette's that even though Ward and I had decided that we would be willing to take the children, I really had no idea how Arlette would feel about our offer. I had told Ward that no arrangements had been made for the children, because Arlette had not mentioned yesterday that any had been made. But I hadn't really thought to ask her. While she was telling me her story, I was already feeling that I had to do something, that I would have to talk to Ward about our raising those children, until Clay came home and I could talk to him face to face about accepting his responsibility. But I hadn't mentioned any of this to Arlette.

I hadn't asked her if she wanted us to take the children. I hadn't asked her if she'd thought about what would happen to the children when she died. Arlette had no family except for Aunt Mabel, and I knew that Mark had no family. So I just assumed that the responsibility would be Ward's and mine, until Clay came home. I assumed that the reason she was telling me the whole story was so that I would offer to help.

I guess it's part of who I am as a person that I always feel that I have to help, if I possibly can. That's what people come to me for, to ask for my help. I always help if I'm able to. I don't always want to, but I do. I can't even remember how many babies I've helped bring into the world, how many sick beds I tended, how many casseroles I've baked for funeral dinners, how many Grange suppers I've organized. I'm used to helping; it's what I do. I never had any idea, though, that with the age of fifty staring me in the face I would be asked to undertake such an important and taxing task as raising three children—two of them babies. But that was just the point, wasn't it? Nobody had asked me, really; I had asked myself.

And then I had another idea, and it hit me like a bolt out of the blue. I didn't know why it hadn't come home to me before, except that I'd been all wrapped up in what I thought was my duty. Lord, what was this going to do to Clay's wife Angela? How would she take this? Right then I wanted to wring Clay's neck. What could he have been dreaming of to be unfaithful to her? She was a good wife for him.

I wasn't sure I'd feel that way at first. I think a mother tends to mistrust that a beautiful woman will make a good wife for her son, so from my point of view her looks were against her. And she'd always struck me as being a very independent sort, especially after she came back from that fancy business college in Massachusetts. They did make a handsome couple, but I didn't know how she'd fit in with our family. I thought she'd be too la-di-da for us, but once Ward and I got to know her, we found out that she was down to earth—just folks. She loved our son, and she was a good match for him. We came to realize that Clay had found himself a gem.

She was a decent daughter-in-law, better than most. And a good mother, too. Generally speaking, I'd have to say she was a less cranky mother than I had been. This past summer I'd found her moody, but I think the war was wearing on her. I knew she missed Clay. Oh, that boy! What was wrong with him? I couldn't understand it. They always seemed to be so well-suited to each other. And what was this new turn of events going to do to their marriage? I didn't know.

I stopped on the first bridge and just stood there looking down at the water. The river churned steely and sullen underneath me, as though it were thinking about gray skies and winter coming on as it swept away west. I'm not sure what I was thinking about right then, except about how complicated life can get. It was strange; I could remember as a girl standing on this same bridge looking at the water when nothing was more complicated than where I was going to go berrying and get enough berries for a shortcake and still be back in time to help with the milking.

As a girl sometimes I would stand on this bridge and watch the water, and all of a sudden it would seem that the bridge and I were moving backwards, and not the water moving forwards. It had been ages since I'd allowed myself time to do that, and it might seem a foolish idea, but that's what I did right then. I cleared my mind for a moment of all these questions that were coming at me from every direction, and I looked down at the river, at the water slipping away under my feet, gallons and gallons of water flowing underneath me from little brooks and mountain streams and springs. In almost fifty years I had never seen the river completely dry. There was always water flowing past on its journey to the lake and eventually, I suppose, to the sea. And as I watched the water, I could feel myself moving back, back as though I were moving back in time to a simpler era.

I stood and watched the water for a while, not thinking of much of anything except the sense of motion. Then I heard the train whistle blow as it pulled into the station a mile away. I looked up, and I knew why Clay had gone into the navy so quickly after Mark died. He'd said that he needed to be a part of what might prove to be the most important event of his lifetime, that he wanted to be a part of history. There may have been something of that in his decision to go to the war, but now I knew what else there was. He needed to get away—from Mark's death maybe, maybe from Arlette and Angela, from his responsibilities here at home.

Clay was not like me. I always had this sense of duty and responsibility. There was always work to be done. When you're raised on a farm, everything is tied up with responsibilities and work. Not that there wasn't pleasure in it or that we didn't have any fun, but pleasure and fun were almost always tied together with our work. But from the time he was a boy, Clay always wanted to have fun just to have fun, and it had nothing to do with work. He wasn't raised on a farm. Sure we always had a few animals while he was growing up, but still and all it wasn't a real farm such as Ward and I had grown up on.

Clay wasn't like Ward either. Ward, like me, had a keen sense of responsibility, but Ward was a tinkerer and a thinker. He might be somewhat eccentric, but he always saw deeper into a problem than I did. He always thought about not just what people said or what they looked like, but what was going on behind their faces in their heads and in their hearts. I think that's why he liked locks so much; it wasn't just the part everybody could see that he was interested in, but what was inside the lock that made it work. Ward was always a thinker.

Clay, on the other hand, was not a deep thinker like his father. And now I remembered the words that Ward had said yesterday, "And what if their son doesn't come home?" And I realized that it had already occurred to Ward that Clay might not come home and that Clay's not coming home might have nothing to do with the war overseas at all, but with the war inside himself.

If Arlette agreed that Ward and I should take the children, Clay would know it shortly. We would write to him; Angela would write to him. And what kind of additional pressure would that put on him? Or would that take the pressure off him, that his mother and father were shouldering his responsibilities and that he wouldn't need to feel the whole weight of this burden? And how was being in the war going to change him? He certainly would have responsibilities in the navy, responsibilities that he couldn't shirk or run away from. Maybe that was just what he needed. Maybe it would help him grow up. He may have been a man—husband, father, policeman; and he may have had duties and responsibilities that went with his job and the rest, but he never did seem completely grown up to me.

I don't know how long I stood looking at the river and thinking, but I stood there quite awhile. My mind seemed full of questions and no answers, but finally I realized that the river and I were alike. We both could feel winter coming on, but we both had to do what we had to do. The river had to flow west and keep on flowing, and I had to do my duty as I saw it and just trust that I was doing the right thing.

When I got to Arlette's, Mabel was outside hanging up clothes on the clotheslines. She had already completed a whole line of diapers, and it came home to me that without electricity she must have done the washing all by hand—pumping the water, heating it on the stove, using the scrub board. I'd almost forgotton how much work that could be.

"Mabel, you must be exhausted doing all this wash by hand," I said.

"Oh, bless your heart, Ida! No, most of these I didn't wash by hand, just the soakers and a few other woolen things. Dad Ames picked up the washing yesterday evening on his way home from the drug store. He got up early this morning and did a wash and dropped the clothes by on his way to work, so that I could hang them out to dry. And what with the babies and Arlette, I'm just getting around to it now, don't you know."

"Well, let me lend you a hand, as long as I'm here."

"Oh, that's all right, Ida; I can get it. And I need the exercise and the fresh air anyway. Why don't you go keep Arlette company; she was awake a few minutes ago when I left her."

"I don't know about fresh air, but with this household to run, I'm sure you get plenty of exercise, Mabel," I said. But I took her suggestion and went inside to see Arlette. Mabel didn't want my help hanging out the clothes, and I really knew that. We're funny about certain tasks. We each have our own way of doing them, and we think of our way as the right way, and we'd rather do it all ourselves than to have the help of someone who won't do it just right. Somehow it doesn't seem reasonable to refuse assistance when you're already so busy, but I understood it perfectly.

"Am I disturbing you, Arlette?" I asked at the entrance to her room.

Arlette had been reading, and she put down her book and laughed an embarrassed little laugh. "No. No, Ida, please come in. I'm—I was reading Robert Louis Stevenson's *Treasure Island*. I never read it, and right now Aunt Mabel is reading it to Alder. I've been listening in, and I want to know how it ends . . . in . . . in case I don't get a chance to finish it with them." Her eyes filled with tears. This was the first time I'd seen her shed a tear at the thought of her death.

"Oh, Arlette, this must be so hard for you." I could only imagine how difficult this must be for her. "I'm so sorry!"

"It is hard, Ida! It really is!" Arlette took a hankerchief from inside her sleeve and wiped her eyes and blew her nose. "I feel as though I'm being torn apart. Part of me is all right with knowing that I'm going to die, with the thought that I'm going to be with Mark again. You know, I really do believe in my heart that I will be reunited with Mark. And I'm almost . . . no, I really am looking forward to that, to being able to tell him how much I really love him. I really do love him, Ida. I know he knows that, but I'd like to tell him to his face."

She wiped her eyes and blew her nose again. "But then—then I think about those beautiful little babies and Alder, and I feel that I shouldn't leave them, that I need to be here for them. And it's just tearing me up inside that I don't have a choice. But, maybe—this is going to sound awful or crazy—but maybe, if I had a choice, I'm really not sure what I would decide. I might decide to go anyway. When I think about that, Ida, I feel so guilty about the children."

"Have you made any plans for the children, Arlette?" I asked her.

"Aunt Mabel and I have talked about that in the last couple of days. When I used to want to talk about it, she would say that she didn't want to hear any of that sort of talk. She'd say that I was just talking nonsense, that I was going to get better, and that I just had to put my mind to it. But in the last couple of days she's been willing to talk about it. I know that she and Dad Ames will take the children. It's such a lot to ask of them at their time of life. I pointed out to her that neither she nor Dad Ames is as young as they used to be, but she said, there I went talking nonsense again."

I decided that the time was right to say what I had come to say. "Arlette, Ward and I have talked it over, and we've decided that we would like to take the children, at least until Clay comes home." I didn't take a breath, but I just kept right on going. "They're really Clay's responsibility, of course, and I mean to see that he accepts it when he returns. If he doesn't return, then they'll always have a home with us. I haven't talked to Mabel about this, but I don't think that she'd object. We can ask her, though, if you think that she might have other ideas."

Arlette was looking down at her hands that were busy making folds in the bedclothes. "Ida, I didn't tell you about Clay and me to make you feel that you should take the children. Or to make sure that Clay took them either. That wasn't why I told you."

"I know that, dear," I said. "Now that you've brought the idea up, though, why did you feel that you needed to tell me?" She could have taken this secret with her to her grave. Aunt Mabel and Dad Ames would have raised the children, and I might never have been the wiser. Ward might never have told me. Clay might never have told me.

"You have been so good to me, Ida," Arlette began. "You've taken care of Alder. You helped out when Janine was born. You were here for me with Nadine and Nathaniel." At that point Arlette took in a strange breath, which sounded as though she were trying to say the word "oh," while she was breathing in. It was the shuddery kind of breath children take after they've been crying too much. Arlette's eyes fluttered, and she put her head back against her pillows. I wasn't sure if she put her head back or if it fell back.

"Arlette? Arlette, are you all right?" I stood up and went to her bedside. She was unconscious. I shouted for Mabel, but Mabel couldn't hear me. I took Arlette's wrist, but I couldn't find her pulse. I put my ear near her mouth and my hand on her chest. She wasn't breathing. And then I knew she was dead. It all happened so fast; it was over in an instant. "Arlette?" I said. "Arlette?" I just stood there holding her hand;

I didn't know what to do. The thought that went through my head was that she had died before we had managed to settle anything.

It was all over. So quick—just like that. She looked so frail lying there. Frail and peaceful. A minute ago she was talking to me, and now she was gone. I don't know how much time passed. I don't know what I did while it was passing. As I brushed the hair back from her forehead, she gasped, and life seem to come back into her body. She moved her head weakly from side to side. "Arlette, are you all right?"

"I'll be all right . . . in a minute," she said. Her voice was so soft that I could barely hear her. There was a look of pain or exhaustion in her face. She reached for her water glass, and I placed it in her hand. She drank a sip, and then, keeping the glass in her lap, she breathed slowly for a couple of minutes.

"Are you feeling better now? What happened?"

"Yes, it's better now." Her face slowly regained its composure, and then she began to speak again. "I don't know what . . . happens. I get these waves . . . that sort of wash over me, and then . . . I get pulled under by . . . the undertow." She tried to smile at me. She breathed slowly for a while. At some point I had sat down on the bed, and now I shifted back into the chair. I sat quiet and watched her.

Then she took another sip of water and spoke. Her voice was still soft, but it sounded stronger. "When the doctor said that I needed to put . . . my affairs in order, I knew that I needed to tell Aunt Mabel everything, even if she had figured . . . most of it out on her own. And I also felt that I needed to tell you as well. If any of my story . . . ever became known, it was important to me that both of you would have heard it . . . from me, from my own lips, not from somebody else."

"But now that you have told me," I said, "it changes everything."

"But that really wasn't my intent in telling you," Arlette said.

At that point Mabel came into the room. She had a tray of tea and cookies which she set down on the side table.

"Didn't you hear me calling you, Mabel?" I asked.

"No, I just came in a minute or two ago. What did you need, Ida?"

"Arlette just had a bad turn, and I got a little scared."

"Are you okay now, Arlette?" The concern in Mabel's voice was an apology for not being present when she was needed.

Arlette nodded, "Yes, I'm better now."

"I should have looked in," Aunt Mabel reproached herself. "And it crossed my mind to do that, but I just thought I'd get the tea first. I did think it was strange, though, that things seemed so quiet in here." She poured the tea and handed a cup to Arlette and to me. Her manner seemed to suggest that she was making up for some "negligence."

"Mabel," I said, "I've just told Arlette that Ward and I would like to take the children."

"I see," Mabel said. Her face was suddenly unreadable. It was interesting; I wasn't sure just how Mabel was receiving the news. Mabel could have the face of a lawyer or a poker player when she had a mind to; you often couldn't tell what ideas were circulating in her head.

"My idea," I continued, "is that when Clay gets out of the service, the children should become part of his and Angela's family."

"And how does Angela feel about this?" Aunt Mabel asked, putting her finger on one of the major flaws in my plan.

"Well, that is a problem, because Angela doesn't know about any of my plans," I admitted.

"And neither does Clay," Aunt Mabel added.

"He knows that they're his children, and I mean to see that he lives up to his responsibilities," I said with determination. "Somehow I just have to have faith that Angela will be able to deal with this."

"And the children are in the middle of all of it," Mabel pointed out.

"I know what you're saying, Mabel," I said. "There aren't any easy answers to this issue, but I don't mean to put the children in the middle any more than I have to. I know how I would like for things to go, and I can only trust and pray that they will go in that direction. If Clay should refuse to deal with this, to tell Angela or to take the children, they will always have a home with Ward and me."

"There are no guarantees in this life," Aunt Mabel sighed.

"The only sure things are death and taxes, I know," I added. "All Ward and I can promise is to do our best. That's all anybody can promise."

"How do you feel about this, love?" Aunt Mabel asked Arlette.

"Well, I told Ida that my intent in telling her about Clay and me . . . and about the children was not to make her feel responsible for taking the children." Arlette looked at Mabel and me, and then she looked away as though she were looking beyond the present moment. "The more I think about it, though, the more I think . . . that it's the right thing to do. Maybe deep inside, some part of me knew that; I don't know. What do you think, Aunt Mabel."

"I agree with Ida that there aren't any easy answers," Mabel said. "My concerns are for you, of course, and for all my little darlings, don't you know. And I know that Ida shares those concerns. Ida and Ward are good people, love, and I know the children will have a good home with them. Even though we might all want to, there is no way that we can protect the children from everything. People will talk and say cruel things no matter how much we wish they wouldn't. Hopefully, we can help them deal with it. I don't pretend to know how everything is put together, but somehow it seems to me that the vicissitudes we deal with in this life help us to grow. If it seems right to you, then I would trust that, Arlette. I fully intend to remain a part of their lives, though. I am their Aunt Mabel, after all."

"Oh, and I mean to see that you do, too!" I said. "I'll need all the help I can get. At my age I'm a little long in the tooth to think of raising these children without taking advantage of all the assistance available to me." I thought about Mabel's refusal of help at the clothesline.

"Well, if you're a little long in the tooth, what does that say about me?" Aunt Mabel asked with a chuckle.

"I can't speak for you; I can only speak for myself," I answered.

Mabel took a sip of her tea, and her face took on a puzzled look. I thought that she was going to say something, but she took a bite of her cookie and chewed it with a kind of thoughtful expression on her face. I waited for her to speak. Finally she pressed her lips together, and then she opened them and gave voice to her thought, "There is one other notion that's going through my mind. So, I figure that I might as well say it."

She hadn't been looking at either Arlette or me, but at her finger circling the rim of her tea cup. She looked as though she were concerned that her finger might fall in. Now she looked at each of us in turn. "Alder and Nadine are obviously Clay's children, but it looks as though Nathaniel is Mark's son. How is Clay going to feel about that?"

"Yes, I've thought about that," I admitted. "But I think it's the least Clay can do. I think that he owes Mark that." I didn't want to tell either of them what I had heard yesterday about Mark's death. I felt that that was best left alone. I thought about the twins though, about Nadine's belonging to Clay and Nathaniel's belonging to Mark. I believed it as much as they did, but I didn't know if anything like that had ever happened before. Oh, I knew it happened with puppies. I'd seen more than one litter with pups from different sires. But I'd never heard of such a thing happening to people before.

Mabel had said something yesterday about people in stories, twins having different fathers in stories, but those were people in stories. I wasn't at all sure if such a thing happened in real life. That question was going through my head, and I was gnawing on it like a bone. I couldn't leave it alone. That was something I was going to have to get an answer to.

Actually I didn't have to wait very long for an opportunity to get an answer to my question. The three of us had decided that I should wait there until Alder came home from school, so that I could be present when he was told what was in store for Arlette and what plans had been made. Then we could all talk with him together and help make him as easy in his mind as we could. We all knew that it wasn't going to be easy for Alder. He and Arlette were very close. But before Alder came home, Doctor Bonsecours stopped by to look in on Arlette. He talked with Arlette and examined her, while Mabel and I were taking care of the babies. When he came out into the living room, I was rocking Nadine and feeding her her bottle. Aunt Mabel was playing with Nathaniel.

"Well, it's good to see that Arlette is feeling so much better in her mind," he said.

"Yes, well, I think it's because we've settled some things, in fact quite a few things," Mabel said.

"Well, that's good," the doctor said. "I'm glad to hear that; I think that's what she needed to do. I'll check back in a couple of days, but if you need me before then, just flag somebody down who's going by the house and get a message to me. I'll come as soon as I can."

I made up my mind in an instant to talk to him about the twins. Part of me didn't want to tell him what I felt was none of his business, but another part of me reasoned that he'd probably already figured everything out anyway. He wasn't a stupid man, even if he wasn't quite my cup of tea. I figured there wasn't any point in hiding what I was thinking from Mabel; we'd almost become like relatives. "Doctor, before you go," I began, "there's something I want to ask you."

The doctor turned and looked at me. "Yes? And what is that, Ida?" He pushed his glasses up on his big nose. (His glasses made his eyes look large, and I thought of Little Red Riding Hood's wolf, "The better to see you with, my dear.")

"I'd like what we say right here to stay just among us," I said.

"Of course, Ida," he said. He put his black bag down on the floor and sat in the straightbacked chair across from me. He seemed to be giving me all of his attention, which was unusual. "How can I help?" he asked.

"It's just a question I have," I said, "but it won't be hard for you to put two and two together, after I've asked it. If you haven't already, that is."

"I see," he said. "What's the question?"

"Is it possible for twins to have different fathers?" My question seemed to hang in the air for a full minute. Mabel looked at me and then at the doctor, but I couldn't tell what she was thinking. I wished that Ward had seen that look; he might have had some ideas.

"It's rare, but it happens," the doctor answered. "With the kind of twins we call fraternal twins, each of the mother's ovaries produces an egg, and each egg is fertilized by a different sperm. So the mother can have a boy and a girl or she could have twins of the same sex, but they can look very different. It is possible for a woman to produce two eggs, but for one egg not to be in a position to be fertilized yet. She could have relations with one man, and his sperm could fertilize the egg that's ready. Then later when the other egg is in position, she could have relations with another man, and his sperm could fertilize the second egg. There are documented cases.

"There is something which is more rare but still possible. A woman could have what we call a bicornate uterus; it's sort of a uterus with two pockets. And she can become pregnant in one pocket, and then a couple of months later she can become pregnant in the other pocket. She would be carrying two babies at the same time, but one would be born a couple of months before the other. In such a case as that, there could be different fathers also."

"Well, I never heard of such a thing," I said. "I guess I've learned something today." Actually it was pretty interesting, and I appreciated the fact that Doctor Bonsecours had answered my question without mentioning Arlette or the twins. He had just treated it as a medical question and let it go at that. I almost liked him for that.

Over the course of Arlette's illness I had sometimes been present when Alder got home from school, so I knew it wouldn't be a complete surprise for him to find me there. Mabel had the babies' schedule down to a science, and she had them all settled down when Alder came through the door. Usually Alder spent his first few minutes at home alone with his mother. Today Mabel suggested that we all go into the bedroom to talk with Arlette. This was something out of the ordinary, and I saw a startled look come into Alder's eyes. He was an awfully smart boy; I think he already suspected what was coming.

"Alder, why don't you come and sit on the bed by me," Arlette said. "I've asked Aunt Mabel and Mrs. Holden to be here because there are some very important things that we need to talk about today."

"What things?" Alder was looking intently at his mother, and there was just a hint of a quaver in his voice. I was watching them both. I had no idea how she was going to say this thing to her son. And then she just said it out, all in one breath.

"Alder, I'm not going to live much longer, and we need to make plans."

"Ma, don't say that!" He turned his head away from her, and looked past us out the window.

Arlette put her arms around him, placed her cheek next to his, and looked out the window with him. "Alder, we've always talked things out, you and I, and I need you to listen now. You remember those sunflowers that you grew for me this past summer, so I could see them from this window. Well, those sunflowers are gone now, but you saved some of the seeds from them, so you could plant more next spring. Those sunflowers were lucky that you were there to take care of the seeds. Alder, you and the babies are my seeds, and I have to make plans so I'll know you're going to be well taken care of. Mrs. Holden has offered to take care of the seeds I love so much."

Alder was crying; I was crying. Even Mabel was dabbing at her eyes, and she never cries. Arlette had a tough job to do, and she managed it well. She told Alder that he and the twins would come to live with me and Ward, and that Aunt Mabel would still be their Aunt Mabel. She didn't give him any of the other information. Even though Alder was very grown up, we decided that the time wasn't right for that. Alder took it awfully hard, but at the end he said that he wasn't giving up hope. It was a sad time.

The next day Mabel and her lawyer and Arlette drew up a will that expressed Arlette's wish that the children live with Ward and me until such time as we should find guardians who Mabel, Ward, and I all thought were more suitable. In the event that something should happen to Ward and me before that time, the children would be placed in the guardianship of Aunt Mabel and Dad Ames. Arlette also expressed the wish that Mark's house not be sold, but retained as rental property with the proceeds used to help defray the cost of raising the children. With no electricity and no telephone, I wasn't so sure that it was going to be that easy to rent Mark's house. Mabel knew a lot more about that than Ward and I did; that was for sure. She had been a landlady for years. Arlette signed the will, and Ward, Dad Ames, Aunt Mabel, and I all witnessed it.

From that point on, I was at Arlette's more than I was at home. For one thing Arlette took a turn for the worse, but for another thing I felt that the babies should get more used to me than they already were. When I couldn't be there, I asked Angela to help out. I told her that Ward and I had decided to take the children. I wasn't sure how she was going to react to that.

At first she looked a little surprised, I thought, but what she said was, "I'm glad. That must have helped put Arlette's worries to rest." It wasn't always easy for me to understand where Angela was coming from. She didn't confide a lot in me. That whole summer she had been edgy and sullen, but with the fall she seemed to come out of her dark mood and be more her old self. I didn't know then the trial that she had gone through.

"Who? What?" It was late at night, and Arlette sensed that someone was with her in the bed. Both in and out of sleep, she'd had such strange reveries lately that she couldn't be sure she wasn't still in the grip of another troubled dream. Clutching at her chest, she tried to catch her breath from the sudden jolt of leaving sleep. And yet she wasn't sure she had, but as she struggled for her quick, shallow breaths, she knew for certain that she felt beside her the heat of another body. As painful as it was for her, she turned quickly to her right and saw the head of thick, blond, wavy hair. The kerosene lamp burning low on the chiffonier afforded her little light, but she would have known that head of hair anywhere. It was Clay's!

"What are you doing in my bed?" Her tone of voice was imperious, and it belied the panic she felt in her chest. Clay didn't move, and for a moment Arlette wavered and was lulled by her illness into a sense that this was just a dream after all. But unlike dreams where one's focus seems to shift and merge, the details of this experience remained clear and constant. And the physical realities of her illness were too real. This was not a dream! In a fright Arlette found herself possessed of a strength that she didn't know she could command. She lifted Clay to a sitting position. "Why are you here?" she demanded.

The chin came up, and the blue eyes of Alder's face blinked open. "I guess . . . I guess I fell asleep." Alder rubbed at his left eye; she had frightened him awake. "I had a bad dream."

Now, she wrapped her arms around him and pulled him close to her. "Oh, my sweet boy, I'm sorry! I didn't know who you were. I must have been on the other side of the world. You gave me such a start." There was energy in her voice that had not been there for weeks. There was strength in her arms. She was holding her son, and she was not in pain. She took a deep breath and let it out slowly, as she felt Alder relax against her. "Tell me about your dream."

"I don't remember it now, but I was scared and worried, and I just wanted to be here with you."

"Well, good! And here you are. Don't be scared and worried anymore."

"But it's not just tonight, because of the dream. I'm scared and worried all the time."

"You are?" She put her hands on either side of his face and looked at him closely. Alder was always so self-possessed. "Scared and worried" were not words he applied to himself. But he looked scared and worried; his face was haggard. "Why, sweetheart, tell me what's wrong?" In the rush of adrenalin she almost forgot what there was to be afraid of or concerned about.

Alder looked at his mother without comprehending how she could ask him such a question. His head wavered from side to side as he felt again the hard hands of his nightmare twisting his reality. How could she not know how hopeless he felt to be facing her death? How could she sit so still and almost calmly ask him why? Her gentle concern, her smooth mother's voice searched the center of his spirit, wound bony fingers around his infinite sense of loss, and squeezed his anguish out into the room. "Ma-a?" He was lost and trying to find her.

"I'm here, sweet boy. I'm here."

"Ma-a!" This time it was louder, desperate for her to understand. Tears sprang suddenly from his eyes.

"Tell me what it is!" She held him close and rocked him as though he were a baby. "Tell me what's the matter!"

"Ma-a, I-don't-want-you-to-die! Don't die! Please don't die!" The words shook from him as he convulsed in sobs against his mother's breast.

She saw it all with crystal clarity. She was really going to die. And he was "scared and worried" because she was leaving him. And the odd thing was that she'd been dealing with the concept of her death for several days, making plans for the children, writing a will. But her death had never truly been a *fact* to her until this moment, when her son pronounced the words. She held his sobbing body and felt his blond hair brushing softly against her cheek. And with this tender act of motherhood, she realized that they were both facing her death at the same moment.

"My sweet boy," she began. "I love you so much! Do you know that?" She felt his nod against her shoulder. "And I know how you must be feeling right now. I know; I really do." She inhaled in a long shuddering, "Oh-h-h!" A memory of loss stabbed at her heart like a knife. The emotional force locked in this memory which she had hidden from herself took her by surprise and overwhelmed her, and she realized she was weeping.

"When I . . . ," she wiped her eyes on the sleeve of her nightgown. "When I was a girl, my mother left me." Her crying gave her voice a nasal quality which made her sound like a little girl. "She left me, and she never came back. And I never heard from her again. I felt as though she didn't love me. She never told me that she did." She looked up at the ceiling and became aware of her breathing, as she held her son and let go of her own memory and centered on his need.

"But it's different with us, sweet boy. We love each other. You and I. You taught me that!" She inhaled, "Oh-h-h!" But the pain of this breath was beautiful and sweet, and she found herself again in the throes of her emotions. "You taught me that!"

Concerned but curious, Alder drew back from her to look at her. "What did I teach you?"

"You taught me how to love. Before you came into my life, I didn't know how to love. But I began loving you while you were growing inside my body. And then, when you were born and I saw your beautiful little face, and I held you in my arms, I fell in love with you. You were the first person I ever loved. You taught me how. And once I loved you, I was able to love Aunt Mabel, and then Mark, and Janine. Because of you, I discovered what a precious gift love is. You're the one who made me able to love."

"I don't remember doing that."

"Oh, you've been doing it all your life, sweet boy. All your life!"

"But, Ma, if you love me, don't you want to go on loving me? I want to go on loving you!"

"Oh, we'll never stop loving each other, Alder. Let's never stop."

"But, if you die . . . " His eyes opened wide trying to make her understand. His tears welled up again.

"When I die, I'll still keep loving you, and I hope you still keep loving me. Dying is not the end; dying is like being in a different room. When you're in the kitchen and I'm in the bedroom, we can still love each other. Love can pass right through the walls. When you're at school and I'm at home, we still love each other. Love is not bound by distance, or time . . . or even death. Death is a part of all life."

"But I want to be with you. I don't want you to leave me."

"Alder, I will always be with you. In here." She touched his head. "And in here." She touched his heart. "Just look inside yourself, and I'll always be there."

"I wish I could come with you."

"One day you will. And I'll be there. But you have things to do first. So many things. You have your whole life ahead of you." She suddenly felt weak. In a moment all of her energy was gone. She needed to lie down. Her hips were aching, her knees throbbed, her shoulders hurt. "I have to lie down," she said simply. But her body took a quick, sharp breath, and she clutched at her heart.

Alder's hands reached for his mother as she lowered herself painfully down onto her pillow. Her face was drained of color. "Ma, are you all right?"

She seemed to be swimming in a murky agony, which strangely enough was somehow enticing. But for the sake of her son, she fought to control her senses. "It's okay," she breathed. "It will pass . . . in a moment." Her eyes were concentrating at some point inside herself. Another sharp, shuddering breath grabbed at her.

Alder leapt from the bed, seized the handbell from the night stand, and rang it with all his might to call Aunt Mabel. He wasn't leaving his mother's side. He sat beside her and petted her hand while she tried to catch her breath. "I love you, Ma. I love you, Ma," he kept saying over and over like a mantra, as though those words would keep her at his side.

"It's . . . okay." Arlette held onto her chest as she struggled to breathe. She took his hand and lapsed into unconsciousness.

"I'm coming; I'm coming. Don't wake the babies." From the kitchen Alder heard Aunt Mabel's loud whisper which preceded her headlong entrance in her night bonnet and long flannel gown. She had one arm through a sleeve of her kimono, and she was frantically trying to find the other sleeve. "What's happened? What's the trouble?"

"Ma's having a bad spell."

"Oh, no! Oh, dear! How do you feel, Arlette?" From force of habit she put her hand on Arlette's forehead, but with her eyes she noted that Arlette's lips and fingernails had a bluish tinge. Her forehead was cool. She was still and unresponsive. "Arlette?"

Breath reentered Arlette's body in a swift shudder, and she opened her eyes slowly, weakly. "I just . . . gave Alder a . . . scare. . . . I'm sorry . . . to get you . . . up."

"That's perfectly all right dear. Don't you give it a second thought." She stroked Arlette's hand but frowned at the blueness of the fingernails. "But Alder, what are you doing up? Did I sleep through the bell?"

"I had a bad dream."

"Oh, my. I don't think you should bother your mother in her condition. She needs her rest, you know. Oh, Alder, and look at the time; it's after midnight. And you've got school tomorrow; you'd better get . . ."

Arlette interrupted, "It's all right. . . . I wanted . . . . . . I'm glad he's . . . here. . . . I'll have lots of . . . time to rest." She could feel the pain and weakness easing a little; she held onto Alder's hand. "Perhaps tomorrow, you could . . . stay home from school. . . . Ordinarily I don't . . . approve of missing school, . . . but maybe this is . . . a special occasion. . . . But promise me that you'll . . . study hard in school. . . . I want you to do . . . your best."

"I promise, Ma." Alder was studying his mother's features, trying to memorize every detail of her countenance.

"I want to be proud . . . of the boy I love."

Then Aunt Mabel understood. She gave a quick brush at her eyes and drew herself up. "Well, if this is going to be a party, I guess that I had better make some tea. How does that sound?"

"That would be very . . . nice." Arlette knew how reticent Aunt Mabel was to show her emotions to other people, even those she loved.

"Alder, . . . I'm lying here looking . . . ahead into your future, . . . I have so many . . . hopes and dreams for you. . . . The Holdens are good people; . . . they'll take good care . . . of all of you. . . . I want you to help . . . them out with . . . Nadine and Nathaniel."

"I will, Ma."

" . . . Remember that . . . what they say . . . goes. They are here . . . in my place."

"I understand that, Ma." He was heedless now of the streams of tears that ran down either side of his face. He knew why he wouldn't be in school tomorrow. Time had slowed down for him, and he was completely focused on his mother. Each moment was precious.

"You're lucky to have so . . . many wonderful . . . people . . . who care about you: . . . The Holdens, Aunt Mabel, and Dad Ames . . . here. . . . And Mark and me on the . . . other side. . . . And we all want the best . . . for you. . . . Mark will always be your first Dad, . . . but one day you may come to . . . know your natural father."

"My father?" This was a question which Alder had always been discouraged from asking.

"I say you 'may' come to know him. . . . He's a good man, and you favor him . . . a lot."

Aunt Mabel bustled in with the tea. She proceeded to make a production of it to cover her feelings. "Alder, I've got yours all ready for you here: plenty of milk and more sugar than you should have, but I know that's the way you like it." She handed him the cup which he took absently. "And Arlette, I'll set yours right here: just a little milk and a little sugar. And mine is here, so now we're all set. Here, Arlette, let me help you with that. My isn't this cozy." She tried to manage her bravest smile.

"I love you . . . Aunt Mabel! . . . You've been wonderful . . . to me!"

The walls of Aunt Mabel's emotional dam burst asunder, and for a full minute she busied herself by putting her large handkerchief to good use wiping her eyes and blowing her nose. "I love you too, Arlette! You've been my daughter. And I've been only too glad to help in any way I could. And don't you fret, I'll keep on helping just as long as God gives me the strength to do it."

"You've got the right . . . idea, you know. . . . It should be a party. . . . It doesn't feel like a sad . . . time to me, except . . . that I feel your . . . sadness. Oh there are . . . so many wonderful times ahead . . . for you all." Arlette's awareness shifted, and she seemed to be wandering in a separate space, but her voice continued. "It's November now . . . and just ahead there's . . . Thanksgiving, and Christmas, and New Year's. . . . I want you to think of me . . . on those days, . . . and be happy. I won't . . . ever be far away. . . . Not really." She felt her breathing change, but she continued to speak.

"Alder, I want you to . . . promise me to enjoy . . . this winter. You've stayed . . . at home cooped up . . . too long. Get outside . . . do winter things. . . . Go sliding. Learn to ski . . . and skate. Aunt Mabel . . . the children will need . . . skates and . . . . Oh-h-h." Another sharp, shuddering, intaken breath, and she was in a silent space, a place where she no longer felt pain or loss. Her senses seemed to float effortlessly on a stream of peace and love. The room was filled with light, and there in the center of the light she saw him walking toward her, smiling, reaching out his hand.

She sat straight up in bed and stretched out her right arm. "Mark?" She smiled. "It's you!"

"Ma!" Alder grabbed her. She sighed and relaxed into his arms.

"Arlette!" All of Aunt Mabel's grief was gathered in the utterance of the name.

• *Grandmother Holden* •

Once Ward and I had agreed to take the children and she'd settled her affairs, Arlette's worries did seem to be put to rest, because after that business was over, she seemed to sort of fade away. She faded in and out. Sometimes she seemed to be in pain, but mostly she seemed to be at peace.

Arlette died on November 9th, 1943, one year to the day that Mark had died. For some reason that coincidence reminded me of what she had said on the night the twins were born about bad things happening in threes. First there was Janine's death, then Mark's, and now her own.

Chapter Fourteen

1943-1944

• *Michael Holden* •

After Arlette's funeral Alder, Nadine, and Nathaniel came to live with my grandparents. The funeral was on Friday, and over the weekend Dad Ames and Aunt Mabel helped my grandparents move much of the furniture from Arlette's house to Aunt Mabel's attic, and whatever was needed was transferred to my grandparents' home.

My grandmother thought that Alder should stay out of school for a few days to recover a little from his mother's death and to adapt to his new surroundings. But on the Monday morning after the funeral, Alder went off to school as though it were an ordinary day, and not the first Monday after the death of his mother. He said that he had to go to school.

"My Ma never let me miss school when she was sick," he said. "She would want me to go to school now."

When I went over to my grandparents' that Monday, I expected Alder to be there, but he was gone. In the last few months Alder and I had spent a lot of time together, and we had become very close. In the days after his mother died, though, he seemed different even with me. He wasn't mean or anything, but he was so sad and serious, and he wanted to be alone. I had hoped that Alder would feel better this morning, and since he wasn't going to school, I thought he and I could do something together. When I discovered he wasn't there, I felt kind of lost. I never used to feel that way at my grandparents', but I did today. The house where I had never expected to find Alder before, now seemed somehow empty without him. My grandfather was sitting in his rocking chair "catching up" on his newspapers. I crawled into his lap and sat there for a while with my head on his chest while he read. Finally, grandfather cleared his throat.

"How is that young man doing today?"

"I thought Alder was going to stay home today," I complained. "I wanted to do something with him." With my grandfather I never had to beat around the bush or pretend I felt one way when I felt another. He always seemed to know what was going on inside me anyway, so I said what was on my mind.

"Is that boy worried about Alder?" Grandfather put his paper down and put his arms around me.

"He's not the same since his Ma died," I said.

"Does that boy remember how he felt when his dog Pepper had to be put away?" Grandfather held me and rocked me while he let his question sink in. I remembered how I felt when Pepper died; it was a feeling I didn't think I'd ever forget.

"Yes, I was sad, and I was sick." I remembered wandering alone inside myself and then hearing Alder talking to me as he sat by my bedside.

"These things take time," grandfather said. "When Pepper died, the hurt inside was very strong at first, but with time it eased. Alder has lost his Ma, and it will take time for him to deal with his loss. Everybody needs to be patient and keep caring about him until he's ready to go on with his life. Maybe he needed to go to school today to get his mind off his pain," grandfather said. "He will always miss his Ma, but with time it won't hurt so much. In time it will be easier for him."

I thought about Pepper and about how I still missed him, but grandfather was right. It was easier now than it had been in the beginning. I thought I would never get over it, but I had Punkin now, and Alder and I had become close friends. Pepper would always be my first dog, and I would never forget him. I thought about how I would feel if my mother died, and I could understand a little the way Alder felt.

"Things have an interesting way of working out," grandfather said with a hug. I didn't know then how interesting it would be.

We had the family Thanksgiving dinner at my grandparents' as usual, but this year the "family" was different. This year my father wasn't there, but Alder, Aunt Mabel, and Dad Ames were. The babies weren't big enough to sit at the table, but they were there too. When grandfather said grace, he said that it was important to remember those who were absent, who were missed by those who were present. I was thinking of my father and Pepper; I knew Alder must be thinking about his mother and Mark and his sister Janine.

After dinner grandfather said, "This old man thinks those two boys grew a little during that big dinner, and he wants to measure just how tall they are. Stand up straight there against that doorjamb so this pencil can mark how high they're up to." Grandfather put marks at the top of our heads, and then he had us reach as high as we could, and he put a mark on the doorjamb at the end of our fingertips.

Alder and I found out the particular significance of the second set of marks at Christmas, when we each got a pair of skis from my grandparents. Grandfather said, "The skier should be able to fold his fingers over the end of the ski for it to be the right size." My mother got us each a sled, and Aunt Mabel and Dad Ames got us ice skates. So Alder and I were completely outfitted for the winter.

By Christmas time Alder seemed more like his old self again, and that winter we had a lot of good times together skiing, sliding, and skating. We skied behind my house. From the hill road the land sloped fairly sharply down to a terraced strip of apple trees and then continued its slope down to the level of the garden. It wasn't a long slope, but it was perfect for us to learn on. Grandfather showed us how to ascend the hill on our skis by sidestepping. And after we had mastered that, Ira showed us how to climb even faster by making a herringbone pattern.

"Now what you've got to do is, you've got to walk like a duck," Ira explained. "You just keep your toes pointed out, and put one foot in front of the other. Use your poles for balance." Alder was better at it than I was; I kept stepping on my own skis. But we both learned to walk like ducks, and we quacked at each other all the way up the hill.

Once the hill was packed down, it got to be a pretty fast run: swooping down the first slope, leveling off between the apple trees, then swooping down the second slope, and passing by the side of the garden, going further and further each time into the field. Alder fell fewer times than I did; I was in the process of collecting a relief map of the entire terrain on the surface of my backside. When I fell, one ski would invariably come off and go sailing on down the hill. Alder usually retrieved the errant ski and encouraged me to keep trying.

"Now, when you want to slow yourself down," Ira said, "point your toes together a little, as though you were pigeon-toed. Keep your knees bent, and don't let one foot get ahead of the other. That's it! You're getting the idea!" So Alder and I quacked like ducks on the way up the hill and cooed like pigeons on the way down. Alder said he guessed it helped you ski if you were a little bit bird-brained.

Once the slope was packed, we used it for sliding as well, but a better sliding place was the road past Alder's old house. His old house was the only one on the road that went down that slope of the hill, and since the house wasn't rented yet, the town closed the road on weekends so kids would have a safe place to slide. That was a long, exciting slide! We started just behind the Cote Drug Store and ended where the land leveled off between the twin bridges near the lower road.

Sometimes we went down the slope in a sitting position, managing the steering mechanism with our feet. Other times we went down on our bellies, pretending we were otters. I knew about otters; Alder had started reading *Little Joe Otter* by Thornton Burgess to me. He said that his mother had read it to him, and that it was still one of his favorite books. After *Little Joe Otter*, Alder said we would read *Buster Bear's Twins*. Alder said when we slid down the hill on our bellies, we were like otters; but when we sat, we were like bears. So at the top of the hill he would say, "Okay, what are we this time: bears or otters?" Sometimes we were twin bears and rode down together on the same sled. Combining our weight made for an even faster ride.

Grandfather flooded a small space near his chicken yard for us to skate on so that we could practice and "get the hang of it," before we went to the town skating rink. The town rink was a perfect place to go after dark, because it was well-lighted and had a shack with a blazing wood stove, where we could put on our skates or go to warm up. During the day, though, our favorite place to skate was on the oxbow of the river, a kind of large bay on the side of the river, a short way before the river emptied into the lake.

Grandfather said the oxbow was part of the old course of the river, but that the river had been made to change its course when the causeway was built for the town road and the railroad. On the lake end of the oxbow there were cattails; on the other end there were stones to sit on for changing into our skates. The road went along one side and the river along the other side. We stayed away from the river side, because the ice was unpredictable there.

We learned first just to walk on the ice in our skates. This we did at home, and we looked rather like chickens walking on the ice, but then grandfather told us to try pushing off with one foot and gliding, then pushing off with the other foot and gliding. In that way we came to look more like swans gliding on the river. Alder said that he'd never been so many birds and animals in his life.

Even though he was in school, Alder and I spent some time together almost every day. Often on Saturdays we went to the movies. Since we were both under twelve, it cost us only eleven cents each. The movie theater was a mile away downtown, and my mother wouldn't have let me go by myself, but she didn't mind if I went with Alder.

On Saturdays there were always two cartoons, not just one. Then the man on the screen swung around with his camera and began the newsreel, which always had news about troops and battles and reminded me of my father on the other side of the world fighting in the war. Then we plunged into the war itself or the Wild West or some swashbuckling adventure or musical extravaganza. We loved them all; we didn't have favorites, and it was always a surprise.

From the movies we usually walked home the long way so that we could stop at Dad Ames's drug store for a soda. We did have a favorite soda. It was called a "haymaker," and Dad Ames made it by mixing soda water with a little squirt of every flavor from the fountain. After we drank our soda, we might sit in a booth and look at comic books, which we called funny books. We had to look at them after we finished our soda, because Dad Ames said that he couldn't sell comic books that had been soaked by a haymaker. Sometimes we even bought a comic book, and sometimes we just sat and talked with Dad Ames, if he wasn't busy.

Dad Ames knew lots of interesting things, especially about nature. Once he told us that what we called frog spit on the tall grasses in the field is not made by frogs at all. It's really made by a small bug. He said that if we took the spit off the grass and spread it out carefully on our fingers we would find the little spittle bug inside. Alder and I looked forward to summer so we could see it for ourselves.

One early spring day in 1944, we were walking the long way home from the movies on our way to the Cote Drug Store to spend some time with Dad Ames. Alder stopped and pointed at the sky, "Look at that!" I looked at a blue sky where a platoon of puffy, flat-bottomed clouds floated toward the horizon.

"It's really nice," I said.

"Look at the moon, Mike!" I looked at it; it was sort of a half moon, or more than a half moon. "Did you ever see that before, Mike?"

"Sure, it's the moon, Alder!" I said it in a way that suggested maybe Alder had just gone "round the bend."

Alder rolled his eyes, "I know it's the moon, for heaven sake; but did you ever see the moon in the sky at the same time as the sun?"

I thought about that, and I wasn't aware that I had, but I didn't want to admit that to Alder, because sometimes he liked to pull my leg about things. Alder was never mean to me, but just because I was younger than he was, I didn't like to have him think that I was a dope. "Have you?" I asked.

"No. I don't remember ever seeing the moon in the sky during the day," Alder said in his investigating-scientist voice. "I think we'd better ask Dad Ames what that means." I could tell now that Alder wasn't kidding; he was excited about this, maybe worried about this. But when we got to Dad Ames's drug store, Alder didn't blurt out his question right away. I had learned to let Alder do things in his own way; it was always more interesting. After we finished our haymaker and when we were the only ones in the the store, Alder brought it up casually, "Dad Ames, did you see the moon in the sky this afternoon?"

"No, I didn't," Dad Ames answered. "Just where is it? Let's have a look at it." So all three of us stepped outside to look at the moon. "I always think it's interesting when the moon and sun are in the sky at the same time. Don't you?" Dad Ames said.

"Yes, it is interesting," Alder said. I started to say something, but Alder nudged me, and I decided to keep to myself the fact that we were both worried about this phenomenon.

"Now, is this moon getting smaller or getting larger, would you say?" Dad Ames asked.

"I don't know," Alder admitted. Then after a few seconds he added, "But if we wait a couple of days and check it, we could tell."

Dad Ames was still looking up at the moon, and he put his hand on his chin, "Yup, you could do that, I suppose, if you wanted to wait. But do you know how to tell without waiting by just looking at the moon?" Alder and I both knew by his tone of voice that Dad Ames was beginning a nature lesson. This was one of the best parts of visiting Dad Ames, because he knew interesting stuff, like grandfather.

"No, how can you tell?" I asked.

"Well, you see, whenever you have a partial moon like this – a quarter moon or a half moon, one side of the moon is always smooth and round, while the other side is sort of blurry and ragged. Do you see that?"

"Yes," Alder said; "I see that. Do you see it, Mike?"

"Yes," I answered; "What does that mean?"

"Now, sometimes the smooth side is on the right, so that you can kind of cup it with your right hand. Sometimes it's on the left, so you can cup it with your left hand. What hand would you use to cup the smooth side of this moon, would you say?" Dad Ames asked.

"The right hand," Alder said, putting his hand up to cup the moon. I followed his lead.

"Okay, so here's the dope," Dad Ames began. He used the word "dope" to mean "important information." Alder and I used the same word to mean "a stupid person." We had learned by now what Dad Ames meant by the word "dope."

"When you can cup the smooth side of the moon in your right hand, it's in the process of getting bigger; we call it a waxing moon. When you can cup it in your left hand, it's getting smaller; that's a waning moon. There's a little rime that will help you remember it: "In your right, growing bright; in your left, losing light." There are "r's" in the first part, so it helps you remember that that's for right hand, and there are "l's" in the second part to make you think of left. Now, have you got all that?" Dad Ames made us repeat the rime and cup our hands a few times, so that we'd remember. Then he asked us to come over to Aunt Mabel's and his house sometime, so that he could show us with a flashlight and an orange just how the phases of the moon work.

We did go one evening to stay overnight with Dad Ames and Aunt Mabel when the moon was just past full, so that Dad Ames could finish his nature lesson, but really it was only the beginning of many lessons that were to follow. Dad Ames said that we couldn't see many stars that night with the moon so bright, but he pointed out the big dipper. And he told us how to draw an imaginary line up through the two stars farthest from the handle of the big dipper.

"The next star up is the north star," Dad Ames explained.

"It's not a very big star, is it?" Alder said. "I thought the north star would be one of the biggest, brightest stars in the sky."

"It's not the brightest star, you're right," Dad Ames agreed, "but it's a very important star, and it's also the star at the end of the handle of the little dipper." That's the way lessons were with Dad Ames; one thing led to the next, which led on to the next. Everything seemed related to everything else in some way.

The names Ursa Major and Ursa Minor for the big and little dippers led to a story of how bears lost their tails, and the north star led to a discussion about the underground railroad, which had helped his mulatto great grandmother escape from slavery to the North. Dad Ames's talk flowed like the river carrying us to places of wonder and mystery. Aunt Mabel joined her voice to his like a stream entering into the river, and together they helped make us aware of the power and depth of the world around us.

At last Aunt Mabel said that we needed to get ready for bed. At first Alder and I demurred, but Aunt Mabel said that she would make us some cocoa while we put on our pajamas. Then she and Dad Ames would sit in our room and talk with us until we were ready to sleep. After the cocoa, Alder and I brushed our teeth. Then we lay and listened to their talk flow on about things they remembered in their lives, until we were each caught by an eddy and drifted into dreams of our own.

At the end of April, Alder began to build what he called our "platform." He used old pieces of lumber which grandfather let him have, and he constructed a platform about six feet by eight feet. I helped hold things and fetch things, but Alder did the carpentry work mostly by himself. Grandfather and Ira helped us to carry the finished platform into the field to a place which Alder had selected. Grandfather called the platform "Alder's Special Place," and it was just that.

That platform could be transformed in our imaginations to whatever we wanted it to be. It became a raft; Alder was Huck Finn, and I became Tom Sawyer as we poled it down the Mississippi. It was a bunker from which we shot enemy aircraft from the sky. It was my father's ship from which planes took off for enemy targets. The war was very much on everybody's minds, and the talk around us assumed a prominent place in our fantasies. But our fantasies were not limited by the war, for the platform could just as easily become a flying carpet on which we soared over Baghdad in search of magic lamps and secret caves. Sometimes the platform was a stage, where we performed for the benefit of the crickets and field mice.

As my grandmother's birthday approached, Alder came up with the idea that we should have a surprise party for her. He talked my grandfather into it and enlisted the help of Aunt Mabel, Dad Ames, Ira, and my mother. Alder and I saw ourselves as the backbone of the entertainment committee, and the platform was put to good use as we spent afternoons, when Alder came home from school, practicing songs and skits for my grandmother's party. Dad Ames volunteered to bring his accordion; grandfather said that he would play his guitar, but only if Aunt Mabel agreed to play her harmonica.

The adults became as enthusiatic as we were. My mother was bringing the sandwiches: egg salad, ham and pickle, and peanut butter and jelly. Aunt Mabel was making the cake; it would be grandmother's favorite, spice cake with coffee frosting. Grandfather and Ira said that they would take care of the punch. Ira said that we needed two kinds of punch, a soft punch and a one-two punch.

On the Friday afternoon of grandmother's birthday, my mother agreed to watch the twins while grandfather took grandmother shopping, so that she could pick out what she wanted for her birthday. When my grandmother bought for herself, she tended to buy practical items: cloth or yarn so that she could make clothes for someone else, dishes or kitchen utensils, a small piece of furniture for the house. But grandfather had bought her a cameo brooch, just in case she came back to the party with a hassock as her birthday present, he said. It was necessary for her to go shopping with grandfather, so that we could decorate the house in her absence and get everything ready.

Everyone took turns keeping an eye on Nadine and Nathaniel, who were both walking all around by now holding onto the furniture. Sometimes one or the other of them teetered ominously and sat down suddenly on the floor with a crash and a look of surprise, but quickly each was back up, traveling to wherever something interesting was going on. Nadine was a smiling, pointing babbler; Nathaniel was a serious, thinking observer. They were both very interested in all of the party preparations. When everything was ready, mother scooped up Nadine and carried her around to show her the decorations and the sandwiches and the cake, while Ira helped Nathaniel to a cup of the soft punch. Ira had already satisfied himself adequately that the hard punch contained ingredients of the finest quality.

When grandfather and grandmother returned, we were all quietly waiting for them to open the door from the hallway to the living room. We all heard them come in, but the door didn't open right away. A couple of minutes later grandfather stuck his head in and whispered, "That good woman has gone upstairs to visit her Aunt Minnie." Alder and I tried to stifle our giggles over grandfather's message, which meant that grandmother had gone to the bathroom. Mother said that grandfather should come into the living room and wait for grandmother to find him. "But she might decide to start supper without coming in here," grandfather whispered.

"If I know Ida, she'll check on the babies as soon as she comes downstairs," mother said aloud, while she bounced a giggling Nadine on her knee. I tried to shush mother, but she said, "She knows I'm here, so I don't need to be quiet. In fact, if she hears Ward and me talking, she's more likely to come into the living room right away." And that's just what grandmother did. When she opened the door, we all yelled out, "Surprise!" and "Happy Birthday!" Nadine laughed and threw both arms into the air; Nathaniel looked from one person to the other as if he were trying to figure out what was going on.

"Well, my word! This is a surprise!" grandmother said. Then she turned to grandfather, "Were you in on this too, you old secret keeper?" Everybody laughed. "My, would you look at the decorations! Someone's been busy! Doesn't everything look nice: sandwiches and punch and cake. You people shouldn't have gone to all this trouble!" Then grandmother smiled one of her genuine smiles and said, "But I'm awfully glad you did. Of course at my age, I should just stop having birthdays, but this makes me feel like a queen. Whose idea was this anyway?" she asked.

"It was Alder's idea!" I said.

"Well, Alder! You sweet boy, you come over here and let me give you a big hug. If you'd waited another week, you know, we could have celebrated the twins' birthdays. But really, this is one of the nicest surprises I've had this year."

Actually though, it was grandmother who surprised all of us. She hadn't bought a sensible something for the house on her birthday shopping trip. She had bought a very pretty blue dress covered with tiny white polka dots, and she had worn her birthday dress home. Grandmother almost always wore a housedress with a full apron. Her only dress-up dress was a plain black frock, which she always wore with a simple gold pin at the neck. In this new dress she looked younger and pretty. Grandfather gave her the cameo brooch, and she put it on. Aunt Mabel and Dad Ames had gotten her a fancy gold wrist watch with a gold wrist band. Grandmother rarely wore a watch, but when she did, it was a sensible watch with a black strap band. Grandmother put on her new watch and modeled it for us, sashaying around the room in her new dress with her right hand pointing to her brooch and her left hand stuck out to show off her new watch. Mother had bought her a dusty-blue hat that grandmother had admired in the milliner's shop window, and on mother's advice Ira had gotten grandmother some blue gloves to match the hat. Soon grandmother had all of her gifts on, and to me and Alder, she looked indeed like a queen who had just stopped in for afternoon tea.

After we had sung happy birthday and eaten cake, Alder and I announced that it was time for the entertainment portion of the program. While my grandparents had been shopping, Alder and I had spent a few minutes going over our songs with Aunt Mabel and Dad Ames to find the appropriate keys for our voices. Even though grandfather had not heard us sing the songs we had prepared, he could pick up any key on his guitar after just three or four notes.

I was singing my song first, and the song I had selected was my favorite, "Pistol Packin' Mama." To me it was simply a rollicking tune which I had heard on the radio so many times that I had memorized all of the words. I confess that the lyrics held little meaning for me at that time. I was as amused as the rest of the country at the thought of an irate wife waving a gun and chasing her faithless husband around a cabaret. Everyone clapped in appreciation of my efforts, and I bowed and beamed.

Alder and I had talked my mother into singing the second tune, and she sang "You Are Always In My Heart." It was a song she sang almost every day, while she accompanied herself on the piano. I knew that she sang it for my father, and Alder and I thought that it was appropriate as a way of bringing my father, at least in spirit, to his mother's birthday party. It was a pretty tune, but it seemed to put everyone in a pensive mood. Alder said that the song made him think of his mother, who was in his heart even though she was "far away." I came to realize that evening that probably everyone has someone whose memory they guard carefully and fondly in their thoughts.

The next song was a ballad performed by Alder. The story was of the kindness of a railroad conductor to a ticketless little girl who was on her way to seek a pardon for her imprisoned father. "The East Bound Train" had been one of his mother's favorites, and Alder and I had decided to perform it as a skit. In one of my grandmother's full aprons and a kerchief, Alder sang the song as the little girl. Wearing a blue jacket and a cap that my mother had helped me to construct, I took the conductor's part, pantomiming and mouthing the conductor's words while Alder sang. At the point in the song when Alder sang, "My brother and my sister would both be very glad, / If I could only bring back my poor dear old blind dad," grandmother reached her hand out to touch grandfather's shoulder, while she dabbed at her eyes with her handkerchief.

At the time I thought simply that she had been moved to tears by the touching story. I remembered her reaction, and in later years when I thought of the program that Alder and I had planned, I wondered what had moved us to make the selections that we had. Even our closing number "You Are My Sunshine," to which everyone knew the words and which we encouraged everyone to sing, dealt forebodingly with the concept of faithless love.

Chapter Fifteen

1944-1945

• *Michael Holden* •

In the spring of 1944, my grandfather's prize chinchilla rabbits had a litter of bunnies. The gentle gray doe and her eight growing offspring occupied an enormous pen in one room of the barn. The buck was housed apart in a separate room in his own small pen; he was a surly individual, who preferred solitude and valued his privacy. One day, when grandfather went out to feed the animals, he discovered that the great pen was open and held only the mother rabbit. She was complacently dozing, apparently enjoying this rare moment of tranquility and oblivious of her forsaken duties.

Perhaps like mothers in fairy tales, she had sent her children off into the wide world to seek their fortunes. Or perhaps she was simply resting, secure in the knowledge that her errant progeny would return at dinnertime. In any event, her children were away and were hopping all around the barn, exploring every corner and crevice of their newly expanded home.

Alder and I had been playing "raft" on the platform when we heard grandfather holler that he needed our help. A distress call from grandfather was an unprecedented event, and we both instantly sprang to our feet and sprinted to his assistance. Alder's long legs enabled him to reach the barn first.

When Alder opened the door, grandfather shouted, "Get inside and close that door quick!" Grandfather was diving unsuccessfully here and there; the barn floor was alive with panicky little rabbits darting everywhere, bent on eluding imminent capture. When I opened the door, grandfather and Alder both yelled out simultaneously, "Close the door!"

I stood there for a second trying to decide whether they meant that I should close the door with myself on the inside or on the outside, and in that single moment one of the baby rabbits vaulted past me out the door and streaked into the field. I knew that rabbits were quick, but never in my life had I seen a rabbit move that fast.

"One of the babies is loose!" I screamed guiltily.

"They're all loose!" grandfather shouted back from somewhere in the recesses of the barn.

I realized, as I chased after the fleeing rabbit, that grandfather had not understood that I meant loose *outside* the barn. I was running as fast as I could go, but the little escapee already had a substantial lead. Shrieking and leaping, the rabbit headed across the tussocky field toward the swamp. I knew that I had to catch that rabbit before it managed to reach the swamp, where I wouldn't be able to follow or find it. These blue ribbon chinchillas were more important to grandfather than his own eye teeth. I could only imagine his distress if I were to be responsible for losing one of them, because I didn't know if he wanted my help anymore, now that he had Alder.

I saw with dismay that the distance between this precious little coney and me was steadily widening, but just at that moment Alder's long legs went pounding past me. I had never seen Alder move so swiftly before; he was bounding like a deer in flight. Just yards away from the swamp, he caught the running rabbit by its flattened ears and lifted the stuggling creature into his arms. As soon as I was sure that Alder had succeeded in our mutual quest, I stopped running and sank to the ground panting and enjoying the wave of relief and gratitude that washed over me.

Alder walked back toward me cradling and petting the little fugitive, who had ceased his struggle and now blissfully nuzzled the crook of Alder's arm. "Are you okay, Mike?" Alder asked with genuine concern.

"Thank you for catching that rabbit," I breathed. "Grandfather would have killed me if it got away."

Alder laughed, "Your grandfather? Your grandfather wouldn't even blame you, Mike; he's nuts about you. Don't you know that? You're more important to him than any old rabbit. Isn't that so, Mr. Bunny?" He addressed this last question to the now placid troublemaker, "You were just scared, weren't you? You didn't mean to cause all this disturbance, did you?" Alder smoothed the little rabbit's fur during this gentle interrogation. My racing heart had returned to its normal pace, but still I eyed with suspicion the seemingly innocent ball of gray fluff cuddling Alder's arm; I was neither so philosophical nor so forgiving as Alder.

When we got back to the barn, we slipped carefully through the door and learned that grandfather had successfully recaptured three babies. Alder deposited the fourth in the pen, and I immediately caught another, who came right up to me as if to apologize for the anxiety her brother had just caused me. Each of us retrieved one more, and with all the babies safely back in the pen with their mother, the great rabbit roundup was over.

"How did they escape?" Alder asked grandfather.

"The door was open, but how the door got opened is a mystery," grandfather said. "This old man thinks the babies wanted to go visit their father in prison," he chuckled. "Maybe they hoped to release him and bring him back home to live with them." Grandfather consulted his pocket watch, "Look at the time!" he said. "It's just amazing how a little excitement can help pass the afternoon!" Then he held the watch out to me. "This is for the young grandson. It's his to keep."

Alder and I stayed to help grandfather with the chores. With animals there's always something to be done: shoveling manure, getting hay down from the loft, lugging feed, carrying water. Alder milked Buttercup while grandfather and I finished feeding the other animals.

That summer before I began school, Alder and I took over more and more of the chores with my grandparents' animals. Neither of us minded; we both liked the animals, and the work wasn't too hard for us. It even got so that I almost didn't mind the pungent odors of the barn. Alder seemed not to mind them from the start; he dealt with the smell of manure with the same equanimity and humor that he dealt with everything that touched his life.

"When it gets too strong, just breathe through your mouth, Mike," he said. And that worked for the most part, with the exception of pig manure. The smell of pig manure seemed to have direct access to my tear ducts and gag reflex, but Alder always comforted me in my distress over this fact. "Don't worry about it, Mike. It's not written anywhere that you have to be in love with pig crap."

Even with the chores to do, we found plenty of time to play and fish. And we went berrying, which didn't seem like work to us, because we joked around so much and ate as many berries as we brought home. We helped out in my grandparents' and my mother's victory gardens. Alder took special care of the sunflowers. We played with Nadine and Nathaniel and helped look after them. Of course, Punkin was a companion on many of our escapades, and she was very patient with the twins, who liked to pull her tail and bite her nose. There was always plenty of time to do everything we wanted to do; that summer seemed to go on forever.

We went to the swimming hole around the bend almost every day that it didn't rain. I had trouble keeping my head above the water without my water wings, but Alder showed me how to hold my breath and swim like a frog under water. As long as I didn't go to places where the water was over my head, I was free of the water wings, and I could swim for as long as I could hold my breath, which over the course of the summer became an increasingly longer distance. Fortunately Alder kept an eye on me, because I nearly swam headlong into one of the wooden piers that separated the shallow water from the deeper waters of the river.

"Wow, you've got to watch where you're going, little buddy!" Alder cautioned.

"I can't always guess just how far the pier is, so sometimes I don't know if I'm getting too near," I complained.

"Then open your eyes and look," Alder said matter-of-factly.

To him it was an obvious suggestion; to me the idea that one could see if one opened his eyes under water was a revelation. After that I always swam with my eyes open, and I discovered a whole new world where fish darted by just out of reach and crayfish scuttled under rocks. One day I swam face to face with some kind of large rodent. I went from horizontal to perpendicular in an instant. I shot straight up out of the water spluttering and gasping, "A rat! A rat! I just saw a rat!"

"What kind of a rat?" Alder asked casually from the pier.

"How do I know what kind of a rat? A *rat* rat!" I scrambled up onto the pier. "We almost bumped into each other. It could have bitten my nose off!" I shouted, letting my anxiety build in the face of Alder's nonchalance.

"But it didn't, did it? It was probably much more afraid of you than you were of it, Mike. You're much bigger than any little old rat, you know," Alder said. "I wonder if it was just a river rat or maybe a muskrat. Or do you think that it could have been an otter? Maybe it was

Little Joe Otter's son, the one with the missing toe. Did you notice if he had a missing toe?"

"I didn't look at his toes; all I saw was his ugly rat face," I said flatly. "It didn't look so cute as an otter, though." We spent the rest of our time at the swimming hole that day diving and looking for the rat to see if we could determine what kind of rat it was. To my relief, we were unable to find it again. As long as we visited that swimming hole, I was always wary that I might again see a rat in the water, but I never did. Alder always continued to hope that we might; I refrained from telling him that I did not share his enthusiasm. I had found the singular underwater encounter sufficient.

In September I started school. I was in the first grade, and Alder was in the sixth grade at the same school. The teacher said that I was "way ahead" because I could already read and write. Grandfather, mother, and Alder had helped me learn. Actually I didn't write; I wrote my name in cursive, but I printed everything else. Alder said that he was proud of me because of my reading and writing.

Really, though, I was both envious and proud of him, because he was a member of the school patrol, the student crossing guards who had the power to stop traffic so that students could safely cross the street. Not only was Alder a patrol, he was the captain of all of the sixth graders on the force of school patrols. Patrols also got to be legally late for school every day, because they were on duty until after the principal tolled the final bell. Then the patrols left their various posts and slowly shuffled through the fallen leaves or strolled in a leisurely manner to school. They were the elite and were expected to be late.

The patrol *uniform* was an adjustable, immaculately white, diagonal chest and back strap that was sewn to a white belt. Alder wore a grand red and silver badge on the chest of his patrol belt. If Alder were chosen the seventh grade captain, he would wear a blue and gold badge; being the seventh grade captain of the school patrol was like being the president of the student body. The school patrols were in effect the deputies of the Duncansboro police, and they were highly respected by both students and adults alike.

There were some early meetings between my teacher, my mother, and the principal to talk about moving me into the second grade, because I could already read and write. But eventually, it was decided to leave me where I was for social reasons. I was happy enough in the first grade, and my teacher did a great job of supplementing the materials available to first graders.

That fall Alder joined the Boy Scouts. He had a scout cap and a splendid red neckerchief that he donned every Thursday evening for his troop meetings. On Saturday mornings he rehearsed with me the knots he was learning for his tenderfoot rank. I got to know their names and how to tie some of them: the square knot, the sheet bend, the bowline, the sheepshank. One Saturday morning when I went over to my grandparents' to learn knots, grandmother said that they were waiting for the doctor.

"Alder's got the chicken pox, or I miss my guess. I don't really need Dr. Bonsecours to tell me that. He'll go in and look at Alder for two minutes, and then he'll come out and say, 'Well, he's got the chicken pox.' Then he'll slap a quarantine sign on the front door and leave. Of course he'll scold me and say that you shouldn't even be here, Michael, because now you'll catch it too. Well, as far as I'm concerned, that's exactly why you should be here. My idea is you might as well catch it and get it over with and out of the way. Go up and talk to Alder, and tell him not to scratch. I'm waiting for the doctor to look at him before I bathe him in baking soda and water."

Alder did indeed have chicken pox, and when grandmother wasn't watching, he scratched. When the doctor returned to remove the quarantine sign two weeks later, he tacked it right back up again. The twins now had chicken pox, and so did I. When the doctor left, both houses were sporting quarantine signs on their entrances. I was running a fever, and I didn't feel very well, so mother put me to bed. Punkin curled up in a ball between my right arm and my chest and kept me company.

As it turned out, grandfather was sick too, about as sick as he'd ever been, grandfather told me later. Grandfather didn't have chicken pox, though. Mother said that he had shingles. I wanted to see him, but mother said that I had to stay in bed. I thought of the word "shingles," and I pictured my grandfather as looking like a walking rooftop. Actually, it was difficult for me to think of grandfather as being very sick. Grandfather was really too sick to work or to do the chores, and I wasn't able to help. But Alder and Ira managed to keep things going. Still grandfather and the twins were a care for grandmother, but Aunt Mabel and mother helped out.

Mother went over and got Nadine every day and took care of her at our house all day in order to give grandmother a break. Mother loved Nadine and would spend hours taking care of her: rocking her, singing to her, trying to amuse her or to coax her to eat something. With the chicken pox, Nadine was a much more subdued child than she ordinarily was. Mother brought my old crib out of storage and put it near the sewing machine, where she sewed little dresses for her while Nadine slept. Mother said that she had never been able to cuddle me and fuss over me whenever I was sick, because I always just wanted to be left alone. That was fairly accurate. When I was sick, I was like my grandfather's buck chinchilla rabbit; I wanted to sleep, and I didn't want to be disturbed. Nadine, on the other hand, seemed to enjoy the attention.

Winter was late that year, and we had a green Christmas. My grandparents speculated that Santa Claus would have to use his airplane instead of his reindeer. Alder and I fretted about the lack of snow, since we were looking forward to skiing, sliding, and skating again. Eventually the snow did come, and we were able to participate in all of these activities, even though it was for a shorter season.

At the end of January, I got to go on a sleigh ride with Alder and his Boy Scout troop. The scouts were encouraged to bring their little brothers, and Alder brought me. The clopping hoofbeats of the team of great, black horses and the jingling, harness bells rang through the frosty air, and the sled sped swiftly over snow-covered roads. There was laughter, singing, and hot chocolate, and the experience more than made up for the disappointment of a green Christmas.

As winter was coming to a close, grandfather and I got to accompany Alder on another Boy Scout outing, a sugaring off party. We got to see the boiling vats of sap turning into syrup in the sugar house. It was fascinating the way the syrup maker was able to control the height of the frothing liquid with a single strip of salt pork rind. We all ate sugar on snow, twirling the solidifying syrup on forks. We followed that cloying superabundance with donuts and sour pickles, and then we resumed our attack on the maple sugar until none of us could hold any more.

A few days after my birthday in April, I returned home from school to find mother sitting by the radio crying. I couldn't remember ever seeing my mother cry. The radio announcer was droning on, and my mother was weeping inconsolably. My first thought was that perhaps something had happened to my father.

"Mom, what's the matter? What's happened?" I put my hand on her convulsing shoulder, and she managed to get some control over herself.

"It's the president," she blubbered. "President Roosevelt has died." At that time I had a very simplistic understanding of adult concerns, and I did not appreciate fully the depth of feeling that leaders can generate in the hearts and minds of other adults. In my mind such a tearful response was appropriate to the death of a family member or a close friend.

"Was he related to us, Mom?" I asked. My mother explained how important the president was to her, to the nation, and to the war effort. But I couldn't shake my original impression that President Roosevelt must somehow have been related to our family.

The president's death woke my interest and made me more aware of the news about the war, which I had until then been rather successful at screening out. But radio announcers and other adults in my life and in my town sounded increasingly optimistic. Alder said the war might be over soon, and then my father would be coming home. When Germany surrendered on May 8, people were glad, but their celebration was reserved and tempered by the fact that we were still at war.

That spring and summer my grandparents and my mother put extra effort into their victory gardens, as though somehow that connection with the earth and the production of that garden would add emphasis to their prayers for my father and would hurry the end of battle in the Pacific. Alder and I helped in the gardens, and although we also found time to fish and swim, the entire summer was tense with hope and waiting.

When V-J Day came on August 15, pent-up emotions burst like a dam and swept away all of the townspeople's cautious reserve. Everyone who owned a car paraded it through the Main Street adding their horns to the din of celebration. Grandfather took Alder and me on a ride through downtown. "It's a day in history they shouldn't forget!" he said.

The streets were packed with people waving, hugging, slapping each other on the back. Everywhere flags were flying and smiles were flashing. The air was filled with confetti, balloons, and streamers. It was a general madness that no one sought to contain. It celebrated a victory long in coming and dearly bought with lives and sacrifice. Duncansboro had never seen such an all-out party, and it is yet to be equaled. It is one of the chief memories of my childhood.

The war was over, and soon my father would be coming home. We were still waiting, but now the waiting had a completely different aspect. We were still counting days, but the pall of war was lifted from our patient endurance of the passage of time. I became more and more excited that my father would be returning. He had left when I was only four, but I retained several memories, and my grandparents and my mother had told me stories about him. But, the more excited I became about his return, the more tense my mother and grandmother grew.

Chapter Sixteen
Home from the Sea

• Grandmother Holden •

The war ended in August of 1945, but Clay wasn't mustered out until the end of November. Ward and I hadn't seen him since January of 1943, when he was furloughed home for a few days after basic training. Except for a call to Angela in February saying that he'd be shipping out soon, our only contact with him after that point was through the letters we sent and received. He wrote frequent letters to Angela and to us, but sometimes it would be weeks before his letters came through. Then we might get three or four letters at once.

Sometimes they were full of holes from the censor's scissors, if someone thought he'd communicated something that might endanger the war effort. Once, the whole body of a letter was missing; there was the date and the salutation—Dear Mom and Dad, and the closing and signature—Love to all, Clay. We never did figure out what that letter was all about.

Mostly, his letters asked for news of home and said that he was fine, but that he missed us all. He would write about his daily routine, the food, the weather, or occasionally something interesting or funny that had happened to him or to a buddy aboard his ship. Often he wrote about home: things he remembered, people he wondered about, what he wanted to do when the war was over and he came back.

It was strictly forbidden for him to tell us in his letters anything about his missions or where he was. Those were the things that got cut out by the censors, but he often managed to let us know where he was anyway. In one of his letters he wrote, "I can't really tell you where I am or what is going on here, but what's important to me is that all of you are in a safe *place, and that is the key* to my happiness." He had underlined the words "place, and that is the key." Nothing about that seemed particularly unusual to me. Later in the letter he wrote, "When all this is over, I look forward to the day when I can sleep in my own bed at our place and wake up to the sound of robins singing and the smell of bacon frying." The idea that he missed home was what I got out of that sentence, but Ward got something very different out of it.

"It looks as though his ship was at Wake Island when he wrote that," Ward announced.

"Now, just how do you figure that?" I asked. I thought that was a strange thing for Ward to have said.

"Their son knew that this old man would figure it out, and figure it out he did. Just look at what their son says. In his letter Clay writes that 'place is the key,' and he underlines it. The next time the word 'place' appears, the nearest important word is 'wake.' So it seems to this old man that he is trying to tell us that the place he is in is 'Wake' Island," Ward concluded.

"Well, that seems like a pretty far-fetched idea to me, Ward," I said.

"Maybe so; maybe not." Ward dismissed the topic for the time being.

Ward likes being mysterious and thinking that he's good at solving puzzles, and of course he usually is. This time I thought he was wrong, but anyway I let him think what he wanted, even though I didn't believe a word of it. Another letter, though, convinced me that Ward did know what he was talking about. Clay wrote, "I was glad to read in your last letter that the place Gilly and Bertha bought is just down the street from you." When Ward said that Clay was in the Gilbert Islands, I knew that he must be right, because we didn't know any Gilly and Bertha.

Ward bought a map of the Pacific and put it up in Clay's old bedroom. He began sticking pins in it for the places that Clay mentioned. We never told anybody outside the family where Clay said he was or how we knew the places he had been. There were quite a few pins in that map by the the time the war was over. I don't remember now where they all were. I remember there was one letter that informed us that he was in Saipan. The line he wrote was, "I'll never forget the joke Dad told on that last Thanksgiving Day at your place and Uncle Sy's deadpan expression." I think my favorite was the Okinawa clue, because I figured that one out all by myself without any help from Ward. Clay wrote, "When I come home, I'm going to cut down part of the woods and build a place where the oaks now are." Ward was right; Clay knew his father would figure it out.

When the ship that brought Clay home docked in San Francisco, Clay and a couple of his buddies wanted to get messages to their families that they were back home in the states. They had no money at that point, because they hadn't been mustered out yet, so they went to the Red Cross to ask if that organization could get a message home for them. The Red Cross worker said that she would be happy to place the calls, but when she learned that Clay and his buddies had no money to pay for the calls, she said that she couldn't help them.

The men had only a few minutes before they had to rejoin their units, and they were about to give up. But then Clay talked with a Salvation Army worker who agreed to place the calls for these returning sailors, even though they had no money. He said that, if they wished, they could repay the cost when they received their mustering out pay. Clay and his buddies did return to pay for the calls. Later, when Clay called us himself, he told us the whole story and said that he'd never again pass a Salvation Army tambourine without making a donation. It's funny how some little thing like that will stick in your mind, but Clay said that it meant a lot to him and that he wasn't going to forget it.

Clay told us about that when he called on the day before Thanksgiving. After just being mustered out, he phoned us first and then Angela to let everybody know that he wouldn't be able to get home for Thanksgiving. He said that he didn't want to spend Thanksgiving Day on the train, and that he and his buddies had decided to stay on in San Francisco and celebrate the holiday together.

It seemed fitting, Clay thought, for them to share dinner and give thanks for getting home safely from the war. He said that they wanted to spend a couple of days together as sort of a farewell celebration. After this, he said, they might never see each other again, and they'd been through a lot since they first shipped out together and assumed their duties on board the *Essex*.

As it turned out, there was a little more to their celebration than a couple of days. It was about a week and a half before Angela heard anything from Clay again. She got an envelope in the mail. It had a cashier's check for three hundred dollars made out to Angela and a scrap of paper with a scrawled note, "Poker Winnings." That was it, nothing else, not even a signature. There was no letter that followed.

He hadn't called; he'd just sent the money and those two words: Poker Winnings. The idea! I'll tell you, I wanted to poke him! Angela didn't seem to be terribly upset about it, at least when she talked with me. She was taking it better than I would have. She said that maybe Clay just needed a "blow out." His father agreed that probably Clay just went on a "toot," and he'd be home in a few days.

At the end of two weeks, though, Angela was worried. She came over to the house one morning after Alder and Michael had both left for school, and I could see that she'd been crying. Her eyes were all red. Nadine and Nathaniel were sitting in their highchairs in the process of making a mess of their jelly-covered toasts. I didn't say anything until I'd poured Angela a cup of coffee and set it in front of her.

"Are you all right, Angela? You don't look good. Has something happened?" I said then, as if I were just noticing it for the first time.

"What are we going to do?" I could hear the pent-up anxiety in her voice. "Something must have happened to him. It's been two weeks, and he still hasn't come home! He hasn't written; he hasn't called!"

What I thought was, "That no good louse! What does he think he's doing? He's gone and decided not to come home at all. That's what he's done." What I said aloud to Angela was, "I guess we'll have to do what we've done throughout the whole war, Angela. We're just going to have to wait. Now, we do know that he got back to the states safely. He sent some money home. I can't say that I like it any more than you do, but I guess we'll have to have faith that everything will be all right." I was trying very hard to sound calm and to contain my anger at Clay, but I was aware that there was a sharpness in my voice that made my annoyance poke out like thorns around the edges of what I said.

In his most irritatingly reasonable manner, Ward said, "War can be a very difficult thing. He's been through a lot. Coming out of the service must be a big adjustment as well. Maybe he just needs some time alone, some time to himself to sort things out before he's ready to come home."

I had tried to say the right things in front of Angela to keep things on an even keel as much as possible, but all of a sudden my anger broke like a flood through a dam. "But why doesn't he call? Why doesn't he let us know what's going on with him then? Why would he put us through this, if he cared about us at all? Why isn't he thinking beyond the length of his nose? Sort things out! I'd like to sort him out!" I was almost yelling.

I heard a squawk come out of little Nadine. With her bottom lip thrust out, Nadine shook her hands at Nathaniel and raised her voice in a scolding babble. It was like looking in a mirror. Nathaniel frowned, puckered his little mouth, and took in a shuddering breath of air. I picked poor little Nathaniel up to comfort him. "Oh, don't pay any attention; Grandmother's just making noise," I said, patting him gently on the back. He put his head down on my shoulder and whimpered.

Now, I'd called myself grandmother and Ward grandfather from the time those babies first came to live with us. I never explained why I used those terms, and Angela never asked. Angela helped Nadine with her glass of milk, smiling in spite of herself at Nadine's little scolding performance, and probably at my little performance as well.

"That good woman asks some difficult questions," Ward said slowly. "Their son hasn't been accustomed to thinking about his family in that way for three years. He's been looking out for himself and for his buddies. It's different; it takes some adjustment."

I couldn't think of a good response to that, and I'd already said more than I wanted to say, and said it louder than I wanted to say it, especially in front of the children. I knew that I just wanted to wring Clay's neck for being so irresponsible. But then, as I began to calm down, my thoughts took a sharp turn right into my heart, and I began thinking like a mother. I wondered to myself, "My God, what if he's really hurt, lying in a ditch somewhere?"

I hated the idea of his drinking and playing poker, but I knew he did it. "What if he'd gotten in with the wrong crowd, and something had happened to him. What if he'd gotten beaten up or something, and he wasn't able to call? What if he was in the hospital? But we would hear about that, wouldn't we?" My mind was going down all sort of paths like that at once. Of course, those are the things that Angela was thinking too, but I have to confess that those ideas weren't the first ones that had crossed my mind. I'd been angry because I was really afraid that Clay might not come home. There was nobody to call; there was nothing we could do but wait. The longer we waited, the clearer it became to me that Clay was not going to return. He had made his decision, and we wouldn't see him again.

"Hey, sailor! Looking for a good time?" The voice was sensual and more alluring than Marlene Dietrich's.

Clay had been walking, not paying much attention to his surroundings. He looked up at the woman, who could have been beautiful with less makeup, he thought. Her voice intrigued him, and he wanted to hear her speak again. He flashed her a genial smile in the hope that she might say something, at least repeat her offer.

"Oo, honey, you've got a gorgeous smile! But Nina could make you smile all over." She ran her tongue around her lips and smiled back at him.

He renewed his smile and said to himself, "I'll bet she uses up a lot of lipstick that way," while he considered her offer. "Now there's a way to forget!" he thought, but he countered it with, "but it's also a way to remember."

"What do you say, handsome?"

"Thanks, but no thanks." He said it gently. Somehow he felt a kinship with her. He didn't judge her; he was too involved in judging himself. It was just noon, and he'd already had too much to drink. He wasn't really drunk (according to his definition of the word), but his mind had a comfortably numb, teetering feeling. He walked on.

"Hey, sailor! Looking for a good time?" The same voice. His thoughts tilted with a sense of deja vu. He looked back and saw that she wasn't speaking to him, but to another sailor. He looked away quickly; the man's eyes reminded him of something, someone he didn't want to think about. By the time he reached the corner, the couple had already vanished.

His buddy Paul was taking a bus home this afternoon, and Clay wanted to be there to see him off. The old gang was breaking up—was almost broken up; when Paul went, Clay would be the last one left. An amateur photographer, Paul was spending the morning sightseeing in San Francisco, "capturing the light" with his camera. Clay felt that he'd already trolleyed up and down enough hills watching Paul snap pictures, so he said, "I'll tell you what; I'll see you back here later before you leave. You go catch the light, and I'll go catch a rainbow." Paul knew what he meant. A shipmate once told them that every true Irishman knows the pot at the end of the rainbow is really filled with the gold of Irish whiskey. Lately Clay had caught a lot of rainbows.

Paul was waiting for him, almost ready to leave when Clay returned to the room. "So, when are you taking off, Clay?" Paul was stuffing the remainder of his belongings into his duffle bag.

"I don't know. It's already winter back home. I'm not that anxious to see the cold weather, I guess. I thought I might just stick around here for a while longer." Clay didn't really want to talk about "home" to Paul.

"Don't tell me you've fallen in love with Frisco?" Paul was looking forward to going home, and he had already tried a few times to find out why Clay wasn't. But Clay wouldn't talk about what was bothering him.

"I'm just not ready to go home yet; that's all." When they docked, none of the four of them had been ready to go home yet, except perhaps for Paul. It was difficult leaving one life behind and picking up the other one right where you'd left off. Clay had been the major promoter of the idea of hanging around for a bit, adjusting to their "land legs" before they went their separate ways. They'd partied and found poker games together. They'd swapped addresses and promised to keep in touch, but all of them knew that they'd write a few letters, and then just Christmas cards, until their daily lives displaced the sense of camaraderie they now felt.

It wasn't easy saying goodbye to friends you'd trusted your life to every day, and Clay had not wanted to be alone. This morning had been an experiment in being alone, and when Paul left, it would all be over, and Clay would have to deal (or not deal) with the rest of his life. It had been easier at sea, but in a different sense he was still "at sea."

"Why aren't you ready to go home?" Paul hadn't wanted to leave Clay, because he'd felt that Clay needed him. Now in these last moments Clay might tell him why.

"I don't know. I'm just not ready. Do you mind? What difference does it make to you?"

Paul looked at Clay's face—closed, depressed. "All right, tell me this, then. How long can you stay drunk, buddy?" Paul was concerned about Clay. When you live in close proximity on shipboard, you acquire a kind of sixth sense about your friends. And he knew that something was eating at this man. In the years they'd spent together, he'd never seen Clay put away as much booze as he had in the past few days.

"As long as it takes!" Clay's answer was sullen. He resented Paul's intrusion, and now as far as he was concerned, he'd already said goodbye to Paul, the best friend he'd had in the war.

"Haven't you got a family waiting for you back East—parents, a wife and son?"

"Yeah. That and a few other things."

"What things? What the hell's eating you, Clay?"

"Nothing!"

"All right, then. The war's over, buddy; it's time we got back to the life we were fighting for. If you don't want to talk about what's chewing at you, fine. I don't know what it is, but I can tell you one thing. There aren't any answers at the bottom of the bottle."

"Look! Stay the hell out of it, will you? I know you want to get home to your wife and little girl. So go!"

"Come on, Clay. Lighten up."

"Oh, bullshit! You only agreed to hang around here because of me. I know that. And now I'm telling you to take off! So what are you waiting for? You got a bus to catch. Just get on it, and go home, and leave me alone."

"Look, I've still got some time before the bus. I thought we'd get a bite to eat first. What do you say? I don't want to say goodbye like this, Clay. After all we've been through, buddy, this isn't the way I want to go."

"Well, that's the way you're going. So go!" Clay turned his back, took out his wallet, and started counting out his money on the bed. He'd dismissed Paul, and now Clay was wondering how long he could last on the money he had. The room was paid for, until the end of the week. He'd been lucky at poker, and he sent money to Angela, but he kept for himself more than he sent home. He could hear Paul picking up his things, and he hoped Paul would just leave. He heard the door open. Paul hesitated.

"Clay?"

Clay pretended to be busy counting. The door closed. Paul was gone. Clay heaved a sigh, stretched out on the bed, and closed his eyes. "Once a lousy bastard, always a lousy bastard," he said to himself." . . .

. . . "Counselor, will you call your next witness, please." The judge looked over his glasses at the lawyer standing before the bench. "And let me remind you, counselor, this court will not tolerate any more grandstanding. If you've got a case to make, then make it!"

The lawyer called Clay to the stand and waited while he was sworn in. After the identifying preliminaries, the lawyer, with his hands on his lapels, looked first at the full courtroom and then at the jury. Finally he turned to address Clay, "Now, Mr. Holden, will you tell the court if in fact you were responsible for this man's death?" It was an accusation more than a question, but the words didn't make sense to Clay. The *man* was sitting right there, before him in the court. The man's dark eyes searched Clay's face for an answer.

Remembering his instructions though, Clay said the words he had rehearsed, "On the advice of counsel, I refuse to answer this question on grounds that may tend to . . . " The courtroom erupted; people were yelling, throwing things. Everyone was standing. The jury reached out at Clay and intoned together, "You miserable son of a bitch!" Then people began falling over like dominoes—falling, falling, crashing to the floor. The noise was deafening. The judge banged his gavel for order. The judge's face was livid.

"Order! Order!" The rap of the gavel could barely be heard above the din of people calling Clay's name. Rap! Rap! Rap! "I will have order in this court, or I will instruct the bailiff to clear the court!" . . .

. . . Rap! Rap! Rap!

The knocking at the door woke Clay in mid-snore from what seemed like a long sleep. Clay sat up and listened to another series of raps. The voice on the other side of the door said, "Clay? Clay, open up!" Clay opened the door, and there stood Paul with his duffle bag at his feet.

"Stuff it, buddy!" Paul said. "I'm not going this way, and you can't make me." Everything in Paul's stance said, "I dare you!" His legs spread apart, his clenched fists on his hips, and the scowl on his face. Clay just looked at him for a minute and then smiled in spite of himself. Paul was a friend. "Look, you say you're not ready to go home. Fine! You need some time. Fine! So, why don't you come home with me. It's not sunny California; I'm sure it's raining up there. But still, it's not winter the way you know it, either. What do you say?"

"I'd . . . I'd just be in the way."

"We all live together on my parents' farm. There's plenty of room. If you want to be alone to think, there's lots of country you can ramble around in. My mother's got a big table that seats twelve, sixteen if people sit on the corners."

"I don't know."

"Well, I'll tell you what! I do know! I'm not leaving you here to brood and drown yourself in whiskey. And I was thinking—if I have to—you're not *that* big; I could probably take you. Knock you over the head. Drag you to the bus. People will just think you're drunk; that's all. And maybe, by the time we get all the way to Portland, you'll have sobered up."

Clay laughed, but he went. He was feeling almost sober by the time they'd gotten only as far as Petaluma. Paul took in a great whiff of air. "Man oh man! Get a load of that. If that don't smell like home!" Clay tested the air and identified clearly what he smelled over the exhaust of the bus. His nose wrinkled.

"Whew! That's chicken shit!"

"You got it! Man, and I always thought you didn't know shit! I take it all back."

"Is that what home smells like to you? Where the hell do you live?"

"In the great state of Washington, just north of the Columbia River, son. Biggest chicken ranch in the county!"

"Oh, shit!"

"Yeah, you said it; ain't it great!"

Clay spent time with Paul's family. It was a large, extended family devoted to their work and to each other. He was taken in, given chores to do, and made to feel at home. Paul had never seen his little daughter Aurora, because his wife was pregnant when he left for the navy. Aurora was shy and clung to her mother while Paul took snapshots of them both. His wife apologized for Aurora's bashfulness, but Paul said, "Honey, we've got all the time in the world to get to know each other. Just give us time. We just need to get acquainted. That's all."

Paul told Clay about his dreams of becoming a "real photographer" one day. "I've got to study up on it, but I've learned some things just out shooting on my own. The light's got to be right; that's important. You've got to be aware not only of what's in the foreground, but of what's in the background as well. For me, the main thing I'm trying to achieve in a composition is balance. Balance is a key concept. It's a lot like life: focus and balance."

Being with Paul in the setting of his caring family made Clay think of home, and there came a day when he was ready to return. Paul saw him to his train. On the platform he hugged Clay and said, "Take care of yourself, good buddy; and stay in focus. Focus and balance."

• *Grandmother Holden* •

It was almost Christmas before we heard from Clay again. It was late in the evening when Angela came over all out of breath to tell Ward and me that she'd gotten a call from Clay. He'd had a layover in Chicago, and nothing was moving because of a snow storm. But unless we heard different, he expected he'd be coming home on the 11 p.m. train the next day.

My reaction during this whole waiting time was like that of a mother who waits up late for her child—a child who has been out beyond the time he's expected home. At first she feels anger because he's late, and she thinks, 'He knows what time he's supposed to be in, and he's not going to talk his way out of the consequences this time!' Then as time passes, she begins to worry. She wrings her hands, she frets, she starts pacing the floor going from window to window. She hopes nothing has happened to her precious child. She prays. Everything can be forgiven if only her child is safe. Then, when he gets home and he's all right, her worry turns to anger all over again. And now, I was angry all over again. I was relieved that Clay was on his way home, but I was angry.

"This old man will meet his train tomorrow night," Ward said.

"It's only a mile from the station to here. As far as I'm concerned," I said, "he can walk it."

"A man returning home from a war, deserves to have his train met," Ward countered placidly.

"Well, you meet his train if you want to," I said. "I plan to be asleep." I knew Ward so well. If it hadn't been for him, I wouldn't have been able to let myself get so angry or be unreasonable in this way. I knew he'd meet the train. I even wanted him to meet the train, while I simmered in my anger. I wanted to be angry when I met with Clay. I don't know if that makes any sense, but it's the truth. Ward and I made a good team. He didn't have to get angry, because I did it for him. I knew him so well, and he knew me just as well. I knew that he wasn't worried about my anger; he knew that I'd come around, maybe even before Clay came home. I didn't offer to take care of Michael so that Angela could go to meet the train as well. My idea was that Ward should meet Clay alone.

Clay's train was on time. Ward opened his arms and drew Clay to him in a big hug, "Welcome home, Clay! It's good to have his son home again."

"It's good to be home, Dad," Clay said. "How is everybody?"

"Well, they've all been pretty worried, because there haven't been any letters or calls for a while."

"So, how angry *is* Mother?" Clay asked.

"His mother has had a lot to contend with. She – she's been about as concerned as this old man can remember," Ward said, defending Ida as he always did.

"That bad, huh? You know, Dad, facing that woman is half the reason that I put off coming home as long as I did."

"What was the other half?" Ward asked.

"Facing Angela," Clay admitted.

"His mother is planning dinner for them at noon tomorrow. She has a few things she wants to talk over."

"Yes, Dad, I'll bet she does! I'll just bet she does. Man, it sure is *wonderful* to be back in the bosom of my family! It kind of reminds me of what I was fighting for over there. I'm looking forward to that dinner in a big way. Did you say she was serving it with Bromoseltzer?"

"It's better to get it out in the open and settled now, so that everybody can move on with their lives," Ward said.

"I know, I know," Clay answered. "It's just not my idea of fun!"

Ward told me about their conversation sometime later, of course. I don't know if Clay thought that this was *my* idea of fun. I never asked him. Bright and early after Alder had left for school the next morning, I took the babies over to Aunt Mabel's for the day. On the way home I was thinking up all sorts of schemes to get Clay by himself and away from Angela, so that I could talk with him alone. But Angela didn't come with him to the dinner I had planned. She said that Clay needed some time alone with his mother and father. I remember now that I wondered a little about that at the time, but mostly I was relieved that I'd be able to have it out with Clay without having to worry about Angela's being there when I did. I had tried to plan out just what I was going to say to Clay, so I would say things the right way. But somehow whenever I talked with Clay, things never seemed to go exactly the way I planned them.

"I'm glad you came home," I said, trying to put genuine warmth in my voice as I hugged him.

"It's good to see you too, Mother."

The trickle of sarcasm in his voice was unmistakable. He sounded as though he wanted to pick a fight. I was controlling myself; I had finally decided that I didn't want to go in that direction, at least not yet and not unless I absolutely had to. Holding him away from me, I looked him over closely. "You've lost a lot of weight, Clay. Are you feeling all right?"

"I'm fine, Mother. War just doesn't agree with everybody, I guess."

I was determined to be as pleasant as I could be, "Well, I've got a beef stew with dumplings ready that will put meat on those bones of yours and make you feel fit as a fiddle in no time."

We ate, and while we ate, we didn't talk about the children. We didn't talk about the war either; Clay said that he couldn't talk about the war. We did talk about the map in his old bedroom upstairs. He and Ward both became lively and humorous as they discussed the clues that told us where Clay had been in the Pacific. It was almost pleasant, but everybody knew that I was biding my time until after the dinner was over, and *that* was what was in the back of everybody's mind.

Finally I knew that I couldn't put it off any longer, so I cleared my throat and just dived in. "Clay, we have to talk about Arlette's children." Clay studied his cup of coffee; he didn't look up. He didn't move a muscle. "They're your children, Clay. Alder is your son. Janine was your daughter. And one of the twins, Nadine, is your daughter as well."

Clay's head jerked up. "That doesn't make any sense, Mother!" he said. "They're either both mine or they're both Mark's. That's what makes them twins."

"That's what I used to think, too," I said as gently as I could. "But it turns out that it's possible in some cases for twins to have different fathers. Clay, you'd only have to look at them to see that Nadine is yours and Nathaniel is Mark's. He's got Mark's eyes. Even if Nathaniel isn't your child, you should raise him. Alder and Janine were yours, and Mark was raising them as his own. And he was ready to raise Arlette's unborn child as his own as well, even if it turned out to be yours. Your father and I know the whole story, Clay. Before she died, Arlette told me herself, so that I would never learn it from someone else. Ira was sitting behind you at the Bar and Grill on the day that Mark died, and he overheard what Mark said to you."

Clay's eyes had returned to his cup of coffee, and his head bent over it, as I talked, as though he were looking for something in its depths. He didn't say anything. He seemed almost to be holding his breath.

Nobody spoke. The room was so quiet that I felt the need to hold back the waves of silence that seemed about to engulf us. "They're beautiful children. And now they're your responsibility. Your father and I have done the best we could while we waited for you to come home. But you're the father. We haven't told Angela anything, Clay. We both felt that that was your place." I stopped talking and endured the silence that came flooding back into the room. Over the last couple of years, I'd gotten used to the house being full of noise. Clay didn't speak. Then, for a moment he seemed to be gasping for air. He didn't look at his father or at me. His eyes were focused either beyond us or inside himself; I couldn't tell which. When he finally began to talk, he spoke in a low voice that was almost a memory of his voice, as though he were speaking only to himself. "I can still see his eyes," he said. "Awake or asleep, I can still see his eyes: accusing, pleading, forgiving. I never saw eyes look like that before. He reached his hand out to me, and I tried to grab it, but the table was between us, and I couldn't get to him. He cried out my name, but his eyes never left my face as he fell. I closed his eyelids, but I couldn't shut out the memory of his eyes.

"I thought if I went away to the war, I would leave them behind me. But they followed me everywhere I went. They were the eyes of every dying man I saw. No matter how much I drank, I couldn't drown them. When I got back to the states, I thought maybe I could still run away, but those sad eyes stayed with me. I can't run away anymore; I know that."

When Clay looked up, he had tears in his eyes. Ward and I knew then that our son had come back to accept his responsibilities. He had always been willful and carefree. But now we saw him burdened as we had never seen him before in our lives. And he seemed almost to have lost a part of himself. All the fight was gone out of him now, and when I considered the change, I wasn't sure that I hadn't preferred him the way he was before.

Chapter Seventeen
Angela's Secret

• *Angela Holden* •

The night Clay came home, the two of us stayed up most of the night talking, catching up, getting reacquainted, making love. When morning came and it was time to get Michael off to school, we'd only slept for a couple of hours, but neither of us was really tired. I got breakfast started, and I woke Michael earlier than usual. "Michael, you need to get up and get yourself ready for school. Don't dawdle, because there's a surprise waiting for you downstairs."

"What kind of a surprise?"

"I can't tell you that, Michael. Then it wouldn't be a surprise, would it? So what you need to do right now is to get up, wash your face, brush your teeth . . . "

"Mom, I know the list. By heart, I know the list."

"Then let's get yourself moving on it, so that you'll have some time to enjoy your surprise for a little while before you have to leave for school."

Michael rubbed the sleepy seeds out of his eyes and snuggled into his pillow. "M-mm, give me a hint, so I can decide how much to hurry."

"Okay, this is a big surprise, something you've looked forward to, and you'll be glad you hurried. So hop to it!" I hadn't told Michael when Clay was coming home, because I didn't want to get Michael all excited until Clay actually got home.

Michael was not long getting ready, and when he saw his father sitting at the kitchen table, he just exploded with joy, "Dad! Dad! You're home! I guessed right! You're back!" He threw himself at his father. "You're the best surprise I ever had!" From that point until I finally pushed him out the door to go to school, Michael talked nonstop, hardly taking time to chew the pancakes I'd made.

It was a pleasure to see Michael and Clay so happy, and I was trying to do everything I could to support the mirth and excitement of their reunion. But part of me kept wandering away from this warm family scene in our kitchen into other rooms, rooms in my mind, rooms which brought out very different feelings in me. Some of the rooms I had partitioned off and tried not to visit very often, because they made me feel angry or sad.

There was one room where I felt trapped and desperate. It looked something like a railroad station where I was making plans to get on a train and travel until I ran out of rails, at which point I'd board a ship that would take me to some faraway place. Clay had done this. He had gone to some faraway place, and he had come back. I envied him that he had had the opportunity to run away. And I chafed at the thought that the same option was not available to me and that, even if it were, I probably couldn't really bring myself to exercise it.

There was another room I kept trying to avoid, but I knew today I would have to deal with it. It was my memory of a bedroom furnished with a beautiful old, dark oak bedroom set. The dresser, chiffonier, and commode had marble tops. I didn't like looking at the bed.

In a trunk in the closet of that bedroom was what I called my patchwork quilt. It was an imaginary quilt I had made from scraps of information about Clay and Arlette. And after I had completed that quilt, the only person I ever told about it was my mother, and her reaction had been, "You made your bed; now you have to lie in it."

I should have expected that, because when Clay and I got married, neither Clay's parents nor mine had been enthusiastic about our marriage because of religious differences. There was no big wedding, but a simple service with only his father and my father in attendance as witnesses to the contract. After the wedding, my parents put on a polite and joyless breakfast for family and friends. I was completely and blindly in love with Clay then, and neither of us could wait to escape the stifling atmosphere of that wedding breakfast to begin our honeymoon in Quebec City.

In my mind I left the quilt and that bedroom and stepped into another room, a room where I was still in love with Clay. This was a fantasy room kept vibrant by romance novels, sentimental songs, and my ability (at least on the surface) to pretend my marriage was perfect. I had spent last night in this room, keeping the doors shut tight against the other rooms that I didn't want to think about. I was surprised that being with Clay was easier than I had thought it was going to be. In spite of everything, I did still love him. I wanted to kill him, but I still loved him; I wasn't sure how he felt about me.

Last night I had been struck by him all over again, and those old feelings returned. Clay was still breathtakingly handsome: tall, blond, blue-eyed, muscular. He had had all the advantages of being beautiful his whole life; women had no choice but to watch him when he walked by. His looks, his deep, resonant voice, and his easy, self-assured manner made him the envy and the idol of every other man. I was in love with him from the first day I saw him. My mother told me to be careful what I wished for, because my wish just might come true. I had never been with another man, but I couldn't have imagined a more tender, considerate, or accomplished lover.

Last night in his arms I almost forgot those things that I knew, and for a few hours I was able to feel secure in this room where I loved Clay. In the months before he went into the service when I was in this room with him, I had fought to keep other thoughts out, but sometimes the door to that other bedroom would fly open. The quilt I had pieced together would be all spread out on the bed, not in the trunk; and I would feel myself go cold. Actually, I had been cold with Clay for several months before he enlisted in the navy and left Michael and me to fend for ourselves.

Next to that room in my mind was the room where I was Michael's mother. It wasn't for lack of trying that this room wasn't a warmer room than it was. This room was full of shelves that held projects which I had helped Michael to complete. There was a Valentine's day box for school, several Halloween costumes, inventions, dioramas, puppets, collages, models, drawings, paintings. Sometimes I had been an active participant in the projects; other times I was needed primarily to provide supplies and occasional encouragement.

I did love Michael, and I tried every way I knew to get close to him, but nothing I did really worked. Michael would never let me hold him, cuddle him, or fuss over him. Although he was very independent and could be a stubborn child, he usually accepted my authority over him, but warmth and closeness were reserved for his Grandfather Holden, for his father, and for Alder. Today I realized that I might as well say, at least in my own mind, for his *brother* Alder. The Holdens had never talked to me about this story which I had pieced together. So I was sure that they didn't know I knew—or that they didn't care. This was the patchwork quilt that I had made and which I was going to have to deal with today.

If Clay and I were going to stay married, we were going to have to talk about his relationship with Arlette and about their children. Clay's parents, perhaps with Clay's blessing, may have decided to raise those grandchildren and to keep me in the dark. But I wasn't really in the dark, and I wasn't going to close my eyes anymore and pretend that I didn't know what I did know. I had tried doing that before Clay enlisted, and it was ruining our marriage then.

For the last three years, I had put my life on hold while he was away. And I didn't bring any of this up last night, but I knew that we needed to talk about it today. Part of me was still in love with him, but I needed to know where I stood, where we stood. I needed for us to be dealing with the truth for once in our lives. I also wanted to know if those children would go through their lives living a lie or if they would ever get to know the truth. Alder and Michael were best friends, but they had no idea that they were really brothers.

Michael's brother Alder stopped by early every day to "pick up" Michael for school. Because of his patrol duty, Alder had to start out early, and Michael also left early in order to accompany him. Michael would have walked with Alder whenever Alder left, but it was an additional bonus to be in the company of the seventh grade patrol captain, easily recognizable by his bright blue and gold badge. When Alder knocked on the door this morning, I called, "Come in!" as cheerily as I could muster. Then I stood back and watched the intensity with which Clay studied Alder. I knew that neither of the boys noticed it, and Clay didn't see me watching him.

I could see that this was very difficult for Clay. I wanted to hate him, and I had hated him, but I knew that that wasn't the answer for me anymore. I always wound up hating myself more than I hated him. Now, I was really more hurt than angry. I just wanted to run away. And I knew I couldn't. But I knew that I had to find the right moment to deal with all of this.

After Alder and Michael left for school and while I was doing up the dishes, through the kitchen window I saw Mother Holden bundling the babies onto the long sled I'd given Alder. She was taking the twins to Aunt Mabel's for the day. Mother Holden had invited Clay and me to dinner, but I'd already decided that I wasn't going to go. I knew that she would probably want to talk to Clay about his and Arlette's children; my presence would make that awkward. I expected that she was going to chew at Clay for not coming home promptly after his Thanksgiving with his buddies.

What Ida didn't know, that I did know, was where Clay had been until he came home. Clay had called me from his friend Paul's. He told me that he wanted to spend some time with Paul, and that he'd keep in touch. And he did; he called me four times from Washington.

Strange to say, once I knew where he was, I was okay. In fact I was almost glad that he wasn't coming home right away. For a long time I'd wanted to face him, to settle things. But now that the time had come to deal with it, I didn't feel that I was ready. I felt that I needed a little more time to prepare—or to avoid. I'm not sure which. Maybe Clay felt the same way. In any event, I understood his not coming home right away.

The first time he called, I said that I'd let his mother know where he was and that he was okay, because she was fretting about his not coming home. And Clay said that he was not calling me to ask me to deliver messages to his mother. He said, "I think she likes to fret. I called you so *you* would know, Angela. She can expect me when she sees me. I don't feel that I have to account to her for my every move anymore." I didn't feel right about keeping this a secret. I told him that, but I didn't argue with him. I told him, "Well, she's your mother, not mine. I just don't want to be in the middle of it."

And that's just why I didn't want to be there today. I didn't want to be in the middle of it. Mother Holden had a well-deserved reputation for being a good cook, but I wasn't really that hungry today. Clay and his folks needed some time together anyway, and it would probably be healthier for all of us if I found something else to do with myself during that dinner.

What I decided to do was to go to Aunt Mabel's myself and spend some time with her and the twins. I have to confess that I had a particular fondness for Nadine. She was such a little sketch! Aunt Mabel called her a "live wire," and that was a pretty good description. That little girl was born happy, funny, and mischievous. She kept us all amused.

Unlike Michael, Nadine responded to all the attention that I gave her. She reminded me of myself when I was a little girl. She loved to be hugged and cuddled. Somehow taking care of her was like taking care of myself. I had been a happy child too, but now the little girl in me needed to feel loved, and I was able to fill that need in myself by lavishing attention on Nadine. Also, whenever I took care of Nadine, I felt like a mother, the way I should have felt with Michael.

Some people maintain that children are like blank slates when they're born, but I don't think that those people ever raised any children. I didn't have a whole lot of experience with children, but just observing Michael, Nadine, and Nathaniel taught me that each of them brought a good part of their own personalities with them into the world. And I was sure that all three of them were not the exceptions that proved the rule.

Michael had always had his own agenda from the very beginning. He was never really bored, even though sometimes he complained that he was, and until he and Alder teamed up, he seemed to prefer his own company to anybody else's. From the time he was a baby, Michael had projects, and he was always very good at getting other people involved in them.

Nathaniel was quiet and watchful from the beginning; even as an infant he was an observer. His dark, thoughtful eyes noticed everything. Even though he could be bullied by his sister, he wasn't usually shy or easily intimidated. He walked almost a month before Nadine did. But Nathaniel didn't get the attention that his sister got.

Nadine didn't have to work at getting attention; people just gave it to her, almost pressed it upon her. I could see her growing up to be one of those women who could simply walk into a room and everyone would be aware of her presence. Nathaniel would probably be able to spend the whole day in that same room, and no one would notice he was there. Michael would spend his time in that room getting everyone involved in whatever he was doing.

I'd gotten to know the twins pretty well over the last two and a half years, and I liked them both. But two-year-olds can be a handful, and I was sure that Aunt Mabel wouldn't mind a little help or the company. I told Clay where I was going and suggested that, when he and his family were through with dinner, he could give me a call at Aunt Mabel's and I could bring the twins back to Mother Holden and save her the trip.

When Clay called me, he sounded strange, subdued; when I got home, he looked strange, beaten. That self-assured, kind of cocky attitude that I liked so much in him was gone. But that attitude was more than self-assurance. It was a phenomenon I had rarely encountered in my life. Clay loved himself. And once, I had felt that he loved me with the same intensity as he loved himself. Now, that special quality seemed to be missing. I'd had a sense of this last night, but now it was obvious to me. I'm not sure that it was so clear to others, but to me it was like an open wound, a hole in the center of his being.

"How was your visit with your folks?" I asked.

"Angela, we need to have a talk," Clay said, "before Michael gets home." He lit a cigarette, and I noticed that his hands were trembling. He had the look of a caged animal, trapped and desperate.

"What do you want to talk about, Clay?" I was surprised at how gentle my voice sounded.

"Alder and Nadine are my children," he began. I sat down. I closed my eyes and swallowed. I opened my eyes again, gripped the arm of the sofa, and forced myself to listen to Clay's story. I had wanted the truth, and here it was without any preamble. My patchwork quilt was unfolding itself on the middle of the living room floor. Clay didn't know that I knew any of this story; I let him tell it and tried not to interrupt. Even though I had lived with this knowledge for three years, hearing him explain it was like being ripped apart. There were parts of the story that I knew, but other parts were different from the way I'd had them figured out.

I found out that Mother Holden had not learned that Clay had fathered Arlette's children until Arlette revealed this information on her deathbed. When she found out, Mother Holden hadn't said anything to me, because she felt that it was Clay's place to tell me, not hers. At that point she intended to see that Clay told me as soon as he came home. I had been angry with Mother Holden because I thought she had been aware of this state of affairs all along and that her silence condoned Clay's actions.

"Why did you marry me, Clay?" I asked him.

"I married you because I loved you and I wanted to share my life with you."

"You wanted to share your life with me, but you didn't want to share with me that Alder was your son and that Arlette was pregnant with your child?" It was a question; I tried not to make it sound like an accusation.

"Arlette made me promise not to tell that Alder was mine, and I didn't know that she was carrying my child. She didn't know it was mine either; she thought it was Mark's."

"Did you love Arlette?" I was trying hard to convey with my voice that my intention in asking Clay these questions was not to accuse him. I had done plenty of that over the last three years. Now I needed to get everything straight in my mind.

"I cared about Arlette, but what was between us wasn't love. We gave each other pleasure, but it wasn't love. We needed each other at the time; we were both lonely."

Lonely? Lonely seemed like a strange adjective for Clay to apply to himself. "How could you have been lonely, Clay?" I wondered aloud. "You were the most popular boy in school. You had the admiration and friendship of everyone. Every girl in school wanted you."

"That's just it. They wanted me, but they wanted something from me. I always felt as though they needed me to make them feel good about themselves, to make them feel complete in some way. They wanted to own me. Arlette never put any pressure on me. She was different; she wasn't trying to catch me. We enjoyed each other with no strings attached. I never felt that she was grabbing at me; with Arlette I was free."

"If you wanted to be free, Clay, why did you marry me and not Arlette?" I had often compared myself to Arlette over the past few years. Arlette and I could have passed for sisters. We both had brown, naturally curly hair, gray eyes. She was heavier than I was, but we had similar builds. Over the past few years I had wondered if Clay really wanted to marry Arlette, but that he had married me instead, because he thought I was more socially acceptable than Arlette. I didn't like thinking that Clay was that small minded.

"Marriage is not what Arlette and I were about." Clay seemed to be thinking this out as he said it. "To be honest, there was a quality that attracted me—that you had in common with Arlette. You didn't need me to make you whole; you were your own person. But you—you had everything going for you: brains, personality, beauty. Every guy's heart skipped a beat if you even looked in his direction. Angela, you could have had anybody you wanted, too. Somehow the two of us seemed to fit together. You always brought out the best in me. I felt as though we brought out the best in each other. With you, I never wanted to be anything but the best I could be, and I came to want to be with you all the time."

"But you didn't give up your relationship with Arlette."

"When we first started going out, I didn't; but when I realized that I was falling in love with you, I knew that I had to end it with Arlette. We ended it by mutual agreement, but we ended it too late. She was already pregnant with Janine. She married Mark, and I married you. And we were all happy with our choices, I thought."

"But then afterwards, you and she found that you weren't able to end it after all, that you still wanted to continue your relationship."

"I don't think that she ever felt that way. I know that I never did."

"Then why did you keep seeing her after we were married?" I had such a clear picture of them together on that old, dark oak bed, the picture that I had tried to avoid looking at for so long now, the picture that suggested itself to me whenever I felt weakest.

"I didn't keep seeing her, Angela."

"Clay, Nadine is your daughter. She's the spitting image of Janine. When Michael was so sick, I asked the doctor if were possible for Nadine to be your daughter, and he said it was. I thought we were talking the truth here. How could she be your daughter if you weren't still seeing Arlette?" I realized that this sounded like an accusation.

Clay didn't bridle; he sat looking at the cigarette in his hand for a moment. He put the cigarette to his lips and drew on it thoughtfully. After he exhaled, he began speaking slowly. "Angela, you and I were really happy together, and I never looked Arlette's way again. I can't remember ever having a glimmer of a thought in her direction. You and I were a match; I believed that. I loved being with you, just breathing the same air. Then something happened to you, Angela. You started pulling away from me. It's such a clear memory for me. I remember I asked you why, but you wouldn't talk about it. You just didn't want to be with me anymore. We didn't laugh anymore; nothing I did seemed to make you happy. Nothing was right. You were distant; you were cold."

"And so you started seeing Arlette again." I wanted him to admit this.

Clay's voice was level. "No, I didn't start seeing her. Dad asked me to tell Mark that he had a job for him. After lunch I stopped over to leave a message for Mark, because I didn't know where he was working. He and Arlette had just had a big fight. She was crying; I was lonely. I'm not trying to excuse what we did. It happened . . . that once. Once! Neither of us meant for it to happen. We had both been happy in our marriages, but now we were both hurting, and it happened. I never knew what went wrong and why you stopped loving me."

"I never stopped loving you, Clay!" I protested.

"I didn't just dream this, Angela. Don't you remember I kept asking you, 'What's happened? What's gone wrong between us? Did I do something wrong?' And all you said to me was, 'Nothing's happened. Nothing's wrong. I don't want to talk about it.' You shut me out. I felt closer to you overseas than I felt those last few months when I was here. While I was in the service, you sent me wonderful, cheerful letters. While I was gone, I felt that you loved me; before I left, all I got was the cold shoulder. To the best of my knowledge, I never gave you any reason to draw away from me, but you did. You say that you want us to deal with the truth here. Then I think you need to tell me what happened to us, if you know."

"I know," I answered. I had never told anybody this. "Clay, you remember that last New Year's Eve party we went to before you went overseas?"

"Yes, I remember. What about it? We danced, we laughed, we had a good time. I know I had quite a bit to drink; you drank too. I danced with other women; you danced with other men as well, but I don't remember doing anything out of the way there."

"When we came home, you wanted to make love, and while we were making love, you called me Arlette. That's what happened. I had never put you and Arlette together in my mind before, but the minute you said that, I could see Alder and Janine, and I knew in my heart that they were your children."

"God, Angela, I'm sorry!" We had each been sitting on our own side of the sofa. Clay moved closer to me and put his arm around me. "But why didn't you say something—tell me, yell at me, something?"

"I couldn't talk about it. I just couldn't talk about it. I felt like ice, all cold and hard. I felt as though nothing could touch me anymore, as though nothing could break through to me. And a few days later, Janine was dead. We went to the funeral, and I watched you. That little girl's death didn't seem to move you any more than any other neighbor's death, and somehow that made me feel even colder about you. Your own daughter, and you just sat there politely sober, like everybody else."

"I didn't know she was my daughter then," Clay explained. "I didn't know until the day that Arlette and I were together. She had never told me, and I never realized."

"I know that now, but I didn't know it then. I remember at the time I felt as though I had married a man that now I didn't even know. I doubted everything about us. I doubted myself. I thought you had married me because I looked like Arlette."

"You think that you look like Arlette?" Clay looked puzzled.

"Don't you?"

"It never ever crossed my mind before. Angela, I never saw you as anybody but you. I loved you! You were the best thing that ever happened to me. You made me feel really alive. I love you, Angela!"

It was strange the effect those few words had on me. I felt a frost in me melting. I felt like a river that had been frozen solid and now began to flow again. The secret Clay had kept from me had made me doubt myself, and the secret I had kept from him had driven him away from me.

"What are we going to do, Clay?" I put my head on his shoulder and my left hand on his chest.

"I want to fix it, Angela." He closed his arms around me and pulled me to him. "I'm sorry about all the pain I've given you. Maybe it can't ever be the way it was before, but I do love you, and I want us to be together."

"I love you too, Clay." I slid my right arm around his waist. "I'm sorry, too, for the pain I caused you. Clay, I'm willing to work at it, but with no secrets this time. You're right, though; it won't be the way it was. It can't. There are the lives of four children to consider now. And I don't want them to be imprisoned by secrets."

Clay's parents had insisted that I be told the truth about the children, but they had come to realize that they could not insist that Clay and I raise the children. They felt that Arlette's children were Clay's responsibility, but at the same time they understood that they were not my responsibility. And they wanted Clay to convey to me that they didn't want to place me under any pressure to take the children. I felt that I needed some time with Clay, some time to talk, some time for both of us to get to know each other again. Clay agreed that we needed time to adjust to what we'd learned about ourselves and about each other. We were both clear that Michael and Alder needed to be told and that they needed to be a part of whatever we decided to do.

That evening we took Michael over to his grandparents. We sat down with the Holdens, and we told Michael and Alder that they were brothers.

"How did you know?" Michael asked, clutching guiltily at his wrist to hide a straight white scar. "We never told you about it."

"What do you mean, you never told us about it?" I asked confused.

Michael looked at Alder, and Alder cleared up the mystery. "After Mike and I became blood brothers, you wanted to know how we had cut ourselves; we told you that we had snagged our wrists on the barbed wire fence."

It took a while for us to make it clear to them that they had been blood brothers even before their childhood ceremony. There were questions that were uncomfortable to deal with, as we had expected, but we all dealt with them as honestly as we could without offering any more information than was asked for.

Finally Alder looked at Clay, and he said, "I'm lucky that I know who my father is. My Ma never knew who her father was. I'm glad!"

When the questions were over, the boys understood and accepted that they were brothers. Alder in his typical fashion had found something to be glad about in this new and unexpected twist to his life. For Michael it was the most splendid day he could remember, for on this day his father came home to him, and he learned that his best friend in all the world was really his brother.

Chapter Eighteen
Michael's Family

• *Michael Holden* •

My father brought home a boxful of glossy cowrie shells from the South Pacific for my mother, and he brought me a sweet potato. The morning after he got home, he gave me the sweet potato at breakfast. He smiled and said he'd won it in a card game from a shipmate who could play it "like nobody's business," and he thought I'd like it.

"Its real name is an ocarina, I guess," he added, "but everybody on the ship just called them sweet potatoes."

Along with the sweet potato and a quick lesson on where to put the fingers and how to blow into it, my father told the story of what had happened on the previous night when he tried to demonstrate for my mother his own virtuosity on the instrument with his rendition of "Twinkle, Twinkle Little Star." Ready to amaze my mother with his skill, my father said he put his lips to the sweet potato and blew, but no sound was forthcoming.

Telling the story this morning, my father frowned at the memory, "'That's funny!' I said to your mom. 'What's wrong with this thing? Even on my worst days I can usually get a squawk out of it at least.'" I watched as he turned the sweet potato over in his hands, recreating his movements of the night before.

"So I started checking it over to see if it had a crack in it or something, and when I flipped it over just right in my hand, I felt something sort of rattle inside. I told your mom, 'There seems to be something inside it.' I thought maybe it was a little dirt or a stick or something, and I tried shaking it out, but nothing came." My father gave the ocarina a puzzled look, showed me the look, and then continued.

"'Maybe I can blow it out' I said. Then I put my mouth on it here," my father pointed to the mouthpiece, "and I blew into it without stopping up the holes. This time when I blew into it, though (You see this bigger hole right here?), out came the biggest cockroach your mother ever saw in her life! No fooling, Mike, it was a *big one*! I have to admit it!" My father could not contain his laughter. "I don't even know how it squeezed itself out of that hole. You should have seen it; it sure was a corker!"

I wanted to see the cockroach. Unlike my mother, I had never seen whatever this thing was—large or small, and I had no idea what one looked like. My first mental image was of something like a mushroom, ballooning out of the hole as my father breathed into the instrument.

"How big was it, Dad?" I asked, trying to get a fix on what sort of thing a cockroach could be.

"Oh, it was about yea-big." My father indicated an approximate size with his fingers. "You should have seen him wiggling back and forth, Mike, trying to get out of there."

The pronoun "him" helped me to the assumption that it was an animal, perhaps an exotic reptile. Now I had a vision of my father blowing into the mouthpiece and of the "cockroach" rising like a miniature king cobra out of the biggest hole, waving back and forth to the music that couldn't get out of the sweet potato and which only the cockroach could hear.

"What happened to the cockroach, Dad?" I asked, still reluctant at that point to reveal my ignorance of the subject.

"Well, I have to say, I don't know for a fact if it fell or jumped or what, but it landed on the floor." My father pointed to a spot on the kitchen linoleum. My eyes followed the direction suggested by his finger, and as he continued, I searched the floor for anything that looked as though it might be a cockroach. "And let-me-tell-you, Mike! Your mother let out one incredible yell that would have awakened my Uncle Stoney, when he was dead drunk and snoring. Man-oh-man, I'm surprised you weren't down here like a shot! Anyway, at the same time as she yelled, her left foot shot out as though it was spring-loaded, and she stepped right on that little bugger."

"Why did you step on it, Mom?" I was really annoyed with this turn of events.

"Why did I step on it?" she repeated incredulously. "I stepped on it because I'm not going to have those filthy bugs in my home. That's why! They're disgusting! They get into everything."

So it was a bug, I thought to myself. That changed my picture once again. Now I could see the poor little creature struggling, pushing with its tiny feet, flapping ineffectually with its little transparent wings, wriggling slowly out of the hole, waving its antennae to the unheard melodies my father played.

"So, where is it now?" I asked. At least I thought I would be able to view the crushed body of this incredible bug.

"Well, when she took her foot off it, Mike, it was still moving its legs a little," my father said. "So your mother picked it up like a bad smell and flushed it down the toilet. And that was that." That was the end of the story. My father stuffed half a pancake into his mouth and followed it with a gulp of coffee.

"The biggest cockroach you ever saw, and you flushed it down the toilet?" I was furious with her, and I was searching for some way to convince her of the enormity of her lack of consideration in depriving me of a major learning experience. In order to do this, I was even willing to admit my complete ignorance of cockroaches. "I've never even seen a cockroach, and now this one's in the river! Thanks a lot, Mom! I don't even know what one looks like, and now I probably never will!"

"Well, let's hope you don't!" my mother said. "You wouldn't be thanking me if I had let them infest this house and they were crawling all over your food and your face in the night. But you're welcome anyway. I did what I thought was best, Michael."

After the cockroach had emerged from the sweet potato last night, every single thing my father had brought home with him had to be quickly marched outside into the cold. And there in the triple glare of the street lamp, the naked porch bulb, and a flashlight, every article had to be shaken out over the snow, turned inside out, prodded, and minutely examined to make sure it was safe to be brought back into the house. The box of cowrie shells had to be abandoned outside until my mother could buy a pesticide spray, since every shell was suspected of harboring an enemy.

"It would be just my luck that you've brought home a pregnant female," my mother said. "Then in no time we'd have them all over the house."

My mother lived in fear for weeks that some hidden eggs might yet hatch and that we would be overrun by hordes of insects, like the plague of locusts upon Egypt. She began asking around for the name of a good, reputable exterminator. My father said that really my mother was right, that cockroaches were an incredible nuisance and very difficult to get rid of, once they established themselves. My mother said that it gave her the heebie-jeebies just to talk about them. I thought it was sad that our cockroach had come all the way from the South Pacific secure in his little sweet potato house, only to be forced out, evicted, exposed, crushed, and sent to a watery grave in the river.

At that time all of the toilets in our part of town emptied into the river. They emptied at a point below our swimming hole, but not below our fishing holes. Alder and I could sometimes see the sewers emptying as we fished, and we never gave it a second thought. It was simply a fact of life about which no one seemed to evince concern. I wondered all day if some yellow perch under a patch of thin ice in the freezing river had breakfasted that morning on the biggest cockroach my mother ever saw.

I told Alder about it on the way to school that morning, and during lunch time we found a picture of a cockroach in the encyclopedia on the big bookshelf that the school euphemistically called the "library." The picture helped diffuse my anger with my mother; the encyclopedia artist had managed to depict the cockroach as an ugly and menacing insect, a formidable enemy to right-thinking mothers all over the world. Alder said that we were probably lucky that my mother had drowned it in the river.

That same evening Alder and I found out that we were brothers. My father, my mother, and my grandparents explained it to us. I was the half-brother of Alder and Nadine. And Nathaniel was also the half-brother of Alder and Nadine. But Nathaniel and I were not related. It took a while to understand that, and I wasn't sure that I really did. Alder understood it better than I did, and when he finally explained it to me the next day, I understood. Alder knew how to make things plain.

• *Angela Holden* •

As it turned out, it was only a month before Clay and I brought Arlette's children to live with us. Actually, we had reached this decision just before Christmas, but we felt that it made more sense to leave them where they were during the holidays, and in that way there would be more time for us to make preparations and more time for them to become accustomed to the idea of living next door to their grandparents.

After that first confrontation with Clay and the long talks which followed, I decided that I was really ready to accept the children. It had been on my mind for a month before Clay got home, and once the two of us got it straightened out concerning who did what and who felt what, I realized that I was all right with it. Going from being the mother of one child to being the mother of four children was obviously a major leap.

It would certainly require some fundamental readjustments in my thinking. But in a very real way, it wasn't so much that I had to accept the children as that I had to truly accept Clay. And once I did that, once I was really comfortable with him, it suddenly felt like springtime to me. I could feel crocuses pushing through the snow all over my body, as soon as I really believed in my heart that Clay loved me, that he had loved me from the start and that he continued to love me.

Through our talks we discovered that, although we had kept things from each other, we had never in our lives actually told one another a lie. I had never confronted Clay about Arlette, but he said that, had I asked him about it, he would have told me the truth.

"I wanted to talk to you about these things, but I was so afraid that I might lose you. I didn't tell you about Arlette and me, but I didn't tell you a lie about it either," Clay maintained.

We went round and round for a while concerning sins of omission vs. sins of commission. In view of the fact that he had not been candid with me concerning the nature of his relationship with Arlette, even though I had not requested the information, Clay's "not lying" to me may seem like a moot point. But it was a significant issue for me. At some very important level we had been honest with each other. And that was a place to start. With that knowledge, we began to explore our relationship more openly, more deeply. There were no taboo subjects for either one of us anymore. We learned to trust each other and to trust the strength of our love for one another. We became real human beings and best friends together.

For me, however, there was something essential still missing in Clay, some attribute of his personality that had been present before the war, but which now seemed no longer to exist. We talked about it. Clay could see the change in himself, but it wasn't easy for him to account for its cause. Mark's death had haunted him, but he believed that in accepting responsibility for the children he had dealt with that, that he had somehow fulfilled an obligation.

We decided that it was perhaps an internal wound which the war had left, something we would both have to live with. He was changed, and neither one of us knew how to change him back. He didn't seem to miss that part of himself so much as I did. I wanted him to love himself again.

• *Michael Holden* •

After Christmas father returned to his job on the police force, and later in January of 1946, Alder, Nadine, and Nathaniel came to live with us. Alder, Nathaniel, and I shared the same room. Our parents bought bunk beds for Alder and me; Nathaniel inherited my twin bed. Alder and I both wanted the top bunk, so we solved that problem by alternating every week when the linen got changed. Mother converted the smaller room, which had been her sewing room, into Nadine's bedroom. Mother said that we were not really crowded, that we were "cozy." Actually, I don't remember ever feeling that we were crowded. I enjoyed sharing my room with Alder, and Nathaniel was so quiet and private that we hardly noticed he was there. Alder nicknamed him "Noisy Nate," because he always kept to himself and never spoke. Nadine, on the other hand, assumed that wherever she was was center stage. She laughed, she performed, and she was often humorously imperious. Father said that she commanded attention. Early on, father started calling her "Princess," but I decided that a better name for her was "Queen Nadine." And after a while Alder and I shortened her title to "Queendeen."

Far from being offended, Nadine relished the appellation and wielded it like a scepter, except that she pronounced it "Keendeen." When she had finished her supper and was ready for dessert, she'd hold up her empty plate, point her chin up, and announce, "Beserk for Keendeen." The smile playing around the corners of her mouth and the sparkle in her eyes told everyone that this was a display of mock-haughtiness. Nadine knew how to get what she wanted. She already understood, instinctively perhaps, Aunt Mabel's maxim about catching more flies with honey than with vinegar.

It appeared that Nathaniel either did not know how to get what he wanted or that his wants were few. He seemed to be satisfied with whatever he got. Because he was Nadine's twin, he tended to be treated in the same way as she was and to share in the fruits of her requests. And with that he was contented and quiet. His demeanor with his twin sister was almost worshipful; his dark eyes took pleasure in all of her antics. But he did not speak. He silently complied with our parents' requests. It was clear to us that he understood language, and we found out that, even when he looked preoccupied, he was very aware of others in his vicinity.

One day Nathaniel was sitting in a corner of the living room playing with his little penguin that walked on an inclined plane. Father in the same room, almost oblivious of Nathaniel's presence, lit up a cigarette and a moment later asked himself, "Now, where did I put that stupid ashtray?" Nathaniel immediately stopped his play, went to the dining room, and returned with the ashtray for my father. Father was astonished, amused, and pleased, but from then on we knew that Nathaniel was tuned in to us, even though he seemed in some ways to dwell apart.

Nathaniel was also tuned in in other ways as well, as we were to discover that winter. That was the winter that mother decided that Alder and I needed to expand our horizons and acquire a bit of culture. So she found a piano teacher for us, a woman with a long nose and hands like chickens' feet. Mother took us to an interview with Mrs. Handshaw, an interview which ended with the teacher's deciding to "take us on" as pupils.

She played a piece for us so that we could appreciate how we would someday sound ourselves, if we practiced diligently. Her henna-dyed head bobbed up and down enthusiastically in time to the music as though she were pecking out the tune. I was fascinated by the backs of her hands and the rapid oscillation of the tendons under their thin, liver-spotted skin. In reality Mrs. Handshaw proved herself to be a very gentle and patient teacher with the lackluster students she had just acquired, but that in no way diminished our delight at having dubbed her "Mrs. Henclaws."

So it was that every Saturday morning, Alder and I found ourselves trudging up the hill with a dollar apiece to pay for piano lessons. From my point of view, mother had added insult to injury by making us perform household chores during the week to earn the necessary dollar. Alder didn't complain and pointed out to me that we should help with the dinner dishes and the dusting anyway, but this dubious reward for services rendered rankled me. It didn't help that I was not a star pupil, and practicing scales was an additional and unrelished chore from my point of view. I'm not sure that Alder really enjoyed the task any more than I did, but I was the one who grumbled at having to toil endlessly over something as inane as "Twinkle, Twinkle Little Star."

After our practice sessions, Nadine would kneel on the piano stool, bang along the keys with the palms of her hands, and shout over her own accompaniment, "TINKLE, TINKLE, WIDOW TAR!" After one of Nadine's prolonged concerts, father scooped her up and said, "Thank you, Princess, but I think that by now the Widow Tar has an empty bladder and full ears." Mother clucked her mild disapproval of father's words. But Nadine beamed, Alder and I howled, and Noisy Nate just watched.

One Saturday morning as mother was doing up the breakfast dishes, she heard drifting from the living room a simple melody Alder and I had practiced all week. She smiled in her satisfaction that at least one of her reluctant musicians was at last acquiring a sense of timing and could finally play a brief piece through without an error. Her patient endurance of our poor and uneven pounding upon her favorite instrument might be paying off after all. Then she remembered with a start that Alder and I had already left for our music lessons. At the piano she discovered little Nathaniel playing better than either of us what his careful observation and keen ears had taught him. He was little more than two and a half years old. He didn't talk, but obviously he had a talent.

Nathaniel was the only child in the family that was not to carry the Holden name. Our parents decided to adopt Alder and Nadine, because they were father's children. Nathaniel was Mark's only child, the only Handy left. Mark had wanted so much to have children to carry on his family name that father and mother felt they couldn't adopt Nathaniel and rob Mark of his wish. But somehow this decision, as well-intentioned as it was, seemed to set Nathaniel more apart. It was true that he kept himself apart, but now we would be five Holdens and one Handy. This name difference in a subtle way set Nathaniel aside in our minds and somehow made his physical and emotional distance less remarkable and more acceptable to everyone.

When we sat around the radio as a family to listen to "Baby Snooks" or "Fibber Magee and Molly," Nathaniel would sit apart. When we went to our grandparents or to Aunt Mabel's, Nathaniel would sit apart or sometimes wander off, and somehow the role of knowing where he was became my responsibility. I had an eye for details, and I tended to notice where he was or where he went, but I didn't tend to worry about him because he was always well-behaved. He just seemed to prefer to be by himself.

This is not to say that Nathaniel was isolated from the family. He participated in family events. He helped Alder and me build a Statue of Liberty snow sculpture. He looked at the Sunday comics with us and listened to Alder's and my readings and explanations of them. His favorite was "The Little King." Nathaniel still didn't speak, but he would point to the comic strip, and either Alder or I would interpret it for him, since "The Little King" never spoke and the story was told simply by the juxtaposition of the pictures. Nadine liked "Maggie and Jiggs." Alder's favorite was "The Phantom," and mine was "Mandrake the Magician," who cast wonderful spells by saying the words of the spell backwards.

When spring came, father bought a car—a used, blue Lincoln Zephyr, which was on the cusp between being a serviceable family vehicle and a maintenance liability. On weekends, mother would pack a picnic basket, and we would go for drives in the country. Nadine always sat between our parents in the front seat; Nathaniel sat between Alder and me in the back seat. Punkin always rode grandly on the package tray and looked out the rear window. Father said that, just as it was his job to watch where we were going, it was her job to watch where we'd been. He called Punkin the rear guard. Father enjoyed exploring the back roads, and after the ride was over, our parents and Alder would talk about the interesting houses and wild animals they had seen along the way. We could never be sure what Punkin had seen. I never saw much of anything, because I almost always fell asleep as soon as we left the driveway. So did Nadine and Nathaniel. Father started calling the car, our Lincoln Sleeper.

I enjoyed the rides, nevertheless, and every weekend I was the first to suggest one. Alder would smile and say, "I think Mike needs another nap, Dad." Alder called father, Dad, and mother, Mom. He said that he'd always called his own mother, Ma, so he preferred calling mother, Mom. He had called Mark Dad, but he explained that Mark was his "first" Dad. Nadine followed his lead, but Nathaniel still didn't speak. Mother said that Nathaniel just hadn't found anything worth talking about yet.

As soon as school was out in June, the whole family was shepherded into the car for a trip to Niagara Falls. Our parents were going to leave Punkin behind with our grandparents, but I teased until they agreed to bring her along. With Punkin and the rest of the family in their usual places, we set out on our first real journey as a family, and the last one in the Lincoln Sleeper without a major mechanical malfunction. Between the front and back seats and packed around Alder's feet (the only feet in the back seat that reached the floor) were baskets and boxes of fruit, pies, and sandwich materials brought along to defray the cost of stopping for food on the way.

Since mother didn't drive at that time, the total burden of driving rested on father. When he had driven until he "just couldn't see the road anymore," we stopped at some roadside cabins for the night. A sign at the desk warned, "Positively No Pets," so father discreetly refrained from revealing that Punkin was with us because there was "no way" he was driving any further. In a room with two double beds and a cot, we managed to make ourselves relatively comfortable. I sneaked Punkin into the room after the proprietor had left.

In the morning, my father told mother to take us kids to the little restaurant, which doubled as an office for the cabins. There we could start breakfast while he packed the car, checked the oil and water levels, and secured Punkin before he joined us. The service was very efficient, and we had already started on our donuts and milk when an old man opened the door and Punkin darted in between his legs. Because of his advanced age, the man's legs were wide-spread for the maintenance of his balance, but it was a good thing that he had one hand on the door and the other on his cane. "Whoa, Nellie!" he croaked, as an orange ball of fur went whizzing between his ankles. His straw hat flew off, his glasses were knocked askew, and he caught his balance at the last moment by tightening his grip on the side of the door and employing his cane as some sort of stabilizing rudder in the waves that seemed to rock him. By the time he regained his composure and could focus, Punkin had already assumed her "sit-up-and-beg pose" in front of our booth, as she waited for someone to toss her a bit of donut.

Everyone stared. The proprietor's face was a study in conjecture. Mother and I were nonplussed and tense. Nadine giggled delightedly, and Nathaniel grinned and pointed. But before anyone could ask an uncomfortable question, Alder said simply, "This dog doesn't belong in a restaurant." With complete composure he rose from his seat, bent over to take Punkin by the collar, and escorted her out. When Alder returned with father, none of us said anything about a dog, and strangely enough no questions were asked.

That day we saw Niagara Falls from the American side, but we were not able to appreciate the better view from the Canadian side, because we didn't have Punkin's license or immunization record with us and, therefore, were not permitted to cross the border. I felt guilty because I had been the one who insisted on bringing Punkin with us, but mother said that it wasn't my fault. She said that no one knew beforehand that we would need to bring those papers, and besides, Punkin's escapade in the restaurant had provided us with a memory none of us would ever forget.

Another memory I would never forget was walking under the falls. Mother stayed behind with the twins, while father, Alder, and I took off all of our clothes and donned hooded, one-piece uniforms. Looking like a gathering of Martians in our khaki-colored, cotton suits, we joined other determined tourists and paraded along wooden stairways and walkways which seemed to cling precariously to the cliffs under the falls. Gallons of water from the falls poured relentlessly over our heads. I tried walking fast and holding my breath as we passed under the cascading torrents, but at the end of the trek I was still convinced that I had swallowed more water than I had ever bathed in. Even father admitted that it was "quite a baptism," and Alder said that he felt that now he could better empathize with our sweet potato cockroach.

Chapter Nineteen

Nathaniel

• *Michael Holden* •

After a rainy, early summer morning, the road up the hill outside our house was alive with little toads hopping everywhere.

"Wow, look at all the little hop toads, Nate!" Alder pointed his fingers to a hundred places at once.

Nathaniel squatted beside us and watched the toads for a while with Alder, Nadine, and me. He seemed interested, but not particularly excited about the phenomenon. After a few minutes he stood up and walked slowly back to the house. When Nathaniel left, we assumed that he had simply gotten tired of looking at the toads and had decided to return to some activity more interesting to him. It was nothing out of the ordinary for Nathaniel to withdraw after observing for a few moments. We watched what Alder called the "toad road parade" for a few more minutes, and then we moved on to catching cabbage moths in the garden.

So we were not present minutes later, when Nathaniel came back to the road carrying a Doeskin Tissue box. Without asking mother's permission, he had removed all the tissues to convert the box into a receptacle for collecting toads. He lifted the small creatures carefully one by one and set them gently down in the smooth cardboard room he had created for them. Within a short time Nathaniel had gathered enough tiny, dark, jumping forms to cover the box's gray bottom. But then, he had to interrupt his collecting to return to the house to go to the bathroom.

In the hallway Nathaniel first placed his pets delicately down on the stairway in their new, tissue-box home. He watched them hop about, hugging each other, happy to have been rescued from the hot tar steaming in the noon sun. Now they were in a cool place where they wouldn't be squashed by cars or mouthed by stray dogs. For a moment Nathaniel gazed fondly at his minions until finally compelled on his way by the pressing needs of nature.

When he returned a few minutes later to rejoin his little friends, he couldn't believe his eyes. The box was empty. It didn't make sense. Moments ago the bottom of the box had been alive with little toads. Now there were no toads. There were no toads in the box, no toads on the stairs, no toads on the floor, no toads under the box, no toads anywhere to be seen.

Nathaniel was turning round and round in the middle of the hallway searching in every direction for his pets. He was just coming to the conclusion that some other agency must have been responsible for removing the toads from the box, when father returned home for lunch. When the door opened, Nathaniel stopped turning and thrust the empty tissue box out at father. The picture of the little doe on the box looked benignly at father in his policeman's uniform, as Nathaniel scowled and accused him, "Where my hop toads, Dad?" No one had ever heard Nathaniel's speaking voice before, and for a child it was a deeper voice than one would have expected. It seemed almost to come from his feet, which were planted firmly apart as he sought to block father's passage.

Father started, but not at the belligerence of the demand concerning hop toads. "Nathaniel, you spoke!" father announced, more to himself than to the angry little presence confronting him in the hallway.

"My-hop-toads!" Nathaniel persisted implacably, pushing the box into father's stomach.

"Your hop toads?" asked father taking the box into his hands. He looked into the box and then at the child standing resolutely before him. His wonder at Nathaniel's speech was still fresh in his face, but he was recovering from his shock and was now beginning to understand Nathaniel's concern. "You had some hop toads in the box?"

"Whole bunch-a hop toads!" Nathaniel corrected him.

"And you think I took them. Is that it?" father asked.

"Put 'em back!" Nathaniel commanded.

"I didn't see them, Nathaniel. I just came in," father reasoned.

"Who did?" demanded the child interrogating the policeman.

"I don't know," the suspect replied. "The other kids are down in the garden, and your mom is at the clothesline hanging up a wash. So, I don't think anyone took them. I wonder what could have happened to them. Maybe they just got out of the box. What do you think happened?"

Nathaniel's dark eyes joined those of the tissue-box doe as he looked closely at father, who seemed really to have no idea where the hop toads had disappeared to. Then Nathaniel turned away. He shrugged, and threw his hands into the air, "All gone! Hop toads all gone!"

The toads seemed simply to have vanished. There was no evidence of them to be found; they were indeed gone, lost. But on that day Nathaniel's voice was found, and it was found for good. Afterwards, mother swept up tiny, desiccated carcasses from under the living room furniture for a week—every time she swept, it seemed. It remained a mystery why none of the delicate amphibians were seen hopping away or were discovered while they were still alive. Father said that they were probably obeying a natural instinct to escape and hide, but that unfortunately, they were unable to survive in an environment so hostile to them.

Now that Nathaniel was able and willing to speak, mother enrolled him with Mrs. Handshaw to begin studying the piano, a consequence which Alder and I saw as a punishment for killing the toads rather than as a reward for finding his voice. A couple of months before, mother had brought him to Mrs. Handshaw as soon as she discovered that he seemed to have a natural talent for the piano. Mrs. Handshaw played small phrases of music to Nathaniel and observed as he played them back to her, but this musical game was the only type of communication in which she could tempt Nathaniel to cooperate at that time. And after a few minutes he tired of the game. Consequently, although she was delighted with Nathaniel's possibilities, her enthusiasm was more tempered than mother's.

"My, your little boy has a wonderful ear, Angela; and I believe that you may be correct in thinking that he has a gift for music. But I think that I would like to hold off just a little while longer from taking him on as a pupil. I say this, because at this point I believe that you can do as much for him as I can. Of course, if you didn't play yourself or if he had no one at home to encourage him, I would feel different. But he has you to help him."

"But, what if he's a Mozart?" mother protested. "I'm not a piano teacher."

"But you're his mother," Mrs. Handshaw observed gently. "And even a Mozart needs a mother. Right now, playing the piano is a game for him, and maybe it's a game best played at home with his mother, rather than with a stranger. I'm not sure that I'm in favor of pushing children too early. It takes the enjoyment out of the game and turns it into work. Right now he's having fun with the piano, and I think it's important that he keep on having fun. Until he learns to speak or until he's willing to speak, you can cultivate this talent yourself better than I can."

So this was the way that Nathaniel came to acquire an undivided portion of mother's attention and time. Although Nathaniel wasn't speaking yet, playing the piano was a medium of communication which they shared. He would watch her and listen to her play, and then he would return the musical message. They encouraged each other and enjoyed each other. Even after he learned to speak and he began to take lessons from Mrs. Handshaw, mother stayed at his side when he practiced.

Although Nathaniel and mother had discovered this singular avenue of intimacy and although Nathaniel had finally decided to speak, he continued to remain aloof from the rest of the family. He was enthralled by Nadine, but he seemed to worship her from afar. He looked up to Alder and me, but he maintained a distance. With Nathaniel there was always a sense of distance, even when he was sitting beside you. And it wasn't easy to determine how that distance was maintained—if it was something in Nathaniel's nature or experience that kept him apart or something in us that initiated or encouraged the separation. Trying to understand that puzzle was like trying to discover which came first, the chicken or the egg.

It was clear to me early on that there was something about Nathaniel that seemed to bother father. Though there was nothing in their behavior that suggested any animosity, the distance between father and Nathaniel was as palpable to me as a stone wall. Yet it wasn't so much a barrier as it was a space, a gulf, a chasm—as though they were on separate banks of a river with no connecting bridge between them. I once heard father say to mother that Nathaniel had eyes just like Mark's.

And I observed that father almost never looked directly at Nathaniel's eyes, but that whenever he did, he looked sad or uncomfortable. Perhaps Nathaniel sensed this as well, because he rarely looked directly at father either.

To an outsider the tension and distance between father and Nathaniel might not have been easily observable in our first summer as a family, because father tended to spend much of his free time with Alder and me. That summer saw the advent of baseball gear and bicycles in our home. Father spent hours teaching Alder and me the rudiments of baseball. Or he would run panting behind me, as I pedaled awkwardly from my perch atop my wobbling bicycle. Father kept one of his hands on the fender, trying to help me evolve a sense of balance on this tricky vehicle, and though he succeeded, it was a long and exhausting process. Alder was an eager and natural athlete; everything was harder for me. A three-way game of catch was an exercise in patience for them, because I often failed to catch the ball and wasted time chasing after it to retrieve it. I tried to enlist Punkin's help in this matter, but she was uninterested in fetching baseballs. She just smiled and pretended not to understand what I wanted her to do.

During these play sessions, mother and the twins might also be outside, but they would be observing us or involved in a game of their own. There were two distinct family groups: father and the boys, and mother and the twins. To an outsider this might have looked perfectly natural: the father with the older boys, teaching them skills boys need to learn; the mother with the younger children, nurturing and entertaining them. But it seemed to be something more than that to me; it seemed an easy way for father to avoid getting too close to Nathaniel.

We did do many things as an entire family, and weekends were almost always family events—sometimes with my grandparents, or with Aunt Mabel and Dad Ames, or simply as a family. On these occasions there were various combinations of pairings and groupings which occurred within the family unit—groupings other than father and the boys vs. mother and the twins. One was the way we always sat in the car; another was Alder and me vs. father, mother and the twins; or Alder and me, mother and Nathaniel, father and Nadine. Considering all the possible combinations and permutations, some of them should naturally have included father and Nathaniel as a pair, but I can't remember one time on those weekends that that combination occurred.

On one such weekend, father discovered that I did not know how to swim. Mother had written to father about Alder's and my swimming at the swimming hole, and those letters, together with the pictures I had drawn and sent him, had clearly given him the wrong impression about my level of competence. I could swim underwater for as long as I could hold my breath, but I could not keep my head above the water, so I was restricted to the shallows where I could touch bottom. With one foot on the bottom, I could make a good pretense of swimming, but from father's point of view pretense at something so important was unacceptable and even dangerous.

The occasion for father's discovery was a cookout at the park on the lake. Swimming was the first activity on the agenda, since after we ate, we would have to wait for an hour to return to the water. Mother played in the water with the twins while father, Alder, and I swam. Of course, from my point of view I was a veritable frogman; from father's point of view I needed lessons. Even Alder did not swim as well as father thought he should, while I had been convinced Alder's skill was sufficient to earn him a place on the Olympic team. Watching father swim, I had to reassess radically my understanding and appreciation of excellence. Father tempered his disappointment and encouraged Alder and me by saying that a summer of swimming lessons would make a world of difference in us—we would see. He said that after a few summers of lessons, he would lay odds that we would be better than he was. It was a bet I should have taken.

After we had swum with father for a while, Alder and I tossed a beach ball with the twins, while mother and father swam together. They dived into the water like two otters and disappeared from view in their race away from shore. After a time mother surfaced and continued to breast stroke slowly away from us, but father was nowhere in sight. I stopped playing with the twins for a moment. My entire attention was riveted on father's failure to surface, as mother moved placidly into the distance. I took a breath and held it, but I had already released all of it before father's head bobbed out of the water far beyond mother. Father was a fish!

Afterwards, while our parents worked at preparing the meal, Alder and I decided to involve Nadine and Nathaniel in building a sand castle. We lugged pails of sand to one spot. Then we got the twins busy scooping out the moat while we formed sturdy ramparts and tall towers. Nadine continued to remain interested while we gathered stones for the windows, but Nathaniel withdrew a few paces away and began digging a hole with his little shovel.

"Look, Nate is digging the lake for the people in the castle," Alder observed. "Hey, Nate, we're building the castle, and you're digging the lake for us. Okay?"

"Okay," Nate replied. Alder could always think of a way to include his brother, even when Nathaniel withdrew. When we ate, we all sat at a picnic table, except for Nathaniel. He sat a little apart under a sugar maple.

Mother called, "Come sit with us at the table, Nathaniel."

"Not now," Nathaniel answered simply.

"I know what," Alder suggested. "Nate can be the lookout and make sure it's safe, while we sit inside the castle and eat our feast."

Nathaniel grinned at Alder, who seemed to understand him. So Nathaniel ate under the tree, while the rest of the family ate at the picnic table. And we had almost finished the meal when a cloudburst took us by surprise. We all scrambled, gathering up things as we raced to the car. Safe from further soaking inside the Lincoln Sleeper, father inclined his head to Alder and gestured with his hand; even from his sitting position in the front seat of the car, father managed to create with this small action the impression of elaborate deference and homage.

"Sire, if I may make a suggestion," father began. "The next time you invite us to dine at your castle, please be sure to repair the leak in the roof."

"Oh, God, that was so great!" Clay held Angela in his arms and spoke his words softly into her ear. He gently kissed her neck, stretched his body the full length of the bed, and heaved a contented sigh.

"It's always great! Haven't you figured that out by now?" Angela teased, as she rolled the left half of her body over onto him and rested her head on his chest.

"I know. That's what makes it so great!"

"That's really nice to hear." Angela wrapped her arms around him and lay still in his embrace.

"Are you tired?" He ran his fingers through her hair.

"Yes."

"It's a lot of work, isn't it?"

"What is?" She yawned. Her words sounded sleepy.

"The children. It's a lot of work for you."

She tightened her hold on him and rubbed her face against his chest. "Yes it is. But I'm enjoying it."

"Are you really?"

"Yes, I am. Really."

"You're the most amazing woman!"

"Thanks, you're pretty amazing yourself." She said it lightly and stretched up to kiss him on the lips.

"No, seriously, are you honestly okay with all this? With the kids and all?"

Angela propped herself on her elbow and looked at Clay. Now she didn't seem so sleepy as before. "You know, it's funny. There was a time when I couldn't have imagined that I would be okay with it, but I'm fine now." She paused. "I don't think I could do it alone, but I'm not alone. You do as much as I do."

"I love you so much!"

"I know, and I love you! *That's* what makes it fine." They held each other again while the question formed inside her mind, a question that only waited for another opportunity to present itself. "Are you okay?"

"Sure, I'm great! I couldn't be better."

"Are you sure?"

"Yeah. Why?"

"I don't know." She knew he didn't have the answer to her real question, even if he understood it. So for that reason she shifted her ground. " . . . Well, tonight at supper you seemed sort of preoccupied and distant."

"When?"

"When the boys were talking about the swimming project."

"Oh, yeah. That. Well, to tell you the truth, I'm just not really in favor of their going around the streets begging for money like a couple of ragamuffins."

"They're going to help raise money for the project."

"The Duncansboro Swimming Project should be supported by the town."

"It is supported by the town—partly. And it's partly supported by donations." Now Angela was wide awake. Because he had wanted the boys to learn to swim, she had gotten involved in the town's new swimming project. "All of the administrator's time is donated. She doesn't get a red cent for all the work she does; she does it for the kids. That's a big donation, and besides that, she's already raised a lot of money for the project through private contributions. What she's asking the kids to do is to collect additional donations around town. Everyone who gives money will get a little tag that says, 'I support the swimming project.' In that way she not only gets contributions, but she makes more people aware of the project at the same time. And, not only that, but the kids get to feel as though they have a real part in it, that they're making a contribution too."

"What the hell do they need so much money for? It's just teaching kids how to swim."

"That, my love, is exactly the kind of thinking that accounts for the town's only footing half of the bill. For one thing the project has to pay to use the beach, even though the cost is very reasonable. Also, they have to hire a bus and bus driver. Then, there are several instructors. Fortunately, the Red Cross is providing a portion of the instructors' salaries."

"Well, it's nice to see that the Red Cross is doing *something*."

"You have got a real gnat up your nose about the Red Cross, haven't you?"

"Well, when I got back to the states, they refused to place my call."

"That doesn't mean they don't do a lot of good things. You need to let this go. Besides, I thought that the woman was willing to place the calls, if you were able to pay for them."

"Same thing!"

"Not exactly. It sounds to me as though she was following a policy, something over which she had no control."

"But that doesn't make it right. She probably could have done something if she wanted to."

"Okay, Clay, tell me this. When you give somebody a ticket for . . . say parking beside a hydrant, do you ever wish you didn't have to?"

"Sure, but I don't have a choice. It's the law."

"Exactly, and probably other people have to live with rules over which they have no control as well."

"I see your point."

"The Red Cross is also providing some training for the instructors, manuals for the junior and senior lifesaving courses, and emergency medical kits."

"Okay, okay, I give up," Clay laughed.

"Oo, I love it when you surrender." She wiggled against his body. Her voice was mock-sexy.

"But that still doesn't mean that our kids should go around begging on the streets."

"You wouldn't object to their going out 'trick or treating,' would you? Isn't that begging?"

"It's not the same thing."

"All right. When Salvation Army workers go around with their tambourines, aren't they begging?"

"They're trying to support a cause they believe in. That's . . . the way they raise money." A weak smile was forming at the corners of his mouth.

"And that's what our kids are doing too." She smiled back at him. He had seen the checkmate coming, but too late. "And the boys believe in this cause, because you want them to learn to swim, and they love you, and they want to please you. And so do I."

He took her into his arms. "God, I love you, woman! You're the best!" Clay realized that he didn't have a leg to stand on, and he always loved the way Angela did this to him. Not that he didn't also do it to her, but he appreciated her skill. She seemed better at it than he was now, though; he seemed to have gotten a little rusty.

"Rusty" was the word he used to articulate to himself the elusive sense of loss which had now become a part of his daily experience. It was as though Clay had misplaced an essential skill over which he had once had mastery, like riding a bicycle. But trying to recover the loss was not simply a matter of practice, since he was unable to grasp just what it was that was missing. In many ways his life was better than it had ever been. There were no more secrets. He loved Angela; they were great together. He had told her tonight that he "couldn't be better," and in a very real sense that was true, because he didn't know how to be better, how to recover whatever was lost. It was as though he no longer had access to a fundamental part of his personality.

• *Michael Holden* •

Alder and I joined the Duncansboro Swimming Project for three mornings a week until school started. With our bathing trunks wrapped in a towel, we caught a yellow school bus at a stop in front of our school and rode out to one of the best beaches on the lake. Riding the bus made the experience seem very special, because at that time our town did not provide any transportation to and from school.

Once at the beach, boys and girls quickly changed in one of the two modesty cubicles on the borders of the woods. The boys would look furtively (sometimes openly) at the girls' cubicle, where they could see the girls' feet and legs and the heads of the taller girls. Seeing parts of the girls while they were in the act of changing their clothes seemed to activate the boys' imaginations. While they watched the girls pull their skirts over their heads or step out of intimate articles of clothing, the boys amused themselves by speculating about the parts of the girls' bodies that couldn't be seen. I asked Alder if he thought that the girls were amusing themselves about the boys in the same way, but Alder wasn't sure if girls had the same sorts of thoughts as boys did.

After we were all suited up, we formed a straight line on the beach to receive our instructions for the day. There were four instructors: an adult and three high school students. All of them sported whistles on cords around their necks and American Red Cross senior lifesaving or instructor's patches on their bathing suits. The instructors stood facing us with their backs to the water, blew their whistles for attention, and divided us into groups: beginners, junior intermediate, senior intermediate, and advanced.

I was happy that I didn't have to start with the beginners, because I had already mastered the dead man's float. With the help of a special board, I learned to keep my head out of the water, a feat which (like many of life's skills) seemed to be primarily a matter of belief, confidence, and practice. By the end of the summer I could dog paddle, do a fair sidestroke, and remain floating effortlessly and endlessly on my back. Alder had a command of the breast stroke and backstroke, and his Australian crawl was smoothing out. Just before school started, Alder spent a week at Boy Scout camp where he swam twice every day and earned his swimming merit badge.

In September when we started school, Alder went to the eighth grade on the other side of town, while I went to the third grade at our old school. It was different not having Alder there with me, but this year I was able to leave for school a little later, because I wasn't accompanying Alder to his school patrol post. Alder pointed that out as an advantage, but I didn't see it in the same light. Alder had to leave as early as he used to. He didn't have patrol duty this year, but now he had to walk a mile and a half to school.

This school year Alder was very involved with school and scouts. It seemed to me that he was always busy after school with homework, scout work, and piano practice, when he didn't have troop meetings or patrol meetings for scouts. On weekends there were piano lessons (which we went to together), but sometimes there were scout outings, fund raisers for scouts or school, or football games with some of the boys from his new school.

Also now there were after-school rendezvous at a soda fountain on the other side of town with Barbara Hildreth. Now, whenever Alder was free to go to the movies with me on Saturdays, it wasn't the way it used to be. Now Barbara always met us there and patronized me as Alder's "cute little brother." Alder thought Barbara was wrapped in a rainbow; I thought she was a simpering pain.

Chapter Twenty

Early Spring

• *Michael Holden* •

That fall and winter grandfather began teaching me how to play cribbage and chess. We played at least one game of each almost every day after school. As usual, grandfather always played to win, but afterwards he would carefully explain his winning strategies to me and show me how I could have played a better game. "In these games a player has to watch, and think, and make careful decisions," grandfather cautioned. "Both cribbage and chess require patience and perspicacity, and they can teach him a lot about life."

Unlike most of the games I had learned, these both involved more strategy than luck, and although I didn't beat grandfather very often, I got to be pretty good at both of them. Alder was learning how to play them too, but he had less time to devote to them than I did. When the two of us played together, I was completely ruthless and usually managed to beat Alder two out of three times. On weekends, when the family went to our grandparents, sometimes there would be a game of four-handed cribbage. When grandfather and Alder played against father and me, the teams were fairly evenly matched. But when grandfather and I teamed up together, we were the indisputable champions.

When the four of us played chess tournaments (which could go on for several weeks), grandfather invariably won. Father said grandfather won because he had been playing the game forever, and as grandfather was fond of pointing out, "experience counts." The real contest in those tournaments was for second place, which I usually took. Father had not played very much for a long time, and like Alder, he had less time to spend studying the intricacies of the game than I did. Father and Alder liked to try to needle grandfather by telling him to watch out, that I was gaining on him fast and that it wouldn't be long before I overtook him. Grandfather's eyes would light up as he crowed, "Good!

That's the dream of every teacher worth his salt, to have his pupils outdistance him!"

One of the areas in which father was trying to outdistance his teacher was in playing the guitar. Grandfather had been father's teacher and had taught him all he could, but father was out of practice because he had not played for the three years during the war, except for an occasional tune on a borrowed guitar on shipboard. Now during his free time father was practicing to rebuild his skills.

"I've gotten rusty," he said, "but it's like riding a bicycle or swimming. Once you know how, you don't completely forget, but it takes a lot of practice to get good at it again." Father strummed thoughtfully on his guitar. "I used to be able to make this thing talk, just like my dad, but now I'm going to need to practice and practice, just like you boys on the piano."

Father practiced by himself, and he played for us and sang us songs which he thought every child should know. Especially at bedtime he would play and sing us songs such as "Sweet Betsy from Pike," "Oh, Susannah," and "Clementine."

"These songs are part of our culture," Father said, "and in their own way they're as important for you to be familiar with as *Oliver Twist*, I think." Dicken's *Oliver Twist* was the story that mother was reading to us at bedtime. Aunt Mabel had suggested that mother make a habit of reading to us every night before we went to bed, and she had provided mother with several books which she considered "worthwhile for building an appreciation of literature, enriching the vocabulary, and providing an understanding of the culture." Aunt Mabel called them mind stretchers.

Father said he wasn't sure that the songs he sang to us stretched our minds in quite the same way, but he felt they were important nevertheless. As it turned out, one of the songs he sang to us came to require some stretching of his own mind. It also proved how attentive the twins were to the lyrics of these evening sing-a-longs. "Did Clementine die?" Nathaniel asked. Father had just finished the verse in which Clementine's ruby lips were blowing bubbles under water and the narrator was unable to rescue her because he was no swimmer.

"Yeah, she died, because the man couldn't save her," father answered.

"Clementine can't die, Dad!" Nadine said, her voice full of concern.

"I know it's sad, Princess, but that's the way the song goes," father said.

"That's a bad song," Nathaniel offered his judgment.

"But Clementine can't die, Dad!" Nadine repeated.

"I'm sorry, Princess, but that's the end of the song."

"Clementine can't die! Can't you do something, Dad?" Nadine persisted.

"That's the song, Princess. What can I do?" Father was at a loss.

"Fix it," Nathaniel offered his solution.

"Well, I'll think on it and see what I can do," father concluded.

The next night, father said that he wanted to sing "Clementine" again for us. "See what you think of this," he said. He played and sang the original version all the way through. I saw Nadine and Nathaniel's looks of concern as father repeated Clementine's death scene, but when father had finished the original verses, he went on to add two more:

Toward the e-nd, came a frie-nd,
Who could dive and float and swim,
Jumped in the water and saved the daughter;
She's hale and hearty, thanks to him.

Oh my darling, oh my darling,
Oh my darling, Clementine,
You are safe and sound forever,
Very happy, Clementine.

"Okay!" Nathaniel said, awarding his stamp of approval.

"Good!" Nadine said at the same time.

After that, "Clementine" came to be Nadine's "most favoritest" song, and she would sing bits of it to her dolls while she rocked them to sleep. So it was not surprising that she should have decided to perform "Clementine" for Aunt Mabel's birthday party. It wasn't really Aunt Mabel's birthday; because she was born on February 29, she wouldn't have a birthday for another year. But we celebrated her birthday anyway on February 28.

Grandmother said, "We can't let her forget that the years are passing her by, even though she's got this idea that she should only add a year to her age every four years."

There was talk about a surprise party, but Dad Ames said that Aunt Mabel didn't have a good feeling about her birthday this year, and he wasn't sure if a surprise party was such a good idea. So grandmother and mother told Aunt Mabel that it was "all settled"; she was going to have a birthday party this year whether she liked it or not, so she might as well reconcile herself to it. "Just because you're getting old," grandmother told her, "it doesn't mean that we shouldn't have a little fun at your expense." Aunt Mabel got stubborn and said that they were free to make as many parties as they liked, but that in no way obligated her to come to any of them. Grandmother countered this mock objection as only grandmother could, "Why, Mabel, I had no idea of asking you to bother your head about coming to the party. Don't you worry about it. We'll bring the party to you. We'll hold it right in your own home, so you won't have to stir a step."

"Well, if you think that I'm cleaning my house so all of you can come over and mess it up with some silly party, you can just think again," Aunt Mabel rejoined.

"Who's asking you to clean your house?" mother chimed in. "I know where you keep the broom and dustpan. I'll come over and clean it myself." Everybody laughed at mother's ludicrous proposal. As mother was fond of saying, Aunt Mabel was so neat that "you could eat off her floors," although I don't remember that anyone ever did, except for Punkin.

"And if you try to lock me out," mother added as an afterthought, "I'll just get in by breaking a window. And it's still winter, so I don't think you really want any broken windows."

"I could just call the police," Aunt Mabel said.

"Oh, by all means, go ahead and do that!" mother said. "Clay or one of his buddies will come over. Now, whose story do you think any of them will believe?"

"I give up!" Aunt Mabel threw up her hands.

"You might as well. It's all decided anyway," grandmother concluded.

So in preparation for Aunt Mabel's birthday party, Nadine and father were practicing father's new version of "Clementine." Mother thought it would be nice if the three of us boys performed pieces on the piano. Neither Alder nor I wanted to do a solo, so we opted to perform the duet "Heart and Soul," which mother had taught us. Nathaniel was going to play the beginning of Debussy's "Claire de Lune." Mrs. Handshaw said that Nathaniel didn't have enough of a reach to play the rest of the piece, so they adapted it by having Nathaniel play the first nine measures twice and adding an ending.

When the day came for Aunt Mabel's party, mother did go over to Aunt Mabel's that afternoon, but not to clean the house. In order to decorate for the party, she packed Aunt Mabel off to grandmother's house. "I've talked Dad Ames into taking off from work a couple of hours early, so that the two of us can decorate this house for the party," mother said. "And you're not going to sit around and watch us do it. At least that much of the party is going to be a surprise for you." Aunt Mabel knew that it would do her no good to object.

At the end of the school day that Friday of the party, father picked me up at school. He already had Alder and the twins with him. The plan was for all of us to go ice skating in order to occupy our time until the party and to free mother to do the decorating. My parents thought it would please Aunt Mabel if we could tell her that we had gone ice skating on her birthday. Aunt Mabel and Dad Ames had given Alder and me ice skates for Christmas for the third year in a row; they said that growing boys couldn't be expected to fit into the same ice skates more than one winter. Alder and I enjoyed skating, and we knew that we needed new skates. So we didn't really mind getting them for Christmas, except that by the third year in a row there was no element of surprise. Mother felt that we both had displayed less enthusiasm about the gift this year than we should have. This year Aunt Mabel and Dad Ames had also bought little double runner skates for the twins as well, along with a copy of *Hans Brinker; or, The Silver Skates.*

"You just never know about children," Aunt Mabel had said. "Nathaniel has a gift for music. Nadine might be another Sonja Henie."

Before the birthday party mother pointed out that we hadn't skated nearly as much this year as we had in past years. She was concerned that Aunt Mabel and Dad Ames might feel that we didn't appreciate their present. She herself had several times taken the twins over to skate on the patch of ice that grandfather created near his chicken yard, but mother wasn't a skater, so that wasn't one of the activities we did on weekends. At one time father had been a fair skater, and after Christmas this year he dug his old skates out of the closet and had them sharpened. He said that he was going to start skating again, but that was as far as he had gotten so far this winter. When mother suggested the skating party, father thought it was a good idea since there might not be many more opportunities to skate, with spring just around the corner.

Because the town rink would not open until five o'clock, we were going to skate on the oxbow. When we got there, I could see that Barbara Hildreth was already there, skating in little circles on the smooth ice while she waited for Alder to join her. That explained why Alder had turned himself into a contortionist and put on his skates in the car on the way to the oxbow.

While Alder was struggling into his skates, father had cautioned him that a person could break his neck trying to negotiate the path from the causeway to the oxbow wearing his ice skates, but Alder said he'd walk through the snow on the side of the path. Father parked the car on the side of the causeway, and Alder sprang through the door and leaped through the snow as though he were wearing seven league boots in his eagerness to reach Barbara.

On the way to the oxbow I had thought that Alder was going to skate with *us* and that he was just eager to get started. I hadn't understood his plan, and I had decided to put my skates on also, so that we could get started together. That was why I had one skate on when Alder shot out of the car. So while father and the twins went down to the rocks to put on their skates, I sat sullenly in the car muttering about Alder and Barbara, while I pushed my foot into my other skate and slowly laced it up without much enthusiasm.

I struggled through the snow down the side of the path to where father was bent over helping Nadine into her skates. By now Alder and Barbara were holding hands and laughing, while they skated down at the far side of the oxbow among a scattering of other skaters. I looked around for Nathaniel, and I saw him standing apart as usual. But he was standing out on the thin ice where the oxbow joins the river. He was standing directly over the drop-off, which years of river currents had scooped out. Nathaniel was completely oblivious of his extreme danger.

"Dad!" I yelled, as I jerked frantically on father's coat sleeve. "Dad! Nathaniel's out on the thin ice!"

"Jesus!" Father's head jerked up, and he wheeled around; he had a terrified look on his face. At that moment there was a crack like a gunshot from the ice. Father's eyes went wild; he yelled, "Don't move, Nate! Stay right there!" Father hurtled around the shoreline on the near side of the oxbow. I knew father was a good runner because he could keep up with my bicycle, but I had never seen him run this fast. He ran like a hunted animal. Even the deep snow did not seem to slow him down.

I could see now that he was trying to get to the small spit of land that stuck out between the oxbow and the river, so he could get as close to Nathaniel as possible. Nathaniel watched father racing toward him, but he didn't move. A few feet away from Nathaniel now, father stopped and stepped cautiously off the safe, small crescent of land. He reached his hand out to Nathaniel. "Take my hand, Nate!" I heard him say. I heard the words plainly, even though father and Nathaniel were several yards away. The world seemed to be completely still, as if it were holding its breath. Out of the corner of my eye I could see people gathering silently to watch.

Nathaniel extended his little hand to father, but they were still too far away from each other to touch. Time stopped while they stood straining their bodies, trying to reach each other. Father was leaning out as far as he could, aware of the need to keep his weight on the thicker ice near the shore. He reached out as far as he could extend his arm, and his hand looked to be little more than a foot away from Nathaniel's. Nathaniel reached for father's hand, and his dark eyes were glued to father's face.

Then Nathaniel took a faltering step toward father. At that same instant there was another sharp crack as the ice broke apart. Nathaniel teetered backwards. Father's body went rigid, as though trying to hold Nathaniel back by the force of his will. "Dad!" Nathaniel cried. His little hand reached out pleadingly to father. His dark eyes never left father's face as Nathaniel fell backwards into the gaping, black hole of icy water.

At that moment I became aware of Nadine's voice wailing, "Nathaniel! Nathaniel! Nathaniel!" over and over again like a small siren. I knew then that she had been crying his name all along, but I had not heard it until that second when I saw the water close over Nathaniel's body. I watched Nathaniel disappear; and in the same breath, almost as though it were part of the same motion, I saw father dive into the swirl of freezing, black water after him.

I tried to scream out, "Dad!" The scream echoed in my head, but nothing came out of my throat. I wanted to go after father, but I stood staring numbly at the hole in the ice. I couldn't move. It was as though the blades of my skates had frozen solid to the ice. My body was frozen stiff. I felt like a statue; I felt as though I might never move again. I was holding my breath. And when I realized that I was holding my breath, a thought formed inside my head, "I wonder how long dad can hold his breath." But I had to breathe.

And as I took a breath, I became aware that I was holding Nadine by the hand. I was holding onto her tightly; I had probably been holding her hand all along. And now I also became aware that Alder had his arm around me. I looked at him, and I saw that tears were streaming down his cheeks. It was as though I were seeing him in a dream. Then I saw Barbara holding onto Alder's other arm; she was sobbing luxuriously. And there was a crowd of people standing around us. The causeway behind us was lined with parked cars, and more people were getting out and gathering around the oxbow. There were a hundred conversations surrounding us now. We just stood there numbly staring out at the hole in the ice where Nathaniel and father had disappeared. The voices rose and fell around us:

"What happened?"

"I don't know."

"A kid just fell through the ice!"

"Oh, my God!"

"Who was it?"

"Did you see it?"

"No, I just got here."

"Did anybody see what happened?"

"Some guy dived in after him."

"Oh, my God!"

"There's nothing anybody can do."

"They're both goners."

"What a terrible way to go!"

"Oh, my God!"
"Who dived in?"
"I don't know."
"That Holden fella!"
"Oh, my God!"
"Officer Holden?"
"The cop who gave you a ticket yesterday?"
"That's the one."
"Oh, my God!"
"Somebody, call the police!"
"Was it his kid?"
"Well, there's a story behind that!"
"Shut up, fool! Those are his kids right there!"
"Oh, my God!"

I could hear the litany of conversations reverberating around me, but I just stood there, letting them flow over me without sorting them out. Nadine had stopped wailing and was crying great hiccupping sobs. Then I felt my head bending backwards. I was looking up, looking at the sky—an early spring blue with soft feathery clouds. I think I was trying to say a prayer, but I'm not sure what was really going on in my head. I saw the sky; I didn't seem really to be thinking.

I saw a white, quarter moon, and without any effort on my part the thought formed itself in my mind, "In your right growing bright; in your left losing light." It was the mnemonic device Dad Ames had taught Alder and me. In my mind I could see the smooth side of the moon fitting into my right hand. So it was a waxing moon; the moon was in its first quarter. Nathaniel and father were gone, and here I was looking at the sky and thinking about the phases of the moon. I pushed myself away from this thought as though I had betrayed them.

Now Nadine had stopped crying, and she was singing. I thought simply, "What is she singing?" The idea of her singing was no stranger than anything else that I felt, or didn't feel. I accepted it as one accepts incongruities in a dream. I listened to her sweet, tearful voice raised against this ugly disaster, and the innocent hope in it seemed to close my throat even tighter, and I felt tears stinging my eyes.

Toward the e-nd came a frie-nd,
Who could dive and float and swim.

It was a bad dream. We were drowning in a nightmare. I wanted to wake up and stop swimming in this ugly, icy strangeness I felt.

Then someone shouted, "There he is!"
"Where?"
"Down by the bridge!"
"Oh, my God!"
"Look! He's got the kid with him!"
"Well, I'll be damned!"
"Praise the Lord!"
"There's no way that child's alive."
"Oh, that's so awful!"
"What's he doing now?"
"I can't see!"

The crowd was surging down the oxbow to the place where the river ran into the lake, to the place near the bridge where there was open water. Somehow we were flowing with the crowd, our skates sliding over the ice. I don't remember moving my feet. Alder was holding onto me; I was holding onto Nadine. Barbara was hanging onto Alder. We were all stuck together as we moved along like the little parade of characters who made the princess laugh in the fairy tale. We were being swept along with the crowd. Their mood had changed; there was cause for hope.

"Somebody call an ambulance!"
"Do you think they'll make it?"
"You just never know!"
"The kid's lying on the ice!"
"Where's officer Holden?"
"He's still in the water."
"Oh, my God!"
"What's he doing to the kid?"
"He's pressing on his back."
"He's trying artifical respiration."
"It's too late; the kid's dead!"
"Oh, my God!"
"Well, at least he got the body."
"He'd better save himself."
"How can he get to shore?"
"Somebody should try to help!"
"They'd go right down with them!"

"Somebody get a rope at least!"

"He's going to freeze in that water."

"Oh, my God!"

Somehow the crowd parted and let us through, so that we could see father struggling. Nathaniel was lying unmoving on the ice between us and my father. My father was in the water. He pushed Nathaniel's body as far as he could away from him on the ice. He put his hands on the ice and pulled his weight out of the water. The ice under his forearms gave way, and father swam closer to where the ice had broken off. He pushed Nathaniel away from him again and repeated the same procedure: pulling himself up, breaking the ice, and swimming closer. He did this four times before he got to a place where the ice would bear his weight.

By then the ambulance had arrived. (It was really a hearse that doubled as an ambulance.) When father finally crawled out onto the ice, people surged forward to help him and to carry Nathaniel. As he went by me I tried to shout out, "Dad! Dad!" But no sound escaped my throat, and father did not turn towards us. Half carried, he stumbled by in a daze without seeing us or even knowing we were there.

All of a sudden I saw Ira standing beside us with father's ice skates slung over his shoulder. He was holding Nadine's boots. "Come on, kids, I'm going to take you home," he said. Ira took us to our grandparents', because mother was at Aunt Mabel's house.

"What are you children doing walking on my linoleum in your ice skates?" grandmother bristled.

Ira told our grandparents and Aunt Mabel what had happened. He said that he knew father was alive; he didn't know about Nathaniel. Ira and grandfather went back to the causeway to get father's car. When they returned, grandmother said that we were going to go pick up mother and Dad Ames, and we were all going to go to the hospital. Grandmother had already called mother, who had just finished decorating Aunt Mabel's house for the party.

"They won't let the children into the hospital," said grandfather.

"Well, Alder is over twelve. He can carry a message out to the car. You'll stay with Michael and Nadine, won't you, Ira? Ward, these children have a right to know what's happened," grandmother said with a finality that would not be denied.

Alder and I got our shoes out of my father's car, and as soon as we had changed into them, we left for the hospital. Grandmother rode with Alder, Nadine, and me in Ira's car. Aunt Mabel rode with grandfather. When we got to Aunt Mabel's house, mother and Dad Ames were waiting in front of the house. Mother was crying. Mother and Dad Ames got into the car with grandfather and Aunt Mabel, and we all drove to the hospital.

Nadine and I stayed with Ira, while everyone else went inside. I knew my brain wasn't working right. I hadn't said a word since I had warned my father about Nathaniel. I could see everything. I understood things. But I couldn't speak. I was just observing. I felt the way Nathaniel must have felt before he could talk. I didn't want to talk; I didn't even know if I was able to talk. It seemed as though an hour passed before Alder came out to the car to tell us what he'd learned.

"Nathaniel's alive!" he said. "He's going to be okay. Dad's going to be okay, too. They're both frozen, so the doctor says they should stay in the hospital for a day or two, so they can keep an eye on them. But everything's going to be all right!"

When Alder went back inside, Ira said, "I've just had me an idea, Mikey boy! I don't get them that often, so when I do, I have to grab ahold of them and hang on. If Mohammed can't come to the mountain, then the mountain will come to Mohammed, as the saying goes. What say, we go get Aunt Mabel's birthday party and bring it over here to the hospital? This calls for a celebration! What do you say?"

"But they won't let us go inside!" I whined. I'd found my voice. More than anything else, I hated to be left out of anything.

"Well, I know that! Don't you think I thought of that. That's what they say, that you can't go inside. That's the rule; but, Mikey boy, the Lord didn't give me the gift of gab for nothing. I never kissed the Blarney stone, but you just leave it to me. And we'll see what happens."

We went back to Aunt Mabel's and got the birthday cake. Ira took a couple containers of punch, regular and high test. We gathered up some plates, silverware, and decorations; and we headed back to the hospital. I had no idea how Ira was going to smuggle us in, or whatever he was going to do. When we parked the car at the hospital, Ira gave us our instructions.

"Now, the two of you just look real sad. Look very, very sad and whatever you do, don't talk to the people. Just let me do all the talking."

Just before we went through the door, Ira stopped and cautioned us, "Remember, sad faces. Don't forget. Come on, let's see those sad faces. Ah, Nadine my precious, you'd melt the heart of Snow White's stepmother. Mikey, you're just great. Now keep it just like that. And don't talk."

Ira stopped at the front office to ask where father's room was. The starched, big breasted nurse consulted a chart and then looked at us over her spectacles and announced that father and Nathaniel had been put in the same semi-private room on the third floor. "Much obliged," said Ira, and he started ushering us out of the office.

"Wait a minute!" commanded the nurse at the desk. Her big, rosy cheeks wobbled as she shook her head. "Those children can't go up there." She pursed her cupid's-bow mouth and drew herself up until she looked like a general. "We have a very strict rule here. Children under twelve are not permitted to visit patients in the hospital."

"Oh, and I'm sure it's a good rule, too," agreed Ira. He softened his voice as though he hated to offer any sort of objection to such authority. "I don't know if you've heard all that happened down by the lake today. These two youngsters here saw their father and their brother nearly drowned. They were on their way to their Aunt Mabel's birthday party when it happened. And with their own eyes (God help us!) they witnessed their brother and their father fall right through the ice right in front of them. Can you imagine it? It's an awful thing! They're—they're in shock, I think. They can't believe that their father and their brother are still alive, you see. Unless they can see them right away with their own eyes, I'm afraid we're going to have two more sick ones on our hands. If they could only see them for a few minutes, I'm sure it would do them a world of good."

"Well, there's nothing I can do," the round nurse said flatly, and now she made her red lips very thin and small. "The rule is the rule. The children shouldn't even be in here. I'm sorry; I can't help you."

"Ah, there it is! Yours is not an easy job, I know," sympathized Ira. "You've got so much heavy responsibility resting on your shoulders. Anybody could see that. And you have to have a heart of gold to be a nurse; I'm sure of that. I'm sure it must be a terrible burden for you to watch these children suffer, them believing they've lost their father and their brother. And I know you'll feel awful if they're taken sick because of their loss and their grief. You can see their sadness." Ira dropped his left hand slowly in our direction. I looked at Nadine. Her face was woeful, the most pitiful sight I'd ever seen.

"Well, I'm sorry, but what . . . " the nurse faltered.

"Oh, if there was only a way that you could talk to the doctor for us," Ira pleaded. "I'm sure whoever made the rule never had a case like this before them. It's not an everyday situation. I know I don't have to tell you. You're an angel of mercy (God love you). You make life and death decisions every day. If there were some way you could just intercede for us with the doctor. If I could only explain the situation to him."

"I—I could try to locate Dr. Bonsecours and see if he's available to speak with you," the nurse offered.

"Bless you! I'm sure you'll be rewarded for your thoughtfulness," Ira assured her. It was magic! Ira was better than Mandrake the Magician. Ira didn't say the words of his spell backwards the way Mandrake did, but he sort of had to think and talk in the opposite direction of the facts before him. There was nothing about this stiff, fat nurse that remotely suggested a heart of gold or an angel of mercy, but here she was— on the phone to the doctor trying to convince him that we were a special case.

The nurse had to make a couple of calls before she located the doctor. When she reached him, she told him that she had an unusual situation on her hands. She briefly explained it and said that she felt it warranted his personal attention. A few minutes after the nurse called him, Dr. Bonsecours came down to the front desk. Ira asked if he could speak to the doctor privately for a minute; they went aside into the hall. Although they were talking low, Ira possessed one of those voices that carries, and I heard some of the words that Ira said: "witnessed," "shock," "can't believe," "sick ones." I was sure that Ira was giving him the same line of patter he'd given the nurse. As Ira went on though, I caught other words: "if you remember," "very high strung," "his dog," and "unconscious for weeks." The words puzzled me, but I couldn't make anything of them at the time. Now I know that he was talking about Pepper and me.

After a few minutes Dr. Bonsecours came over to Nadine and me. Nadine's face seemed frozen into something that looked like the mask of tragedy. It was marvelous. I only hoped my sad face was as good as hers. Dr. Bonsecours looked at us thoughtfully. I tried to look as morose as I knew how. Then Dr. Bonsecours reached his hand out and placed it on my head. He petted me like a dog.

"I think that maybe we can make an exception and bend the rules just this once," he conceded.

When we brought Aunt Mabel's party to father and Nathaniel's room, Aunt Mabel said that this was the worst birthday she'd ever had, but that at the same time it was the best birthday she'd ever had.

"Sometimes as you're getting older and things aren't going well," Aunt Mabel said, "you get to wondering just what the point of it all is, don't you know. But then a thing like this helps you remember how really precious life is. Now, just look at these two here. As far as I'm concerned, that's a picture that's worth a thousand words."

We looked at Nathaniel cuddled up next to father on the same bed. Father's hands were bandaged, but his arms were around Nathaniel, and Nathaniel was holding onto father. There was no space separating them anymore. Nadine and I hugged them both.

"Are you awfully unhappy, Princess?" father asked her, concerned.

"No, I'm happy," Nadine answered, but her face was set in a look of grief.

"Oh my ears and whiskers, I forgot!" Ira boomed. "You don't have to look sad anymore, sweetheart. It's okay now. You can smile again. My, but you were wonderful, Nadine darling! What a little Shirley Temple you are."

Nadine beamed.

"Well, I'm glad it was just a funny face," mother said.

Nadine laughed.

"I'm sure glad we're all here to hear you laugh, Princess," father added.

"That's a mighty brave thing you did today!" Ira said to father.

"I had to save my son . . . and myself," father said. He looked into Nathaniel's eyes, and Nathaniel looked back. They laughed, and father kissed his new son on the head and ruffled his hair. Nathaniel nuzzled in as close as he could to his dad. Then father looked at Alder, Nadine, and me, the warmth of his gaze resting on each of us for a long moment. "The lives of all of my children depended on it." He smiled at mother and took her hand in his. "And our life depended on it."

We sang "Happy Birthday" to Aunt Mabel, and we all smiled and laughed at the happiness we shared in that moment. Despite the flow of good feelings, Aunt Mabel good naturedly refused to reveal the secret of her age, but she said that today she did not feel old. As she handed around the cake, Aunt Mabel said, "In this life bad times are a given, but good times are a gift, and right now I feel truly blessed."

Somewhere in the South the wood thrushes were only beginning to think of their long flight northwards, but in that hospital room it was already springtime. Afterwards, mother and father both agreed that father had finally refound his lost "focus and balance," and grandfather said that his son had come home at last.

About the Author

Born in 1940 in Newport, Vermont, Jay Kendall attended grammar school there and graduated from Newport High School in 1958. As an undergraduate, he attended Cornell University and the University of Vermont, where he completed the B.A. in English in 1963. In the same year, he married Ellen Arrison, and they had two sons, Matthew and Aaron. The couple divorced in 1983.

The author has taught at several New York and Massachusetts high schools, including Mahar Regional School in Orange, Massachusetts, where he has been since 1969. He holds an M.A. in English and an M.Ed. in counseling from the University of Massachusetts, Amherst.

For three years at Mahar, the author taught English before becoming the first supervisor of the school's cooperative work experience program. From 1981 to 1995, he was a full-time counselor and then director of student services. He returned to the classroom in 1995 to teach English.

To help him teach writing, he attended summer seminars offered by the Western Massachusetts Writing Project at UMass, Amherst. There he was encouraged to write every day, and *The Secret Keepers* began in the first summer seminar as a character sketch of a grandfather seen through the eyes of his grandson.

The author makes his home in Tully Village in Orange. Besides teaching English and American literature, he continues a study of the English/American language and its history and evolution. He describes himself to students as a fashion consultant in the language. Solely for personal amusement, the author plays guitar and piano, occasionally accompanying himself on guitar as he sings ballads for his English classes.

Hobbies include cross-country skiing, snow-shoeing, swimming, walking in the woods, reading, writing, and watching television. He tries to spend some time each day reading both French and Spanish.